PRAISE FOR ADA

'A tense, original thriller that perf<
and shocks of *Silence of the Lambs* and *Shutter Island*.
—John Marrs, bestselling author of *When You Disappeared*

'A brilliantly original idea, with a terrifying villain at its heart.'
—Claire McGowan, author of *What You Did* and the Paula Maguire
series

'*Trance* is a creepy, dark and highly original debut. I couldn't put it
down!'
—Victoria Selman, author of *Blood for Blood*

'Fast, furious, and very scary, *Trance* is a hugely enjoyable and original
thriller. Adam's going to be one to watch.'
—Simon Kernick, bestselling author of *The Bone Field*

PAIN

ALSO BY ADAM SOUTHWARD

Trance

ADAM
PAIN
SOUTHWARD

THOMAS & MERCER

Text copyright © 2019 by Adam Southward
All rights reserved.

Published by Thomas & Mercer, Seattle

www.apub.com

Amazon, the Amazon logo, and Thomas & Mercer are trademarks of Amazon.com, Inc., or its affiliates.

ISBN-13: 9781542092302
ISBN-10: 1542092302

Cover design by kid-ethic

Printed in the United States of America

For Kerry, Isla and Daisy, without whom none of this would be any fun.

CHAPTER ONE

Mia stared through the rain. The bus shelter offered little protection and her feet were already soaked, her face and body numb. But still she stared.

The glaring lights of the hospital blurred in front of her. Three ambulances were parked in the emergency bays across the street and Mia's heart fluttered with anticipation. *Hold it*, she thought. *Wait until shift change. Safer that way.* Emergency departments never slept, but the night shift meant fewer staff and fewer visitors. She glanced at her watch. Five minutes should do it.

Mia wished she'd eaten. Hunger pains gnawed at her stomach and she pulled a bottle of water from her coat pocket, taking a long swig, ignoring the hollow feeling as the warm liquid flooded her gut.

A police car turned into the road ahead, slowing as it approached. Mia pulled up her hood and stood rigid as the car drifted by. It stopped, turning into the hospital entrance. She watched two officers jump out and disappear inside. There was always a steady flow of police into the emergency room on Saturday nights. Mia knew Sunday was better, Monday not so good.

The horror of what she was about to do snarled and griped from deep in her stomach. She'd feel it in the hours afterwards, when the shame and regret took her in sweats and shivers. But she buried it, as she always did. No time for that now.

A crowd of nurses and doctors exited the building. Mia couldn't hear their voices above the rain, but she saw smiles, handshakes, hugs and waves. Friends, colleagues, leaving each other for the night, promising to be back tomorrow.

Mia wondered what it felt like. To have someone who cared if they saw you again. She closed her eyes, remembering. Brief flashes of a loving smile, torn away in pain. Mia clenched her jaw and shivered. She waited until the thumping settled in her chest before opening her eyes. She watched two of the nurses cross the street towards her. They huddled under the bus shelter, talking to each other, pausing briefly to acknowledge Mia's presence behind them.

Mia tucked her head down, tilting it to study them both. The two nurses were tired but happy. Excited at the prospect of a good night's sleep and motivated to return. They talked of patients and colleagues, affairs and gossip. Mia thought she detected a limp on one; she kept shifting her weight around, but it was minor. The other squinted, a headache, nothing serious. Both women were healthy and happy. Mia sniffed and turned away.

A bus came and went and the nurses departed. Mia was alone again. Hardly noticing the rain, she left the shelter and walked at a steady pace across the road. She paused at the row of ambulances, checking the rear doors. All were closed, which meant the patients were already inside.

The door hissed open and the noise of the waiting room hit Mia. Raised voices, footsteps and alarms, beds squeaking on the lino floors. And patients. Lots of patients.

Mia focused.

Patients in pain, moaning and weeping; the long, deep sighs associated with extreme trauma. Mia's heart fluttered, strong and urgent. She turned. Mia knew this department well. St Mary's was one of her more regular haunts.

The emergency room was chaotic, more than usual. Patients and visitors spilled over the benches and on to every spare foot of flooring.

The triage area for ambulance arrivals was full, with paramedics leaning on trolleys, waiting for their patients to be checked. The sheer number of patients and visitors tonight would make it difficult for Mia to get close to anyone.

She paused, keeping her head down, surveying the room before deciding on her backup plan, the AMU. In the acute medical unit patients had stabilised, or at least they should have done. It was the next stage on after the emergency room, a short stay while beds were found and tests were run – bloods, ECGs, scans. Fewer staff and fewer visitors. In the AMU patients were often left unattended for long periods.

Perfect.

The security was minimal. Mia walked along the corridor linking the two departments. She paused at the double doors, glancing down the network of corridors snaking off into the rest of the hospital.

Her vision tunnelled. The usual memories surfaced, but they wouldn't settle. Sometimes she followed them, treading the corridors of this hospital or the next, searching. But not tonight.

Tonight was for a single purpose.

Mia blinked, took a breath and pushed open the double doors into the AMU, still wearing her coat, hood up, her heavy boots leaving a trail of dirty water on the floor.

Eyes darting, adrenaline spiking, she observed the room. It was separated into four sections. Eight patients in this section, two with curtains pulled closed around the bed. The attending doctor stood surrounded by colleagues at the nurses' station, some distance away in the centre. The doctor's attention was focused on a huge whiteboard which listed patients and their status, and most of the nurses had their backs to the door. Mia kept her chin low and sauntered over to the first curtain.

The patient slept peacefully, although his chest rattled with every pump of the respirator. Mia studied the man's face. His eyelids fluttered, his skin was clammy and his mouth trembled. Mia watched his chest and traced his arms to his hands. They were loose, relaxed.

Mia placed her hand at the centre of his chest. She felt it move for a few moments before pushing, resisting. Increasing the force with each breath, Mia leaned in, putting her weight behind her hand.

Nothing. The ECG registered a slight change in heart rate but not enough to trigger an alarm. The man's breathing slowed but his face remained unresponsive.

Mia lifted her hand, disappointed. She slipped out of the bay, checking the nurses' station. Still in shift handover, they'd be there for some time.

Mia paused, shivering but focused, her chest tightening. The sensation wrapped itself around her, hugging her body in a demanding embrace. She tasted it on her tongue, in her throat and in her nostrils as she breathed in the warm air of the ward. The growing pressure throbbed at the base of her skull. Mia forced her breathing slowly in, slowly out.

She continued to the next bay.

It held a younger man. Mid-thirties, perhaps. Mia smiled when she saw his face, which was tense and drenched in sweat. Mia took in his condition with a practised scan: road accident; left leg mangled. Splinted – probably waiting for X-ray, then surgery. He would be pumped full of painkillers, but it was only taking the edge off. He panted, his eyes clamping shut every few seconds. His hands grasped the sides of the bed, knuckles white with tension. He wasn't hooked to an ECG or any alarm. He wasn't near death, just in excruciating pain.

Mia approached the bed, standing over the man, watching the damaged leg. She didn't have long, but this would be over in a matter of minutes.

With her left hand, she pulled a strip of pre-cut duct tape from her coat pocket, took off the backing and affixed it over the man's mouth, leaving his nose clear. She pressed the tape down, checking it was firm.

4

Her eyes locked on his face as she reached out with her right hand. She rested it on the leg, below the knee, where a bloodied bandage bulged outwards. An open fracture; a knee joint. A horrible combination.

Mia exhaled. She held his leg – a firm caress on the jagged bone draped in fabric. The man's face contorted, his breathing quickened, his blood pressure spiked and muscles tensed. His pain intensified, second by second, as Mia's grip tightened. She grabbed the broken bone and twisted.

Her hand was wet, bloody, her fingers under the bandage probing beneath the skin into the damaged tissue beneath. The bone was jagged and sharp. Mia laughed, a small hiss escaping her lips. With every movement, the pain shot through the man's body – almost too much, almost enough to send him into unconsciousness. But Mia was practised and she teased.

Part of Mia's brain objected, screaming at her to stop, but the more primal part, the part that was damaged, was in full control.

The man tried to speak, but the tape held fast and a muffled groan emerged. He writhed and shuddered. Mia's stare had never left his face and now their eyes met. He looked at her in terror; Mia's eyes shone. The fear gave her an extra jolt of pleasure as the main surge began to subside.

Mia already felt the sluggishness taking over. The lethargy after the hit. She needed to be away from this place before she succumbed.

The man reached out, weak from pain and blood loss, his hands trembling. But his arms collapsed to his sides and his pupils dilated. His eyelids flickered weakly.

Mia frowned, but the rush of warm blood on her hand explained it. An artery, perhaps nicked by the accident, now severed by her twists and abuse. She tore her eyes away from his face and to the leg. Her shoulders sagged as her ecstasy departed, switched off like a light.

Blood poured from the man's leg on to the floor. Two pints, maybe more, were already pooling at her feet.

Time to go.

The curtain flew open as Mia turned to leave. A hospital porter with a clipboard stared at the scene in front of him. A big man – shaved head, tattoos on both forearms. He might be used to seeing all manner of terrors in this place, but at this his face twisted in confusion. Mia's right hand dripped blood; her forearm was covered in it. Behind her, a man bled out through his leg, his mouth taped shut.

Mia didn't give the porter a chance to think, kicking him as hard as she could between the legs. She saw the pain register in his eyes but resisted the urge to watch and sprinted for the exit. She pounded open the double doors to the AMU and ran for the emergency room. Shouts came from behind her and she risked a look back. The porter she'd kicked was already up and after her. A tough guy. Unexpected. Hospital staff usually hated a fight.

Mia was quick and nimble, athletic after months of running and living rough, but the after-effects of her high were already kicking in. Her legs stirred but they moved in slow motion, wading in syrup, while her mind began to fog. She barged her way into the waiting room, knocking over an elderly lady on crutches. The howl from the woman was matched by the screams of onlookers. A security guard appeared from the left and lunged. Mia lashed out, her fist catching his cheek as she stumbled past. He cried out but recovered, charging after her.

Scores of people jumped out of her way, but Mia could hear the stomps of the guard, joined by the porter, who kept up his pursuit.

The main exit was open. The glass doors hissed as a stray trolley blocked one of them from closing. Mia sprinted, picking up the pace, dodging between two ambulances, pausing for a fraction of a second before picking her escape route. The rain still thundered and she considered her options: Paddington Station to the right; Hyde Park to the south; or head east, towards Regent's Park. She picked south, darting out on to the main road, heading for a cut-through along the side of Imperial College.

A few more paces and she would make it.

She heard another shout and made the mistake of looking round. The guard was a fair way off, but he raised his hands and his face opened in horror as the bus hit her.

The corner of the vehicle hit Mia side-on with a crunch, sending her spinning several yards into the far kerb.

Mia's head spun. She lay on her back on the wet tarmac, feeling the rain pounding the skin of her face. Her body tensed and she tested her extremities. Her right hand and arm moved with ease, so she patted the rest of her body, quickly and methodically, starting with major bones, sockets, vertebrae and her skull.

She would recover. Her left shoulder was dislocated, left forearm fractured and two fingers on her left hand broken. She rolled on to her side, pushing against the tarmac until her shoulder popped back into place, feeling the bones scrape as they connected. She raised herself up, wiggling her joints. The little finger was at an awkward angle so she pulled it out of its socket and tried to straighten it. It wouldn't go, so she jammed it together with the third finger. She'd splint it later. It'd heal in time.

The bigger issue was her pursuers, who had caught up but remained at a distance. The guard was talking into a radio and the porter looked as white as a sheet, no doubt regretting chasing this young person into the street and straight into the path of a bus. The driver, a middle-aged woman, hovered by the bus, promising everything would be OK, telling Mia not to move.

'OK, son,' said the porter. 'Help is on its way. You stay there.'

Mia stood up, thankful that neither of her legs was broken. She pulled her hood closer, not daring to think of what had been caught on CCTV and what would be examined by police. She was thankful they hadn't clocked her gender, but the risk of ever coming back to this hospital had just shot up.

Fighting the fog and the increasing effects of her comedown, Mia turned and raced off, sprinting as fast as her damaged body would carry her. Her lungs laboured and her mind drifted, but the shouts from the hospital faded and nobody pursued as she hit an alley and disappeared into the night.

She was safe. It was her first mistake, and almost fatal, but she'd survived. At least for tonight. Perhaps in a few weeks it would be safer.

Until then, she would search elsewhere.

CHAPTER TWO

'You need to help me,' said Dr Alex Madison to the young man in front of him. The suspect was skinny, dressed in a T-shirt and jogging bottoms, a gang tattoo of a spider's web covering his arms and neck – a black widow under his jaw. Alex's heart had dropped the second he'd walked in and seen him.

'Fuck you,' came the reply. James, Jimmy, Jim: Alex had tried them each in turn until he got the least violent response.

Alex twisted in the interview chair, feeling the cheap plastic flex under his weight. The session wasn't going as planned. He'd been here for half an hour so far, going around in circles for most of it. He glanced at each of the walls of the small police interview room in turn, thinking of a hundred other places he'd rather be on a Sunday afternoon.

Detective Laurie, sitting next to him, raised her eyebrows. It was her fault Alex was here. He tried not to let his mood show.

'What does your mother call you?' said Laurie.

A pause. 'Jamie.' It came out in a grunt, but it was progress.

'Jamie,' said Alex, nodding his thanks. 'Good. Do you know why I'm here?'

'Because they think I'm a retard,' Jamie said, nodding to the detective, who kept her face cool and her response cooler.

'No. Because we don't think you should be the one sitting here,' said Laurie. 'Your friends Franco and Jay. They—'

'They're not my fucking friends.'

Detective Laurie nodded. 'But you know them.'

'No.'

'You don't know them?'

'Never heard of them.'

'But they're not your friends?'

'That's right.' Jamie smiled, and something in it sent a shiver down Alex's spine. He leaned in to study Jamie's expression. It was vacant, no emotion, not even a hint. The man was in control. Not enjoying himself, but . . . Alex wasn't at all sure the police had got this right.

'Can we have a word?' he said to Detective Laurie.

She nodded. 'Interview stopped at sixteen hundred at the request of Dr Madison.' The door buzzed and two uniformed officers came in.

'Please take Mr Brooks back to holding,' said Laurie.

The suspect's expression was pure poker face, but he flicked his eyes at Alex on the way out. Alex saw something in that instant, a familiar feeling of unease. He'd seen it before in clinically psychopathic patients. He shivered as the man was led from the room.

'It's Sunday,' said Laurie, pacing ahead of Alex towards the office. 'I get it – I don't want to be here either. But he ticked all the boxes for a psych assessment and your name came up.'

Alex nodded, trying to shake his annoyance. Detective Laurie was right. He could at least give her the courtesy of a proper assessment. Part of his agreement with the Metropolitan Police and the CPS was being on the regular psych roster. One weekend in four he was on call. When the police suspected mental health issues in either a victim or a suspect, Alex got an automated text message asking him to drop by.

It was low-level work and the least rewarding part of his life by some distance, but he'd agreed to do it. Keeping on the weekend roster meant he stayed top of the list when the more interesting work came along – work that involved more than just violent reoffenders with little chance of rehabilitation.

'What am I missing?' said Alex, thinking of the brief notes he'd been emailed ten minutes before he arrived.

Laurie stopped by the water cooler and tucked her long blonde hair behind her ears. She filled a plastic cup and drank it in one. Alex wondered how she managed to look so fresh and motivated on a weekend. Younger than him by a few years perhaps, and with confidence exuding from her every move.

'Three on one,' she said. 'Stabbing. Rape – we think. One of the suspects being sought is the victim's boyfriend. The victim is hanging on for her life. Thirty years old, female.'

'I read the brief. But why am I here, really?'

Laurie frowned. 'Like I said, he ticked the boxes.'

'You think this guy has mental health issues. You think he was left as the fall guy.'

She nodded, offered Alex a cup.

'But that's not it,' said Alex, declining the water.

Laurie smiled. 'Ah, there it is. They said you were good. No, that's not it.'

Alex tried not to react. His last major case for the Met had ended a year ago. The serial killings of Victor Lazar had been huge, but ultimately unresolved. Alex had helped stop one of the most prolific killers London had ever seen, but in the process he'd nearly got his own daughter killed. Victor had escaped his grasp and remained at large. The killings had ceased, but the case remained open. Alex was briefed once a month and the message was always the same – nothing to report, the threat to Alex and his family considered low. Victor had disappeared off the face of the earth and taken any evidence with him. Dr Alex Madison had earned a mixed reputation for his part in the whole thing, in some places a good one, in others bad. Detective Laurie had obviously heard only the good bits.

'I'm a psychologist,' he said. 'It's kinda my job.'

Laurie stared at Alex, her smile fading. 'Something about Mr Brooks doesn't feel right.'

'I know. I see it too. But it's hard to deduce much from one short interview.'

'I don't want him released, not yet. I need a thorough assessment. You know what I mean?'

Alex nodded. He got it. The police had a tough job. Even tougher were all the rules and regulations that meant guilty suspects were often released before enough information could be gathered. Good police had good hunches. They knew when they had a bad apple in their holding cells. When Alex looked at Detective Laurie he saw one of the good ones.

'I'll see what I can do,' said Alex. 'Give me an hour and we'll reconvene?'

Laurie looked at her watch, a white Casio digital. *Trendy*, thought Alex, tugging his own sleeve down to hide his Rolex.

'Tomorrow,' she said. 'You can go home, Dr Madison. We've got enough to keep him for forty-eight hours. His story doesn't add up, that's all. I appreciate you coming out and agreeing to help.'

'Until tomorrow,' said Alex, thankful for the reprieve. His weekend was almost over and he wanted to go home, open a bottle of red and binge-watch something on TV.

Solitary, but as good as it got these days.

Alex headed out to the parking lot. The rain had cleared and the day was bright with broken cloud. It would have been a good day to take his daughter, Katie, out, had he not been on call. Booking something in and then having to cancel would be worse than booking nothing at all.

His relationship with Katie had grown stronger over the last few months. She was still recovering from the major incident last year when Alex's suspect had decided to make the fight personal. But Katie, like her mother, was silently strong and resilient. She'd dealt with the trauma and tried to get on with her life. The problem was that most of her life continued without Alex. Grace hadn't forgiven Alex so easily and quashed any thoughts he had of patching things up.

Grace knew how difficult the year had been for him. Losing his own father had conjured a lifetime of complicated emotions and so far Alex had kept them locked away, stifling the grief, pretending it would go away. Grace sympathised but she was independent – fiercely so. She didn't need Alex as much as he needed her, and she knew it. Grace wasn't hostile but she'd made it clear Alex had a long way to go to prove himself – as a father first and foremost.

Thoughts of his familial mess caused Alex's mild mood to evaporate. Sinking into the seat of his car, he reached into his jacket pocket and pulled open the packet of Xanax he always carried. He'd been cutting down, but the thought of his empty house and an evening alone caused the familiar sinking feeling; his throat narrowed and his stomach tightened as the anxiety crept outwards from his chest.

He swallowed the pill dry, took a deep breath and pulled out into the main road.

It was a short drive home to Harrow. A familiar car waited outside his house, lifting his mood as he pulled in behind it.

Speak of the angel.

Grace had a key – he'd insisted, part of his proving that she could drop in any time and be welcome. His string of unsuitable girlfriends had ended and he was single. Single and responsible. But Grace rarely used the key, most often waiting in the car when dropping Katie off.

Today it looked like she'd caved. The car was empty.

'Hi, honey,' Alex shouted, slamming the front door behind him. Grace and Katie were in the kitchen. Grace looked unamused at his entrance, but Katie jumped up, throwing her arms around his neck. Although thirteen years old, she still weighed next to nothing and hung off his neck while he walked.

'Happy Sunday,' she said, planting a wet kiss on his cheek.

'You too, although mine wasn't great.'

'Work?' Katie pulled a face.

Alex nodded, glancing over at Grace. Their eyes met and he saw warmth in them, but restraint. Forgiveness would be a long time coming.

She'd cut her hair into a bob. It suited her, he thought, curving perfectly around her face – the face Alex still pictured in his dreams. He tried not to let his eyes stray but he couldn't help it. She looked great, athletic and glowing.

'Been working out?' he said.

Grace smirked. 'A little. You?' She pointed to his belly, which had relaxed a little over the last year. His exercise routine had taken a back seat with the stresses of work and lack of time. At least, that's what he told himself. He had a long list of ready excuses. He sucked his belly in.

'Don't have to,' he said, smiling back. 'Naturally svelte.'

Grace raised her eyebrows. 'So,' she said, 'the reason we're here—'

'You're invited to my party,' said Katie, releasing her vice grip around Alex's neck and dropping to the floor.

'End of term,' said Grace. 'Katie persuaded me to let her fill the house with her classmates.'

'Brave,' said Alex, pulling out a stool from the breakfast bar.

'And she wanted you to come. We wanted.'

Alex forced a smile. Grace hadn't invited him to the house in a long time. The family house in Ealing was hers in the settlement. He didn't resent it, but he wished it wasn't like this.

'And there's something else.' Grace turned to Katie. 'Can you give us a minute, love?'

Katie huffed and went out into the back garden. The door clicked behind her.

'Sounds serious,' said Alex.

'It's not,' said Grace, 'but I wanted to tell you, otherwise Katie would.'

Alex felt an unsettling in his gut. Brief, panicked thoughts raced through his head. 'Are you sick? Is Katie sick? What—'

'I'm seeing someone,' said Grace. It took a few moments to process. She looked away, awkwardly playing with her hair, pulling a strand from her face. 'It's not serious, just . . . someone from work.'

'Who?' Alex caught himself before continuing. His tone was demanding, as if he had a right to be. 'Sorry,' he said in a softer tone. 'I mean . . . shit.'

'Life goes on, Alex,' she said, turning to face him. Their eyes met and again he saw the same warmth, mixed with hurt. The hurt he had caused. She still felt that way. He still meant something to her.

He wanted to say something light, something jokey. He didn't want to admit how he felt, as if she'd punched him in the gut and kicked his legs out from under him. The anxiety bubbled again and he forced out a few small breaths.

'How long has it . . . How long have you been seeing each other?'

He didn't care. Or did he? He stared past Grace and through the kitchen window. Katie sat on the lawn, playing on her phone, her face a picture of feverish concentration. This was the wrong future for her. Her future was supposed to be with him and Grace, back together. Alex had almost convinced himself of it. It dawned on him slowly. What an idiot he was.

'Not long, and it's not like we're getting married, but John will be at the party.' Grace reached out and held his arm. He didn't deserve her sympathy. He'd had several girlfriends after they split up. What right did he have to judge her for this?

He nodded, biting the inside of his cheek with such force he tasted blood.

John. Grace's new partner. Lover. Future husband?

'Thank you for telling me,' was all he could offer before turning away. He rummaged in one of the drawers, found the corkscrew and pulled a bottle of red from the rack.

'Stay for a drink?' he said.

Grace shook her head. 'Thanks, but we've got to go. We were driving past, on our way back from a friend of Katie's. Katie insisted we stop in and wait half an hour to see if you showed. She tried calling. No answer.'

Alex pulled out his phone. Flat battery. It must have died while he was at the station. The second time this week. He made a mental note to get a new battery or a new phone.

Grace stood, picking her bag up from the worktop.

'How are things, Alex? You know, with your . . . health?'

'OK,' he said, pouring a large glass of Rioja, swirling it around. 'Under control.'

'Talking to someone? Therapy?'

'Yes. Sometimes.'

Grace knew about his anxiety. It had almost crippled him after a particularly distressing case several years ago. She didn't know about his benzo addiction, though. He'd been longing to tell her, to come clean, but he'd never found the right moment. Now wasn't it.

Grace's eyes narrowed. Why did he lie to her? She always knew when he did. He regretted it but it was too late.

'You said you would.'

'I will – I have a name. I'm busy at the moment. You know how it is.'

He grinned, fake, and her expression said it all. She returned the smile and called for Katie.

'Bye, Alex. I hope you come to the party.'

It was two hours later when his landline rang. Alex had polished off one and a half bottles of Rioja, and his mood was dark, plagued with visions of Grace and her new lover, John. The worst bit was that he hadn't seen it coming. He'd tried, not as hard as he could have but more than ever before, to focus on his family, Katie and Grace, and win their hearts back. He had Katie's – she adored him and he her. But he'd assumed Grace would follow. As someone who studied the human mind for a living, he was disappointed at his failure to see his own delusion. These last few months hadn't been about Grace preparing to come back into his life. They'd been about her preparing to leave it.

The incessant ringing cut through the haze. He checked his phone and recognised the number immediately.

'Good evening,' he answered, trying his best to sound lucid. 'It's been a while.'

'It has,' said DCI Hartley, her voice booming down the line. 'Why the hell is your mobile switched off? Don't tell me, I don't care. Anyway, I've got something for you.'

Alex swallowed. He reached for his wine glass, thought better of it, and walked through to the kitchen.

'Go on,' he said, pouring a glass of water.

'We thought it was a one-off, but we've pulled CCTV and found a string of them.'

'Of what?' Alex's ears pricked up. Hartley sounded excited.

'Killings. At several hospitals in London. One perp, or so it seems. It's serial.'

Alex frowned. Some doctor on a euthanasia trip, no doubt.

'Not a doctor,' said Hartley, pre-empting his question. 'Not an employee.'

Hartley paused. Alex could hear her breathing.

'You need to prepare yourself, Alex,' she said in a softer tone, as if choosing her words carefully. 'The scenes aren't typical of anything I've ever seen. Our perpetrator is . . . Well, that's why I need you. There's something wrong with this person, Alex, very seriously wrong. I need you to figure out what.'

CHAPTER THREE

Mia laid her tools out on the workbench. She'd slept fourteen hours straight, a big comedown, but woken to find her left forearm swollen and bent. It needed re-breaking and straightening. An hour's work at most, but not pleasant.

She rested her arm on the rough wood, trying to remember. She'd done this once before, three months ago – or was it four? She didn't mind having a bent arm, but even though it didn't hurt, it might be permanent. Mia knew there were two bones in the forearm. If too badly damaged, it would limit her ability to rotate her wrist. It would be a handicap, and one she wasn't willing to risk. Besides, it looked odd. Distinctive. The sort of thing she didn't want. Mia blended in. She kept her light brown hair tied back tightly under her hood. She wore black, loose clothes, hiding her thin muscular body. A bent forearm might be hard to hide. It would invite questions, create memories in people she wanted to forget her.

At first she tried to pull the bone straight. Taking hold of her left hand with her right, she tugged. Her joints cracked but the forearm didn't part. The muscles and tendons were strong, pulling it together. She needed to break it again.

The club hammer was a recent item, lifted from a hardware store five minutes' walk away. She raised it, then put it down again. With the fingers of her right hand she tried to feel where the break was, prodding through the fast-swelling tissue.

There, she found it: an uneven fracture a third of the way between the elbow and the wrist. Again, she raised the hammer, twisting her arm around so she could strike the bone without the muscle getting in the way.

She brought the hammer down as hard as she could. A satisfying crack echoed off the walls and concrete floor. Mia was pleased to find the end of her forearm malleable enough to straighten. Blood rushed to the site of the fresh trauma and she picked up the two lengths of metal rod she'd already prepared, laying them alongside her arm. She grabbed the duct tape next, using her mouth to rip off several long strips.

It was tough and frustrating, but eventually Mia's arm was straight and strapped to the metal rods. She'd leave it like this for a few weeks to heal. It should be strong enough then. If not, she'd break and splint it again.

She rested for the next few hours, deciding not to venture out of the warehouse. The police would be searching. The chances of her being found were slim but Mia found these hours the hardest, as her conscience battled its way to the fore. She was drowsy, distracted and worried.

Mia sat in an old car seat, long ago ripped from its vehicle, and gazed at the ceiling high above. Rusty metal stanchions supported huge sheets of corrugated iron, and birds nested in the nooks, watching Mia suspiciously. An intruder in their world.

Although abandoned, the warehouse still had power and water. Mia stole everything else she needed, which wasn't much. Situated in north-west London, it was close enough to walk into the city but remote enough to ensure privacy and seclusion when she needed it. Mia had been living here for as long as she could remember – twelve months according to the calendar on her phone, which she'd stolen from one of her first victims. Mia had no idea of where she'd been before that time.

She knew her name and little else, but she had memories and she had dreams. She could make sense of neither.

Tension crowded her chest, and hopelessness threatened to draw the darkness closer.

She picked up a stray nail from the concrete. It was short, rusty but still sharp, and she examined it in her hand, then forced it under her left fingernail, watching the spike break the skin, edging upwards. Pushing harder, she jammed the nail deep into her finger.

Blood dripped on to the floor, seeping around the foreign object, and Mia felt a dull scratching sensation. She stared at the nail, wondering how many times she'd performed this experiment.

No pain. Not for Mia. But the memory of pain . . . it was in her somewhere. Mia knew this should hurt, and could almost remember what it felt like.

But not today.

Mia pulled the nail out and hurled it across the floor. She held her finger until the bleeding stopped before lying back in the seat, her lips trembling, her heart breaking.

A single tear escaped, then another.

To cry because of a lack of pain. But also because of what that made her.

It was almost too much to imagine. Almost too much to bear.

CHAPTER FOUR

The man's left leg was mangled, blood visible on the sheets and metal guards. The photo was in close-up, brutal and sickening. Hartley tilted her monitor and Alex nodded, remaining silent. He breathed through the feelings of nausea. Nobody ever got used to seeing dead bodies, Alex was sure of it.

He stirred two sugars into his coffee, staring suspiciously at the brown liquid, then sipped and winced. It didn't taste any better sweet.

'Not what you're used to? Sorry. This is public-sector coffee,' said Hartley. 'If you want luxurious, you'd better hop back along to Harley Street.' She slurped her own, hammering her keyboard at the same time.

Alex watched her face – alert and focused. More than he could say for himself at eight o'clock on a Monday morning.

DCI Hartley had found Alex during the case of Victor Lazar, and although she and Alex hadn't seen eye to eye, she'd been professional and let Alex run with his theories. Since that case their relationship had been courteous yet distant. Hartley ran big cases – murder, trafficking, serious organised crime – and liked to do it her way. She reluctantly brought in outsiders, but at least it showed she knew what she didn't know. Alex had worked on several cases for her over the months, mostly profiling and minor assessments for the CPS. Nothing as big as Lazar.

'I'm supposed to be somewhere else today,' he said.

'Holborn? Yes, I contacted Detective Laurie, told her to find someone else.'

Alex wasn't sure whether or not to be put out. Detective Laurie had been nice, but her suspect was bound to be a dead end. Anybody could work it; it didn't need to be him. Besides, although Hartley hadn't told him anything about her case yet, she was clearly agitated. That in itself was intriguing.

Despite Hartley's jibe, Alex had been reducing his private practice over the last twelve months. He was down to two days a week in Harley Street, which was necessary to pay his exorbitant mortgage and the luxuries he hadn't yet figured out how to let go of. His new Mercedes was one of them, replacing his Porsche, which Grace and Katie had both hated. His collection of expensive watches was another. But he was turning a corner. His extravagance was on the decline and he was happier for it. These days he found a simple smile from his daughter was worth more than all the luxuries he'd accumulated over the years.

As a clinical psychologist, his private clients were real, but their needs were mundane. A lot of money and a lot of anxiety. Alex could have retired at fifty with his hourly rate, but after the events of the previous year and the death of his father, he'd promised himself he'd make better use of his profession and expertise. He could do better than provide CBT to millionaires struggling with their first-world problems.

So Alex offered the rest of his time to the CPS and the Met, working on a standard contract for a fraction of his private salary. It was worth it, though. Big cases like this made it worth it, particularly when the psychological aspect was so unusual. He craved this type of work, and that's how he'd managed to drag himself out of bed at six on a cold morning.

He glanced around at the modern office. The Metropolitan Police HQ on Victoria Embankment in London was famous for its revolving sign at the entrance. The press liked to camp out and film this gleaming mark of London's finest, but the interior of the building would have shown a different picture. Particularly on a Monday morning, where chaos reigned and overburdened officers fought to stay above water.

'OK,' said Hartley. She stared into her mug, taking a few deep breaths, and then glanced back at the screen. 'This is Paul Shaw, thirty-three, father of two. Motorbike accident, serious but not life-threatening.'

Alex raised his eyebrows. 'He looks pretty dead to me.'

'He is, but not from the accident. He broke his tibia – open fracture – and popped his kneecap out.'

Alex winced. 'Painful.'

'Indeed. He was stabilised at the scene, conveyed to St Mary's, where he lay in AMU on pain relief, waiting for an X-ray and a surgical team. They planned to reset the leg with a plate and pins. He'd have been home in a week or so, back to his family.'

Alex studied the photo. 'So he bled out?'

'Yes. But only after he'd had a visitor.' Hartley flicked away from the image and opened a folder containing video files.

'He lost four pints and went into shock,' she said. 'He couldn't be stabilised. Died at 23:36.'

Alex nodded, watching Hartley's monitor.

'These are from St Mary's Security – emergency room and AMU. Low quality,' she said, opening the first file. A black-and-white video of a hospital corridor.

'This is the link corridor between the emergency room and the AMU.' Hartley referred to her notes and fast-forwarded the video to a particular time. When it reached 23:04, she pressed play.

'This is our suspect,' said Hartley.

A figure came into view. The camera pointed towards the emergency room, so it captured the front of the person. The figure ambled towards the AMU, pausing for a few seconds to stare past the camera along the corridor. The lighting and poor quality made it impossible to pick out the face.

'Dark clothes, hooded, boots, slim build,' said Alex.

'Young.'

'Male?'

'Probably.'

'Why?'

Hartley shrugged. 'If the appearance is indeterminable, we go by their actions. What follows is sadistic violence. This sort of crime is unusual, but statistically he's male.'

Alex conceded the point. Seventy-eight per cent of violent crimes in the UK were committed by men. Out of those, the vast majority were aged between twenty-five and forty. Young and male was the obvious deduction without even seeing the CCTV footage. It didn't help much, though.

'So why am I here?'

Hartley closed the first video and opened the second.

'Inside AMU. Quality is as bad, but it gives a decent angle of the bed over the top of the curtain.' Hartley paused. She swallowed. Alex gave her a moment. He forgot how much mental trauma senior inspectors such as Hartley were forced to experience on a daily basis. She acted tough and in control, but Alex knew it hurt. Deep inside, Hartley hated watching this crap as much as the next person. She pressed play.

The figure approached the nearest curtained bed. The angle was awkward and distorted by a wide-angle lens. Alex noted the medical staff huddled half out of view at the station.

'Handover?'

'Yes. Bang on.'

So the timing was planned, thought Alex, as he watched the suspect slip inside the first cubicle and stand over the patient. A few seconds passed. Assuming the suspect was male, he appeared to watch the patient before reaching out, touching their chest. Alex kept one eye on the clock – it was hard to judge the seconds due to the jerkiness of the video. The suspect then stepped away and out of the cubicle. Less than a minute had passed.

'Strange,' said Alex, wishing the video was high resolution. 'What are they doing?'

'No idea,' said Hartley.

'Injuries?'

'No. That one was in for a minor heart attack. Stable, pain free and ready to be transferred to a ward.'

Alex watched the figure slip behind the next curtain into the bay holding the now-deceased, Paul Shaw. The suspect paused, as before, examining the patient, peering into his face. He put something across the man's mouth.

'Tape?' said Alex.

Hartley nodded. 'Standard duct tape, branded.'

The man reached for Mr Shaw's leg, feeling under the bandage. Nothing happened for a few moments until the arm jerked, visibly wrenching the damaged leg left and right.

'My God,' said Alex, peering in more closely, his eyes blurring at the grainy image. The patient writhed on the bed, clearly in agony, arms thrashing. The suspect continued, his arm moving, shifting forcefully on the leg, pulling one way then the other. He used his whole body weight to push into the joint, twisting and grinding. Given the original injury, the pain must have been unbearable.

'He's torturing him,' said Alex. 'For what reason?'

The suspect threw his head back. The hood covered the top of his face, but the lower half was visible. His mouth dropped open and he swayed, chest heaving. The movements lasted a minute or so, before his head dropped again.

'What was that?'

'You tell me?'

Alex shook his head. He watched the next three minutes. A porter pulled back the curtain; the suspect lashed out, kicking the porter before sprinting away. Alex stared at the grainy fuzz of blood dripping from the leg of the patient. The floor turned dark grey around the bed. The hairs on the back of Alex's neck prickled. Hartley was right to be worried.

'Any more footage?'

Hartley huffed. 'Nothing from St Mary's. Two other hospitals have submitted files. That's why the case was created and I was assigned.'

'Same MO at the other hospitals?'

Hartley nodded. 'Very similar. Spaced less than three months apart. Two others dead, that we know of. The CPS is going crazy, wondering how many post-mortems they're going to have to request. A lot of people die every month in London hospitals, Alex.'

She left it hanging. Alex sat back in his chair. He tore his eyes away from the monitor and Hartley paused the video.

'Security has been tightened at the ten biggest city hospitals,' she said. 'Uniformed officers on rotation at the emergency entrances, but we can't keep it up for long. Without a decent lead, I'll be forced to pull the officers away again in a week or so. Besides, it causes panic. Patients start asking awkward questions.'

She checked her watch. 'I'm headed over to re-interview one of the witnesses from St Mary's. Officers recorded strange testimony from outside the hospital. I'm not sure whether to believe it.'

'Strange?'

'I'll be back later,' said Hartley. 'I'll take you through it then.'

Alex nodded, processing what he'd seen, resisting the urge to push Hartley too hard for information. She'd be under pressure from above. Giving a case like this to Hartley meant the commissioner wanted it solved yesterday.

'Good,' said Hartley, the strain in her eyes clear. 'I can see the cogs turning. You have the case notes so far. I want your thoughts. That's why you're here, Alex. Read the notes, watch the footage. Tell me what the hell is wrong with this person, and tell me quickly.'

CHAPTER FIVE

The dream lingered for several seconds after she woke, fractured and incomplete. Mia shuffled on to her knees on the torn mattress, hugging herself, arms wrapped tight until the shaking subsided.

Rain hammered overhead, shaking the metal roof, dripping through on to the hard concrete below. Mia shivered, trying to grasp fragments of the memory before it left her for the day.

The car. Faces in the darkness. One of them turned to her. Mia recognised the woman, felt a rush of familiarity and emotion. Mia loved this woman and saw herself in her face.

Mia closed her eyes but the face faded. The features blurred into grey and only the woman's eyes remained. Flashing lights, overhead. They blinked out in an instant, and Mia was again left with blackness and longing.

Not just longing. Hunger.

So soon, she thought, and so strong.

Mia threw aside the thick blankets she slept under. Dressed only in her underwear, she examined her bruised body, running her finger over the familiar scars. She had a small one running from her belly button straight down three inches. The large one, under her left breast, was raised and ugly, stitched in a hurry perhaps. She had two more scars on her back, over her spine. She had no idea where any of the scars came from.

Otherwise, she was in great shape. She flexed her muscles, watching her slender thighs tense and relax. Her left arm remained taped and splinted. She couldn't tell how well it was healing, although the swelling seemed to have subsided. Her shoulder joint moved with a grinding sensation, but it moved. It was enough.

She rummaged in her small pile of belongings for the thermometer. Sticking it in her mouth, Mia shuffled towards the office at the back of the warehouse. She washed in the metal basin, shivering again in the frigid water, rinsing her underwear before hanging it on a rail, slipping on a dry set in its place.

She spat the thermometer out. Normal range. Good. Infection was hard to judge and she'd formed a habit of taking her temperature every few days, just to be sure.

Black jeans followed, a black hoodie and a dark grey trench coat. Black boots completed her look, which was intended to blend in and hide. Become a shadow to most people. For some, a nightmare.

A cracked mirror reflected her young face. She stared at herself for several moments, wondering why she looked like the woman in the dream. Mia had no family that she could remember, and yet . . .

Pretty, on certain days. Mia would look at herself and liked what she saw. She compared her face and body with people in the street, with women in magazines, with billboards and lingerie posters. She compared herself with the women in suits who strode around the city, with the politicians on TV in the store windows. She compared herself with the doctors and nurses who paced the corridors of the hospitals she visited.

How old was she? Younger than the doctors in the wards, but older than the schoolchildren she watched crowding the pavements of London. Her features were dark and she blended in, yet she sensed she didn't belong. Not from here. Then from where?

Perhaps one day she would join the crowds. Perhaps one day she wouldn't need to compare.

A noise broke her thoughts. A scratching, scraping coming from the far side of the warehouse near the door. Mia froze, listening. Rats were common, but they rarely came close and Mia paid them little attention. This was a different sound, made by a larger creature.

Mia crept across, approaching the sliding door from the side, tiptoeing, pressing her ear against the thin metal. Visitors were rare in this neighbourhood. Mia had seen off the odd vagrant, but most people had better places to be. More scratching and a whine. A pant. Heavy breathing. Not human.

Mia slid the door back slowly and crouched to meet her visitor. A small black dog, knee height. It stepped back and stared at her, its wide eyes pleading through matted fur. Skinny and dirty, the stray shook with nerves, forming the beginnings of a bark. A faint whine emerged.

'Are you lost?' Mia tilted her head, examining the animal. At her voice the dog approached, trying to nuzzle one of her hands. Mia let it, for a second, before pushing it away.

'You can't stay here,' she said, seeing the hope in its eyes, wondering if it could see the sadness in hers. Too risky, too noisy. Much as she craved a companion, it couldn't be this one.

'Go away.'

Again the dog stepped forward. It managed to bark this time, gently, into her face. It licked its lips and sat. Mia saw the stumpy tail begin to move.

Mia shook her head, but the dog laid itself across the threshold, its eyes widening, staring up at her. It wanted her, needed her. It had presented itself at her mercy, ready to be her friend.

But Mia didn't have friends.

'Go,' she said, harshly this time. She pushed the dog and it stumbled to its feet. It stood a few feet away, waiting.

Mia took a chipped brick from a stack near the door. She weighed it in her hand. The dog didn't move, calling her bluff. Mia watched as the dog sat again, shuffling a little closer. She raised the brick, pulled her arm back and hurled it as hard as she could.

The brick flew high, well into the distance, crashing into the waste ground beyond. She cursed as the sound echoed around the buildings. The dog followed with its eyes but didn't move.

Mia cursed again but the dog seemed to get the message. It sniffed the air in front of her, raised itself on all fours and backed away slowly. Its eyes had lost their initial curiosity and the tail had stopped wagging. Mia watched as the dog turned. Their eyes met and she saw sadness. It gave her one last look before scampering out of sight.

She stared after it, biting down on the loneliness until she felt a tooth crack. She spat the fragment on to the floor, wondering if it hurt.

CHAPTER SIX

The PC blinked into life. Two new video files were available, labelled as STBARTS and LONDONBRIDGE, both large city hospitals. These would be the other instances of their suspect caught on CCTV. Alex double-clicked on the first one, leaning back in his chair, notepad and pen at the ready.

Thoughts of Grace and John had plagued him on the way in. His morning Xanax wasn't working and he popped another as the video loaded. Two each morning, he registered with some discomfort. Grace was right – he should seek help. But Alex had been saying that to himself since his early twenties. It was much easier to medicate than to seek therapy, and cheaper. He should know.

Alex checked his watch. Hartley hadn't been in the Met office when he arrived, but he got waved through with a visitor's badge and a signature; they had his name and photo. He was on their list and had been allocated a desk with a terminal.

It took forever to load and he scanned the bustling office while he waited. Uniforms and detectives scurried around. A few glanced his way, sizing him up. He tried to remain discreet, but was aware of his tailored suit and Barker brogues. Essential for impressing private clients, but way out of place in this office. Why couldn't he shop in the high street? He heard Grace's voice, her amused tone, and his mood dropped again.

The first video finally started playing. From St Bartholomew's, dated three months ago, it was better quality than the one from St Mary's. Alex watched the clock in the top-right corner of the screen. 23:08 – almost the same time. Shift handover – the perfect time to slip around inside a hospital while the staff were distracted.

There he was, a silhouette at the entrance to the ward, lingering, checking the nurses, keeping his head ducked before slinking across towards four curtained bays. Something in the man's posture made Alex pause and rewind the video. He stared, frowning, before continuing.

The angle from this camera was poor. The suspect entered a bay and stood with his back to the camera, blocking out any sight of the patient. Alex watched for seven minutes, then fast-forwarded another twenty. The figure swayed, shifting, but Alex couldn't make out what was happening, and then it was all over. The man left the curtain and walked towards the entrance, seeming less alert, shuffling. At one point he staggered, putting his hand out to steady himself at the doorway. The video ended.

Alex frowned. It looked like the same person, but the video didn't capture anything useful. He brought up the accompanying notes – the medical summary and cause of death. Reading through, he felt sick to his stomach.

The patient had been sixteen years old. Still a child. Alex had a flash of Katie in a few years, lying helpless in a hospital bed, and shook it out of his head.

This girl, Dawn Hitchens, had herniated a spinal disc at her gymnastics centre, where she was training for the regional squad. Alex knew the basic physiology of the injury – a disc ruptures and the gel inside leaks out, causing sudden and severe lower-back pain, often spreading to the legs. Most cases are treatable with painkillers and moderate intervention, but Dawn had been brought into the emergency room because of numbness in her feet and a high fever. Due to be checked out by a consultant the following morning, Dawn was only on mild painkillers and had complained, in some distress, about her level of pain. The parents had also complained to the matron. At handover the nurse had promised to explore stronger analgesics to see her through the night.

Dawn never made it through the night.

She was found dead after shift handover, turned on her side, her back scratched, bruised and swollen. Marks and contusions in the skin suggested the slipped disc had been repeatedly pressed and manipulated. The cause of death was asphyxiation, but this appeared to have taken place after the torture had finished.

The doctor's report, some of which had been withheld from the parents, pending the police investigation, stated that the girl must have been subjected to 'extreme and punishing pain for an extended period' before she died. The local police weren't called until much later that night. Due to a technical oversight, the police didn't request the CCTV until another week had passed. The case was opened, but was the first of its type. They had no idea who the hooded figure was, and no leads whatsoever.

Alex took a moment. He stared at the floor, breathing slowly. As usual, four in, hold, four out. Reading the report had been worse than seeing the video. He knew he should be diagnosing, positing what might cause such behaviour, but found himself unable to think straight. That girl had been taken from her family at such an early age, before she'd had a chance to make her mark on the world. Who had the right to do that? Who would do it, knowing the trauma they would cause? A disturbed mind, either through nature or nurture, or through a temporary influence. But that was hardly a diagnosis. The police knew as much the minute they'd watched the video for themselves.

You'll need to do better than that, Alex, he thought to himself.

Calming himself, he opened up the next video. This was one month ago at London Bridge emergency room. Four in the morning, not shift handover, but a quiet night. Alex scanned the notes first, wanting to prepare himself.

Ian Jordan, a thirty-eight-year-old lawyer, brought in by ambulance with a burst appendix. Risk of sepsis was considered high and the surgical team was prepping. Ian was less than an hour away from having the troublesome appendage whipped out, being settled with a dose of antibiotics and having a few weeks off work.

The paramedics handed over and the patient was left in a bay, in full view of the CCTV.

The suspect appeared at the edge of the screen at 04:09, hovering, same posture, face down, hoodie up. He waited until three of the nurses ran out to deal with another situation – the report said a road traffic accident with four casualties was incoming.

As soon as the nurses were out of sight the suspect ran over to the trolley holding Mr Jordan. Again, Alex narrowed his eyes. Something in the way the suspect walked bugged him.

This time, Alex had an uninterrupted view of the suspect's handiwork. His face remained in shadow, but his right hand went straight for the patient's lower abdomen while his right slipped a strip of tape across the mouth. Using both hands and his weight, the suspect leaned in, putting pressure on the patient's face, presumably to stop him screaming, and on the area of his gut already in immense pain. Alex watched as the man lifted his hand, bunched a fist and punched repeatedly into the patient's stomach. It went on for several minutes like this, and Alex found himself swallowing, the nausea rising as he imagined the pain this victim must be going through.

According to the clock, the suspect stopped eight minutes later, pulling off the tape and leaving. Again the suspect staggered, crashing into the next trolley before moving out of sight of the camera.

Ian Jordan died shortly afterwards from an internal haemorrhage. It was unexpected and caught the attending doctors by surprise. They assumed sepsis, until the post-mortem revealed the truth several days later. Then the police were called.

Alex rewound the video and watched the suspect stagger off. He did it again, and a third time to be sure. His first conclusion at least was something the police didn't know.

'You look pleased.'

Alex spun in his chair to find Hartley behind him. She looked tired, but less stressed than before.

'I'd hardly call it "pleased",' said Alex. 'I've just watched the other two CCTV videos and read the reports.'

Hartley screwed up her face. 'Yeah. I know.' She nodded and their eyes met. Neither needed to express how sick it made them feel.

'So what can you tell me?' she said, taking a chair, pulling a Thermos out of her bag. Alex was about to answer but Hartley cut him off.

'Herbal tea. Doctor says I drink too much caffeine.'

Alex nodded. He'd have to find his coffee elsewhere.

'So?'

'Not much,' said Alex, 'except he's a she.'

'Beg your pardon?' said Hartley, pouring the steaming liquid into a mug.

'Our suspect is female. Something bugged me in the first video. Baggy clothes hide a lot, but they can't hide certain things.' He rewound the second video and played a clip of the suspect moving away.

'Look here. The hip rotation and extension of the legs. I attended a witness coaching course a few months ago – they covered this and it suddenly hit me. Male and female gait is subtly different. You can't always detect it, but here you can. See.'

Alex replayed the clip, pointing to the suspect's waist and hips. 'It's the way women place their feet,' said Alex. 'Men don't walk like that.'

Hartley sipped her tea, screwed her face up even more, and took the mouse from Alex, playing the video another couple of times.

'Lucky break,' she said, giving him a smile.

'You agree?'

'I agree,' said Hartley. 'I'll get a second opinion, but I think you're right.'

She continued to sip her healthy drink, clearly not enjoying it.

'Does it change anything?' she said.

'Yes,' said Alex, 'I think it does.'

'In what way?'

'In that it rules out a lot of the usual motives,' he said. 'The psychological profile for this type of crime – even though I've never seen anything quite like it, but I mean ABH, GBH, intent to cause severe injury and death – is predominantly male. That means . . .' He tailed off, trying to process his thoughts, pick the right words. 'It means we're dealing with someone rather special.'

'I told *you* that,' said Hartley. 'Tell me something I don't know.'

Alex flushed, a little annoyed. He'd made a contribution, if minor, to the case, but it seemed to go unrecognised by Hartley. He shook his head at her and she gave him another, less convincing smile. Her phone buzzed and she excused herself, heading towards a row of cubicles along the far wall.

Alex watched her go, trying to focus, trying to make sense of what he'd seen so far. He leaned back in his chair, ignoring the anxiety tugging at his gut.

Could it be gang-related? Alex knew little of such things, but the background information on the three victims didn't warrant such a conclusion, particularly the sixteen-year-old gymnast. The individual investigations so far hadn't revealed anything remotely associated with gangs or turf wars. Hartley hadn't mentioned it. She would have done if she thought it had any relevance.

If not a gang or another retribution-style cause, then Alex was left with the simple explanations or the extreme. Simple was more likely to be true: drink and drugs. But what possible combination of narcotics could elicit such wanton violence? These attacks were planned, premeditated. Not necessarily the victims themselves, but the timing, the situation. The location . . . Why hospitals? Full of vulnerable people, but also full of staff and security.

Also full of drugs, but the suspect went straight for the patients, not for the pharmacy.

Unless she had another reason for being at the hospital.

Alex was grasping at nothing. He made a note on his pad to speak to Mikey. Their relationship was mainly business these days but based on a deep friendship that went all the way back to medical school. Mikey was a pharmacist for the NHS and sold prescription drugs on the side to fuel his gambling habit. Alex bought prescription drugs from Mikey to fuel his benzo habit. The two of them also went for the occasional beer, although that was rare of late. As they got older, each had become more conscious of their own failures, and the banter had become strained, serious. Each offered advice to the other. Both knew they were the worst type of hypocrite.

He'd ask, but Alex wasn't convinced this was drugs, and it almost certainly wasn't alcohol.

So if the explanation wasn't simple, that left the extreme. The outlying psychological conditions that could turn a normal human into a monster.

Hartley appeared over the desk partition. She looked puzzled.

Alex raised his eyebrows. 'Progress?'

Hartley shook her head. 'No. I just spoke to another witness.'

'Oh?'

Hartley edged forward, leaning on the partition. 'I think our suspect is high when they're committing their crimes,' she said. 'Seriously high.'

Alex frowned. He didn't tell her he was on the verge of dismissing this. 'It's possible,' he said, 'but there's nothing I can think of that would cause such behaviour.'

'The porter who caught our suspect in the act,' said Hartley. 'He said that when he gave chase our suspect got hit by a bus outside the hospital.'

'A bus?'

'Indeed. He said it clipped her shoulder and sent her flying, ten feet or more into the kerb. The bus stopped, the driver panicked, but guess what our suspect did?'

Alex shrugged, not liking where this was going.

'He or she got up, brushed themselves off and sprinted away faster than Usain Bolt.'

Alex chewed his lip, nodding to himself. 'The porter didn't exaggerate?'

'The bus driver corroborated it,' said Hartley.

Alex sniffed. 'Well, the suspect could just have got lucky,' he said, although he thought getting hit by a bus was a pretty unlikely trauma to run away from.

'Or?'

Alex thought about it. 'OK. Possibly high. Some sort of NMDA receptor antagonist. Angel dust—'

'PCP?'

'Yes, or ketamine. That class of drug could provide enough pain detachment to allow you to walk away. But the person would need to be pumped to the eyeballs with it. I doubt they'd be able to sprint.'

'Would PCP cause any other symptoms?'

'You mean like a desire to sadistically torture somebody?'

Hartley smiled. 'Something like that.'

'No,' said Alex, his voice confident, although he was beginning to feel anything but. 'PCP, ketamine and the like can cause all sorts of symptoms, and yes, mild aggression has been recorded in some patients.'

'Well, there you go—'

'Not like this, though,' said Alex, remembering the video and the medical report. He lowered his voice. 'Not like this, Detective. Our suspect might be taking PCP or any manner of drugs, but it didn't cause her behaviour.'

Hartley looked about to challenge him but saw his face and obviously thought better of it. She tapped the partition and left him to his musings.

CHAPTER SEVEN

Mia's mood descended. She waited on a bench in Regent's Park, collecting her wits, waiting for the right time.

Sometimes several days could pass and Mia would feel almost normal. She'd enjoy the sunrise, take in the fresh air and stroll through the city streets, believing she was just one of many, a normal citizen of this alien city.

But when Mia's darkness fell and she plummeted into her inner nightmare, her body would quiver and scream, her mind falling in line. No matter how much she fought – and she did fight it – she could never hold out for long.

St Mary's was out of the question today, after the incident with the bus and the porter. It wasn't safe to return, not when she'd been seen. But London City Hospital was only five minutes' walk from the park; she'd go there. She knew all the London hospitals intimately. She relied on them. Mia was drawn to these places of suffering. They provided her with easy sustenance, and she didn't know where else might offer the same.

But they were more than hunting grounds. Something else drew her in: a familiarity that tugged at her gut, fleeting and incoherent. It flashed in her mind for an instant, then slipped away, leaving nothing but anguish. She had to go. She had to be there.

Mia chose the direction and moved, her shuffle widening into a purposeful stride. Head down, she remained on the outskirts, always avoiding people, always ducking to the side, into a doorway, or skipping into the road. She had the knack of drifting through the crowds, leaving nothing but a shadow in her wake.

She paused a short distance from the main entrance to City Hospital. Leaning against a railing, she held a folded tourist map, pretending to study it. Two police officers with clipboards stood at the doors, scanning the flow as people passed in and out of the building.

Probably nothing, she thought, edging closer, remaining on the opposite side of the road. Two minutes later, Mia stopped again. One of the officers had hold of a young man dressed in dark jeans and a black hoodie. The officer pointed to the man's head, and Mia watched him pull the hood back. His hands were out, palms up, protesting his innocence. After a few words, the officer let the man go and he continued on his way.

Anxiety coursed through Mia. She heard her heart beating, battling between her desire to continue and her worry at being caught. The decision was made for her as the officer raised his head to scan the road. Panicking, Mia backed into the shadows, slipping down a side street and into an alleyway. She crouched out of sight behind a wheelie bin, cursing the police and herself. *Stupid*, she thought, *and careless*.

Her first mistake. Or had she just been unlucky? Chance had brought the porter to the bedside and prompted the chain of events that followed.

The hospitals were being watched and her frequent visits noticed. She wondered if St Mary's was the only one they knew about. She'd been careful in the others, so many others. In and out. People had suffered and died, but she'd never been caught. Never even come close.

Her luck had finally run out.

Rummaging in the wheelie bin, Mia found an old plastic bag and scrunched both her hoodie and coat inside it. She emerged from the alley in a vest top and jeans, carrying the bag. She was cold, and it left her splinted arm exposed, but she looked different; it was enough.

The whirling panic crept back in as soon as she'd caught her breath. Mia walked and she sweated, her mind a mess. This couldn't be happening. She couldn't access the hospital. Her appetite hadn't been satisfied, and she worried about the consequences. Mia was teetering on the edge and needed gratification. What would it take to tip her over?

They couldn't stop her. They mustn't.

She waited. The sun began to dip and the shadows snaked across the streets. Shivering, she held her bare arms against her body, hugging the heat into her thin chest.

The police remained at the entrance of City Hospital, but there were other ways inside. Mia slunk past on the opposite side of the street, keeping out of sight, her arm hidden and her black clothing in the bag. The underground parking lot could be accessed by a side road, and Mia stuck to the shadows, joining the flow of pedestrians, workers and patients heading in and out.

She followed a group of nurses. They headed down the tarmac ramp, turning at the bottom, not towards the parked cars but towards the staff entrance. Mia had been here before. The door was badge-access only; it led directly up to the emergency departments. But everyone tailgated. She could get through with a little patience.

One of the nurses, a large lady with a rucksack slung over one shoulder, stumbled, grabbing a handrail for support. Mia stopped. The nurse was in pain; her leg throbbed. Mia watched, feeling the tendrils snaking out, teasing and coaxing her. A sprain, or something deeper. Mia couldn't tell, but she glanced around, wondering if she could take a chance.

Two of the other nurses turned. They called and headed back, reaching out to their colleague, helping her limp along. One of them took the rucksack and carried it. Mia clenched her fists, watching as the group swiped themselves inside. The door closed.

Patience. It wasn't one of Mia's strengths, not in her condition. She couldn't linger for too long in one place, and chose to walk a length of cars, keeping an eye on the door and the flow of people, waiting for her chance.

Luck. Mia's was getting worse. Beyond the glass door she spied a uniformed security guard. Not police, but just as much of a barrier. The guard ambled through the door and paused, taking a quick scan of the surroundings. It was dim, the sun unable to find its way into the parking lot, the shadows offering protection. Mia looked away, walking back towards the ramp, cursing under her breath. She risked a glance and saw the guard disappear inside, his rudimentary scan complete.

Mia tapped her splinted arm against a metal railing, trying to distract herself from her increasingly shallow breathing. The clang of metal on metal echoed in the enclosed space. The vibrations travelled up her arm and Mia wondered if the impact would damage the tissue and bone so carefully trying to knit themselves together.

'Are you OK?'

An older man approached her from the shadows. A nurse, dressed in scrubs. He clasped his hands together but held back, apparently wary. Mia considered her appearance and didn't blame him. Her eyes burned into his.

He frowned. 'Can I help you inside? Are you waiting for someone?'

Mia shook her head. She studied his face, the angle of his jaw and the arch of his neck. She traced down his throat to his chest, breathing deeply, trying to catch a whiff of something, anything. She breathed out in a deep sigh, trying to rein in the craving in her chest. He had nothing to offer and Mia hated him for it.

The nurse's frown deepened, the expression sympathetic but unsure. He glanced at her arm, then peered into her eyes.

'Look at me,' he said.

Mia stared, but she was distracted by a siren in the street above, blasting through the traffic. The ambulance flashed its lights as it pulled into the bays above the parking lot, and the glare reflected off every glass surface of every car. The light hit Mia and filled her mind. Her vision faded, the parking lot disappeared and Mia turned inwards.

Her own experience. Her memories. Her waking dream.

Shunted left and right, a blast of cold air and a floating sensation. Her feet were cold and her lungs burned with fresh air. She was being pulled along and couldn't move.

Panic.

The lights flashed.

Mia blinked and the memory evaporated. The parking lot surrounded her once again and the face of the nurse peered in. He stepped forward this time, but Mia's good arm snapped out, grabbing his wrist.

'Do you know me?' she said, gasping as the panic attack took hold. 'Have I been here before?'

She shook, gripping the nurse hard. He tried to calm her, speaking softly, coaxing her to relax, but his words had no effect. He pulled his arm free and she let him go, staggering away towards the ramp, picking her feet up into a shuffle.

She was running by the time she hit the street. The nurse didn't call after her. Perhaps he was scared; perhaps he thought it best if she left. But she could hear her heart beating over the sound of the sirens and the traffic. It thundered in her ears as she pounded the pavement, desperate to get away from the one place she needed to be.

There was no pursuit. Mia stopped a hundred yards from the parking lot, her heart in her mouth and her fists clenched so tightly she could feel the nails cutting the skin. Her breathing slowed, mirroring the calm of the air and the steady flow of cars in and out.

She leaned against a wall, watching the road and the entrance, frozen with indecision. Ten minutes passed. She shivered but remained rooted to the pavement, tucked into the shadows, away from the line of cars parked against the kerb. A solitary street light flicked on, casting an orange glow across the street.

A figure appeared, limping up the ramp from the parking lot before turning and heading towards Mia. Not staff; not medical. A young woman who dragged her leg, shuffling along. The street was empty – a lull in the traffic. No other pedestrians in sight.

The woman crossed over. It wouldn't be long before she walked directly past Mia. But the woman stopped. Mia saw a flash of keys in the woman's hand, and then the parked car in front of her beeped, the hazard lights flashing against the tarmac. It was a dark-coloured hatchback, the interior light failing to come on as the woman opened the driver's door.

Mia stiffened. The woman's face was visible in the faint glow of the evening sky and the street light. Mia saw what she wanted; what she needed. Staying in the shadows, Mia crept towards the car, hidden against the wall, stopping as the woman slung her handbag on to the passenger seat. Distracted, she didn't look up, and Mia slunk past to the rear of the car, alert to the signals radiating from the woman's laboured breath. Her sweat caught the air and flowed into Mia's nostrils, lush and enticing.

A patient in pain. Satisfaction would be hers.

The driver's door closed. Mia reacted, her desperation surging through her muscles as she grabbed the handle on the rear door. She jumped in, reaching forward and dragging the woman by her hair into the back seat.

She had the presence of mind to slam the door just in time to stifle the first scream.

CHAPTER EIGHT

Alex squinted in the morning sun. The pathologist introduced herself as Dr Hickman. Short and nervous, she threw a worried frown at Alex before leading them inside.

'I'm the psych consult,' said Alex, taking a small breath, feeling the energy drain from his legs. The smell in the morgue was hard to pinpoint, like a battle between bleach and death. Neither was winning.

Hartley had called him early that morning. There was another body. A violent death at City Hospital during the night.

They'd met at the station and taken Hartley's car. Alex was surprised to find she drove a new BMW coupé. He realised he shouldn't have been. Why shouldn't a senior detective appreciate a fine car? She didn't hold back on the speed either, and Alex felt a little less guilty about the way he drove around London in his Merc.

Dr Hickman nodded, her frown disappearing. 'That's good,' she said. 'The person who did this needs help.'

They headed straight into one of the examination rooms. Alex saw two metal autopsy tables, one empty, the other with a female body lying on it. The body was pasty and grey, but with dried blood covering a large amount of the skin.

'We brought her out of the cold chamber a few minutes ago,' said Dr Hickman. 'I've done a preliminary exam – we've photographed and taken hair, fingernail scrapes, fibres and an internal. She was mostly naked when they found her, her clothing ripped. We haven't cleaned her yet, hence the blood.'

Alex swallowed, trying to get the taste of the air out of his mouth. He lingered behind Hartley, who stood with the pathologist next to the table. Alex saw that the dead woman's hands were bagged, standard procedure for a murder investigation, but the sight of it still made him shudder. This wasn't a person any more, it was a crime scene and a collection of potential evidence.

'Post-mortem?' said Hartley.

'Scheduled for tomorrow. I wouldn't usually invite the police in at this stage, but I thought you'd want to see the injuries beforehand, given the alert you put out.'

Hartley nodded, holding her hand to her mouth before taking a deep breath. Alex sidled closer, praying this would be quick. He'd avoided looking at the body thus far. Now he had no choice.

The woman looked to be in her twenties or thirties. Slim with dark brown hair. Her features were hard for Alex to determine. His heart thudded in his ears.

'The fatal injury was this,' Dr Hickman said, pointing to a narrow slit through the woman's left breast. 'Possibly a penknife, straight through the heart. No puzzle there.'

Hartley leaned in to look at the knife wound. Alex stared below it, at the woman's stomach, trying to avoid her face. He saw a young woman, killed in the prime of her life. He wanted to cover her in a sheet, hide her away, comfort her loved ones.

'The more disturbing injuries are the non-fatal ones,' said Hickman. She pulled out a biro and moved around the table, starting at the woman's groin. 'Her genitals are mutilated, ripped and bruised. Quite significant damage.'

'Rape?' said Hartley.

Hickman paused. 'No,' she said. 'Not rape. In fact, I don't think it was sexually motivated at all. The injuries are not typical of that type of assault.' She moved on, her voice calm, her emotions held in check, Alex suspected, through experience and practice. Alex couldn't hide his reaction quite so well and looked away, clenching his jaw. He had to count to ten before looking back.

'OK?' said Dr Hickman, pausing.

Alex nodded. Hartley gave an unamused expression, but Alex could see her perspiring, her jaw clenched.

'Both nipples have been ripped off,' continued Hickman, 'bitten, by the look of the tearing. I'll confirm at the post-mortem. Her armpits are gouged and bruised, and her stomach – her solar plexus – it looks like it was punched repeatedly with a fist. See this marking here?' The doctor glanced at Hartley. 'A small fist, I might add.'

'Moving on, her fingertips have been bitten and three fingernails cracked, again with teeth. Her ear canals have had forced entry – perhaps a finger inserted . . .'

Alex had had enough. He stepped away and turned. The room spun, vertigo gripping him.

'Sorry,' he murmured. 'This is, uh . . . I might need some air.'

The doctor paused. She seemed to consider things, then put her biro back in her pocket.

'There are further injuries,' she said, 'to the feet and knees, but they are less severe. She appears to have a swollen ankle from a previous injury.'

'We're tracing her movements to see if she was a patient at City Hospital,' said Hartley, turning to look away from the body. 'But those wound locations . . . All of them are clusters of nerves, hypersensitive to pain.'

Dr Hickman nodded. She looked impressed. 'Yes. Obviously, the genitals, but these other injuries would also have caused intense pain.'

'You're sure all of these were inflicted before death?' said Hartley.

'Yes,' said Hickman. 'Absolutely. My full report will be available after the post-mortem, but that's about the size of it. This woman was extensively tortured before being put out of her misery.'

Alex sucked in the fresh air of the parking lot. He was shaken and had given up trying to hide it from Hartley. She gave him a few moments, stepping aside to check her phone.

Alex had seen a lot of dead bodies during his work with the police. His cases had ranged from domestic abuse and fratricide through to serial killers like Victor Lazar. Alex had always tried to maintain a professional distance, assuming with his training that he could apply his techniques to himself. As he reached into his pocket for another Xanax, he realised he was far from being able to achieve that. He hid the pill from Hartley, slipping it into his mouth, slumping against the side of the car.

He stared at the tarmac, watching a crisp packet drift between the tyres. A cat scooted out from its hiding place and gave chase. It brought light relief to the sickening churn of his stomach. He saw the mutilated body in the morgue. He thought of Grace and Katie. He thought of his mum in her nursing home, her mind gradually slipping away. He thought of his father's death at the hands of a suspect Alex should have stopped. He spiralled.

'Alex.' Hartley tilted her head, looking concerned.

Alex cleared his throat and his mind cleared. Back in the moment.

Hartley unlocked the car and they headed back to the office. She drove more sedately on the return journey, perhaps herself affected by what she'd seen.

'We had a possible sighting,' she said. 'Our suspect outside City Hospital yesterday.'

'What time? Before or after that young woman was murdered?'

'Before, and in the vicinity, spotted in the underground parking lot. The description matches, broadly. A nurse found her. He said the woman's arm was injured, taped up; he assumed she was a junkie. She got spooked and ran off and he reported it to Security.'

Alex pondered. He considered the victims so far, the injuries and the sickening methods employed by the killer.

'It's about pain,' he said.

Hartley turned. 'Torture, sure. A sadist. My question is why, Alex?'

He didn't answer immediately, trying to untangle his thinking. 'That's why our suspect goes to hospitals – they're an easy place to find injured people. But there's something else . . .' He paused. 'Hospitals are staffed and busy. Most have security. Why risk it? If all you want to do is hurt people, why not do it in a dark alley? Avoid the crowds . . .'

'Like she did to that woman in there?'

'If it was our suspect.'

Hartley shrugged. 'The forensics unit isn't finished with the car yet. We'll see what we can find.'

Alex nodded. Perhaps Hartley was right: this was nothing more than a sadistic killer on a rampage. He just couldn't shake the feeling that he was missing something.

They pulled into the Met parking lot, both deep in thought. Hartley excused herself and hurried off, already on another phone conversation.

Alex paused and hung back. Hartley was giving him time and space, but he'd need to start earning his money soon. The problem was that he had so little to go on. To determine a psychological condition and motive behind such acts required more than the evidence presented so far. Alex was at a complete loss.

He pulled out his phone and dialled. It was answered on the fourth ring.

'Hi, Alex.' Grace's voice was warm. It seeped into him, tempering his anxiety, allowing him to escape the vision of the last hour. 'What can I do for you? Katie's at a friend's, sorry. You can call or text her?'

'It was you I wanted,' said Alex. 'No, nothing. I just wanted to . . .' His throat closed, a lump forming. He still found this so hard but he wanted to hear her voice. He needed it. His family was the only thing that kept him sane, even if they did it from a distance.

'Are you OK?' Concern crept into Grace's voice.

'I love you, Grace, and Katie. So much,' said Alex, taking a gulp of air. 'I'm not . . . you know. I'm not trying to suggest anything. I know you have your life . . .'

'Alex—'

'I wanted to tell you. That's all. Just to let you know. I'm here for you if you ever need me.'

A few moments of silence. He heard Grace sniff.

'Thank you,' said Grace finally. 'It means a lot.' She paused again. 'We love you too.'

Alex found himself nodding, a smile escaping at the corners of his mouth. His jaw remained clenched.

'We'll talk soon, OK?' said Grace.

'OK,' he said. Grace hung up and he did the same.

Turning into the wind, his eyes watered. He sniffed until the tears stopped forming, and then headed back into the office.

CHAPTER NINE

Three and a half thousand miles north-east of London, an icy wind crept through the open door of a wooden cabin. The cabin stood isolated on top of a hill, overlooking a complex warren of squat concrete buildings, each connected by covered walkways, each rooftop thick with snow. The buildings sat hidden in the middle of a forest clearing in the shadow of the Ural Mountains, the native Siberian larch trees surrounding the complex like a protective blanket of white and green. The protection was intentional, for this complex was not on any map and its true purpose was not in any government file or account. Very few people came this far north, which was exactly why the directors had chosen the location.

The man in the cabin doorway paused, dusting off his thick jacket, pulling the hood down to reveal matted black hair and a thick beard. Flakes of snow drifted from the fur hood, melting as they hit the wooden floor.

'Shut the bloody door.' A voice from an armchair, near the window, which was set at an angle to the roaring fire and gave the occupant a clear view of the room. The usually warm voice of the young woman who occupied the cabin was cold and tense. She knew something was wrong. She'd already packed her few belongings in anticipation.

The man snorted, but obeyed, turning to slam the wooden door behind him. He remained where he was, dripping, thawing after the short trek up from the complex. The woman in the chair had watched him through the window, insisting he came to see her, to speak face to face.

'It's getting complicated,' said the man. He paused, stomping his feet on the floor, leaving a puddle of dirty water.

'I forget when life was simple,' said the woman. She didn't look at the man, preferring to stare out of the window at the grey skies.

'Not just the girl. There's another party involved. They said you should know. They said you must—'

'Who?'

The man paused. He pulled out a notebook from his jacket pocket, unfolding the cover and turning several pages.

'Dr Alex Madison.' The man pronounced the name with care. 'The UK police are using him. He has been under observation for some time now. Apparently, he . . . Apparently, this is . . .' The man struggled for the right words. 'It's your problem to deal with.'

If the woman was surprised, she hid it well, her eyes barely wavering from the window. Only a person who knew her history would have seen the flicker, the recognition and the emotion that crept up through the cold. Dr Alex Madison. She curled the name on her tongue, enjoying the memories it triggered, scared at what the future held in store.

'When?'

'Now,' said the man.

The woman's head snapped round, her eyes boring into his. The man swallowed, glancing at the floor. 'I mean,' he stuttered, 'the message I was given was for you to leave immediately.'

The woman continued to stare for a few more seconds before closing her eyes and turning back to the fire, enjoying the warmth on her face.

'Very well,' she said. 'At least the weather in London will be warmer than here.'

'*Da*,' said the man, backing away, sensing his message had been delivered and his presence was no longer required. Messengers in this place were frequently blamed for the message, and the mountains never tired of hearing their screams.

The door slammed again at the man's departure. The woman remained seated, taking a few deep breaths before picking up her laptop from the coffee table. She sent two brief emails and then logged out. She had four hours before her transport arrived.

Four hours to figure out how big this mess had become, and how deep she'd need to clean.

CHAPTER TEN

Mia woke with a start. Her legs were slippery with sweat and she kicked off the sheet. Her temperature plummeted and goosebumps appeared on her thighs, but she didn't notice.

Before the flash – a car journey. Vivid and coherent. The face turning towards her became clearer each time she saw it. The eyes were like hers, the features the same. The woman in the car smiled at Mia, and Mia knew the smile was because of her. Mia created joy in this person. Family. Her mother?

So where was her mother now?

Mia stood and paced the warehouse, naked except for underwear, hot one minute and shivering the next. Coming down or hungry for the next hit, she was never sure. Her bodily sensations were not an accurate or reliable indicator. She took her temperature. Not an infection; not a fever. She suffered regardless.

A normal person would find this easy. A normal person could go to the police, ask them to help. They would find her mother. Perhaps the driver of the car was her father. Mia didn't need to be alone.

But Mia wasn't normal. She couldn't go to the police. What if they knew what she'd done? What if they knew what she was capable of? Mia would be arrested and locked away, unable to search for her parents, unable to satisfy her urges.

The only person Mia could trust was herself, which remained scant comfort, for she knew the hopelessness of her position. Of her life.

She stood in front of the mirror, examining her body. Thinner by the day, her muscles stood proud, but her body fat couldn't get any lower. She needed more calories. Getting sick due to lack of food wasn't an attractive option. She could die in this place, wither away. How long would it be before the smell attracted animals? Rats and bugs. Eaten from within by maggots.

She couldn't go to the police, but she had to do something. She had to find answers.

Mia traced her index finger down her stomach. There wasn't much for the maggots to eat.

At least it wouldn't hurt.

But then again, nothing did.

Mia dressed and left the warehouse. The night had brought with it a semblance of rationality. The fact she'd never before needed to alter her appearance was testament to her natural caution, but the time had come.

Mia headed to one of the more run-down but busy shopping streets. The shopper never saw it coming. Leaving a handbag unattended near the entrance to any store was foolish, and Mia, with a practised swipe, removed the bag from the floor and dropped it into her carrier bag, striding away before anybody had the chance to react.

The phone went into a bin with the bag and almost everything else. Mia found ninety-five pounds in cash. She also pocketed a mascara, blusher and lipstick. She had plans for the latter.

Freshly loaded, Mia headed to the nearest pharmacy, before stopping in at a discount clothes store. She was quick, reluctant to spend too long under the watchful eye of CCTV, picking out two pairs of skinny blue jeans, two floral tops – long-sleeved to cover her splinted arm – new sports underwear and a pair of black pumps. The floral tops were a stretch for Mia, but she wasn't stupid. She needed a complete change of appearance. She shouldn't have left it so long.

The shopping spree lasted less than thirty minutes and Mia was back in the safety of her warehouse within the hour. She laid out the clothing and make-up on the mattress. The last item out of the bag was a box of hair dye. Mia stared at the photo of the woman on the packet, tracing the perfect lines of her face, admiring the shine of her hair, the bouncing curls and flawless colour.

Mia filled the basin with water and applied the hair dye. While it worked she chopped another inch off the length, leaving it close around her chin. She stood, naked, glaring at herself in the mirror, counting the seconds.

The dye worked. Her hair was now a dark brown with a red tinge, distinctly different. Dressed in her new clothes with a touch of make-up, she was transformed. Whoever the police were looking for wouldn't be found in this body.

She gazed at herself in front of the mirror. It would take time to get used to it. *I look almost normal*, she thought as she slipped the pumps on to her feet and picked up her bag. Some women would kill for a body like this. Mia killed and got a body like this.

Perhaps it would be a good thing, she considered. Pretty people were treated differently, she noticed, as a rule. They could get away with things others could not. Go places others could not. Persuade people they were right, they were innocent.

Pretty people could persuade other people they were not monsters.

She moved her gaze up, away from her damaged torso to her neck and face. Olive, she decided. Light brown, at a push. She'd often tried to compare her skin tone to the racks of make-up in the high street, never sticking around long enough to find a match. It was important, wasn't it? To know what colour your skin was? If she knew, would that tell her where she was from? But who to ask . . .? Mia put the questions aside for now. Her features were dark and striking, she knew that much. It would have to do.

Again, Mia headed out of the warehouse, carefully locking the door behind her.

She braved it. Her choices were dwindling. Her hand had been forced and she needed answers.

London City Hospital. As before, two police officers stood outside, clipboards in hand, scrutinising the masses of people flowing in and out of the hospital entrance.

Mia didn't pause for a second but crossed the road and joined the throng. Avoiding the police officers' gaze would be suspicious, so Mia tested her own theory, walking right past one of them, a young man. She caught his eye, and he held it for a second longer than was necessary, a glint in his own. Pretty people. He offered a nod and a smile to Mia, who returned it and kept walking.

Inside the doors, she let out the breath she'd been holding, facing the crowd with renewed purpose. Today wasn't about a fix. Not yet. Today was about the memories, about where they came from, about what had happened to her.

Mia forced herself through the emergency room, hearing the occasional cry from a patient and checking her own heartbeat, which fluttered longingly in response. She managed to leave the temptation behind and ventured into the corridors.

A maze, that's how it appeared. But it was organised, colour-coded, clean and efficient. Mia paused with several others to study a map. Names, departments and clinical disciplines jostled for space on the huge sign, but none triggered any recognition in Mia. Stroke, cancer care, endocrinology, ophthalmology, dermatology . . . Mia's gaze jerked down the list, not spotting anything that jumped out at her.

She picked a direction at random and trod the corridor, careful to keep her face forward, unemotional, uninteresting. The corridors were long and busy, full of voices – sometimes shouts, sometimes laughter. Mia walked for twenty minutes or so, taking lifts, stepping around trolleys, circling upwards through the building towards the upper levels.

Occasionally, she would pause at the entrance to a ward – to catch her breath, she told herself, but really to hear a snippet, a scrap of pain. She listened to the suffering and smelled the fear, the noises and odours of human anguish seeping through the air into her consciousness, teasing her about what could follow. But she stopped herself in time. Only just. Several floors up with no easy route of escape, this was the wrong place to satisfy her urge.

She dug deep.

That was not the purpose of today.

Stepping out of the lift, Mia paused to stare at the nurses and doctors milling around. Nothing familiar, nothing at all. It was only when a bed appeared from her right, pushed by a porter dressed in a light blue top and black trousers, that Mia's heart skipped a beat. The porter paused, gripping his end of the bed. The patient lay flat, awake and staring upwards. An elderly lady with severe lower abdominal pain, her skin pasty and beaded with sweat. Mia swallowed and tried to focus.

Two doctors appeared at the foot of the bed. They both wore green scrubs, but nothing on their faces. Their hair was also uncovered. The scene almost formed into something familiar in Mia's mind, but it was wrong, all wrong. She shook her head, approaching the bed. The doctors should be wearing masks, she thought. It was right and proper. It was necessary.

'Where is your mask?' she heard herself say, standing not three feet from the bed. The patient's pain radiated outwards. Mia wanted to reach out and touch her.

The porter and two doctors turned to stare. Mia saw their eyes burning into her, the porter's in amusement, and the doctors' with concern.

'Are you a relative?' said one.

Mia looked up from the bed and met the doctor's eye. Concern and sympathy with a dash of suspicion stared back at her.

Mia shook her head, backing away. This was all wrong. She was sorry she'd come.

As she retreated into the lift, the doctors lost interest and moved on. The doors closed and Mia clenched her jaw in frustration.

Keeping her head down as she exited the lift, she found herself lost, frustrated and angry in the rabbit warren of corridors. She barged into people and ignored their comments as she hastened away.

Finding herself going in circles, she headed into the ladies' room and locked the door, standing against the cold tiles of the wall, eyes closed. Breathe in and breathe out. She tried not to listen to the niggling feeling in her gut. The urge was there, lurking, not quite ripe, but Mia knew it was unpredictable.

She relieved herself, glad of a clean bowl and fresh paper. She washed her hands and splashed her face. Staring into the small mirror, she cursed, realising she'd smudged her make-up. Sighing, she wiped away the smears as best she could with tissue paper and water.

Mia paused to stare out of the window, which overlooked the street below and the emergency entrance, its bays half filled, the others painted with red warning lines. Her vision drifted, her eyes casting into the distance, where they landed on an approaching ambulance. The lights were off until it reached a set of traffic lights, at which point it erupted in sound and light, a cacophony for the senses.

It filled Mia's head and her eyelids flickered. Standing in the corridor several floors up, suddenly she could smell the exhaust fumes, hear the drone of the diesel engine and feel herself drifting.

The memories surged to the surface.

The back seat of a car, driving at night. The seat was black leather and Mia was sitting on her hands – younger but not much, her teenage body planted firmly in the seat.

The car disappeared. Flashes of light and white noise followed. Then she was lying on her back, listening to the rumble of tyres and the drone of an engine. A siren wailed. They accelerated, swerving left and right until she felt dizzy and lost. Someone was talking to her, repeating a question, but she couldn't hear it.

The vehicle stopped and she felt the trolley shift under her, the slamming of doors and shouts. The lights flashed, reflecting off the windows. Mia stared at the ceiling of a place she didn't recognise. Lights flew past overhead.

A feeling of vertigo, lying flat on her back but in motion. A man stared down at her. He said something, but his voice was too deep and slow, muffled by the mask over his face. A surgeon's mask. She knew what it was, but she didn't know why. He bore a scar below his right eye, raised and pink. It flashed like lightning in her eyes.

Mia tried to raise herself up to tell the man she couldn't hear him, but she was unable to move. Her whole body was rigid. Panic took over. Her chest heaved, and pins and needles stabbed at her hands and face. She couldn't breathe, hyperventilating until the light faded and the vision tunnelled into darkness.

She felt hands on her, several at once, rummaging around her body. In her body. Muffled voices overlaid with hisses and beeps.

A voice. 'I said, are you OK?'

Mia snapped awake. The darkness retreated and the noise of the hospital slapped her into the moment. A female nurse was standing next to her, staring with concern.

Mia remained dazed. She turned back to the window, watching the lights of the ambulance spinning their dance. She waited for more, but the moment had gone and reality insisted.

'I'm OK,' she said, turning to the nurse, 'but I have to go.'

Mia stumbled out of the toilet, heading for the stairs, keen to leave this place.

The dream was real – a memory – she was certain of it now. But what had happened to her? And why?

CHAPTER ELEVEN

'A paper tiger?' The young woman stared at Alex with suspicion. Alex placed his cup carefully on the coaster so as not to mark his expensive hardwood desk and nodded.

'It can't hurt you,' said Alex, 'even though it appears frightening.'

He leaned back in his chair, feeling the squeak of the soft leather, breathing in the mild aroma of the diffuser on the mantelpiece. Katie had bought it for him. Pomegranate and something citrusy; he couldn't remember what. He thought the Met's open-plan office could do with one or two; perhaps it would diffuse the smell of sweat and overwork.

He'd committed to a morning of private appointments back in Harley Street. It was useful: a complete distraction from the case and time to clear his head, focus on a different problem.

Jessica, the woman in front of him, had called three weeks ago about her anxiety. After several calls, during which Alex had managed to persuade her that anxiety couldn't be treated quickly or via the phone, she'd agreed to come in and see him.

Outwardly, Jessica was a delightful young socialite. Twenty-two years old, she'd had a privileged upbringing, a university education and more money thrown at her than even Alex was likely to see in his lifetime. Today she sat perched in a Ralph Lauren dress, her Louis Vuitton bag clutched to her chest. Her tan suggested a recent holiday; her jet-black hair suggested an expensive stylist.

But Alex knew all too well that anxiety didn't discriminate. It took its victims from all walks of life, and a millionaire's daughter was no less likely to find herself crippled with panic attacks than someone living in poverty. Alex sympathised regardless and knew he could help most people regardless. Luckily for Jessica, she could afford private therapy quickly and on her terms. Alex had agreed to see her as soon as she was able.

'But it feels so real,' she said. Alex could see her shaking. She sniffed, the tears kept at bay. Alex didn't push; she'd cry when she felt comfortable enough to do so. Sometimes it happened in the first session, with other patients not for weeks. Every journey through cognitive behavioural therapy was different, but the success rate was good. Alex was positive about Jessica.

'It does,' agreed Alex, 'but I want you to think about what we've discussed today. When you next step into a party or a gathering and you feel the panic rising, as you've described, imagine this paper tiger lurking in your head. It's big and fierce and if you pay attention to it, it will grow in size and detail and effect. But . . . it is only there by your grace. It cannot hurt you.'

Jessica nodded. Gazing at her lap, she chewed her lip. She was bright – Alex could tell the minute she'd called – and she listened too.

'And remember,' he said, 'our plan for you. Don't avoid: expose. You have this thing on Saturday?'

'A friend's twenty-first,' she said, taking a deep breath. 'Fancy dress.'

Alex nodded. 'Use it. These events will become part of your treatment. They'll help.'

'How long?' Her eyes pleaded a little. 'I just want to enjoy a party without having a panic attack. It's not normal. How long will I be like this?'

Alex fingered the handle of his coffee cup. How long indeed. He considered his answer carefully. His own anxiety had presented at an early age and he'd hidden it, not having anybody he could talk to. His father was distant and his mother suffered from anxiety so acutely herself she couldn't see beyond her own daily battles. His teachers had been good, but only the most troublesome kids got attention. He coasted through school, bright enough to pass everything, shrewd enough to hide his suffering.

Alex started self-medicating in his teens, using his mother's pills. By the time he hit university his addiction was established and therapy seemed like a distant goal, to be taken at some point later in life.

Now, at forty-one, Alex had spent over half his life on benzodiazepines. The fact he was a respected clinical psychologist changed nothing. Alex could understand the theory, know the practice and deliver lectures on the damaging long-term effects of benzos, but still be no closer to treating his own anxiety than when he'd first popped one of his mum's Diazepam tablets at fourteen. That was life. Being a doctor didn't change it. Alex was still human, his flaws no greater or less than in the average person. Alex would seek therapy when he was ready. He suspected, deep down, that day would never come.

'I can't give you the answer to that,' said Alex truthfully. 'You're young and bright with a fantastic support network. Work hard at it and I'm sure we'll make progress.'

'Progress?'

'Yes. We don't talk about cures for anxiety, we talk about strategies. With work and practice, your anxiety will be manageable. You'll live a normal life and enjoy it. That's what I want you to focus on at the moment.'

Jessica nodded. The grasp on her bag had relaxed. She looked up and smiled. It seemed genuine. Alex looked into her young face and saw his daughter Katie staring back. Pure innocence and the pain inflicted on others when she suffered.

'Can I ask?' said Alex. 'I know we mentioned it, but how is your relationship with your parents?'

Jessica's smile thinned. She sighed and her shoulders sagged. 'Can we do that another time?'

'Of course,' said Alex. 'And it's not something we have to cover, unless you want to.'

Jessica's eyes were piercing. She understood.

'Perhaps when I've tackled my . . . panic attacks,' she said. 'Perhaps then I might talk to you about my parents.'

Alex nodded, palms out. 'I'm here when you need me,' he said.

Once the young woman had left the office, Alex poured another coffee and stretched out in his chair. There was still a certain pride in treating people like Jessica. It was a genuine need and the success rate was good. If he could help these patients get their lives back on track, then at least he was a positive force in the world. She could grow up without the crippling pain or stigma of a mental health condition – a normal human being finding her way.

Alex's good mood tapered off as he completed a pile of paperwork and invoices, checking his next appointment, which wasn't for another hour.

He sauntered over to his impressive oak bookshelves full of periodicals and psychology texts. They were on display more for the clients than for Alex, but he still liked to flick through the odd journal, take in a new nugget of information. At least he could pretend he was still up to date on everything.

The paper tiger example was still fresh in his mind, but as one particular textbook caught his eye, he thought about a far more real animal out on the streets of London. A violent, wild animal taking lives with seemingly reckless abandon.

Psychopathy and Violence: Type and Concepts was an old text, one of his father's, plucked off the shelves after his death. Most of his father's belongings were now in storage, but Alex had kept a few select texts and journals. That was back when Alex had made a promise to follow up on his father's work – to investigate the seriousness of the deception and lies. His father had broken every rule of medical ethics in a grotesque and twisted fashion – and paid the ultimate price for it. But after the case and his father's murder, once Katie and Grace were safe, Alex had put a lid on it – mental and physical. He ignored his conscience, which screamed that he should know – he *needed* to know – the extent of his father's work and that of his colleagues at the university they claimed to represent. It was easier to let it go. In the year afterwards, Alex had needed to rebuild and distance himself professionally and personally from the deeds of his father. His career was delicate enough without dredging up his father's sordid past. He feared what he'd find if he allowed himself to be drawn in.

He fingered the spine of the book. His father's work was far removed from this subject, yet the memories still lurched to the surface. Alex took a breath and forced them under. *Keep the lid on*, he thought.

Alex pulled the book off the shelf, heaving it over to his desk, where he flicked open the cover.

He tapped the first page – a brief introduction – with his finger, skimming the text. It described the subject from an undergraduate perspective, using Hollywood-movie psychopaths as the example, as methodical and controlled perpetrators of horrific violence. In this model, the psychopath's violent acts were predatory: planned, purposeful and emotionless deeds making for great set pieces undertaken casually by cold-blooded villains.

In reality, however, the predatory psychopath was one of two types. Less well known was the affective psychopath – impulsive and reactive, the perpetrator of explosive rages against another person. These were hot-blooded, often passionate and emotive attacks. The important thing to note from a clinical perspective was that in the latter affective type there was often no planning or method.

The hard contrast between the two types bugged him.

Alex picked up his phone and dialled Hartley's number.

'Dr Madison.' Hartley answered on the third ring, her voice curt but polite. 'I'm glad you called. I need to speak to you, actually.'

'Hang on,' said Alex. He paused. What did he want exactly? Methodical, Alex. The police were following procedure. He needed to follow it with them at the very least, and use them. Hartley would have her own perspective on this topic.

'Predatory or affective?' he said, flicking over the pages of the book on his desk.

It didn't take Hartley long to catch on.

'Predatory,' she said. 'She's stalking victims at the hospitals with a cold and calculated plan.'

Alex nodded to himself, except something didn't add up. He thought back to the grainy CCTV footage – the suspect swaying and her head rising up and away from the victim.

'But she's displaying emotion,' he said. 'Or at least a sensual reaction of some sort. You can see it in her reactions. Not what I'd expect from a psychopathic predator.'

Another pause. 'OK,' said Hartley, 'but she's still a stalker. These weren't random encounters. She planned her visits to the minute. She's type one if she's anything.'

Alex nodded. Hartley was making an easy conclusion, if the wrong one. Alex flicked ahead, through the summary into the first few chapters, knowing the answer to his niggling doubt wouldn't lie in here. There was no simple explanation as to why some people suffered crippling anxiety attacks, and why some people suffered crippling violent psychopathy.

'You don't think so?' said Hartley. 'What are you thinking, Alex?'

Alex flicked through the pages in the textbook, not reading, just feeling the paper slipping through his fingers. He considered cases where he'd seen violence like this before. A particular patient sprang to mind, one that he and his fellow students had observed during his training. The patient had been sectioned and sedated. He'd killed four people – all family members – in a fit of rage. Conclusively an affective psychopath, his motive had been a perceived slight by an uncle, who had cut him out of an inheritance. He'd decided to slaughter all the beneficiaries.

'Motive,' said Alex, 'or rather, the lack of one.' He turned away from the desk towards the huge sash window in his office, staring across the street. That patient had been complex and ill, but at least he had had motive, clear and simple.

To try to diagnose the hospital killer based on the evidence they had was incredibly difficult without some idea of motive. Was she a complex violent affective psychopath or something more? Alex couldn't know without more information. Unfortunately, more information was likely to be accompanied by more bodies.

Hartley took a breath. 'Alex—'

'Did Forensics find anything?' he said. 'In the young woman's car?'

Hartley cleared her throat. 'Loads, but nothing of use so far. We've got several sets of hair, blood and fingerprints. After eliminating the victim's, we've got a selection of no matches. They could belong to anybody – friends, family, lovers . . .'

'Or the killer.'

'Of course. But like I said, no matches, so it doesn't help us identify her.'

'It'll help if we catch her.'

'*When* we catch her, Alex,' said Hartley. She cleared her throat again. 'Bloody cold,' she said, sniffing. 'Anyway, I have something else to tell you. I'm being reassigned.'

'What?' Alex shifted in his seat. Hartley was his ally, albeit a distant and cold one. Hartley understood his background and the darker aspects of his cases. Only she understood what had happened last year with Victor Lazar, or at least she pretended she did. Perhaps not.

'Don't worry,' said Hartley. 'I'm not going far. I'm being told to jump up a level, overseeing several cases, which means I can't remain as the senior investigating officer on this one alone. I'm bringing in another detective – I think you've met.'

'Who?' Alex had met a lot of inspectors during the last few years. None stood out as particularly forgiving or supporting of his profession. This case might just have got a whole lot harder.

'Detective Catherine Laurie. Goes by her last name. She said you'd met.'

Alex thought of the young detective who'd dragged him to her station a few days ago. Detective Laurie. She'd seemed genuine, professional. The sort of person you'd want to have your back.

'We have,' said Alex. 'Briefly. She's up to speed?'

Hartley huffed. 'Thank you, Alex, yes, we are competent at handing over our cases.'

Alex caught himself. 'Sorry,' he said. 'It's just . . . this isn't your standard murder case.'

'Which is why you're still on it,' said Hartley. 'And don't sweat it. I know you're beating yourself up at the moment.'

Alex swallowed. Hartley knew him so well. Was he that transparent? 'I need more information,' he said. 'That's all. A motive would be nice.'

'Well, hopefully Detective Laurie can help you find it,' said Hartley. 'She's good, Alex, plus she's worked some hard cases.'

'Hard?' Alex wasn't sure whether to push it. Hard cases meant something different to him and Hartley.

'Trust me, Alex. Now, I've got to go. Laurie will be in touch.'

Alex checked his watch. Time for his next appointment anyway. He thanked Hartley for her time and hung up.

He thought about what Hartley had said. Detective Laurie might be good, but was she prepared for something like this? Was she prepared for the horror of what their suspect was capable of? Alex hoped so, because in truth he was struggling with it himself. He'd waited all year for another big case. Now one had landed in his lap, and with it the distant panic that he was once again out of his depth. He couldn't afford any mistakes this time. Not with this one.

Alex arranged the papers on his desk and went to close the textbook. As he did so he noticed a handwritten note in the margin of the open page, under the chapter heading '*9 – Psychopathy and Emotional Stimuli*'. The scrawl was unmistakably his father's writing – Alex would recognise it anywhere. This was old, faded blue ink from a fountain pen. The note read *Hyper-Empathy Syndrome. Lot 15. DB. Randomised??*

Alex frowned. He flicked through the next couple of pages but found no other notes. Hyper-empathy syndrome was a rare affliction that caused distress due to the inability of the sufferer to observe others' emotions without feeling debilitating effects. Alex had never come across a single case of it in his career, and as far as he knew, his father had had nothing at all to do with this type of condition in his research, either the legitimate or the illegal.

It wasn't associated with violent psychopathy and Alex wondered what might have prompted the note, perhaps many years ago. The memories popped back up and he slammed the book closed in response. No time for that now. The ramblings of his dead father would have to wait indefinitely. Alex had his own life to attend to.

CHAPTER TWELVE

Mia stumbled into a bar – quiet and run-down, but open. After leaving the hospital she'd walked for hours, and her cravings had waned, perhaps as a result of the aerobic strain on her body, her blood and nervous system flooded with endorphins. Part of her wanted to examine this feeling, to use it, but she had more pressing thoughts on her mind, and as she sat down her hunger returned with force, acute and unrelenting.

Perching on a stool near the back, she ordered lemonade from the bartender. She downed it and ordered another, the fluid and sugar gradually subduing her shakes.

She lost herself in her thoughts, trying to grasp the images triggered in the hospital. She searched, but her mind blanked and gave her nothing but blackness and despair. Anger crept in as her future was laid bare before her. Bleak and unthinkable.

What did it all mean?

Mia clenched the lemonade glass so tight it cracked.

'Careful.'

A soft voice to her left. Mia's head jerked towards the stranger.

'Bad day?'

A woman hovered a couple of stools along. Mia took in her appearance. Slender, almost too thin, with a plain but friendly face. Long brown hair in a ponytail; dressed casually. She had her own drink, a small glass of white wine.

And she was in pain.

Mia turned her body towards it. Not bad, but a dull, nagging sensation. She saw it in the woman's face and in her stance; she saw it in the way the woman held her shoulders and arms, in the rhythm of her breath and the tone of her skin. The air around this woman shivered with pheromones, both alarming and sensual, a delicious mixture that blanketed Mia.

Mia saw it all in an instant. Pain, precious pain. She tensed, but with it came another, altogether different feeling. The same feeling she yearned for on the normal days.

Mia smiled, and she saw the desire reflected in the woman's eyes.

'A bad day,' said Mia. 'Yes.' She found her voice an octave too high, but the woman closed the gap between them.

'I'm Clare,' she said, taking a seat. Their knees touched and neither pulled away. Mia took a short breath, both scared and attracted by the touch.

'Mia.' The sound of her own name was strange on her lips. Mia spoke to as few people as possible. Hearing her own voice was peculiar, like a foreign sound. She relished it on her lips.

'I'm Mia,' she repeated, meeting Clare's eyes, which also seemed anxious, yet drawn to her.

Clare talked. Mia listened. Clare was troubled, not just with physical pain but a hundred other woes she was happy to spill to this stranger in a bar. Clare had a job. Mia understood what that meant, but had no point of reference, nothing to compare. Clare's worries seemed minor and pointless to Mia and yet she listened, because it was clear the subject of their conversation didn't matter. It soothed her panic, but stoked her hunger.

'Where are you from?' said Claire.

I wish I knew, Mia whispered inside. *Tell me where you think I'm from.*

'Not from here,' she offered.

'I can see that,' said Claire. 'And your accent. Spanish? No. Greek? I'm rubbish with languages. I had a friend from Croatia once. You sound like her.'

Mia held her expression. She could be Spanish or Greek or nothing of the sort. Mia would find out. One day. But not today.

They ordered more drinks. Mia kept to sugary soft drinks; Clare preferred wine. The more she drank, the more she talked. Hours passed. Mia found herself lost in Clare's eyes. They sparkled as she recounted how much of a creep her boss was. They darkened as she recounted how many times she'd had to decline his advances.

'I think he figures I'll become straight if he asks enough times,' she said, rolling her eyes. 'A complete idiot, and married.'

'You're not,' said Mia. Not a question, more of a statement. Mia had an understanding of how the world worked; she just couldn't remember how she'd got that understanding.

'And you're not,' said Clare, her face twisted into a grin, 'unless you're the world's best fucking actress.'

'Why would I act?' said Mia. She moved closer. Clare intrigued her, drew her in. Her pain shimmered in the background; her attraction pulsed in the foreground.

Mia wanted both.

Clare's flat was five minutes' walk from the bar. She continued to talk and Mia continued to listen, but at the same time doubts formed in her mind. Mia glanced at Clare's arms. Marks, near the veins. Needles, perhaps, which could explain the pain. A kindred spirit, although her addiction couldn't be anywhere near as bad as Mia's.

The flat was small, messy but clean. Mia made no judgement, given her own living arrangements. The talking stopped. Clare didn't offer her a drink, and they stood and stared at each other for several moments. Clare broke the spell, touching Mia's cheek. A wave of mixed sensations shook Mia, her heart thumping, her palms tingling.

They kissed, soft and tender. Neither broke it, lingering until Clare slid her hands further around Mia's body. Mia tensed for a second but relented, letting the stranger explore her, tug at her clothes, leaving them in a pile at her feet and then pulling off her own.

Mia let Clare lead her. The bed was firm and Mia lay back, shaking, awash with emotion and sensation. Clare looked down with a puzzled frown.

'Are you OK, Mia?' she whispered.

Mia nodded. She didn't know, that was the truth, but she didn't want to stop. She embraced Clare and pulled her closer, losing herself in a new kiss, fascinated by the anticipation, which was increasing with each moment.

Clare was experienced; Mia was not, yet she felt a reawakening. This wasn't the first time she had done this. Did she have a girlfriend, a partner, before? Before she woke in a dark London street in the middle of the night with her memories gone and her terrible addiction gained?

The pleasure faded as Mia's thoughts clouded. Clare took her hands away and sat up.

'Touch me, Mia,' she said, taking Mia's hand and placing it for her. Mia tried. She watched Clare responding, her pleasure almost desperate in its intensity. Mia gazed at the body in front of her, its delicate lines, soft curves and rapturous movement.

Clare rocked, her face flushed. She panted.

And then Mia felt it.

'Ouch,' said Clare, stopping her movement for a second. She smiled and carried on. 'Gentle there, gorgeous.'

But it was too late. Mia was lost in an instant. Her hand twisted again, a little too hard, her fingers pushing further.

'Whoa,' said Clare, her smile disappearing. She slid away, holding Mia's wrist. 'Gently, I said.'

It was too late. Even if Mia had wanted to stop, the primal urge lurking all day had finally broken free. The pain jumped from Clare to

Mia and with it an ecstasy that sex could never compete with. In that instant Mia experienced Clare's pleasure and her pain, but it was the latter that won. The most sensitive part of Clare's body was shot through with agony. It was dazzling, full and surging. And Mia needed it all.

Mia yanked her hand out of Clare's grip. She held the woman between her fingers, the soft flesh tearing under her nails. Clare screamed and Mia's other hand shot up, striking her in the temple with a balled fist. Not enough to knock her out, but enough to knock her sideways.

Mia flipped over, straddling the shocked woman. Her hand twisted, sending shock waves of pain through Clare's body. At the same time, she forced her hand against Clare's windpipe, cutting off just enough air to subdue her.

It was Mia's turn to pant and gasp. Her ecstasy was far beyond whatever Clare's had been. She played Clare like an instrument, wrenching the notes from her damaged body, listening to the perfect symphony it created in her own. Her mind flooded with the euphoria, filling her to the brim with bliss. As she turned her fingers, torturing the woman beneath her, their eyes locked again.

Clare's were wide, dilated. Pleading. Tears ran from the corners, her terror evident. Mia saw it all, but she was lost. There was nothing she could do to stop, even as the high peaked before the fall.

Mia writhed and she gasped. She shuddered, tensing her muscles, better than any sex, better than any orgasm. Her pleasure was absolute and without equal.

It became too much, as it often did, and Clare's consciousness yielded within minutes, shutting down. Her body went limp and Mia paused, enjoying the last remnants of pleasure, before sliding off, her naked body covered in blood and sweat.

Mia panted, her heart racing and her skin tingling, unable to tear her eyes from the damaged and twisted body in front of her. Clare was still alive, by a fraction, and Mia's thoughts spiralled. Maintaining her anonymity was essential for survival, but the sight of Clare's face caused waves of guilt and terror to crash through Mia's mind. The nausea hit her and she gulped it back, bringing her bloodied hands up to her face.

Leave, Mia. While you still can. Before the fog descends and you lose all sense. You can't risk staying here.

She didn't want Clare's life to end like this. The realisation was there, even through the departing ecstasy and the relentless surges of despair. The pain might be the last thing Clare felt, everything transferring to Mia in her final breath. Perfect pain and an imperfect death. She had never wanted it. This wasn't what Mia wanted to be.

Mia tortured herself with the thought as her high ebbed away.

Still covered in blood, Mia left Clare on the floor and pulled on her clothes. She left through the front door, pulling it shut, hearing the lock click behind her, ignoring the photo on the wall of Clare with two others, perhaps her parents, embraced in a family hug.

Another family destroyed, Mia. Another life. It's what you do.

Her body began to cave within minutes. The high was gone and the regret came thick and fast, launching itself from her stomach, sending shivers down her spine to every extremity.

She vomited into the gutter until her stomach was dry, tears streaming from her eyes, sobbing into her fists. She stared at her hands, the hands that mere moments before had caressed another human being. A possible friend, a lover, a companion.

But it can never be, Mia, she told herself. *You're a monster. It's what you are and always will be. Your hands are not for pleasure, they're for pain.*

Don't ever forget that. Don't ever forget what you are.

CHAPTER THIRTEEN

Alex shuffled in the seat of his Merc, staring at the old family house. It was the house he and Grace had bought together. The house they'd raised Katie in. It was also the house Victor Lazar had kidnapped Katie from twelve months earlier. Grace had refused to move, asking Alex to promise that the threat had disappeared when the case was closed. Alex couldn't do that, not one hundred per cent. She'd stayed anyway.

He'd been sitting in the car for twenty-five minutes, watching the flow of young teenagers being dropped off outside, all carrying presents and fizzy drinks, some with balloons. He'd brought the same, of course, but for some reason couldn't get his body out of the seat and out of the car.

He knew the reason. The reason was John.

Alex knew this type of jealousy and resentment was typical at this stage of a break-up; in fact, he'd be worried if he didn't feel it. Only a sociopath would wish their ex-wife a happy future with a new man. But he couldn't let these childish emotions turn into childish behaviour. Not here. Not now. Alex needed to show Grace his maturity and respect for her choices, whatever they might be. He just hadn't figured out how to do that yet – not in the twenty-six minutes he'd been sitting in his car.

With his right hand he fingered the packet of Xanax in his jacket pocket. There'd be wine for the adults at the party, plenty, but he knew he'd need more than alcohol to get through three hours of small talk and new faces, particularly one he didn't want to meet.

He popped a pill in his mouth, swallowed it dry, then heaved himself out of the car. Grabbing his present, balloon and a rather good vintage Rioja, he shuffled towards the front door.

It opened before he knocked. Katie stood in denim shorts and a top – she never wore dresses any more – and screamed.

'Daddy!'

'Hi, sweetie,' said Alex, dropping the present and letting the balloon float to the hallway ceiling. He managed to keep hold of the wine as Katie jumped on him, wrapping her arms and legs around his body.

Alex enjoyed the hug. These moments were still the purest and most perfect he knew, and he buried his face into her neck until she giggled and wriggled away.

'What did you get me? You didn't have to do presents, you know. It's not a birthday. Mum said.' Katie pulled a face, but it changed as soon as he picked the box up and handed it to her.

'Well, it is the holidays.'

Katie ripped open the paper to find a gift box containing a matching bracelet and necklace. Alex knew the right set to buy, even without Grace's very specific text messages. He wondered at what point he'd missed the transition from Lego to jewellery, but he didn't mind. Katie would soon be a young woman and Alex would buy her the Earth if he thought it would make her happy – a habit he wouldn't recommend in any good parenting guide but nevertheless couldn't resist. He got to spoil his daughter: it was one right nobody could take from him.

Again Katie shrieked her delight – Alex could tell she was already high on sugar and excitement – and gave him another quick kiss before running off with her friends.

Alex paused in the hallway. Standing here evoked a mixture of complex emotions and memories, most of them pleasant, many tinged with regret. He remembered Katie's first day of primary school, adjusting her red cardigan, unbuttoning and buttoning until they got it right, checking the Velcro on her shoes and pulling her socks to the right height.

He should be standing in this hallway every morning, ready to go to work, waving goodbye to Grace and Katie. Instead, he'd spent his time in this house derailing his marriage, spiralling into self-destruction and forcing Grace to make a choice.

She'd chosen for him to leave.

Alex checked his reflection in the hardwood framed mirror – a present from her parents one Christmas. He looked old, pale with bags under his eyes, growing by the month. He checked his hairline: still holding, but noticeably thinner. *What wonderful things to look forward to in my forties*, he thought.

The shrieks from the garden filtered through, bringing him out of his haze. He took a breath and headed into the kitchen.

'Alex.' Grace was perched behind the breakfast bar, pouring cordial into plastic cups. She nodded towards the far end, where several wine bottles waited, glasses sparkling – desperate to be filled.

Alex put on his best smile. 'Hi, Grace,' he said, kissing her on the cheek, catching a waft of her perfume, feeling her brief embrace and trying not to linger.

Grace stood back, her hand resting on his arm. 'I'm really pleased you came. Katie would have been devastated if you hadn't.'

'And you?' Alex couldn't help it.

Grace's expression softened. Her eyes were full of warmth.

'I'm always pleased to see you,' she said, turning away, playing with a loose strand of hair. 'Now,' she said, turning back, composing herself. 'Would you pour us a glass of wine? I see you've brought a bottle no doubt more expensive than anything we've got. Shall we start with that?'

Alex poured two glasses. They toasted to Katie.

'The most perfect thing I've ever done,' said Alex.

'Ditto,' said Grace.

They sipped in silence, the noise of all the children distant in the moment. Alex watched Grace: the gentle sway of her hips, her hand movements, the nervous playing with her hair. He wanted to go to her, hold her and tell her how sorry he was for everything.

But he'd done that already. Many times over. He didn't even know if he and Grace being back together would be the best outcome for Katie. Grace was stable and in control of her life. Katie, a strong and intelligent young lady, reflected that.

Alex was an addict, pining for a family he'd screwed up, desperately seeking professional accolade away from the trivial appeal of his lucrative practice. Would forcing himself back into their lives at this point be the right thing to do?

'John.' Grace's voice snapped Alex into the present. He turned to see a taller man enter through the French doors. John was thin, wearing chinos and a casual white shirt. Bald, with a trendy beard, he wore sharp-looking glasses.

John extended his hand towards Alex. 'Alex, hi,' he said, his voice deep with confidence.

Alex cleared his throat, taken off guard. He extended his hand.

They gripped, neither wanting to dominate with an absurd alpha-male squeeze but neither wanting to be relegated to second place.

'Hi. John, isn't it?' said Alex, his voice calm and firm. *Well done*, he said to himself. *You managed to say hi without screaming. Check that off the list.*

They released their hands.

'Nice to meet you,' said John. 'Is that your Merc out there?'

Alex nodded. 'Uh-huh.'

'AMG?'

'C63,' said Alex. 'Six point three litre V8,' wondering why he'd felt compelled to say it. *Mine is bigger than yours.*

John tilted his head to one side. 'Nice,' he said, walking over to Grace and slipping his hand around her waist. Alex stiffened, and to his surprise saw Grace do the same. He recognised her discomfort in a second, and noticed John didn't.

A mild victory – Grace's reaction couldn't hide her feelings, however complicated they might be – although the victory was short-lived. John leaned in and pecked Grace on the forehead, before turning to the wine. He proceeded to take Alex's Rioja and pour a large glass, slurping it down.

Alex tried to keep his smile, but it was forced.

'Two thousand and one,' he said. 'Muga.'

John sniffed, glancing at the wine before placing the glass rather hard on the worktop. 'I prefer white,' he said, turning back to Grace. 'Do you want me to round the girls up for food?'

'Sure.'

John nodded to Alex and slipped back out into the garden. Alex heard his deep voice summoning the children to gather round. Alex slurped his own wine, necking the glass and grabbing the bottle for a refill.

Grace put her hand on her hip. She tried to look annoyed, but Alex saw disappointment in her eyes. With him or John?

'What is it with you men?' she said.

'What?' said Alex, sure he'd done nothing wrong.

'Not you,' said Grace. 'John might just as well have urinated in a circle around me, marking his territory.'

'Nice vision,' said Alex. 'Thanks.'

'I'm serious,' said Grace, shaking her head. 'No, I'm sorry. I shouldn't have forced this.'

Alex saw the angst in her eyes. It wasn't her fault. Men were blunt instruments sometimes.

'It's nothing,' he said, but he knew he was lying.

John had come into his family kitchen, grabbed Alex's wife, grabbed his wine, then strutted off to round up his child. Alex felt exactly like the beta male, emasculated and inwardly seething. Was he making too much of it? Yes, but even Grace had noticed. She looked at him with concern.

'Try and be the bigger man, for Katie's sake?'

That got him. An unfair card to play. How could he refuse?

The first hour passed without incident. The second started to drag. Katie's friends were too many to count, polite, but far too grown-up for Alex's liking. They alternated at great speed between physical garden games and huddling around a smartphone, marvelling at some video or social media posting. Alex couldn't pretend to know, and hoped Grace was more up to date than he was. The effects of social media on young people's mental health was a growing concern in Alex's field, but he got the impression that opening the debate today might mark him out as something of a spoilsport. He and John avoided each other, nodding politely but trying not to talk. Alex lingered in the kitchen, enjoying the mix of Xanax and alcohol. He finished his bottle and most of a second. His head was swimming while he scoured the worktop for a suitable follow-up.

'Like a drink, huh?'

John appeared at the breakfast bar. Alex looked in vain for Grace or one of the other adults – the parents of several of Katie's friends from school were milling around, but they were all outside. It was just the two of them.

'Not sure what you mean,' said Alex, in a tone that suggested he knew it was intended as an insult. But even in his inebriated state he saw John's face crease with concern.

'Oh no,' said John, 'I didn't mean it like that. God knows, I like one. I actually came in here to find another glass of something. Didn't realise you were in here.'

Alex paused, studying John's face. He was telling the truth. Did that make it better or worse? The guy wasn't suggesting Alex had a drink problem. In fact, he'd almost admitted to having one himself.

'So you work with Grace?' said Alex, deciding on small talk, pouring a glass of red for John and handing it over. John examined the wine for a moment before sipping at it.

'I do like red,' said John. 'I'm not much of a connoisseur. The one you brought was good.' He indicated the empty bottle of Muga on the side. 'I work in Legal,' he continued. 'I'm a solicitor. Commercial, some property.'

Alex nodded. Professional. Grace would only pick somebody with a brain and the sense to use it. But it made him feel even more threatened. His mind clouded and his thoughts became muddled. This was happening too fast. His family was being pulled away and he was doing nothing to stop it.

The alcohol wasn't helping; he'd already had too much. He should have left after the first bottle. He wasn't getting any quality time with Katie or Grace anyway.

He took a deep breath, observing his own mental state and physical responses. It was a curse of his profession and seldom useful. He needed to suck it up and be polite – it wasn't as though he had to be friends with this man. Whatever Alex's future with Grace, it would not be determined by this lawyer. His interactions today didn't matter; Alex just needed to remain mature and considerate.

'And you're a shrink?' John grinned. It wasn't malicious, just playful, but the comment was full of ignorance and it riled Alex. He counted to three under his breath and tried to let it go.

'Clinical psychologist,' said Alex. He kept his smile and returned the wine glass to his lips, sipping as deeply as he could.

'Are you analysing me now?' said John. He glanced away as a cheer erupted from the garden. The kids were playing a ball game. Alex wished he was out there with them.

'You couldn't afford me,' said Alex. He knew it came out wrong. It was supposed to be light-hearted but came out with a thump. A direct challenge.

John stiffened, leaning back, pulling himself to full height, which was a good few inches on Alex. 'I do OK, thank you.'

Alex shook his head, trying to laugh it off. 'Hey, chill out. I didn't mean—'

'I might not have a private practice, but I have a pretty decent income. Stable.'

Alex heard John punctuate the last word.

'What are you trying to say?' said Alex. He stumbled, holding himself against the bar.

John looked as if he was going to continue, but he backed off, his hands up in surrender. 'Perhaps a coffee instead of more wine, yeah?' he said, edging towards the French doors.

'Fuck you,' said Alex. He hadn't meant to say it out loud. He said it in his head, but the words escaped, stabbing through the air towards John, whose face dropped in astonishment.

'I beg your pardon?'

Alex realised he'd failed. He hadn't even made it halfway through the party.

He reached the hallway before Grace came running after him.

'What happened?'

'Nothing,' said Alex.

She looked worried, but her eyes narrowed as she came closer. 'You're not driving.'

Alex looked at the keys in his right hand. She was right, of course. He hadn't planned to. But he needed to get out of the house.

'I'll grab a taxi,' he said.

'Does Katie know you're leaving?'

Alex considered walking back through the house, past the memories, past John the lawyer. 'I'll call her later,' he said.

His eyes met Grace's. They both lingered. Could she see the pain in his? He could see the confusion in hers.

She finally broke contact, sighing, and smiled as she opened the door for him. 'You lasted two hours,' she said. 'I'd bet to myself you wouldn't make one.'

They stepped out on to the porch. Grace pulled the door ajar, hiding them from the hallway. She gave him a big hug, planting a kiss on his cheek. Alex once again smelled her perfume, her hair, her skin. He backed away and headed to the street.

'Call me tomorrow,' said Grace. Alex nodded, waving over his shoulder, turning away from the Merc and towards the high street.

CHAPTER FOURTEEN

The Grosvenor House Hotel gave a pleasant view across Hyde Park, but the woman at the window leaned her forehead against the glass, letting her eyes lose focus. Her suitcase lay unopened at the end of the bed, her breakfast uneaten on the trolley.

'How did you let it go this far?' she said. There was brief silence on the other end of the phone. 'Well?'

The man's voice was nervous, as well it should be. Forcing a visit in these circumstances, he knew he was treading on very thin ice. Once broken, he wouldn't recover.

'We didn't anticipate it,' he said.

'You failed to,' said the woman.

'The expectation was very different.'

She paused. 'Tell me something useful.'

More silence. She knew they were out of their depth. That's why she was here. Her organisation did not tolerate screw-ups, and remediation would be swift.

'Will it lead to us?' she said, pushing herself away from the glass, staring down at her feet, frowning at a scuff on her left shoe. Valentino heels, purchased as part of her travelling expenses. She'd be forced to throw them away in a couple of days anyway, but still.

'No.'

'You sound sure. Why am I not convinced?' She could almost feel the man's anxiety seeping over the phone line.

'I don't see how it can. They're making little progress.'

'Yet. They will. The police are not stupid. Dr Madison is not a fool.'

She could hear the man's laboured breathing. 'We're watching him. What would you have us do?'

Her turn to pause. Action at this point could be counterproductive. Her own history in this matter was fresh in her mind. The risk of exposure was high, but she had many means at her disposal to mitigate the damage. Better to watch and wait.

'Be prepared to tidy this up,' she said. 'Get the teams in place. Do nothing until I tell you.'

She hung up before the man had a chance to respond.

CHAPTER FIFTEEN

A different entrance. Mia had the presence of mind to do that. Outpatients reception at City Hospital was quieter than the emergency entrance, the patients less urgent, the flow less manic. A waiting room overflowed with people queuing and complaining. Mia caught a whiff from a man nearby; he'd perched on an empty seat, a throbbing pain in his heavily plastered leg. Mia paused for a fraction of a second, enjoying the look on his face and the odour escaping in his sweat. She took a deep breath and hurried on.

Deeper into the hospital, Mia stopped. An image of Clare's body flashed into her mind. Mia shut it down quickly, swallowing and breathing. Her head was clearer, although the hunger surged and waned. It faded almost to nothing as she leaned against a cold wall, feeling the plaster on her palms. Closing her eyes, Mia let the relief wash over her. It would be temporary, it always was, but she'd take any respite she could get.

Her eyes flicked open. It was a busy corridor, but nobody took any notice. Patients were wheeled by porters; visitors paced on mobile phones, reassuring distant loved ones; doctors and nurses hurried to their next location, lost in thought or deep in conversation.

Mia was invisible again. The way she liked it.

She paused, willing her mind to focus, listening to the sounds of the people flowing past. Hard shoes, soft shoes, crutches and wheel-chairs. Squeaks of rubber and the rattle of metal. Sheets rustled against bodies and keys jangled on chains. She'd been here before; it was in her dreams. And not just any hospital – this one. It was there, somewhere, the recognition. Like a noose around her neck that wouldn't tighten but wouldn't let her go either.

The nearby lift pinged. Mia jumped a little, unsettled, but stood immobile, letting it seep into her. A wheelchair creaked past, pushed by a porter. It entered the lift and the doors closed with a soft hiss. The sounds triggered something.

Memories.

She'd been here before. This corridor, or one just like it. This wasn't a dream, this was real, and Mia was here.

Her chances of finding anything were slim, but that wouldn't stop her trying.

Mia headed for the lift. It pinged its familiar sound. The surgical floor was on level two, and she crammed in with nine other people for the short lurch upwards.

Head down, she exited, excusing herself past two men who seemed intent on brushing against her as she left. She was used to it. Perhaps in another life it would have bothered her. She'd have stopped and con-fronted the two men who thought it their right to violate her body and her space. But not today. Not in this life. Mia had a far more dangerous task to occupy her efforts.

Day Surgery reception was quiet and controlled. No security, just a nurses' station with three staff, hammering away at their keyboards. A quick glance to the left – stores, restroom and staff break room. To the right, prep and doors through to theatre. Straight ahead, the waiting area and recovery.

Mia turned right, walking with the assumed confidence of some-body who should be there. She wasn't challenged. Who'd want to be on a surgical ward unless they had to be? Pharmaceuticals were locked away in any hospital. There was little a normal person could do in such a place.

But Mia wasn't normal.

She walked with purpose. It wasn't clear in her head, but as she walked past the bays of patients being prepared for surgery, it became so simple.

You're looking for the surgeon, Mia. One, two, perhaps many. The people in your dreams and visions. This place was in her head. She hadn't dreamt all of it. The faces and the situations were too visceral, too real, for it to be a fantasy. They could be anywhere in the world, she reasoned, but equally, they could be in London. They could be here. Right now.

The double doors to the theatres were closed but not secured. Easy access to and from the ward was more important than preventing intruders. Mia waited for a break in the foot traffic and kicked one of the doors open, stepping through.

Wary of challenge at any point, she scanned quickly. Five theatres were signposted to the right. She heard voices and the squeak of rubber soles. To the left was another set of double doors with a STAFF ONLY sign above them. Mia pushed through, finding herself in another short corridor, the smooth, blue-painted walls broken by the doors of individual offices, each with a silver nameplate.

Mia checked the first, twisting the metal handle. It was locked, so she moved on to the next. Locked too. Frustrated, Mia wondered whether to turn back. Of course they'd lock their offices; they probably left personal belongings in here during their shifts.

The third door, however, was unlocked. Mia turned the handle and the door creaked open. Seeing no light on inside, she slipped into the office, closing the door behind her.

A spartan desk and worn leather chair. Two bookshelves and a smattering of reference books along with photo frames and an ornament of a wooden horse. The photos were of smiling children – Mia counted four – all posing for the camera.

She moved to the desk and the closed laptop, opened it up and was presented with a log-in box. Username and password. Mia sighed. She thought about taking the laptop, but she'd still have no chance of seeing what was on it. She had no technical know-how or resources to extract information from a locked PC. She had no friends or colleagues to help her. She was on her own, and the laptop was useless.

The other wall held a blue cupboard, metal, the kind used for files. Next to it was a wicker wastebasket – empty.

Mia tugged the handle on the cupboard and it clicked open. It had three shelves. The top held a coffee mug and cafetière, along with three bags of ground coffee beans. Behind the coffee she saw a small bottle of vodka. It seemed that doctors were not immune to the temptations of ordinary folk. A small part of her smiled. The second shelf held more books and journals. The third shelf held a large plastic storage container. Pulling it out, her spirits rose a little when she saw piles of brown folders.

Patient records, it seemed. Names, addresses, some diagnoses. Mia flicked through. Hip replacements, colorectal excisions, prostatectomies, breast excision and inguinal hernias. The files were all thin and light. Beyond the name of the form of surgery undertaken, there was nothing. Mia checked the names, twenty-five in all, but found none she recognised. None of the folders had *Mia Anastos* written on them.

Mia placed the tub back on the shelf and closed the cupboard. There was nothing in this room. No hint or reason. Mia let out the breath she'd been holding and stepped back out into the corridor.

The fourth office was locked.

The fifth and last on this side of the corridor clicked open. Mia checked behind her and entered the room.

It was dim, not dark, the blind on the window closed but letting in enough light for her to see her way around. This office was smaller than the last, with a single wooden desk by the window, a row of filing cabinets against one wall and a bookshelf on the other. A long black coat hung from a rack by the door, a briefcase and umbrella lay on the floor beneath.

Mia moved around the desk, pushing the fake leather swivel chair to one side. She tapped the keyboard, bringing the monitor to life. She was presented with a log-in box asking for username, password and swipe card. Mia chewed her lip. She moved away from the desk and rummaged through the coat pockets. They were empty apart from an Oyster card – a London travel pass. She dropped it back into the pocket and frowned.

Heaving the briefcase on to the desk, she checked the locks. Combination, three numbers on each side. Both locked.

Mia thumped her fist on the case. The anger simmered: a mixture of frustration and despair. What was she doing here?

The filing cabinets were next. Four in a row, all unlocked, the drawers sliding out with a greased ease. Mia flicked through dozens of brown folders, glancing at the names and numbers at the top of each one. More patient records.

All Mia had were her dreams of the masked faces who had treated her. They had wheeled her somewhere on a hospital bed, she knew that for certain. And she had the subsequent visions – of being held under a bright light, the tug of her legs and abdomen, the concerned look on the face above her.

Or was it concern? Mia closed her eyes and thought about the expression, so hard to gauge with half the person's face covered by a surgical mask. In her dream, the experience was fragmented, flashing in and out of her vision, her consciousness. But in her waking analysis, it went on for hours. Mia had been subjected to treatment – surgery, she suspected.

And then the darkness.

If the answers lay anywhere, they must be here. In this hospital, somewhere, was a folder with the name *Mia Anastos* on the front.

And in that folder would be written what they did to her.

She searched through the open cabinets, checking every record. Like a needle in a haystack – Mia was aware of the ridiculous odds, but what other choice did she have? The last drawer slid open to reveal three black A4 folders and a few items on the floor of the tray.

A loose envelope contained financial statements. Mia frowned. The name *Nova AG Pharmaceuticals* was stamped at the top. She placed the papers back in the envelope and into the drawer.

A black book lay at the bottom. Mia picked it up and flicked through the first few pages. An address book, mostly empty. A few names and numbers entered throughout, no more than three or four, as far as Mia could read from her first scan. She sighed and dropped the address book back into the drawer.

It clanged as it hit the metal, masking the sound of the door opening behind her. Too late, she spun around to find a man in the doorway.

'What are you doing in here?' He was tall, bald, stocky and red-faced. He wore an expensive-looking suit, no tie. He was staring at the filing cabinet behind Mia.

'I said, what the hell are you doing? Those are confidential.'

The man advanced into the small room. Mia tensed, her eyes darting to each side, instinctively looking for escape. The man appeared unsure what to do. He paused, opening his mouth to yell before closing it again.

Their eyes met.

His eyes widened then narrowed, but Mia saw it. She was practised at reading other people, her unnatural edge heightening her ability. Mia knew what the reaction meant. Autonomic, almost, recognition of a familiar face triggered a response that was impossible to hide in most people.

The doctor knew who she was.

Mia pounced. The surgeon was a large man, but Mia was experienced and he stood no chance. She grabbed a pen from the desk and leapt at him, stabbing her right arm in a wide arc so the pen dug deep into his shoulder muscle below the neck.

The surgeon went down. His first cry was muffled by Mia's other hand, silenced as she wedged her fist into his mouth. Leaving the pen where it was, embedded three inches into his neck, Mia forced her hand against his windpipe and her knee into his stomach, pushing against his diaphragm.

He gasped, but the breath wouldn't come. She pushed the air out of him and his body convulsed. Mia held him for thirty seconds, until he began to drift off. She risked letting go of him for long enough to jump up and kick the door shut, turning the lock from the inside.

The surgeon started to move slowly, in pain. Blood gushed from his neck. It hadn't hit an artery, but the wound was deep. It could be fixed, but Mia thought it best to leave it there.

Taking the roll of tape from her bag, Mia made quick work of securing the man's feet, arms and mouth. He barely had the strength to struggle, already in shock. Mia tasted the pain and licked her lips, feeling her urges surging from the depths. But she stopped it, summoning all the strength she had, and instead fixed her eyes on his, looking down at him.

Fetching another pen from the desk, Mia straddled him.

'I'm going to take the tape off your mouth,' she whispered. Her voice stumbled and wavered, but she held the new pen an inch from his right eye.

'If you scream, I'll stab this pen through your eye. OK?'

The surgeon's eyes widened again, this time in panic. He did his best to nod, wincing and shuddering as the pen already in his neck shifted.

Mia paused, allowing her heart rate to slow, forcing the desire away again. She wouldn't be able to hold this for long. She peeled at the tape. It had stuck hard and ripped the skin, pulling bits of stubble with it. The surgeon's mouth trembled. He licked his lips.

'Wha— what?' He tried to speak, his mouth swollen with panic.

'You know me,' said Mia, the revelation shocking her as much as the man on the floor in front of her. He *knew* her. Was this it? Was this the visit she'd hoped for all this time? Her eyes lit up with hope, but they died again when they met his. His were narrowing, shutting off. Mia knew what he was doing.

'I don't,' the man said. 'Please.' His eyes were panicked, but the recognition was under control and he was lying, denying this miraculous moment.

'Liar,' she hissed. Mia leaned in, reaching for the pen embedded in his muscle. She gave it a push, left and right, trying to ignore the pleasure it gave her, trying instead to focus on the pain in his face.

The surgeon shook and sweated. His eyes closed and Mia forced them open with her fingers.

'If you lie, I will hurt you,' said Mia. An easy threat from her, although she doubted he knew what she was capable of.

The surgeon nodded again. It must have hurt, but he did it anyway. His eyes opened wider. What did Mia see? Sorrow? Regret?

'I can't help you,' he said, coughing, the back of his throat filling with mucus. 'I don't know you. I've never seen you before.'

Mia's eyes filled with hurt, and she knew he saw it. But he didn't waver.

'I'm so sorry,' he whispered, clamping his lips shut, closing his eyes again, perhaps anticipating what was to come. Or perhaps he hoped that was enough, that she'd leave and his ordeal would be over.

Unfortunately for him, Mia had no intention of leaving.

'Then this will be unpleasant,' said Mia, re-taping his mouth, pushing it hard at the edges against the sweat pouring from his face. She raised the pen, feeling the pain starting to seep from his body. She took a breath.

'When you're ready to talk,' she said, 'blink with your good eye.'

CHAPTER SIXTEEN

Alex's head thumped as the Merc hit a pothole, making the wheel jerk to the left. He tried to concentrate on the road, keeping an eye on the satnav, heading for City Hospital.

It took almost an hour to get across town and Alex's hangover lifted a little as he raced through the morning traffic. He'd gone to bed early the night before after an apologetic exchange of text messages with Katie. She understood, she said, showing far more maturity than Alex could muster.

John was OK, said Katie. Kind to her, and Mum seemed happy. Katie assured Alex that John wasn't even round that often, but Mum had given her 'the chat' and explained they were more than friends. 'Gross', is how Katie had summarised the situation.

Otherwise, Katie had long since come to terms with her parents' break-up. It wasn't news. She quickly moved on to other things – the holidays, the promise of a trip to the Italian lakes, without John, and the antics of her friends. Life at thirteen was just as busy and complicated as in your forties, Katie assured him. To that Alex could offer only a knowing smile, signing off for the night, promising to see her soon.

City Hospital loomed ahead. Alex pulled up in a visitor's space and waited in Outpatients reception as per his instructions. He wasn't kept waiting for long.

'Dr Madison.' Detective Laurie appeared through a set of double doors marked STAFF ONLY. Her face opened in a warm smile. As before, she looked immaculate, in a crisp suit, her hair tied tightly back. Alex found himself feeling self-conscious, wondering, in his hung-over state, if he looked as bad as he felt. He returned the smile, shaking hands with her while attempting to smooth his shirt.

'Alex, please,' he said. 'It's great to see you again, Detective.'

'Just Laurie. I ditched my first name in high school and the "detective" bit can get a bit wearing if we're working this together.'

'Laurie it is,' said Alex, finding her manner immediately likeable. Some people had a knack for first and second impressions. He already felt at ease, his head clearing at the thought of a day with Laurie.

'Sorry I didn't get to finish with your suspect,' said Alex as they walked. Laurie ushered him through the doors towards a stairwell and service lifts. A couple of porters hung around chatting. When they saw Alex and Laurie, they moved off, glancing over their shoulders and whispering to each other.

Laurie shrugged. 'Don't sweat it. This case looks way more fun. I can see why you ditched me.'

Alex was about to object, but she grinned, pressing the button for the lift. Alex watched her, observing her posture. She held her head and shoulders firm, a power pose. It was intentional behaviour. It made Alex think about his own posture and he found himself straightening up, sucking in his belly and tilting his hips. He lifted his chin and forced his shoulders back.

Laurie gave him a sideways glance.

'Backache?' she said.

Alex pretended he didn't know what she meant.

'I get it from slouching at my desk,' she said. 'It'll destroy your spine, given time.' This she seemed to find amusing, and smiled again. It was infectious.

'You got me,' he said, thinking she was right. His posture was terrible because of the amount of time he spent at his desk. Perhaps he should ask for some tips.

The lift beeped and opened on the second floor.

'Surgery,' said Laurie, checking her phone and stepping out. Alex followed as she stuck the phone to her ear and entered into a rushed conversation. She beckoned him to follow and they paced down the corridors until they reached the ward. To the left, Alex saw signs for toilets and the staffroom. To the right, patient bays for pre-operative checks and doors through to the theatres. Straight ahead, swarming with uniformed police, was the nurses' station, the waiting area and Recovery. It was cordoned off with bright yellow tape and he spotted three armed officers standing to one side. Their weapons were slung and they looked relaxed. Another officer stood talking to them, sipping coffee from a paper cup. This was a crime scene, no doubt, but whatever had happened here was over already.

'Victim number five,' said Laurie, shoving her phone into her trouser pocket. It created a bulge against the fitted fabric.

'Five?'

'Perhaps,' said Laurie. 'The body is the same, but with an interesting addition.'

'What?'

'Come with me.' Laurie led the way under the tape towards the doors marked THEATRE.

The stench hit Alex's nose before they reached the scene. The narrow corridor lined with offices was busy as forensic officers performed their work, hurrying in and out carrying equipment and making their assessments.

Alex and Laurie were asked to wear plastic overshoes to avoid contamination. Alex hobbled on one leg, followed by the other. Laurie was more practised, slipping the plastic covers over her brogues and looking at him with faint amusement.

'You've done this before, right?' she said, her eyes wide.

Alex was finding it hard to be serious around Laurie. Her tone was cutting, but always friendly, as though she'd invited him into some private joke. She seemed to be making light of what appeared to be a very serious crime scene. Defence mechanism perhaps, or just well-judged detachment. Alex had met many professionals over the years who coped only because they could laugh and joke while dealing with the nastiest crimes imaginable. It was a mixture of training and innate ability to manage stressful situations. Laurie seemed to have it perfected.

'I have done this before,' said Alex. 'Several times, thank you.'

'OK.' Laurie approached the open door. Several forensics markers were dotted about. Alex took care not to touch any of them.

'We're not doing a scene walk-through,' said Laurie. 'I've already done it.'

'Oh,' said Alex.

'And the body's been moved already.'

'Then why—'

Laurie turned to him. Her smile was gone, but her expression firm and controlled. 'The man was mutilated, tortured beyond belief,' she said. 'Both eyes had been gouged out, but slowly . . . with a pen.'

She let that hang. Alex swallowed the taste of bile in his throat as he imagined the pain this person must have been subjected to. And for what?

'You can see the body,' said Laurie, 'if you wish, and all of the scene photography. But that's not why you're here.'

Laurie led them into the room. Alex scanned the small office, nodding to the one remaining forensic scientist, who was scraping what looked like blood out of the carpet. There was no shortage of it to scrape either. The body had lost several pints during whatever trauma it had suffered. Alex put his hand to his nose.

Laurie pointed. 'The body was found supine here. Exact cause of death is unclear; the pathologist will call me when he knows. I'm putting a tenner on blood loss.'

Alex nodded, scanning the rest of the room.

'Dr Paul King,' he said, reading the black lettering on the door.

'A well-respected surgeon,' said Laurie. 'Fifty-six years old, very experienced, well liked.'

Alex pointed at the filing cabinets. One of the drawers was open at the end. It had been dusted for fingerprints, the black residue still coating the handle and edges of the metal. As he scanned the others, he saw that every drawer had been dusted.

Laurie nodded. 'The extra detail.'

'She robbed him?'

Laurie raised her eyebrows.

'Assuming it's our suspect from the hospitals' CCTV, she's a she.'

'Oh, I know that,' said Laurie. 'Only a woman would be clever enough to get away with this many murders in London for this long.'

Her expression held, but Alex could see the sparkle in her eyes.

'I'm kidding,' said Laurie. 'Sorry. I get carried away sometimes. You're a psych – you can probably tell me why I do it, one day.'

Alex opened his mouth to speak but wasn't sure what to say.

'Gender is irrelevant at this point unless it pertains to motive,' continued Laurie. 'But yes, I think the doctor was robbed.'

Alex walked over to the filing cabinet. 'Do we know what was taken?'

'No. But all of the drawers were opened by the same hand. We've had the hospital records staff here and they say a few files are out of order, have obviously been searched. The last drawer – the open one – didn't contain patient records. It doesn't contain anything.'

'So she found what she was looking for?'

'Or she didn't,' said Laurie, shrugging. 'We don't know what was in it. We think the only person who could tell us is on a pathologist's table being cut into bits.'

Alex frowned.

Laurie looked apologetic. 'Sorry, but the surveillance CCTV in these hospitals is shit. We've got nothing of value because the cameras don't cover any of the staff areas. We're tracing the public areas and the proper street CCTV outside to see if we can figure out which direction she headed in.'

'But you're right,' said Alex, trying to ignore Laurie's flippant behaviour, for the moment, anyway. She was a fast thinker and correct . . . This changed everything.

'It's not random,' said Alex.

'See,' said Laurie, waggling her finger at him, 'I told you you were good.'

Alex ignored her, smiling. 'She's returning to hospitals not just because of easy victims but because she's searching for somebody or something.'

'What?'

Alex shrugged. 'Beats me.'

'Then why are we paying you?'

Alex feigned hurt. 'Sorry I let you down.'

They both sobered as the forensic officer stood and excused himself, carrying an array of sample bags. He nodded to them both.

'Later, Laurie,' he said, leaving the office.

Alex glanced at Laurie. She waited until the officer had gone, then perched on the end of the desk, staring at the blood-stained carpet. Her smile had faded.

'Why the torture?' said Laurie. 'I'm used to crimes of passion, but this is different. This is revenge, isn't it? A lone torturer. But why so many victims?'

Alex found his stare following hers. The carpet where a man had died a few hours earlier.

'I don't think it's revenge,' said Alex. 'At least, not in a personal way. Perhaps in a broader sense – revenge against the world.'

Laurie paused for a few seconds before looking up. 'That doesn't help me in the least.'

'And it's probably not true,' said Alex. 'Her choice of victims is so far unexplained but her choice of locations is clear. But she was at City Hospital looking for something or someone. Perhaps today she found that someone.'

'Dr Paul King.'

'Perhaps. Perhaps we need to focus on this doctor. Find out a little more about him.'

'We're good at that,' said Laurie. 'It's what the police do, Alex.'

The sarcasm was back. Alex held her gaze, deciding she was altogether more pleasant to work with than Hartley.

'I just wanted you to see it, the scene,' said Laurie. 'That's all. So you can start working that giant brain of yours Hartley told me about. I thought it might spark something.'

'Thanks,' said Alex, 'and it may have done, I just don't know it yet. However, I expect Hartley's flattery has an ulterior motive. Does she want to cut my rate?'

'At least by half,' said Laurie. Her phone buzzed and she jumped up, pulling it out of her pocket. Her face dropped as she read whatever she'd received. She tucked the phone away.

'The commissioner is sticking her nose in,' said Laurie, beckoning Alex to follow her back out into the corridor. 'I've gotta go. She wants a progress report. This is becoming high profile. The press are downstairs.'

'You're making a statement?'

'God, no,' said Laurie, weaving back out into the waiting area. 'We'll go back down the service lifts. But she's serious. Scrutinising everything. Every resource.' She looked at Alex. 'And every cost.'

Alex nodded as they waited for the lift. He knew what that meant. He had better produce something of value soon or he might find himself scrutinised off the case.

He jumped into the lift, his mood tempered but still somewhat buoyant, in no small part due to Laurie. But she was right, and the commissioner was too. Alex must do better than tag along for the ride, stating the obvious at every scene.

He was better than this, normally ruthless in his analysis. He knew the distraction of Grace and his private life was leaking into his professional life and it irked him. He'd always maintained such a rigid line between the two. He needed to let things go with Grace, for now at least. He needed to focus and provide the expertise the police were paying for.

Thinking hard as they bumped downwards, Alex tried to picture the killer stalking along these very corridors, searching for her next prey. He imagined the thought process that had led her to the private offices of the surgical team and the patient records within. He wondered what had transpired when she met her latest victim. Did they know each other? Did he catch her stealing and she killed him as a result?

No, it was more than accidental. This was no botched robbery. This woman was predatory and disturbed, haunted by a psychosis of some description. No sane person could commit such atrocities against other people, repeatedly and in the same fashion. Her desire – her motivation – was born out of something significant. But Alex didn't have a hope in hell of figuring out what without more information.

The doctor was the key, Alex was sure of it. What was the link between their mass killer and the prominent surgeon who lay dead and mutilated in her wake?

CHAPTER SEVENTEEN

He had a choice. The surgeon could have told her why he knew her. How he knew her. Where he knew her from.

He chose the outcome. He chose to die.

Mia didn't believe it for a second.

The lust had taken her. She'd lost control and drained his body for every last drop of pain. The questioning had quickly turned into frenzy as his pain engulfed her, rendering her powerless to resist. She had wrenched every drop out of his body, impervious to his screams, unable to listen to his pleading.

What could he have told her, had she controlled herself?

The darkness had descended fast. Mia had made it home to her lair, weeping and struggling to keep from screaming, her whole body shaking with revulsion and the after-effects of her fix. Again, it was not enough. She panicked, hyperventilating, pleading with a god she didn't believe in for an end to it, by whatever means.

It was only after several hours of sweat and tears that Mia sank to her knees, her head starting to clear, her body trying to reset into something resembling that of a normal person.

She undressed, heading to the basin and scrubbing herself with the icy water. She kept scrubbing all over until her skin was red in patches. The tape around her arm peeled off and the metal poles clanged on to the hard floor. She retrieved them to re-tape once she was dry. Her bones wouldn't have set yet. She had several more weeks of the make-shift cast.

Why had he resisted? She saw the recognition in his face, his pupils jumping and his body tensing. He'd been surprised, but not scared. Not initially. Not until she'd wrestled him to the ground.

Not until she started hurting him.

He wasn't in her dream. She examined the fragments she could remember, but his face was absent. That didn't mean he wasn't there. Her body had been twisted and violated by many people in her dream; she could see only a couple. The man with the scar, he stood out, his face flashing a warning. But the doctor yesterday had no scars, just a round, pale face that dripped with blood and saliva and finally stopped moving.

Mia dressed and attended to her arm. Her hand shook as she worked, a mixture of adrenaline and fatigue battling in her tired body. But her mind wouldn't rest. She changed into fresh clothes and paused at the mirror, forcing herself to tidy her hair and apply some make-up to try to hide the bags under her eyes.

She sat on the mattress, practising breathing techniques she'd developed herself to settle the shakes and subdue her cravings, if only for a few hours.

Opening her bag, she retrieved the items she'd taken from the filing cabinet in the doctor's office. The black address book she placed to one side. Taking each of the three folders, she emptied their contents in front of her and shuffled them together.

The first pages were stapled. The top sheet was a statement from a UK high-street bank in the name of Dr Paul King. Mia scanned the amounts. A few thousand here, a few there. Mia had no idea how much a surgeon got paid, but the amounts were high. This doctor was making tens of thousands a month, according to this. Mia flicked over the pages. They were all similar, a month per page.

Mia put them down, flicking through the next few pages. Delivery slips, orders for medical supplies. The name *Nova AG* was stamped all over everything, but it still meant nothing. None of the documents meant anything. Mia guessed this was hospital paperwork, the kind you'd find in any doctor's office. She threw the rest of the papers down and closed her eyes.

Food. Mia rummaged in her bag and found a chocolate bar. She ate it in three bites, grabbing a cup of water to wash the thick lumps from her throat. She imagined the sugar already working, seeping into her blood. She wasn't keeping to her promise of more calories. She was getting thinner by the day.

Next, Mia flicked through the address book, black and dog-eared. She'd resisted getting too excited at this find, but she couldn't help wondering.

Seven names in total, spread throughout the pages. Why seven? Mia knew she had no contacts, no friends and no family, but she assumed normal people had plenty. Did this doctor have only seven friends, or were they something else?

Only three had addresses. The others had phone numbers but nothing more.

Mia checked and double-checked the pages. She closed her eyes against the drumming in her head, the relentless beat signalling that the beast within her needed satisfying.

Suicide had occurred to Mia. Several times she'd woken from the darkness ready to do it, the knife poised at her neck. It wouldn't hurt. The blood would drain from her body as she'd watched blood drain from other people. They closed their eyes long before all the blood had escaped. It would no doubt be the same for her. Drifting into sleep, she supposed.

But what if it wasn't like that? Who knew the terrors of feeling your life slip away? Mia was no coward, but she feared the unknown as much as any other.

It wasn't cowardice or even fear that stopped her. It was not knowing. How could she die without knowing what had happened to her? Her parents, her mother in the car – if that's who it was – what became of them? Did they live three streets away, mourning the loss of their daughter? Were they dead and forgotten? Did they suffer the same affliction, addicted to the pain of others, wandering the streets of some other city in the world?

She had to know. She needed answers.

Mia found the first house without trouble. It was hard to stay hidden in a modern city.

It was an upmarket terrace in the north-west. Mia had walked, using the journey to eat and drink, forcing the food into her stomach. Two double espressos woke her up and she felt almost in control by the time she faced the house.

Almost.

It was getting late, the light already fading behind the slate roofline. Mia paused, looking both ways, feeling exposed. She usually hung around busy shopping malls, public areas, hospitals . . . The lack of people was disconcerting and the risk of being seen and reported was obvious.

Another ten minutes passed before Mia made her decision. She crossed the road, jumping up the concrete steps to the front door, knocking three times, hard, firm, panicked.

She was about to give up and leave when the door creaked open. An elderly lady peeked through the gap before opening the door wide, presumably seeing Mia as no threat.

Mia didn't waste any time. She pushed the door and the woman into the hallway, stepping round and slamming the door behind her.

The woman staggered and backed up against the wall. Mia looked into her face and was immediately struck by how ill the woman looked and the radiation of pain from every feature. An oxygen tube fed her nose, secured around her neck, plugged into a cylinder on a trolley next to her. The woman's eyes were bloodshot and weeping. She trembled with fear.

Mia resisted. Such wonderful, gorgeous pain was emanating from this woman. She smelled it in the air, on her breath and in her sweat. This was not what she had intended. This would not end well.

'Kim Norris?' said Mia, struggling to get the words out.

The old lady nodded. Her hands fidgeted. She opened her mouth to speak but gasped instead, drawing a long slow breath. Her chest rattled. The oxygen tube hissed.

'Do you know me?' Mia brought her face to within inches of the woman.

Kim Norris continued to shake but appeared to examine Mia's face. Her eyes dropped, taking in Mia's body, clothing, everything. Mia watched her eyes very carefully.

The frail woman's eyes found their way back to Mia's. The two stared at one another for several seconds before Mia blinked and moved her head back.

This woman didn't know her. Every sign and movement told Mia she was a stranger to this woman. She cursed and rummaged in her bag.

'Do you know this man?' Mia showed her one of the bank statements, pointing to the name at the top, Dr Paul King.

The woman squinted at the name, but her facial expression said it all. Mia knew before she said it.

'He was my doctor,' whispered the woman, her voice cracking.

Mia paced the hallway, walking in circles. 'Are you a doctor?'

'No,' whispered the woman, frowning in confusion. 'I was his patient. He treated me. I have pulmonary fibrosis. Late stage . . . as you can possibly tell.'

The woman's initial fear was fading. Her pain, however, was intense. Mia closed her eyes as tightly as she could, counting the seconds until her urge subsided.

'What did he treat you for?' said Mia. Her visit had been a failure. She should leave, run away before she succumbed.

The woman indicated a door off the hallway. 'Do you mind if I sit? I get dizzy.'

Mia nodded, watching her wheel the oxygen through the door, following closely in case she tried to make a call. Mia hadn't checked if anyone else was in the house, but if there had been, they would have appeared by now.

'He never treated me,' said the woman, sitting in an old floral-patterned chair. 'He said I wasn't a good candidate.'

Mia stood in the doorway. Any closer and she'd be lost, committed. If she hovered, if she left, this woman might be spared the rest of her life, however short it might be.

'Candidate for what?' Mia could see the woman's hands clasping into fists, trembling. Waves of pain flooded her every second. It was delicious. Mia's breathing slowed. She panted, once, then again. She was falling and didn't know how to stop.

'My pain,' whispered the woman. 'He said he could treat my pain. He said he could make it go away.'

CHAPTER EIGHTEEN

Laurie didn't call for two days. Alex made good use of the first day, catching up on his private appointments and paperwork. The second day he moped at home, trying and failing to think clearly about the problems in front of him.

With Grace and her new man at the back of his mind, he tried to throw himself into his analysis, reviewing everything the police had collected so far. He watched the CCTV again, noting the suspect's movements and her mannerisms, looking for any clue that might help. He re-read the witness statements of the bus driver who'd hit her and the porter who'd found her standing over a patient.

He stared at the blank page in his notebook, tapping his pen at the top, producing nothing more than a row of neat ink dots.

The police had gone into overdrive. Standard lines of inquiry and procedure were being followed with double the staff. Laurie was busy herding the team, but Alex could tell she was waiting for him. Waiting for Alex to give her a clue, some insight into this warped mind.

Pain. Alex wrote it at the top. The one thing all the victims had in common was the level of suffering inflicted on them. She didn't just kill, she tortured. So simple, yet to inflict it on others she must be driven by some overwhelming need.

The rational reasons for doing such a thing had been more or less ruled out by the police. They'd gone around in circles looking for gang affiliations and criminal connections of the victims, but they all came up blank. It was reasonable to conclude at this point that the acts were irrational, driven by psychosis. Alex agreed, but it meant the pressure was on him to offer some theory to back it up.

Why pain? What did pain offer the killer?

Sadistic killers were well documented and profiled across the world. A truth often hard to swallow in civilised society, sadistic minds were far more common than most people would like. They weren't all killers, and in fact only a very small percentage of sadists physically hurt people. But sadistic tendencies – the enjoyment gained from hurting others in order to make themselves feel better – lay at the heart of the sadist.

And that is what Alex believed they were dealing with. He wrote *Sadist* underneath *Pain*, adding a double question mark.

To inflict pain on someone in order to see the victim's reaction. The screams, the trembling physical reaction. The tears and the terror in the eyes. Some sadists enjoyed the begging and pleading for mercy – it bolstered their ego and self-worth. They believed themselves godlike in having complete control over a helpless victim. This tallied with most of what he'd seen. The victims in this case suffered terribly, their torment ending only in death.

Something bugged him, though.

Double lives. Alex scribbled it down, pondering. Most sadistic killers had double lives and could control their switch from one to the other. Seemingly normal professional people presenting sales figures in a corporate office by day could be planning their murders by night. Such double lives were part of the control process.

So far, the police knew nothing else about the killer. The prints weren't on file and neither was the description. Perhaps she was a software engineer or a lawyer or a teacher. The last thought sent a brief shiver down Alex's neck. But the appearance of being normal was what enabled these killers to find their victims.

This bugged him too. He made a mark next to his notes. This killer didn't need to know her victims. She wasn't pretending to be normal to get close to people – as far as they knew, anyway.

Rituals. Alex wrote the word with another question mark. Predatory and meticulous in their planning, sadists typically knew well in advance the what, the where and the who. Some killers had been known to script their murders like a screenplay, planning every word, every movement and their timing.

And that was the main issue Alex had with a standard sadist profile. It didn't fit. Every single victim in this case was already in pain from some other cause. Their killer found people in pain – and inflicted more. Puzzling. Inexplicable.

To make matters more confusing, the planning was not meticulous. She seemed to hit inner-city hospitals, but the victims could only be there by chance. There was no way she could know who would be in the emergency departments or the other wards ahead of time. That sort of information simply wasn't available to anyone, not even to the nurses in the hospitals, according to the reports.

So the victims were chosen at random, but all had been in pain already, except for one – Dr King, the surgeon she'd murdered in his office. Why him? Why had she deviated from her usual routine? Perhaps the location of her crimes wasn't purely opportunistic after all. Was she drawn to these hospitals for some other reason?

Alex thought about Dr King and the theft of unknown materials from his office. He double-underlined this note on the page.

He drifted, his mind wandering to previous patients, previous cases. An unpleasant memory reared its head and nudged around, jostling for position. Victor Lazar, the serial killer from his last big case, and the horrific circumstances the man had suffered.

What drives people to do such things? In Victor's case, it was what had been done to him. The worst kind of abuse over his formative years, resulting in a monster who could identify himself as such but could not stop the urge to exact his revenge in the only way he knew how.

Alex wondered what had happened to this killer. Nature or nurture, years of suffering or a snap in the night – a switch flicking on, turning one of those engineers, those lawyers or teachers into the monster they were now chasing?

Alex was snapped out of his thoughts by his phone buzzing across his desk.

'Laurie,' he said, clearing his throat.

'Meet me at City Hospital, thirty mins?'

Alex checked his watch.

'More like forty-five. News?'

'Another victim. Kim Norris. Seventy-eight years old.'

Alex winced. So many, so soon. The speed and frequency with which this killer acted was almost unprecedented.

'In a ward?' he said, wondering how the bolstered security would explain the lapse.

'No. You'll like this – this patient had been discharged from City Hospital many months ago. Pulmonary fibrosis. She was on her last legs.'

'Fibrosis,' whispered Alex. 'In pain.'

'What? Uh, yes. Probably. The only doctor available to comment gave us a brief overview. Horrible disease, and she didn't have long.'

'So what will I like about it?'

'Her doctor. He's our dead surgeon. Dr Paul King treated Kim Norris for her condition nine months ago but suddenly discharged her from his care. The clinical director at City Hospital is going to do some digging, but she wasn't sure what Dr King was doing treating Mrs Norris in the first place.'

'Why not?'

'Because he's a surgeon. You don't treat pulmonary fibrosis with surgery, or at least only as a last-resort lung transplant. She wasn't on the list.'

Alex tried to join the dots.

'Medical records?'

'Nope,' said Laurie. 'The appointments are in the record, but if she had a care plan or consultation notes, they're missing.'

Alex leaned back in his chair, feeling the soft leather wrap itself around him. His heart thumped with the excitement that came with a breakthrough, however minor.

'What are we missing?' he said.

'Plenty,' said Laurie. 'We followed up on Dr King. We have some colleagues we need to talk to, but the man kept himself to himself. We're looking at professional affiliations and sponsorships.'

'Sponsorships?' Something about the term spiked Alex's heartbeat. He'd been here before. 'Relating to what?'

He heard Laurie shuffling papers. 'Not sure. Like most prominent surgeons, he was in demand, bombarded non-stop by private companies – pharmaceutical and medical device manufacturers.'

'And?' Alex caught himself, hearing his demanding tone. A wave of anxiety caught him by surprise, along with the sound of his father's voice. *You'll never understand, Alex. You'll never get it.*

'And I don't know,' said Laurie, sounding defensive. 'This is your world, isn't it?'

Alex's throat dried up. Why did memories of his late father pop up without warning? He knew why. Because of what they were discussing. It didn't make it any easier.

'I'll be there in forty-five minutes,' said Alex, hanging up. He dropped his phone on to the desk and reached into his jacket. *Just one*, he thought. *Two a day, that's my limit.* He popped the pill into his mouth and forced himself out of the chair.

Medical devices, pharmaceuticals. Sponsoring a surgeon in London. Sponsoring him to do what?

Alex sent Laurie a text from the parking lot. Once again, she met him in Outpatients reception, leaning against the staff entrance, hands in pockets. Alex thought her face looked full of mischief and he found it relaxed him more quickly than the Xanax had done. He smiled and stopped in front of her, noting another sharp, fitted suit and a different pair of brogues.

'Eyes up, Doctor,' said Laurie, catching him.

Alex blushed. 'I was . . . You're more smartly dressed than most detectives I know,' he said, hoping it sounded like a compliment, as it was meant.

Laurie smiled, genuine, the mischief fading for a moment. 'And you're a better-dressed doctor than most I've seen recently. Although,' she said, indicating the waiting area, 'most of the people in this place look pretty rough, so don't take much from that. Come with me.' She winked at him.

'We're going . . .'

'. . . To see a colleague of the late Dr King,' she said. 'Dr Piers Tau. A somewhat reluctant interviewee. We managed to corral him in his office. I don't think he can help us.'

'You've spoken to him?'

'Briefly.'

They trod the same route as on their last visit. The hospital appeared back to normal, as it must, the daily patient lists full and the staff struggling to keep up. They headed past the pre-op bays and through the waiting area towards the surgeons' offices.

'The end office on the left,' said Laurie, leading the way.

It was a small but tidy room, one wall lined with bookshelves and filing cabinets, the other with pieces of odd abstract artwork. A man sat hunched over his desk, round-faced, with messy hair and a gut that looked as though it enjoyed the finer things in life. The doctor was scowling at the uniformed officer perched near the door. Alex noticed a large scar below the doctor's right eye, pink and raised. He tried not to stare.

'Thanks,' said Laurie to the officer, who exited, pulling the door shut behind her.

'Dr Tau,' said Laurie, 'so sorry to keep you waiting. My colleague here broke down on the way.'

Alex caught his reaction in time, unsure whether or not to apologise. 'Dr Madison,' he said, extending his hand.

Dr Tau shook it, his hand warm and clammy. 'Dr Tau,' he said. 'Look, I have a full surgical list this afternoon. I can't stay here chatting.'

Laurie dragged a chair over from by the wall. Alex thought she made a point of taking several seconds to line it up with the desk before sitting. The frustration was evident on the doctor's face. Alex remained standing, unsure what game she was playing.

'You must be upset,' said Laurie. She patted her jacket pockets before pulling out a small notebook and pen.

The doctor's eyes narrowed for a moment. Alex caught it.

'Of course,' said Dr Tau, 'Paul's death was tragic and, from what I've heard, horrific.' The doctor's voice cracked. He cleared his throat. *Grief*, thought Alex, *or something else?*

'You were in surgery at the time,' she said. It wasn't a question, but Dr Tau nodded.

'Yes. I've already told one of your colleagues.'

'I know. My apologies,' said Laurie.

Alex watched Dr Tau. He fidgeted, picking at a fingernail. If Alex had been able to see the man's feet, he was sure they'd be shuffling. His expression was tense, his jaw clenching and releasing. Not grief. This doctor was anxious as hell. Not the typical behaviour of an experienced surgeon.

'We're trying to get through all of his colleagues, build up a picture of his life, his contacts, et cetera,' said Laurie.

The doctor nodded, a glimmer of relief evident on his face. Why should he be feeling relief? The hairs prickled on Alex's neck with a feeling of déjà vu. The feeling of seeing a doctor abusing their position of power.

Laurie proceeded to ask Dr Tau a list of scripted questions, mainly about Dr King's patients. Did they have any in common? Had he seen any acting strangely, appearing at the hospital when they shouldn't? Any relations of patients turning up unexpectedly? Any unresolved negligence cases? Laurie ran on for several minutes before closing her notepad and nodding to herself.

'Tell me about your sponsorships,' said Alex. He could tell the question had caught Dr Tau off guard, his eyes shooting to Alex's.

'That's none of your business,' snapped the doctor. Laurie paused, glancing up at Alex.

'I mean, it's confidential,' said Tau. 'I can't discuss my professional arrangements outside of my employment here.'

'That's not true,' said Alex. 'And anyway, my colleague here has already researched your affiliations with several medical suppliers.'

It wasn't a lie, but if Laurie had found out anything, she hadn't shared it with Alex. He tried not to look at Laurie, focusing instead on the doctor's face. Tau swallowed. His anxiety increased.

'And we are the police,' said Alex. 'It would be better to share now, rather than in court.'

Laurie's head snapped around.

Dr Tau paled. 'Court?' he said. 'Don't be absurd.' He swallowed again, his mouth clearly dry with nerves. Alex could read all the signs. This man was fighting his panic.

'Er, Dr Madison,' said Laurie, 'a word?'

Laurie ushered Alex out of the office, apologising to the flustered doctor but telling him to stay put.

'What the hell?' said Laurie. She didn't look angry, just confused.

Alex paced in the dark corridor. The uniformed officer hovered at the other end.

'He's hiding something,' said Alex.

'He's nervous.'

'Why?'

'Because one of his colleagues was butchered in the next office?'

'That's not it.'

Laurie put her hands on her hips. 'We're not interrogating this surgeon,' she said.

'I'm not,' insisted Alex. He paused. 'But what did you find out about his relationships with medical suppliers, pharmaceuticals?'

Laurie frowned. 'Not much, Alex, short of searching his house and office. His name is mentioned against several clinical trials and research programmes. He's a distinguished lecturer at the medical school. Much the same as our deceased Dr King. They're both good surgeons. What can I say?'

'Money?'

'He's not under investigation, Alex,' said Laurie. 'We're not examining his bank accounts. The purpose of this interview is to find out more about Dr King's routine and his patients. Dr Tau is not a suspect.'

Alex sighed, leaning against the wall.

'What is it?' Laurie came closer, examining his face. Alex caught a whiff of her perfume.

'What did Hartley tell you about our previous cases?' he said.

Laurie shrugged. 'Not much. Enough.'

'Such as?'

'Such as . . . you tended to work on the bizarre and the macabre. Unexplained motives, actions. *The limits of the human mind.* Her words, not mine.'

Alex nodded.

'But I expect you're also useful in other ways.' Laurie wiggled her eyebrows. The mischievous smile was back. At least she wasn't angry with him.

'My biggest case involved the medical profession,' said Alex. 'A group of doctors abusing their power, experimenting on patients. Children. The results were . . . horrifying.'

Laurie nodded. 'Victor Lazar? I read about it, although most of the case was restricted by the CPS. Most of us assumed some high-level screw-up.'

Alex shook his head. 'Not exactly. But it brought back memories. I've been mulling this over for days. We know our suspect is targeting hospitals – and not just to get at the patients. She's looking for something.'

Laurie nodded, smiling as Alex once again stated the bleeding obvious.

'And Dr Tau is nervous. I don't think he's nervous because his colleague died. I think he's nervous for some other reason.'

Laurie kept nodding but waved her palm for him to continue. 'Such as . . .?'

Alex huffed.

'Did that huff mean you've worked it all out?' said Laurie. 'Or did it mean you have a hunch and nothing more?'

Alex shook his head. 'Hunch,' he said.

Laurie sauntered back to the office door. 'In that case . . .'

They both stood opposite the desk. Laurie thanked Dr Tau for his time and said they'd be back in touch again. Once more the relief was palpable on his face.

Alex cast his eyes around the office before they left. He spied that one of the filing cabinet drawers was open a few inches. Had it been open when they first arrived? His eyes darted around the room, landing on a brown leather messenger bag next to the desk. It too was open, with the flap thrown over several blue folders.

Alex stared back at Dr Tau, who shuffled in his seat, trying not to make eye contact.

'Goodbye, Dr Tau,' said Alex as they left, Tau's sweaty palm leaving a distinct impression as he and Laurie walked along the corridor towards the exit.

'Coffee?' Laurie exited the lift and stared at the signs on the wall. 'I could do with ten minutes' downtime. There,' she said, 'this way.'

Alex agreed, surprised at the invitation. Laurie was normally racing from place to place. He fell into step beside her.

'Sorry,' he offered.

'No problem,' said Laurie. 'I guess it doesn't hurt for these people to get a dose of fear sometimes.'

Alex was intrigued. 'That was loaded.'

Laurie laughed. 'No. Just these doctors think they're above everyone else.' She glanced at Alex, her hand reaching out to touch his arm. 'Present company excluded, obviously.'

Alex glanced at Laurie as they walked. Her manner was unique – quirky, but still professional – and he found it invigorating. She was friendly, flirty perhaps, although Alex didn't know her well enough to judge. Maybe she was like this with everyone.

Alex had already figured out a few things about her, though. She tended to hide her intentions. She distracted people, including him, with small expressions and comments, her face radiating warmth one minute and sarcasm the next, although she was never hostile. Behind her pleasant façade Alex could sense her mind whirring, racing along at breakneck speed. She was intriguing. Alex was glad of the chance to get to know her a little better.

'Careful,' she said as they approached the coffee shop counter. 'You'll walk into someone.'

Alex tore his eyes away from her, suppressing a smile.

'My round,' he said.

'Obviously,' said Laurie. 'You can expense it through that lucrative private practice of yours.'

Alex narrowed his eyes. 'Obviously,' he said, still smiling.

They took a table at the far end of the café near the window. It overlooked the streets outside. Several floors up, it was easy to get lost staring at the people and vehicles swarming below, thousands of Londoners going about their business. Most of them legitimate, a few criminal. Out of those, a few were the nastiest specimens society could offer.

'I wonder if she's down there,' said Laurie. 'One of those, looking up, planning her next gig.'

'I hope not,' said Alex. He wanted to make a joke, keep it light, but he kept seeing visions of the young woman on the pathologist's table, tortured and murdered in her prime. 'I hope not,' he repeated, sipping his coffee. It scalded his tongue and he winced.

Laurie sniffed, leaving her own cup on the table.

'Do you see your family much?' she said.

The question startled Alex. He'd been hopeful of finding out more about Laurie. He hadn't banked on her starting the questions.

'Yes,' he said. 'Lots.' He thought about it. 'Not as much as I'd like. I'm divorced. One daughter, Katie.'

Laurie nodded. 'Hartley told me.' Alex wondered whether that was quite appropriate. He guessed it was standard for the police to talk about these things. He was in a position of trust with them, after all.

'I ask,' said Laurie, 'because these cases hit officers hard. They relate to their families. Death and suffering become visible, present and real.'

Alex nodded. So true. Was she telling him how hard it was hitting her? Was she asking for help?

'Parents?' said Laurie. 'Sorry, I mean, I know about your dad, Rupert. What about your mum?'

Alex paused. A personal question, but OK. His father's death at the hands of Victor Lazar wasn't a secret, but it conjured a mixture of complex emotions in Alex. He and his dad hadn't been close, and he was one of the people Alex had thought of when talking about the abuse of power. His dad had committed the ultimate betrayal in his position as a psychologist – but in return had paid the ultimate price.

'My mum's in a home,' said Alex. 'She needs 24/7 care.'

Laurie nodded, and Alex noted a change in her. The jokey exterior had faded. She looked serious, deep in thought.

'But I see her when I can.' Alex felt compelled to fill the silence. A classic detective's tactic, although he knew it didn't apply here. Laurie looked troubled, distant.

'What about you?' said Alex. 'Married?'

He glanced at her hand as he waited for the answer. She wasn't wearing a ring. Should it make a difference?

'Nope,' she said, staring at her coffee. 'Divorced too.'

Alex's heart thumped, but he wasn't sure why. Laurie was nice, friendly, professional, pretty . . . Alex bit his bottom lip and turned away. He was not heading down that road. Not today.

'Cheers,' he said, raising his scorching coffee. 'To being single.'

Laurie smiled, but it was forced. Her history haunted her, that much was obvious. Judging by her expression, prying into it now wasn't the right thing to do.

Alex tried his coffee again, concerned about Laurie's sudden change in mood, a different side to her emerging.

'It's hard not to think about those close to you when you witness such atrocities,' he said. 'We all have our ways of detaching.'

He thought of his jacket pocket and the small packet of benzodiazepines nestled there, night and day. Alex coped by drugging himself. He wondered how Laurie coped, other than through jokes and distractions.

She nodded and looked as if she was about to say something, but turned away. Pausing, she then turned back, with a wide smile. It look forced.

'Good coffee,' she said, taking a gulp, almost spitting it back out. 'Still too hot,' she said, fanning her mouth. At the same time her phone buzzed in her pocket. She read the screen and huffed.

'Report due,' she said. 'Time to go again.' She put the lid back on her cup. 'Takeaway?' she said, standing up.

They both headed to the same parking lot.

'I'll call you tomorrow,' said Laurie as they separated by the ticket machine. 'In the meantime, you need to leave the doctor alone.'

Alex nodded. He stared past her, deep in thought.

'I mean it, Alex. Don't stir up a bunch of complaints. You have your theories, but I need evidence, OK? Remember who our suspect is. Clue – it's not one of the doctors.'

'You're the boss,' said Alex as she walked away.

Alex hung back, waiting until Laurie was out of sight before heading back inside. He strolled through reception with his head down, slipping into the first empty lift, his foot tapping impatiently as the floors swept by. He felt bad for going against Laurie's instructions, but she'd forgive him if he turned up a lead. Dr Tau's behaviour warranted further inspection. Laurie might not be willing to do it yet, but she was bound by official process. As long as Alex was careful, he was within his rights to be here.

He hoped he wasn't too late, and as he stepped out, he saw that luck was on his side. Dr Tau was rushing towards him, bag swinging by his side, coat slung over it. The man was leaving in a hurry.

The doctor stopped short in the corridor. The bag hit his leg, his coat slipping to the floor. He grabbed it, scowling.

'Dr Madison,' he said, forming a pained smile. 'Forgotten something?'

'As it happens . . .' said Alex, and then paused. He thought carefully about what to say. He'd rushed back up for a confrontation, but now that he was here, he struggled to form the questions. A straight confession was unlikely.

'I'm busy,' said Tau, moving towards Alex and the lift, his chin jutting forward. 'I told you that already. If there's nothing more—'

'Is it worth it?' Alex blurted it out. He could leave the soft approach for the police. Alex was sure Tau was hiding something. His involvement in the chain of events was not as an innocent colleague, Alex was sure of it.

He watched Tau closely. The man was a practised liar, that much was certain, but Alex's experience won out – the man's body remained firm, but his face betrayed him. Alex was right: Tau was guilty. But of what?

'I don't know what you mean,' said Tau, his voice almost a whisper.

'The trials,' said Alex. It was a guess, but he saw the flicker in Tau's eyes. 'What were they? What were you trying to achieve?'

Tau swallowed. His gaze faltered, but he recovered quickly. Obviously a man used to being in charge and unused to being challenged, he found this questioning an insult.

'If you'll excuse me,' he said, stepping past Alex, 'I'm leaving.'

'Are you next?'

Alex wished he hadn't said it, but it tumbled out, tangled up with memories of his father, of his arrogance and delusion. His father had thought he could play God and get away with it. He'd believed there'd be no consequences. And how wrong he had been: killed for his mistake. Alex saw the same look in Tau's expression now: an incredulity born out of a lifetime of privilege and superiority. Tau considered himself elite and untouchable, and Alex knew the man would not explain himself.

Alex found himself stepping forward, an anger boiling up from his stomach, the anger that had simmered since the revelation of his father's guilt and everything that had come before.

'Tell me what you did,' he said, stopping within a foot of Tau, leaning in, their faces inches apart. He smelled Tau's breath, stale and stressed. The doctor's face was clammy, but his eyes were defiant. 'Your actions led the killer to this hospital,' said Alex. 'Your actions killed your colleague.'

Alex knew he was out of line, his theories running way ahead of the evidence, but it was all he could do to stop his fists balling and lashing out. He resisted only because of the consequences for Laurie and the case. Talking was one thing, but Alex must hold it together. His father had ruined a decent chunk of Alex's life while alive. He wouldn't continue to ruin it after his death.

Tau flinched, his gaze darting over Alex. He moved back a step, then another. Apparently sensing Alex wouldn't follow, he squared his shoulders and straightened up, stepping into the lift.

'Goodbye, Dr Madison,' he said. His stare was icy, though as the doors closed Alex saw a flicker of uncertainty.

Alex let him go, leaning against the wall of the bright corridor, struggling with his frustration. He still had so little information, yet the sense of familiarity was growing.

As his anger settled down, his rational brain began to spin. What had Dr Tau done, and what had gone so horribly wrong?

CHAPTER NINETEEN

More than dreams. More than suspicion. The surgeon had revealed his recognition of her and the papers she'd stolen from the filing cabinet had revealed more. The first name in the black book was a lost soul, just like her, although clearly not in possession of the same desires. The old lady's story was brief, but her words hammered Mia's memories into the fore. Kim Norris had been promised relief from her pain but had never received it. What then did that mean for Mia? What had the surgeon offered her, and why was she now cast out with her vicious and unrelenting urges, while the doctors withdrew and pretended they didn't know her?

If only Mia had been able to control herself. But it was too delicious, too immediate. Mia had apologised, but the woman's pain was irresistible and Mia had taken it from her. Kim was elderly and didn't struggle. Mia watched her eyes and saw a flicker of relief near the end. Mia had done what the surgeon couldn't, permanently and without malice. The comedown was fast and gut-wrenching, but Mia dragged herself up and kept going.

She had a lead, a source of the truth, perhaps. Her mind whirled in confusion, but her motivation was clear. She held the black book in one hand and a map in the other, shivering at the side of the road, crouched against a brick wall, waiting for the shudders to subside.

North London, more wealthy suburbs. Mia stared at the cherry tree blossom in the front garden, the neat lawn bordered by lavender. The driveway held a silver Mercedes. Mia watched her reflection in the car window as she crunched through the gravel towards the front door.

The porch was grand with white pillars on either side of a red-tiled floor. The sash windows to the right were ornate, the woodwork freshly painted, the glass clean. Shutters stopped her seeing through into the room.

Three knocks. They thundered through the house but also through Mia's head. The sound caused ripples of unease in her gut, ominous and menacing.

As soon as the door creaked open Mia lunged inside, pushing the occupant of the house away from it and into the hallway. She kicked the door closed behind her before she'd had a chance to look at them. When she did, she found herself face to face with a tall wiry man with a full head of grey hair and gold-rimmed glasses. His eyes were wide in shock at the intruder, his hands raised to protect himself.

'What on earth?' he said, in a deep and controlled voice. He was well spoken, cultured.

'Do you know me?' asked Mia. She stood, ready to strike him, her right fist clenched. 'Did you treat me? At your hospital?'

The man peered at her, still in a state of shock. He swallowed, his throat jumping. He shuffled backwards.

'Don't move,' said Mia. 'Not until you answer me, Dr Willis. I know who you are.'

'I . . . No, I don't think so.' The doctor's voice remained controlled, even though his body was tense, his fight-or-flight response on the verge of being triggered.

They stared at each other. Mia glanced over at the wall, found the light switch and flicked it on. A chandelier bathed both their faces in light.

Mia leaned forward. The man backed up, his footsteps soft on the dark hardwood floor. He pushed against the banister, which creaked in protest.

'My pain,' whispered Mia. 'Did you take away my pain?'

She saw it in an instant. The doctor's eyes gave him away and his jaw dropped with a gasp. He emitted fear, a mixture of pheromones and sweat, the latter beading on his forehead. His body posture changed, his arms sagging and his shoulders drooping. Mia inhaled, feeling the change in the man's body as he struggled to contain his reaction. But there was no fooling her. Mia's capacity for reading people was unparalleled. She lapped it up, waiting for his reply.

'I . . .'

'You recognise me,' said Mia. 'You.' She brought her right hand to his throat, grabbing his windpipe, digging her fingers in. He struggled in response, clutching her arm, but he was weak and she was full of fury.

'Stop!' Mia shouted, to herself, not to the doctor. Releasing her hand, she gulped as the man's pain became raw and alluring. This wasn't why she'd come here. She wanted answers, not a fix. No matter how hard it might be, Mia knew she must resist again, for as long as possible.

She grabbed his hair and pulled. His head bowed and he went down on his knees.

'If you don't answer me, I'll kill you,' she said, hoping the threat would be enough. Reaching into her jeans pocket, she pulled out a small penknife. Flicking it open, she pressed the blade flat against his throat, standing over him.

The doctor's voice lost its confidence. Raised an octave, it whimpered. 'Please,' he begged. 'I have a family. I'll give you whatever you want.'

Mia paused. *Family.* She had a family. Didn't she? The people in the car? Her mother, she was almost sure, except that it was a dream, no more. The driver, in her more imaginative moments, was her father. A loving father who protected his little girl, drove her around London in a luxury car, perhaps heading home to a house just like this one, with a grand porch and wood flooring and sash windows. Perhaps Mia had had all of this.

Before it happened.

'What did you do?' asked Mia, aware that her voice was a whisper.

The doctor's breathing was laboured. On his knees, with Mia's knife at his throat, he tried to look at her, wincing as the blade nicked his skin. Mia crouched, allowing him to see her. She'd succeeded. He wasn't in pain, not yet.

Mia suppressed her urge. It crept into her mind, wrapping itself around her, hugging her body. It was on her tongue, in her throat and in her nostrils as she breathed in the fear emanating from the doctor. Pressure throbbed at the base of her skull and along with it the distant panic that she would be overcome. Mia forced her breathing slowly in, slowly out.

'Please,' she said. 'Tell me.'

The doctor trembled. Mia heard a car pass by the house. A bird sung outside the front door. A whistling sound came from the back of the house.

'We tried,' said the doctor. His eyes watered, with fear or regret, Mia wasn't sure. 'When you came in, you . . . An ideal candidate, that's what they said.'

'Candidate for what?' Mia moved in even closer. Her hand juddered and the knife slipped against his throat, causing him to gasp in shallow breaths.

'Where did I come in? To a hospital?'

The doctor nodded.

'Where?'

The doctor gulped. 'London City Hospital.'

Mia's mind swirled. The mass of questions she'd prepared spun and disappeared, knocking into each other, confusing her. City Hospital. It was unravelling faster than she could grab it.

'Why was I there in the hospital? What was wrong with me?'

'A crash,' said the doctor.

Another faint noise from the back of the house. Not a whistling, but a scraping. Faint but audible.

'You were in a crash. Terrible . . . We tried – we saved you.'

Mia shook her head. Crash. The car. The dream. Where were the others?

'My . . . the woman in the car,' said Mia. 'Where is she?'

The doctor closed his eyes and shook his head. A bang from the back of the house, a door closing in its frame. Mia's head darted up.

'Catherine!' screamed the doctor. 'Call the police!' The man wrenched his head away before Mia could stop him. She still had hold of him as he did it. One hand on the side of his head, the other holding the knife to his neck.

She couldn't have stopped what happened.

The warm gush of blood hit Mia's fingers before the doctor even realised what had happened. Her hand snapped away, pulling the knife with it, but she was too slow. The doctor scrambled backwards, registering the wound as he did so. His right hand went to the gash in his throat, groping around. Blood dripped through his fingers and on to his white shirt. His expression was desperate as he gasped with the trauma.

Mia didn't pause. She heard footsteps at the back of the house and knew the sirens would be next. She left the immaculate hardwood floor of the hallway and barged through the large front door surrounded by the grand porch. She didn't glance at the sash windows or the silver Mercedes as she raced across the gravel driveway.

The one odd conclusion Mia did come to as she sprinted away from the scene was that bleeding out through an artery obviously didn't hurt. There had been very little pain from the doctor, she thought, as she tucked her penknife away and picked up the pace, hitting the side streets and alleyways, zigzagging to shake off any pursuit.

Mia ran for thirty minutes before stopping, realising she was shaking from head to toe. Not from withdrawal, nor desire or addiction. She was shaking from adrenaline born of excitement. The doctor had told her. He was part of it. Which meant her journey had finally turned a corner. That doctor would be dead before the police arrived, but there were others. There was one more name.

And Mia would find him.

CHAPTER TWENTY

Alex held the phone to his ear. Laurie had relayed the information at breakneck speed, pausing only to make two sarcastic comments, both about Alex. She paused at the end of the conversation.

'So?'

'Can we speak to him? Can he talk?' said Alex.

'Yes,' said Laurie. 'His carotid artery was sliced open but not severed. He managed to apply enough pressure until his wife arrived. She called the police, sat with him – she's a midwife, by the way – and stopped him bleeding out. He's been sutured and is in AMU. They think he might need further surgery. It's serious.'

'So . . .'

'So I'll see you there, Dr Madison,' Laurie said. 'Don't keep me waiting or stand me up. A girl hates that.'

Alex smiled, tucking his phone in his pocket, grabbing his jacket off the chair and his keys from the holder.

Another victim. Another doctor. But this time, still alive.

Alex raced through town, swerving across lanes, trying not to look at the screen of his phone. Dr Willis was the name of the victim. Alex had texted *Associate of Dr Tau?* and was checking if Laurie had replied. The phone buzzed as he screeched up to a red light.

Yes. But Dr Tau out of town. Are you nearly here? Your coffee is cold.

What a coincidence. He wouldn't say 'I told you so' in those exact words, but Alex's desire to investigate Dr Tau in greater depth could at least go on record. Tracking him down would use precious time they might not have.

The lights changed and Alex roared off, his mind processing and preparing. The wounded doctor was stable, but their time with him would be limited. He might resist their questions. Despite being the victim of attempted murder, he wasn't an innocent bystander. He was involved, connected somehow. The attack on him had been targeted, and Alex needed to know why.

The acute medical unit at London City Hospital appeared calmer than the other floors. Visitors were restricted and the doors kept closed. Uniformed officers stood guard at the entrance, challenging Alex for his ID before they let him through.

Laurie greeted him on the other side. Alex made a point of not looking her up and down, staring instead at the two coffee cups she was holding in a carrier.

'One for me?' he said.

Laurie narrowed her eyes. 'But I'm wearing a new suit,' she said.

Alex glanced at her clothes.

'Made you look,' said Laurie, handing him one of the coffees. 'It's an old suit. Follow me.'

Alex sipped his lukewarm drink and followed Laurie past the nurses' station into the ward.

'Dr Willis is in a private room at the end. Doctors say we have fifteen minutes. His condition is deteriorating. They didn't stop the bleed. He's scheduled for surgery this morning – they've got a specialist vascular surgeon travelling in.'

Alex nodded. The single rooms in AMU were for infectious disease control or patients with compromised immune systems. Alex supposed attempted murder was also a good reason to put somebody in one. He just hoped they found out something of use.

The room was brightly lit, small and very hot. Alex found himself tugging at his collar as they closed the door behind them. Laurie took in the room. Alex watched the way her eyes darted around before she picked up one of the spare visitor chairs and lined it up with the end of the bed. She sat, indicating Alex should stand to the side.

Dr Willis lay flat, hooked up to an array of monitors. ECG, oxygen and a drip. A woman sat next to him, holding his hand. He was awake, staring at the ceiling, breathing slowly into the mask.

'Mrs Willis?' said Laurie. 'I'm Detective Laurie from the Met. This is Dr Madison.'

Mrs Willis's eyes were bloodshot and weeping. She glanced at them both before returning her gaze to her husband. 'They told me you were coming. He's going into surgery again,' she said. 'He's still bleeding.'

Laurie nodded. 'I'm sorry, Mrs Willis.' She paused. 'We won't be long. Dr Willis, can we ask you some questions?'

The doctor swallowed, the bandage on his throat jumping. The respirator hissed and he pulled the mask away.

'Why don't you give us a minute, dear?' he said, his voice a whisper. His wife gave his hand a squeeze and stood, nodding to Laurie and Alex on her way out.

They waited a moment. Alex watched the ECG monitor tracking the doctor's heartbeat, waiting for Laurie to lead.

'I know what you're going to ask,' said the doctor after his wife had closed the door, 'and you'd be right to.' He swallowed again. 'Truth is, I was never one of them. I was intrigued, but never convinced.'

Laurie frowned, glancing at Alex. The shiver again. Prickles on his neck. He'd been right. This was about experimentation.

'Tell us about the trials,' said Alex. 'What were they for?'

Laurie's frown deepened, but she remained silent. Alex wanted to cut to the heart of it, and this was the best place to start.

The doctor looked as though he was shaking his head.

'Dr Tau said this was the one. I didn't argue . . . The father was dead. The mother was in a terrible state – unlikely to make it. The girl, though . . . She had . . .'

Dr Willis tailed off. He swallowed twice, appearing to struggle. His heart rate jumped momentarily before settling.

'Are you OK?' said Laurie.

Dr Willis closed his eyes and took a few breaths.

'They were illegals. It's what we were told. The paperwork was fake. It made it . . . easier.'

'Easier to do what?' said Alex, aware they didn't have long with this man. 'You mention Dr Tau. What does he have to do with this?'

'What's her name?' said Laurie.

'I was a member of Dr Tau's trauma team,' said Dr Willis. 'Hand-picked, only on shift once a week, seeking candidates. Very few passed muster or arrived at the right time when we had complete control of the trauma pathway – we needed everything from emergency triage to surgery and recovery.'

Alex leaned in, resting his hands on the safety bars at the end of the bed.

'Candidates for what?' Alex checked his voice. It was raised, demanding. His temper was simmering. He needed to know more but worried he'd snap at hearing it. What the hell were these doctors involved in?

'I didn't know about the result,' said Willis. 'They told me they'd discharged her when the treatment showed serious side effects. That's all I knew. I didn't know she'd come back. Why did she want to hurt me? To kill me? I don't understand.'

Alex paused. He glanced at Laurie, who shrugged. Did the doctor not know the extent of their suspect's rampage? Alex guessed not. Nobody would have told him.

'What was her name,' Laurie repeated. 'The girl?'

'You don't know what's wrong with her?' said Alex, cutting in.

Again the doctor shook his head. He tried to clear his throat and stopped, clearly struggling. Laurie glanced at the door.

'She was in pain,' said Willis. 'Terrible pain. So was her mother. That was what we were doing.'

'Explain,' said Alex. He caught a sharp look from Laurie but ignored it.

'It was legitimate. At first, anyway. Stage two clinical trials. We were being sponsored directly by the pharma, but who isn't these days?'

Alex took a deep breath. In the pockets of a pharmaceutical company. Plenty of doctors weren't, thank you very much.

'What—'

'Her name,' said Laurie, standing, leaning over the bed. 'Dr Willis, we suspect this young woman of several murders over the last few months. Tell me her damn name.'

Dr Willis blinked rapidly. 'Murders?' he said.

'Dr King was one of them.'

Willis shook his head. Alex could see his hands trembling. 'But why?'

'Her name!' Laurie shouted, slamming her hand on the bed. Alex jumped back. It was the first time he'd seen Laurie angry. He supposed she had a right to be. Their goal was the same but their priorities subtly different.

Laurie needed to find her killer.

Alex needed to know why she was a killer.

'Mia,' whispered the doctor. 'I was told her name was Mia. Anastas. Anastos. Something like that. But it was probably fake. Ethnically, I think she was Greek, possibly Albanian.'

Laurie typed the name into her phone and sent it off in a text. Alex had no doubt the wheels of her investigative team would go into overdrive. He also suspected they wouldn't find anything.

'I need to know what happened to Mia,' said Alex, glancing at Laurie, checking she was OK for him to continue. She nodded, her anger gone.

Dr Willis paused. His breathing was laboured. He shifted on the bed, wincing a couple of times as he did so. His heart rate rose and stayed elevated.

'I don't think I can,' he said finally. 'As I said, I wasn't one of them. I wasn't party to the strategy discussions – the talks with the drug company. I didn't know the plan. All I did was be part of the trauma team.'

Alex considered this. 'How much did they pay you?' he said.

Dr Willis huffed. Out of arrogance or reticence, Alex wasn't sure.

'Enough,' he said. 'More than enough. They paid very well. But they stood to make a fortune if it worked.'

The ECG monitor alarm went off. The doctor's brow was visibly wet with sweat. He closed his eyes as a nurse rushed into the room. She watched the ECG for a moment before switching off the alarm, checking Willis's vitals. She turned to Laurie and Alex.

'Time's up,' she said. 'He's in no state for this.' The nurse looked concerned, responsible for having let them question him.

'Dr Willis,' said Alex. 'Information. Where can I find information on the trials?'

'I said, enough.' The nurse raised her voice, ushering Alex away from the bed, but Willis responded.

'I'm sorry,' he said. 'Truly I am.'

'The information.' Alex dodged the nurse as she moved to wrestle him out of the room.

'Alex,' said Laurie. 'We'll come back. Stop it.'

'It's OK,' said Willis. He seemed more composed, still in pain but under control. 'My office,' he said, 'at home. Catherine will show you. But please,' he said, 'before you judge . . . we were trying to help them. Trying to achieve something great.'

Alex let himself be pushed through the door into the corridor. He hadn't got what he wanted, but at least they hadn't left with nothing.

He walked on ahead, deep in thought, his heart hammering in his chest. Shrugging off Laurie, he found a men's room and locked himself inside, drawing a few breaths, searching for his pills.

Dr Willis's words. *Achieve something great.* A flood of memories hit him as he crunched the Xanax between his teeth. Those words, spoken by people in power, used to justify all manner of horrors. He'd been here before and had hoped never to see it again.

What did they do to this poor girl, Mia, and what had they created as a result?

CHAPTER TWENTY-ONE

The phone call came later that day. It was a surprise to Alex, but Laurie confirmed it.

'They couldn't stop the bleeding. He died in surgery,' she said.

A brief panic took hold of Alex. His actions in the hospital room flashed in front of him, his questions and manner. Dr Willis had been agitated, stressed by their visit.

'Don't worry,' said Laurie. 'The vascular surgeon confirmed that his bleed was far worse than they'd thought. The knife had torn the artery and several other structures. He went into arrest and they couldn't revive him. It was a wonder he lasted so long.'

Alex breathed out, feeling relieved, and guilty for it.

'Matches on the name?' said Alex.

'No, nothing. We're going through Interpol, but we're not hopeful. Fake names, passports or whatever, it's very hard to trace – could take months.'

'Mia Anastos,' said Alex.

'Possibly. Or her name might be Betty. Who knows?'

'We got a fraction of what we needed,' said Alex, feeling the ruthless processes in his brain spinning up. 'Her family, her mother. Where is Dr Tau?'

He heard Laurie clear her throat. 'Still out of town,' she said.

'Willis's office?'

'His office at the hospital was cleared by my team an hour ago. Everything is at the station being catalogued.'

'Home?'

'Tricky,' said Laurie. 'His wife and family are all there, grieving and understandably hostile towards us at the moment. I decided not to barge in today and strip it for evidence.'

Alex nodded. 'But you can search Dr Tau's office?'

'We did. I had to go up a level and get permission. All the records were legitimate surgical patient records and notes. The team are searching through with assistance from the hospital, but nothing relating to this so far.'

'Then search his home.'

'Is that an order?'

Alex paused.

'I'm kidding, Alex.' He heard her sigh on the phone. 'He's not a suspect. I can search the hospital because it's not his property – the files all belong to the National Health Service, but I can't barge in and search his house.'

'Not even with Dr Willis's admission?'

'What admission, Alex? He gave us a few fragments we haven't even corroborated yet. It's not enough to put out a national search on Dr Tau. Our suspect is female and has killed several people – priority number one is catching her. These shady doctors, if that's what they are, can wait.'

Alex held his tongue. She was right, of course. He'd started to notice that about her. Police protocol was strict, and she wasn't about to start bypassing it all. But she hadn't drawn the same conclusion from their conversation with Willis as Alex had. She hadn't heard a doctor admit to conducting hidden trials on humans 'to achieve something great'.

'When can we go to Dr Willis's house?' he said.

'Maybe tomorrow,' said Laurie. 'I've got some PR to do with the family.' She huffed. He heard her tapping away in the background.

'Until then?'

'Go home? See your family? A round of golf?'

'Golf?'

'Whatever it is you rich doctors do.'

Alex had never played golf and didn't intend to start. 'And I bet you're just going to sit around and wait,' he said, goading her.

She sighed again. 'Actually, no. But I've got something to clear up. Probably your fault too.'

'Really?' Alex wondered if he'd managed to screw something else up without even realising.

'I've been called back to Holborn to address some "administrative errors" in a previous case.'

'Sounds like fun.'

Laurie's tone darkened. 'Administration is never fun, Alex, and I don't make mistakes. But I'll let you know when we can get on with some real work.'

Behind the joke Alex could detect her mood as genuinely peeved and a little puzzled. He found himself wanting to support her, help her out. He didn't like the idea of her getting into trouble.

'You follow protocol,' he said, hoping it was true. 'You're diligent. I'm sure it's nothing.'

Laurie paused for a few moments. Alex could tell she'd stopped typing. 'I think so too,' she said. 'Let's hope my superiors agree.'

Alex didn't try golf. The other doctors in the building had already invited him into their club – several of them played – but Alex had never fancied it. He tended to shun social activities on principle. There was something deeper in his reluctance, he thought, but he put it to one side.

Instead he drove to his office and ploughed through the invoicing, wondering why he didn't use the PA service downstairs. He'd figured that going part-time should mean he'd do all the admin himself, but as he filed the eighth client email he was beginning to regret it.

Another niggle to add to his worries. Would Laurie be OK? He had a pang of fear she'd be pulled off the current case and sent back to Holborn. He was growing close to her – they understood each other, or so he reckoned.

His focus on work wavered so he picked up the phone.

'Hi, Dad.' Katie's voice always sent a smile straight to his lips. He wished it wasn't mostly on the end of a phone.

'Hi, sweetie,' he said. 'Just checking in. How are things?'

Katie reeled off a list of teenage woes, mostly to do with her friends and Instagram. Alex listened, half wishing he hadn't asked, but half just pleased to hear her voice.

'That's tough,' he said, not really following. 'How's Mum?'

'She's fine. John's taken her out for dinner again.'

'Again?'

'They do it a lot.'

Of course they did, thought Alex. He remembered when he and Grace first dated – endless dinner dates. He could probably count on one hand the number of meals he'd taken Grace out for in their final year of marriage.

He huffed.

'Sorry,' said Katie.

'Why don't we go out?' he said. 'For dinner. Anywhere you like.'

'OK. I can't today – I'm seeing Jess. Tomorrow I'm round Sophie's with Freddie. Thursday I'm going to Fran's. Maybe Friday?'

Alex marvelled at his daughter's schedule. When had his baby girl turned into this raging socialite? 'Friday is great. Pick a restaurant and let me know. I'll book it.'

'Sure thing. OK. Gotta go.'

'So soon?' Alex could listen to his daughter's voice for hours. She clearly had better things to do than listen to his.

'Friends,' she said. 'I've got messages to send, people to talk to.'

'Oh, before you go, will you have time to see Grandma at the weekend?'

An awkward silence. Katie found visiting Alex's mum in the care home a stressful experience. Her grandmother had deteriorated fast after his father's death and was confused, agitated. Her questions triggered memories for Katie of her ordeal at the hands of Victor Lazar the year before. Alex didn't know the right thing to do but couldn't bear the thought of his mum being cast aside after everything his father had put her through. He owed it to her to try and maintain some semblance of family.

'I'm not sure,' said Katie. 'Perhaps in a couple of weeks? I promise.'

'OK.' Alex didn't push it. He had just wanted to mention it.

'See you Friday then. Love you, Dad.'

'Love you.'

Alex hung up, feeling a little better but conscious that his general levels of anxiety were peaking. He'd need to watch himself. He fingered the packet of Xanax in his pocket, spinning the small container around, feeling the label peeling at the corner. Another before bed or a glass of wine? Perhaps both.

Still holding his phone, it buzzed with a message.

Meet me at Dr Willis house tomorrow at 10. Family are out. Address below.

Alex left the Xanax unopened. Laurie was as good as her word. She made things happen, and this was progress. Alex decided to get an early night, figuring he'd need to be on form tomorrow, whatever they found.

CHAPTER TWENTY-TWO

Alex Madison looked exactly as she remembered. He'd aged, but so had she, not so much in years but in experience. She'd read the reports but preferred to conduct her own observations. His office was nice, better than any place she got to work in – she watched it from the other side of the road, watching him enter and head up the stairs. She remembered his private practice and his obvious ambition, but also recognised his faults and his failures.

Her phone had been glued to her ear for the last twenty-four hours. They were failing to keep a lid on things – the mess was spreading. The clean-up was imminent. It rang again, buzzing in her hand. She stared at the immaculate blockwork across the street, admiring the simple patterns and the wealth that could create such structures. She was no stranger to money, not any more, but the opulence of London was still fascinating to someone of her background.

'Yes,' she answered.

'Tau is with us.'

She snorted. The doctors had proven themselves untrustworthy and incompetent. This one in particular was a complication that needed fixing.

'Keep him there.'

'In what condition?'

She sighed. 'Treat him with the respect he deserves. Just keep him there.'

The caller hung up. They'd call again. A constant stream of questions, requiring a constant flow of answers. Get one wrong and she'd be the one to suffer, not them. She knew only too well what would happen if the true extent of this work was exposed. She had her role and the responsibility that came with it.

She paused before leaving the road, a doubt springing up in her mind, just a fragment, lingering for a second, a moment of panic. What she was doing; what *they* were doing. The thoughts would never sit comfortably. Knowledge was powerful, but it was also painful. She felt more of the latter than was healthy or useful.

Doubt would do no good here. She forced it from her mind, tucked her hands in her pockets and headed back to the hotel.

CHAPTER TWENTY-THREE

Dr Willis's house was imposing, with a neat lawn and expensive gravel driveway. Alex couldn't suppress a stab of envy, casting his eyes over the huge porch and the sash windows. Surgeons earned more than psychologists, it seemed. Then reality hit him, and he remembered Dr Willis was dead, murdered by the suspect they'd failed to catch – the one he'd failed to identify.

But why? What secrets had Dr Willis not passed on before his death? What had led his killer to take revenge? What had the doctors done to earn such hatred?

He crossed the road and sidled up to Laurie. She'd seen him but remained leaning against her black Mini, arms folded, staring over at the huge house.

'Surgeon,' she said. 'It was a toss-up between that and police officer. I chose wrong.'

'You're alive,' said Alex, turning to her.

She looked shocked and slapped him on the shoulder. 'Hey, I do the inappropriate comments!' she said. 'You should know better. Right,' she continued, 'house is empty and we have permission to search Willis's study for items relating to patients – private or NHS.'

'That's it?'

'That's it. We're not rifling through his underwear today. Maybe another day.'

Laurie pushed herself away from the car and crunched up the drive. Alex followed, thinking Laurie looked tired today, not her usual sharp self.

'How did the administration go?' he asked. 'All fixed?'

Laurie glanced back and smiled, but it was weary and false. 'OK. Not a problem.' She approached the front door, and Alex knew she was lying.

She fumbled with a key and pushed it into the lock. The heavy door swung open with a creak and they both entered the hall.

'The study is at the back of the house,' said Laurie.

Alex paused. After the door closed behind him he heard something else. Footsteps, the creaking of floorboards.

'I thought you said the house was empty?' he said, looking up the stairs. No, the sound came from this floor. Laurie and Alex glanced at each other.

'Hello?' said Laurie. 'Mrs Willis?'

Silence. They both strained their necks, listening.

'It's Detective Laurie!' she shouted.

Still nothing, but then more footsteps, louder this time. Somebody running on a hard floor.

'Through there,' said Alex as Laurie approached the end of the hallway, Alex close behind. They entered a reception room. The wood flooring gave way to thick woollen carpet. Two sofas faced each other, a walnut coffee table between them. A large marble fireplace provided the centrepiece, and above a huge watercolour loomed, a scene of an Italian coastline, the bright houses lighting up the landscape. Laurie paused. Two doors led off, one straight ahead to what looked like the kitchen, the other to a further reception room.

'Stay here,' said Laurie, choosing to head away from the kitchen, deeper into the house. The noise had stopped, but she crept across the carpet in silence. Alex ignored her request, heading to the kitchen. As he reached it, they both heard a door slam at the back of the house.

Laurie's head snapped around. Alex ran into the kitchen in time to see two figures sprinting away through the garden.

'Out there!' shouted Alex. 'The garden – quick.'

There was no exit from the kitchen, just a single window overlooking a lawn bordered by mature shrubs. The garden curved around to the right and the intruders had disappeared. Alex sprinted back into the reception room to follow Laurie.

She'd raced on ahead and Alex weaved through the furniture, into a small room housing nothing except a grand piano on a hardwood floor. In front of the piano stood a set of French doors, open to the garden. Beyond the piano lay a larger room. The door was open and Alex could see inside. It was a mess. Lined with bookshelves, most of the books had been pulled on to the floor, documents and journals strewn everywhere. A desk stood at the centre, its surface covered with papers and folders.

The study.

Alex paused. 'Laurie!' he shouted. When she didn't answer he tore himself away, through the French doors into the garden. It wasn't as large as he'd thought, and the bend he'd seen from the kitchen ended abruptly against a high fence with a trellis running along the top.

Laurie stood in front of the fence, one hand on her hip, the other holding her phone. She shouted a few more words into it before hanging up and turning to Alex.

'There's an alleyway behind here,' she said. 'No idea which way they went from there.' Her face clouded and she gripped her phone tighter. 'Shit!' she shouted into the bushes.

'Was it our suspect?' said Alex. There were two people, which didn't make sense, but perhaps Mia had an accomplice. It was unlikely for a sadist or a psychopath, but not unheard of.

'I don't think so,' said Laurie. 'I caught a glimpse of their backs. They were both running.' She shook her head, thinking. 'No,' she concluded, 'they were both too tall. One was thickset, male. The other . . . not sure, but not our suspect. I'd put money on it.'

Alex nodded. Their eyes met. Alex didn't want to say it.

'Yes, we should have searched the house yesterday,' said Laurie, her eyes on fire. 'Shut up, Alex.'

With that she stomped back towards the house. Alex followed at a distance, his mind spinning, considering all the options, none of which was particularly attractive.

'The question is, did they find what they were looking for?' said Laurie. They both stood in the study, trying to avoid stepping on the books and journals. There wasn't much room to move and Alex gave up, making his way to the desk, wincing as a book spine cracked under his shoe.

'Let's hope we disturbed them before they had a chance to,' he said, peering at the desk. Several folders were stacked on one side. A few of the same type lay ripped open on the floor. *The intruders were caught mid-search*, he thought. Did they get lucky, or would he and Laurie?

'Uniform is on its way,' said Laurie, not seeming too convinced they'd find anything.

Alex leaned against the desk, casting his eyes around the room. It was unnerving, and he knew why – his father's study had been very similar. An old-style refuge from his family, a place of secrets and thoughts, lined with a library's worth of knowledge, crammed into old bookshelves and cupboards. Alex had never been allowed in his father's study alone while his father was alive. After he'd died Alex had put the stuff he couldn't face reading into storage. Alex had found his father's secrets – details of his own sordid pursuit of greatness, breaking every medical ethics standard in the process. His father was killed because of what he'd done. Was Dr Willis of the same breed? Arrogant to the point that they couldn't see right or wrong? Gods of their own world in which they played with people's lives?

'Where do you keep your secrets?' he said to the shelves.

'They weren't accomplices,' said Laurie. 'I presume that's your theory?'

Alex shook his head. 'Nothing's certain, but no. I think it's far more likely they were here for the same reason we are.'

'To find Dr Willis's links to all of this?'

'Or to cover them up,' said Alex. His mind drifted once again. If this was some case of experimentation or clinical trial, the people sponsoring it would be hastily covering their tracks. Pharmaceutical companies had very deep pockets and liked to keep them full. Alex knew they wouldn't think twice about interfering in a police investigation if it served their purpose.

'We need to scan and file,' said Alex, pushing himself up. He wished he'd had more coffee. 'Anything related to pain medication or treatments put in one pile. The rest can go to one side.'

'Yes, boss,' said Laurie, although her tone, usually light, seemed heavier and more distracted.

Alex watched her as she knelt, sorting through books. She looked younger today, perhaps in the way she held herself. The power posture had sagged and she looked vulnerable.

Alex wished he could help her and figured the best way of doing that would be to work out what they were dealing with. Progress in this case should take the spotlight away from her other worries.

They sifted for an hour or more in near-silence. Five uniformed officers, two detectives from Laurie's team and a forensics officer arrived, all but the last sad they'd missed the party. The forensics officer busied herself dusting for prints, despite Laurie's insistence that the intruders had been wearing gloves. Alex watched the scientist diligently work her way around the study before moving to other parts of the house.

Uniform checked the fence and started door-to-door inquiries, hunting for information, anything that could shed light on the intruders or anything else out of character in an upmarket street.

'What did Mrs Willis say?' said Alex.

Laurie shrugged. 'She's grieving, as can be expected. We told her as much as we could, not implicating her husband but suggesting she stay away from the house while we investigate. She wasn't really processing the news, but she'll stay with her sister for the time being.'

Alex nodded. Grief was an unpredictable emotion. He sympathised with Mrs Willis and wondered how much, if anything, she knew about her husband's work.

'I assume we can't speak to her?'

'You assume correct,' said Laurie. She picked up a textbook, showing it to Alex. 'Any interest?'

'*The Challenge of Pain*,' read Alex. 'Melzack and Wall. I've heard of them. I think they proposed the gate theory of pain, back in . . . let's see, must have been the sixties.'

'Gate theory?'

'It describes a gating mechanism in the spine – it opens and closes, allowing the signals to the brain. I can't remember the details, but it was pretty fundamental. The important thing was it established a physiological basis for the complex phenomenon of pain.'

'It's not all in yer head?'

'Exactly.'

Alex put the book to one side on the growing pile of reference material associated with pain research and management. He nudged over another, the eleventh edition of *Pain Assessment and Pharmacologic Management* by Pasero and McCaffery, without picking it up.

'A lot more books by this Patrick Wall fella,' said Laurie, slinging him another. *Pain: The Science of Suffering* was a thin text, unfamiliar to Alex, but then so were most of these. He'd had some experience of managing the psychological effects of acute and chronic pain in patients, but his understanding of the physiology was limited. Pain remained a complicated process involving intricate interactions between several important chemicals found naturally in the brain and spinal cord. If Dr Willis was researching pain management on patients, it wasn't necessarily a bad thing, *if* he was following the rules. However, if he was breaking them, it was because the drugs or interventions were unproven and the pharma company was having difficulty getting a licence to run trials.

But that's what they needed – patient information. The theory on its own wasn't useful.

After another hour they both stood, knees creaking and backs aching. They'd searched the entire study top to bottom, twice over.

'There are a lot of books on pain,' said Laurie, examining the huge pile of texts and journals near the door. 'Enough to make your head hurt.' She wiggled her eyebrows at the pun.

'There are,' he agreed, 'but he was a surgeon. So what?'

Laurie sighed, leaning against the door frame, cracking her neck, tilting it at an awkward angle. She pulled a face. 'You're right. It means nothing. Medical textbooks in a doctor's study. So what?'

'There must be something,' said Alex, scanning the room. No safe, no locked cabinets. If Dr Willis had secrets, they weren't here.

'I'll call the office,' said Laurie. 'See if they've had any luck.'

Laurie stepped out. Alex heard her speaking to the team in her usual cutting tone, although the weariness was still evident. Alex nudged the pile of books with his feet, exposing a thin journal, *Global Neuroscience, Vol 12, 1981*. The front cover led with an article titled *The Neuroscience of Empathy*. Alex didn't recognise the publication but crouched to pick it up. Something about the age of the journal aroused Alex's interest. He scanned the shelves and floor but couldn't find any other issues.

He flicked through a few yellowed pages, finding the article in question. The abstract was very technical, focusing on firing mechanisms in the temporal and frontal lobes of the brain, and didn't make an awful lot of sense to Alex. He was about to discard it when he saw the list of authors at the bottom. He did a double take, his heart skipping a beat. *King's College: C. Anderson, G. Shaw, R. Madison et al.*

The last name. R. Madison at King's College. There was only one at that time – Alex's father, Rupert.

It couldn't be.

Alex's mind spun. *Hyper-Empathy Syndrome*: his father's hand-scrawled note in an old textbook, now in Alex's possession. And here a decade-old article on empathy, co-written by Alex's father, lying in Dr Willis's study. Alex suppressed his panic before his heart hammered through his chest. He couldn't go there, not now. It was probably nothing – the scientific research community was a small world and there were many legitimate reasons why they'd refer to each other's literature. It happened every day – it was required, in fact, to ensure credit and proper peer review.

But what were the chances?

He felt the dark shadow of doubt creeping in. His father had been complicit in experimentation on children in the seventies and eighties – psychological and pharmacological, working under the reputational protection of King's College. Dr Willis was in possession of an article written by his father from the same time period. Just the one.

The threads spun together in Alex's mind, the connection staring up at him from the page. His father's work had produced a serial killer, Victor Lazar. Dr Willis and his colleagues had produced Mia Anastos. Both individuals were products of illegal experimentation. Were they following the same path, albeit separately, or was this a link, however tentative, the significance and intimacy of which Alex struggled to comprehend? His father's work could easily have extended beyond his deeds in the eighties. Beyond his death. There could be something else at work here. But what?

'You OK?' Laurie appeared at the doorway, hand over the mouthpiece of her phone. She looked quizzically at him. 'You look like you've seen a ghost. Was it Dr Willis?'

Alex stared blankly. Should he tell Laurie what he'd found? He looked down at the open journal. But what had he found? A reference to his dead father and an innocent note in a textbook. Laurie would probably dismiss it and call him crazy. He knew what she'd ask: would it help them find Mia? And the answer was no, how could it? No, whatever this was, it was circumstantial and personal. Alex would need a whole lot more if he was going to raise the lid on his father and everything that came with it.

Laurie stared at him until he turned away, unable to hold her gaze.

'Nothing,' he said. 'It's nothing. I'm OK.'

Laurie put her phone back to her ear, narrowing her eyes at Alex before turning away. 'There you are!' she yelled into the phone. 'You didn't think it useful to call me an hour ago?' She listened for a few moments. 'I'm coming in. Have the files ready for me. Nobody else reads them, OK?' She then did her best attempt at slamming the phone down while on a mobile, pressing the call-end button with a flourish.

Alex waited. His heart rate slowed, his mind cleared. He buried it, like he always did.

'OK,' she said. 'The team found mostly the same stuff from his office at the hospital – texts, journals, loads of boring shit.'

'And?'

'And seven patient records in blue folders tucked away behind one of the cabinets. They weren't registered with the main hospital records – as far as the hospital was concerned, the patients had never been treated there.'

'And . . .'

'One of the patients is called Mia Anastos.'

CHAPTER
TWENTY-FOUR

The urge hit her out of the blue, descending with a violent wrenching into her stomach. Mia's addiction didn't creep this time, it leapt, grabbing her head in a cruel vice, spinning it with desire and adrenaline.

Despite her actions over the last few days, satisfaction had eluded her. She'd hoped perhaps it had faded or at least subsided for a time.

She was wrong.

The final name in the address book would have to wait. She couldn't chase anyone in this condition. Even if she found them, there would be no answers, only pain.

Only death.

Mia paced the warehouse, having enough presence of mind to wash and dress properly. Her shaking hand applied lipstick and a little make-up. It smudged, but it was acceptable. Better than the drawn, pasty skin she wore today. The bags under her eyes could be partially hidden. Hidden enough.

A quick fix, that's all she needed. Could she risk taking somebody off the street? A café or a bar? No. She'd done that once and got lucky, but Lady Luck did not smile on people like Mia. Cruel monsters got what they deserved.

Locking the warehouse door, she prowled, heading south, unsure which location to head for. St Thomas's or Guy's? Both massive, easy to blend into, easy to find a secluded cubicle in.

But they'd be watched, wouldn't they? Mia wasn't naive. They might not know what she looked like, but they knew she was coming. She'd been careless and had left a trail. Her months of secrecy had come to a crashing end the night she was discovered by the porter and hit by the bus. That night was the beginning of the unravelling, and Mia could see no end to the thread.

It wouldn't end until she had answers.

Mia navigated through the crowds, shuffling through, trying not to be noticed. Was she still pretty? Doubtful, and today she wore it badly. Her face was twisted with cravings, her jaw clenched, teeth grinding. Her clothes were clean, but she stooped, hunched with a stiff back and tense neck muscles.

She watched one man as he walked towards her. His head turned her way but didn't linger, turning back just as quickly. As he passed close by, Mia caught a whiff of unease and discomfort. The man limped, not visibly, but his muscles were sore and his right hip ached.

He disappeared into the crowds. Mia slowed, breathed, but forced herself onwards. There was no way she would take somebody in public. Not worth the risk.

Mia's sense of direction was good. Without realising, she was veering towards the centre and St Thomas's. She'd rock up and pause, watching and waiting. Her desire was flowing around her, causing muscle spasms and nausea, but she could hold on, as long as she had her fix today.

Cutting down a side street, she weaved in and out of scaffolding. The crowds stayed on the main street and she found herself in relative quiet, the background din of traffic echoing off the high buildings, several under construction, the white guard sheets wrapping the scaffolding plastered with logos and safety warnings.

Mia was halfway along the street when her ears pricked up. A faint call from within one of the buildings caused her to pause. The call came again. It was familiar and sensual, the call of alarm and fear.

The call of pain.

She turned towards the scaffolding. The darkness beckoned. The noises within tugged at her heart, drawing her off the pavement and into the building. No ENTRY WITHOUT PROPER EQUIPMENT, she read off the sign as she passed it by. Mia needed no equipment. Her ears heard the faint calling, the foreplay, and she continued inwards.

The calls became clearer. The building was huge and Mia picked her way through stacks of plasterboard and gantries. The area was empty, devoid of any workers. Pushing a layer of transparent sheeting to one side, she found herself in a large atrium, dark except for a floodlight in one corner. Groans came from one side. She saw a body, prone, with a second crouched over it.

The crouching man heard Mia and spun around. 'Help! Call an ambulance.'

'What happened?' said Mia, approaching the two figures. They were both male, dressed in workwear, harnesses and hard hats. The injured man looked like he'd fallen from a great height, perhaps landing on his feet. Mia saw a gantry twenty feet above, tracing the line to the ground.

'He came off the platform,' said the worker, still crouching over his colleague, concern creasing his brow. 'There's no signal in here,' he said, indicating his mobile, which was on the floor near his boots. 'Please call an ambulance. I think he's broken his leg. His back's crooked. Hold on, mate,' he said to his friend.

Mia went closer, staring at the man on the ground. He was still conscious, his head twisted sideways, sweat pouring from his face. She concentrated, tracing the waves of pain coursing through his body. The main impact had been on his left foot, on which he must have landed. His ankle had snapped, the tibia fracturing. The blood soaking through his trousers suggested an open wound. His knee had popped out too but had taken enough of the impact to save the main thigh bone, the femur. But the pain didn't stop there. Through his hips, possibly fractured, his spine was in trauma, pulsing with blood. The mixed sensations, apart from the pain, caused sudden and uncontrollable panic. His mind was spinning in a world of hurt.

Mia was beside herself with excitement.

'I'm a nurse,' she said to the fallen figure. She glanced at the face of the concerned worker. 'What's your name?'

'Steve,' said the man. He looked in shock, his eyes darting between Mia and his friend, who groaned again, a deep, throaty noise that sent shivers through Mia's body.

'Go outside and call an ambulance, Steve. There's no signal in the road either – you'll have to get to the main street. I'll stay and stabilise him.'

Steve didn't protest. He jumped up and ran towards the exit, pausing before running back for his phone.

'Wait for the ambulance outside, Steve,' said Mia. 'You'll need to guide them in. Don't rush. Better to get this done properly. Your friend will live if you take your time.'

Steve took a deep breath, pulling his shoulders back. He nodded and paced towards the exit, not running this time.

Mia stared at his back.

'We don't have long,' she whispered to the injured labourer, 'but your pain will be gone soon. I promise.'

CHAPTER TWENTY-FIVE

Alex separated the entries by date and laid them on the desk. Laurie had commandeered a conference room and they locked themselves in with the patient records recovered from Dr Willis's office. Placing six of them to one side, Alex spread out the contents of the folder with Mia's name on the front. It was disappointingly thin – ten loose sheets of paper in total, far short of what Alex would expect in a full patient record.

'Still nothing on Dr Tau?' he asked, lining up the papers with the edge of the desk. He plucked a few clumps of dust from them and flicked them on to the floor.

'Nothing,' said Laurie, 'and nothing from his office. If he had any records, he took them with him.'

Alex remembered their interview. Dr Tau had clearly been agitated. He didn't push Laurie on how hard they were looking for him. The doctor was merely 'out of town' and wasn't a suspect in any crime. That was the official line Laurie was sticking to. Alex got the impression she was under pressure from above. The screw-up with her previous case was inviting additional scrutiny. Alex felt for her, glancing up. Their eyes met for a moment too long. Alex tore his away and placed his hands on the edge of the desk.

'So here she is,' he said. 'Mia Anastos. Demographics: she's recorded as twenty years old, but if she's illegal then this may all be wrong. She may be younger.' He huffed. 'Address?'

'Doesn't check out,' said Laurie. 'The property has been empty for the last three years, according to the development company that owns it.'

'So we can assume most of this is false.'

'No photo,' said Laurie.

Alex shook his head. 'Hospital records don't, as a rule. Images from tests will be in here – if she had an X-ray, MRI or CAT scan.' He sifted through the notes. 'But there aren't any. Perhaps he had them in his home office. But whatever was there . . .' Alex left it hanging, not needing to say it.

'What's that?' Laurie pointed at one of the sheets – faded green paper. The header had *Nova AG Pharmaceuticals* stamped at the top.

'It's a prescription.' He examined it in more detail. 'No, it's not, but it is a list of drugs. Never heard of them,' he said, touching the logo. 'There are only a few big pharmaceutical companies in the world, but thousands of small specialists. This must be the sponsor.'

'I'll look them up,' said Laurie, tapping away at her laptop. Alex scanned the list of drugs, not recognising them. Proprietary brands, he assumed.

'Funny,' she said, clicking through the first few pages of search results. 'No results for Nova AG.'

Alex shrugged. 'They may not be public. It might be a subsidiary business. I'm more concerned about what they were up to.'

Laurie pushed her laptop to one side.

The demographic sheet was probably useless, so Alex moved on to the reasons for current visit – that is, why Mia had been at City Hospital in the first place.

The report was brief. Road traffic accident, car overturned, trauma to lower abdomen and spine. Internal bleeding. Unconscious during conveyance by ambulance, but regained consciousness shortly after arrival.

The report stopped there.

'These are copies,' he said, searching the desk, 'and they're incomplete. There should be more.'

'What?'

'The examination and findings in emergency triage. It should be right here.'

'So what's this?' Laurie tapped the next loose sheet of paper. It was in the format of a management plan, where doctors would normally set down the agreed actions, stating the diagnosis and initial treatment plan. For Mia's record, it simply said *Threshold achieved – Nova trauma pathway.*

'Threshold for what? Nova?'

Alex chewed the inside of his cheek. He reached for his coffee cup. It was empty, with brown stains around the rim.

'Pain,' he said. 'Pain threshold. It's what Dr Willis said. She met the criteria.'

'You sure?' said Laurie.

Alex shrugged. 'What else have we got?' he said, aware there was very little of substance in what they had in front of them.

'We're still hunting the police records,' said Laurie. 'It's a manual process.' She looked peeved at her department's inability to speed things up.

'Can't you just search by the date written on the hospital report?'

Laurie's jaw dropped rather dramatically. 'Genius,' she said. 'Why didn't my detectives think of that?'

'The date on this is false,' said Alex, his face flushed.

Laurie gave him a wink, returning her gaze to the desk. 'These last three pages are handwritten,' she said. 'All headed *Nova Pathway.*'

Alex pulled them towards him, starting at the first, skimming the text. 'This isn't a proper record,' he said. 'Not standard terminology – it's opinion. Dr Willis's, I'd bet. His impression of the treatment.'

'Which was?'

'Let me see.' Alex scanned down a third of the way. 'He talks here about preparation. *14:00 The Nova rep was in the room; inappropriate*, he writes. *He spoke into a voice recorder in English then in Russian.* He makes several notes about the surgery prep and his impressions. He wasn't happy, by the sound of it.'

'Nova rep?'

'A representative from the pharmaceutical company was in the theatre.'

'Is that normal?'

Alex considered it. His limited experience of clinical trials suggested that yes, the drug companies were part of every stage. They funded, sponsored and ran a lot of trials end to end. Such actions were, however, strictly controlled by the industry. Everything had to be published in advance, including the names of the participants. 'It doesn't say who, just that they were part of it. That's normal, I guess.'

'What else does it say?' Laurie shuffled her chair in closer.

'Um, hang on. Page two covers the procedure – emergency surgery followed by the Nova drug programme. Page three is observations . . . Let's see. The rest appears to be a log, journal entries of the subsequent days.' Alex leaned back, scanning the rest of the pages. 'This isn't a patient record. This is what Dr Willis kept secret, for himself. His log. It was never meant to be read.'

Laurie nodded. 'Insurance?'

'Possibly. Perhaps he was in over his head.'

Alex read from page two. '*Driver DOA. Father? Possibly. Shipped over to St Thom's morgue, tagged as homeless. Second passenger: Mother? Severe abdominal haemorrhage. Terrible state. Didn't meet criteria or threshold. Sent to Barts with no ID. (Should I follow up)?*'

'They sent her family to other hospitals?' Laurie's face dropped. 'Bastards. What the hell did they think they were doing?'

Alex didn't try to hide his own disgust but kept reading.

'*15:00 Stabilising surgery took priority. Internal lower abdominal bleed fixed. Spinal rupture – cause of elevated pain, main focus. Dr T worked for three hours repairing. Nova kept rushing him, saying the treatment must start within a four-hour window.*'

'Dr Tau,' said Laurie. 'He saved her.'

'Saved her for their purposes,' said Alex. 'It goes on like this – observations and Willis's role assisting. He says he stitched up her abdomen then asked to leave. They refused.' Alex flicked over to the next page.

Laurie's phone buzzed. She swore when she saw the screen. 'Yes, ma'am,' she said. 'Yes, OK. I'll be right up.' She put her phone away. Alex saw the creases of concern on her face. She looked at Alex and managed a strained smile. 'Hartley wants to see me.'

Alex nodded. 'Shall we . . .?' He indicated the papers on the desk.

'You continue,' she said. 'This is your world. Call me when you can – tell me what you think.'

Laurie left the room, pulling the door closed behind her. Alex's gaze lingered on the door for a few moments before turning back to Dr Willis's log.

Day 1, 18:00 We used the new batch on the female patient, Mia Anastos. Lot 19. She'd stabilised enough, so we brought her round. She was conscious with no painkillers. The levels of pain must have been astonishing. Her spine was still raw – the disc barely in place. She thrashed in her restraints. Her heart rate was elevated. The Nova rep pounced, administering the dose via IV. He stood back, watching her vitals, ordering our anaesthetist out of the way – Dr Robbie wasn't too happy about it.

Day 1, 18:30 A cruel half-hour, watching this girl in extreme pain, but it worked. Dr Robbie left the theatre in disgust. The endorphin catalyst – they're calling it N5 – appears to be working. We woke her up enough to ask her subjective rating. She was confused, agitated, but gave a pain rating of zero. She didn't have any pain at all, even after physical manipulation. Astonishing. She passed out shortly afterwards.

Day 1, 20:30 In recovery. We're all still here, minus Dr Robbie. There seem to be more of the Nova reps than before. Some are rather burly-looking. Mia seems pain free. The action of the endorphin catalyst should be to artificially generate natural endorphins . . . but of course they aren't natural. I read the background material. It's still artificial. When all is said and done, it's still akin to an opiate. She's generating her own heroin fix. Nobody wishes to hear my views. They just point at the girl. I've decided to keep my own records, separate, including this log. I must protect myself and my professional integrity, regardless of how this ends.

Day 2, 10:30 I stayed the night. I'm not sure I had a choice, to be frank. Dr Robbie was back too. She looked scared. I must speak to her when I can. Mia, if that's her name, is sitting up in bed. They're stopping her from walking because of her spine injury, but she still has no pain. She's displaying some confusion, staring at each of us, her eyes piercing. Nobody has told her about her parents, that her mother may still be alive. Should I?

Day 5, 12:00 It's been five days. I was allowed home, as were the others. I flicked through my contract. NDA and penalties spread throughout it. It's quite threatening as a read. I wonder if it wasn't a mistake . . . but the results are positive . . . I must remind myself of that. This young lady had life-threatening injuries causing pain on an objective scale of 10/10. This treatment has reduced it to zero. We're winning?

Day 6, 8:30 I've been back to my usual lists. We have a daily meeting with Nova at Mia's bedside. I walked in this morning to find them arguing. Side effects. Oxytocin levels off the chart. Whose chart? I joked. Dr Tau asked about the long-term effects of elevated neurotransmitters such as oxytocin in the brain. The Nova rep refused to answer, obviously knew something.

Day 7, 8:30 Refreshed my knowledge on oxytocin, 'the moral molecule'. Posited to be at the heart of empathy in mammals. People with higher levels of oxytocin are more empathetic in all scenarios, able to put themselves in another person's position, feeling another person's suffering, wanting to help. We agreed to monitor levels. Talk of moving her to a specialist facility. I asked where and was told to read my contract. I guess that means I won't be told.

Day 9, 16:30 Called in for an unscheduled meeting. Mia left her bed in the night. She was found in one of the emergency wards, leaning over an elderly patient. Escorted back to her bed, she was displaying classic symptoms of opiate withdrawal. More arguments. Against the majority wishes, Nova administered more N5, claiming the dose hadn't been high enough during surgery. Dr Tau looks stressed. He is running the show, so he says. I wonder how much control he really has over Nova. Is he bound by the same contract as me?

Day 13, I had a few days off. I got emailed daily reports, as did the rest of the team. Mia responding well. Asked where she was. Another problem for the team – she appears to have amnesia. The psychological trauma must be hitting her. Nova have refused a psych consult at this point. Argued with Dr Tau. Nova won.

Day 14, Complications. Amnesia is worsening. Oxytocin levels even higher than before, not sure if related. Continuing to monitor.

Day 15, Opiate withdrawal symptoms continuing. Appears to come in waves every twelve hours or so. She suffered vomiting and diarrhoea this morning. I'm being distanced, as I question the efficacy of N5. Dr Tau seems to want me out. Does he not respect my experience and opinion? I thought we were professionals.

Day 16, Mia found in the emergency room again. She was in a near-panic, sweating – symptoms of opiate withdrawal again. I questioned the whole underlying premise of artificial endorphin production – asked for access to the earlier trial data. Request refused.

Day 17, Mia in emergency triage again. Being moved to another private room and restrained at night. Nova are placing a guard(!!) on the door. What do they think she'll do??

Day 18, Oxytocin higher than we've ever seen. Nova suggesting several unrelated tests. She seems alert but often disappears inside herself. Appears to study people in the room, watching them intently. She sniffs people. What is the oxytocin doing to her?

Day 19, Called in by Dr Tau. He says the patient is being moved. We are to wrap up our own notes within the hour and submit them all to him. Nothing relating to the patient is to be stored anywhere else. This seems unorthodox, to say the least. We know we're breaking the rules, but we're assured these are phase 3 clinical trials. The dangerous early stages are over . . .

Alex flicked the page over and found it empty. He scanned the desk, rifling through. Ten pages, ending abruptly with that final journal entry. He took a deep breath, re-reading the last few notes, grabbing his notebook and pen.

It was here, Alex was sure of it. N5 was Nova's drug. Purpose? To obliterate pain, so it seemed. It did so by artificially stimulating the creation of neurotransmitters – in this case endorphins – to interact with opiate receptors in the brain and thus reduce the perception of pain. Alex knew they acted similarly to drugs such as morphine and codeine. Endorphins were the body's natural painkillers, created under all sorts of scenarios. Here, the N5 drug appeared to create a synthetic version, or perhaps the real version, but in an artificial way. Alex wished he had access to more information. Nova AG would be top of his list to question next.

N5 created chemistry in the brain to eradicate pain. Was it permanent or temporary? And what about the underlying cause? Alex noted the questions, underlining them twice. This was no doubt a breakthrough, with potentially staggering implications – positive implications – if it worked.

But Dr Willis's notes were worrying. Elevated oxytocin levels was a puzzling side effect. Alex knew oxytocin was a powerful hormone, also acting as a neurotransmitter in the brain. He thought back to his post-grad study. Oxytocin regulated social interaction and sexual reproduction, playing a massive role in behaviour. It was involved in parent–infant bonding, release of milk for breastfeeding, through to general empathy, generosity and ability to orgasm. It was often called the love hormone because of the stimulus for release – simply hugging a loved one caused oxytocin production. Having sex even more so. The hormone played an intricate part in one's understanding of and interactions with other people. People with higher levels of oxytocin could empathise, understand. He scanned back in the journal entries . . . *feeling another person's suffering.*

Alex paused. Feeling when people were hurting.

He picked up his pen. New line.

N5 removes the pain. Leaves symptoms akin to acute opiate withdrawal. Check.

Oxytocin elevates empathy to an astonishing, unheard-of level. Empathy, not sympathy. An ability to feel the pain of others, with no compassion for it.

Feeling their pain.

Alex placed his pen on the table. He stared at his notes. The evidence was here, and his theory was rational.

Is that what drove Mia? What caused her to attack her victims? Is that what they had turned her into?

A pain addict?

CHAPTER
TWENTY-SIX

The hotel had been left behind, replaced by the dark corridors of a more familiar environment. Her expensive Valentino heels had been discarded in the hotel trash, replaced with black boots, the brief moment of extravagance over.

The woman took a deep breath, leaning against the cold metal wall before turning the handle. She entered the small, windowless room, ignoring the shuffling of the two men already seated in front of the scuffed wooden desk as they sat upright and stared at her. She saw fear and reluctance. These men were scared of her and what she represented. The fear was necessary, and warranted. They didn't know what she would do if they failed her, but the rumours were kept alive, fresh reports always available, most of them true.

In the far corner of the room stood another man, large, with a bald head and an expensive pressed suit. He'd flown in on a separate flight, direct from Moscow. He gave a nod and she returned it.

She turned to the two trembling men, raising her eyebrows.

'We cleaned up as best we could,' said one of them. His eyes darted to his colleague, who remained motionless.

She nodded, waiting.

'But we were disturbed,' he said. 'We can't be sure we got everything.'
She turned to the man in the corner. He gave a small shrug. She knew it was impossible to wipe clean all traces. What they were doing pervaded so much, involved so many people, that remnants were bound to exist. But some were more important than others.

'Very well,' she said. The two seated men appeared to sag with relief.

'Go,' she said. The men scrambled to their feet, almost falling over each other as they exited the room.

She waited until the door clicked closed.

'We need to prepare,' said the bald man. 'I can't guarantee our safety.'

'How much do you think he knows?'

'Dr Madison?'

She nodded.

'Ah.' The man risked a brief smile but wiped it quickly when he saw her stare. 'Too much. We cannot take the risk.'

She raised a finger. 'That is for me to decide.'

The man frowned, but nodded. 'Of course.'

They stood together in silence, their eyes meeting in mutual suspicion.

The man broke first. 'Then what do you suggest?' he said.

'We quieten down,' she said decisively. 'For now. Go dark. When it's time to move, I'll give the order.'

The man continued to stare.

'Understood?' She squared up to him, stepping forward. His confident stance swiftly evaporated. He was not like her, not one of them. He might temporarily have forgotten his place, but it quickly came back to him under her gaze.

'*Da*,' he said, nodding, casting his eyes down in submission.

'Nobody touches Alex Madison until I say so,' she said, with more emotion than was appropriate.

'As you wish,' said the man, nodding again before leaving the room.

The woman let out a long breath. The doubt rose again in her chest as her conviction wavered. Alternative courses of action crowded her thoughts. She considered the risk.

The choice was hers alone.

CHAPTER TWENTY-SEVEN

Mia knew what she must do.

The memory of the builder's face burned into her vision. His fractured skull, caved in, the blood leaking from his ears and nose. Mia was out of the pit and climbing back into normality. She lay naked on the mattress, shivering but hot, tapping her splinted arm absently against the floor.

She'd had her fix. Now she must use this brief clarity to continue her search. At London City Hospital, where it had all started. She needed more information, more memories to feel the triggers and find the truth.

Her high was quick, the recovery quicker. She was poised at the top of a slide, teetering, struggling to stop herself descending into desire. The cycle was speeding up, and Mia plummeted into sorrow and grief. What would she become? Beyond the aberration she'd already achieved lay perhaps a deeper, darker Mia who knew no normality at all – one who would lurch from victim to victim without pause.

How far away was she from such insanity?

Mia washed, examining herself in the mirror, thinking, always thinking; delving into the blackness of her memories, searching for an answer. Her body was young, fit and damaged. Not from here. Who had seen it? Who had touched it? Mia clenched her fists and cried out, biting back the scream before it released, knowing it might never stop.

Love. Mia yearned for the abstract emotion she witnessed daily among the people of the city. To love and be loved was surely beyond her reach. Even if she could find somebody, she couldn't hide her grotesque desires and the murderous actions she was compelled to perform. No one would understand. No one would love her back. Mia knew she was destined to be a solitary animal, a predator and a hunter.

Unless . . .

Mia didn't consider herself diseased so the thought of a cure was hard to process. But it played on her mind nonetheless. Would her search end in a cure, a solution, a remedy? Some way of breaking the possession she was cursed with? What had the doctor promised the old lady? To be free of pain, but ever seeking it. That couldn't be the intention.

Perhaps she needed a priest. At least they might forgive her.

Mia sat at her desk: an ancient and dirty workbench with a stool. The wood of the bench was rough and splintered and the stool wobbled. Mia knocked her arm against the side a few times, listening to the dull clink of the metal rods.

She placed her arm on the bench, palm down, the top of her hand exposed.

Pain. Where was it?

Pliers. Mia had a pair, lifted from the same hardware store she'd stolen the club hammer from. They were cheap, yellow-handled and small, but adequate. A pair of scissors would do.

She chose her little finger this time. She found it useful to alternate – sometimes her toes, sometimes other parts of her body – careful not to inflict too much damage.

One day, perhaps, it would hurt. Mia gripped the end of the fingernail on her little finger in the pliers. It was hard work keeping her finger on the table, but she managed it, as she held the pliers tight and twisted them, up and away. The nail tore with a crack and a brief sucking sound but snapped along the middle. Mia discarded the half-nail, watching her finger ooze with blood.

It should have hurt. If Mia had been a normal person, it would have hurt.

The pliers were needle-nose. Mia used one end, pushing it into the exposed flesh, trying to get hold of the rest of the nail. She managed to dig one point of the pliers in and grab it, the blood making the job difficult. Twice, the pliers slipped off. With a final tug the remaining nail came away, ripping the cuticle and the skin, a thin strip tearing towards the first joint.

Mia stared at her bloodied and damaged finger. She focused on her body, the sensations and the reactions. Her mind registered the pressure and the scratching; the throb of blood rushing to the damaged site was palpable. Her body was in trauma and reacting accordingly. No pain.

Mia dropped the pliers and reached for the hammer and a blunt carpet tack. Pushing the tack on to the delicate exposed flesh, she lifted the hammer and slammed it down, careful not to hit too hard. A broken finger joint would be annoying and could restrict her movement even more.

Her elbow began to throb. Mia guessed it was a result of blood rushing to the arm, her body screaming in alert. Closing her eyes, she looked inwards, searching. A faint haze tended to descend at this point, a mild clouding of her thoughts, nothing more. She observed it. She also observed a greater than usual feeling of calm. It draped itself over her like a warm blanket.

Just for a moment, though. When she opened her eyes, the sensation disappeared, snapped off like a light.

Useless. And pointless. Mia used the pliers again to retrieve the carpet tack from the end of her finger, poking around until it came loose in a puddle of blood and bits of skin and tissue. She could see the bone and frowned, thinking she'd gone too far.

A liberal dousing of antiseptic lotion followed by a layer of gauze and a thick white bandage. Infection was the biggest risk from an open wound. Mia was good at cleaning and disinfecting. She'd change the bandage every night and keep the wound wrapped until it healed. The nail would grow back.

They always did.

CHAPTER
TWENTY-EIGHT

Alex wrestled with the handset as he weaved through the late-afternoon traffic.

'Shall I give you a minute?' said Laurie on the other end of the phone. 'Give you a chance to learn how to use twentieth-century technology?'

Alex managed to get his phone into the holder without hitting the kerb.

'I'm fine, thanks.' Alex would never admit he hated the way his car could automatically connect his calls. He preferred being in control, even if that meant pulling over.

'You wanted to talk?' said Laurie. 'Three messages. I ignored them all, of course, but then you sent a fourth and I felt bad. Didn't want you to think I didn't care. Should I have sent an *I'm very fucking busy* emoji?'

Alex wasn't sure if he was being told off or flirted with. Both, perhaps.

He proceeded to tell Laurie his theory, such as it was, about Mia's condition. He described the actions of the drug N5 and Dr Willis's conclusions about acute opiate withdrawal and the elevated oxytocin levels. Her brain chemistry was fried, said Alex, causing what he suspected to be an insatiable desire to feel pain. When he'd finished there was silence at the other end.

'Hello?' he said.

'Addicted to pain?' said Laurie.

'If you put it like that, yes. Other people's.'

'That's . . .' Laurie cleared her throat. 'Could that really happen?'

'I think it has.'

'Addicted to pain?'

'That's what I said.' Laurie was doing her usual light-hearted sarcasm, but Alex felt his conclusions warranted more. He suppressed his annoyance.

'I've heard people pay money for that,' said Laurie. 'Pain, I mean. As in sexual. As in S&M? God, Alex, why do you make me explain myself?'

Alex held his tongue. He assumed she was having a bad morning. She'd stop in a minute.

'It's fucking crazy, Alex.'

'Thank you for your technical analysis of my conclusions, Detective. Mia Anastos does appear to be crazy, I believe, driven not by sadism or psychopathy or any other psychological condition. I think she's being driven by a physiological condition, caused by her treatment at the hands of Dr Tau, Dr Willis and their team. She's an addict, Laurie. She's doing what addicts do.'

More silence.

'I've never seen an addict do this, Alex.' Laurie's voice was calmer. She was back into sensible mode. 'Never in my long and distinguished career. I'm not saying you're wrong. But I'm saying we need more.'

'What do you mean?'

'I mean, I can't go to Hartley and the commissioner with your conclusion as it stands.'

Alex's face flushed. 'Why the hell not?' He knew his tone was off, but he didn't care. 'Tell Hartley. She'll listen if it comes from me. I'll call her myself.'

He heard a swift intake of breath. 'By all means, Alex,' said Laurie. 'Go around me if it makes you feel better. I thought we might want to do this together, though. I know my job and I know procedure. Your conclusions aren't enough. What do you expect me to do with them?'

Alex tried to calm himself. She was right about most of it, but not if it meant leaving Dr Tau and this Nova pharmaceutical company alone.

'Have you at least put out inquiries into Nova AG?'

'Yes, as it happens. I did it all by myself without you even ordering me to. You know what we found? Nothing. Silence on all fronts. We've put calls in to the major pharmaceuticals, asking for assistance. The ones who've got back to us say they've never heard of Nova AG. It's not listed at Companies House in the UK. We've asked Interpol if they have any knowledge – that might take a while.'

Alex sighed. 'So they're ghosts?'

Laurie frowned. She chewed her lip. 'We haven't *found* them. That doesn't mean they don't exist or that they're not out there right now operating. It just means nobody's telling us anything. There's a difference.'

Alex nodded. He understood. Whatever organisation was running these trials, it wasn't a pharma. Again his thoughts wandered. The test subjects didn't know they were taking part in a trial. They were being preyed on by opportunistic surgeons waiting for the right candidates. So how many had been treated with N5?

'The other six files? The patients? Who were they?'

'We're following those up too,' said Laurie, 'but it doesn't look like any of them had the Nova treatment. Their notes are sparser than Mia's. They all say *threshold achieved*, followed by some reason not to proceed, either age or condition or prognosis. A couple were on contraindicated medication already. The only one of note was Kim Norris.'

'The old lady with pulmonary fibrosis?' Alex took a moment to think. 'Why would Mia go after her?'

'No idea. But Mrs Norris wasn't treated, according to the notes.'

Alex huffed. A bunch of candidates, but only one treated. 'So where does that leave us?'

'The only useful information is what you've read in Mia Anastos's file. She seems adept at staying hidden. No sign of her in the last couple of days.'

Alex pulled over to the kerb. He was too distracted to drive. Annoyed that his theory was being dismissed as incomplete and frustrated they had so little to go on.

'I've got another call coming through,' Laurie said. She paused. 'Hang in there, Alex. You've got something, a thread. Let's keep pulling it and see what we get. I need more material before I talk to my bosses.'

Alex promised he would and hung up. He swerved back into the traffic.

Alex pulled into the restaurant parking lot. When he insisted that he'd pick Katie up, she responded with a brief text: *See you there, Dad.* He didn't fight it. He'd insist on dropping her home, though. The restaurant might be only ten minutes from Grace's house but there was no way he was letting her walk.

Alex thought he'd done a reasonable job of not becoming the overprotective distant dad. She'd been dragged into his murky world and come out relatively unscathed. Victor Lazar's whereabouts were unknown and the investigation remained open – Katie had struggled at first with the lack of closure, but for once, Alex had taken his own professional advice and let her take therapy elsewhere, continuing as normal, letting her live her life and grow into her early teens with the innocence she deserved. Grace took the lead as a wonderful mother, and Alex hoped to follow as a reasonable father, offering as much as he could, knowing he would always be playing catch-up.

As he locked the car he couldn't help the twinge of regret and frustration that accompanied his regular thoughts about Grace. Over the last few days he'd allowed himself a brief reprieve, allowing his mind to focus on the case. But now, as he espied Katie through the restaurant window, the emotions threatened to swallow him up.

'Daddy.' Katie was already seated at her favourite table.

Alex glanced around, looking for an adult.

Katie pulled a face and laughed. 'Mummy dropped me off, literally five minutes ago.'

'Literally?'

'Exactly.'

'How's Mum?' Alex didn't like to interrogate Katie about Grace but found it hard not to ask at least a few questions. Any significant news would normally bubble up.

'Fine,' said Katie, studying the menu. 'I've going to have a calzone.'

'Fine,' said Alex, beckoning over one of the waiters. 'Two calzone and two Appletisers, please.'

Katie grinned. 'We can't have exactly the same.'

'Too late,' said Alex, giving the menus back. 'How fine is Mum?'

Katie shrugged, pulling out her mobile phone. She placed it on the table, glancing at the screen, swiping it before looking up. 'Why don't you ask her?' she said. 'Come in for a cup of tea when we've finished dinner. John's away at the moment. Work trip or something.'

Alex's heart jumped. He let it settle, wrestling with the proposition. Should he leave Grace alone for a while? What good would pushing himself back in do to her or Katie? She'd made her choice. On the other hand, every minute with him was a minute away from John. She'd fallen in love with him once. She might still love him now. Maybe all he needed was time and an audience with her.

The drinks arrived and Alex enjoyed the ice-cold feeling on his tongue. He never drank at meals with Katie, insisting on having the same as her. It was his thing. He had to have a few things, surely? Part of him still wished for a glass of red, though. He needed the release and the comfort.

'Tell me about the holidays so far,' he said. 'What has my favourite daughter been doing?'

Katie tore her eyes away from her phone and began. Her description of the last week was jumbled and overexcited and Alex loved it. Listening to Katie being so enthused about everything from reality TV to animal welfare was a fascinating insight into teen psychology. He tried not to analyse and to simply listen as their food arrived and they tucked in.

'Plus, I'm thinking about becoming a vegetarian,' she said, with her mouth full.

Alex nodded. 'You realise this calzone has cow and chicken in it?' he said. 'Possibly some other things.'

Katie chewed a little more slowly. 'Yeah, but I haven't started yet. But if I'm going to be a vet, I can't eat animals.'

'You can,' said Alex, 'but not the ones you're treating. The owners wouldn't like it.'

Katie pulled a face. 'I'm serious, Dad. You should see what they do to animals. We watched it on YouTube at Beth's. They experiment on them, give them drugs and stuff. It's horrible.'

Alex nodded again. She was right, of course, but it was the way she said it that stopped him arguing. Experimentation. Humans do it on other animals and people largely ignore it, but most people ignore everything. *What about experimentation on other humans?* he thought.

What would people think if they knew humans in the UK were unwitting subjects in a drug experiment? Would they care? Alex liked to think they would, although he wasn't convinced.

He lifted his glass to his lips, gazing at Katie. She was devouring her food and swiping her screen at the same time, her face a mask of intrigue. *Pure innocence, so fragile,* he thought. What would possess people to experiment on a child like Katie? His mind filled with shocking images of her being restrained and mistreated, of drugs being forced into her veins. He shook the visions away, but the reality remained. It happened all over the world, even right here in London.

Mia Anastos had been invaded, abused, molested, Alex was sure of it. The people involved no doubt had lofty goals and ideals, but the cold truth was that to achieve them meant treating humans like animals. Forcing participation, experimenting until results were achieved, good or bad. Harvesting the useful, discarding the useless.

Was Mia a reject? Did Dr Tau and Nova treat and discard her, leaving her to writhe in her incurable condition? Did they take any responsibility for their actions, or did they not even realise?

'Dad,' said Katie. She was looking at him and waving in his face. 'Earth to Dad.'

Alex blinked. The visions faded. The noise of the restaurant increased. 'Sorry,' he said. 'I was miles away.'

'Work?' Katie proceeded to describe how her job as a vet would be far better than his career. Not that doctors weren't important, but there was a shortage of vets and she was needed in that profession.

'Dessert?' asked Alex, unable to resist a smile.

'And more Appletiser,' said Katie.

'And more Appletiser,' he agreed.

Grace looked pleased to see him. Was he imagining it? No, he was reading her correctly. Her face opened up and her eyes invited him in. Katie complained she was stuffed and headed to her room, saying she had literally hundreds of texts to read.

'She was on her phone for most of dinner,' Alex whispered.

Grace shrugged. 'Then it's your role as a parent to forbid it.'

'Do you?'

'No,' said Grace. 'Tea?'

Alex perched at the kitchen bar. Grace was dressed in lounge pants and a vest top, what she always used to wear for a night in front of the TV. Her hair was tucked behind her ears and she'd removed her make-up. Alex cast his eyes down at his mug, blowing the steam away. His heart was racing and he struggled to pinpoint why.

His mind was spinning, focusing on the case, on Mia and what she'd do next. He couldn't help but think of Laurie and her handling of it so far. She was good, no doubt, but plagued by other worries, other cases and personal demons. Alex knew his thoughts were straying on to the wrong side of professionalism with Laurie, but if Grace really had moved on, shouldn't he? Shouldn't he be the responsible father and accept that two families was the way forward? Laurie might not feel the same, but he detected at least a hint of chemistry. Should he pursue it, or was he kidding himself?

'Busy day, huh?'

Alex brought himself back into the present for the second time.

'Sorry,' he said. 'Yes.'

'Tough one? Your assignment? Katie said you had a big case on for the police. She's very proud of you, you know.'

'Even prouder if I was a vet,' he said, bringing Grace's smile out.

'Of course,' said Grace. 'There is no nobler profession. This week, anyway.'

'She's . . .' Alex didn't know how to describe Katie's effect on him.

'Growing up. An adolescent. A complete pain in the arse one day and a delight the next,' said Grace. 'Yes, I know.'

Alex smirked. Their eyes met. Grace was the one to break it.

'How's . . . you know?'

'John?' Grace frowned. 'You don't care.'

'I'm being polite.'

'John is fine. We're both fine. Look, Alex, are you . . . you know? Seeing anyone? Don't let work take over. I know what it does to you. It's not healthy.'

'Do you want me to see someone?'

Grace huffed, her smiled fading. 'That's not what I mean. You're welcome here any time, you know that. It's just . . .'

'Life goes on?'

'You have a great life, Alex.'

They heard Katie calling from the top of the stairs. Grace headed out of the kitchen and Alex sagged in his chair. This wasn't the way he'd planned his precious limited time with Grace. He didn't want confrontation, and he didn't want to talk about other partners.

Alex's anxiety gnawed at his stomach, bubbling, waiting to pounce. Dinner with no wine was to blame, he thought, reaching for his Xanax. He opened the container and popped one into his mouth, washing it down with tea.

'Headache?'

He hadn't seen Grace come back into the kitchen. Her eyes narrowed when he quickly shoved the tub back into his pocket.

'Uh, yeah,' he said.

Grace's eyes stayed on his jacket. 'You're sure?'

They stared at one another, Grace's eyes boring into him. For somebody who'd managed to lie repeatedly when they were married, he found it impossible to do so now.

'They're . . . a little help, that's all. For stress.'

'A little help?' Grace's hands went to her hips. 'Like the help you said you'd get from a professional?'

'Grace, I—'

'So drugs are your answer? What are they? Diazepam?'

He regretted discussing drugs so openly when they had been together. He used to run through his cases with Grace in the evenings, describing his treatment plans and medications. Grace had a fantastic memory and an intellect to match. She knew as much about anti-anxiety drugs as he did.

'Similar, but—'

'How long?'

Alex was not about to admit having been on drugs since before he went to university, throughout their marriage and right through their messy divorce. His lower dose back then had made it much easier to hide; plus, he'd kept the drugs at the office, never at home. Only since the divorce had he taken to keeping a packet on him at all times. He guessed it would only be a matter of time until he got caught.

'Recently.'

'How many? Are you fit to work? To drive? You had Katie in the car.'

Alex jumped off the stool. 'Hey, relax. It's low dose and doesn't affect my driving. I wouldn't put Katie at risk.'

As he said it, he doubted his own words. He couldn't remember a time when he wasn't on benzos. To say it didn't affect his reaction times was naive, if not an outright lie.

Grace took a deep breath. 'You said you'd get help.'

'And I will.'

Her eyes were full of hurt when she looked back up. He had done this to her. Betrayed her trust yet again.

'I should go,' he said.

Grace didn't object, staring pointedly at the floor as he brushed past into the hall.

'Bye, Katie,' he called, trying to inject some cheer into his voice. She called back and Alex turned to the front door. 'I will get help,' he said.

Grace nodded, folding her arms around her body defensively, indicating that the conversation was finished. 'Bye, Alex,' she said, closing the door behind him.

CHAPTER
TWENTY-NINE

The air was clear and cold, and Mia sucked in a deep breath, clean and refreshing in her lungs. She stared upwards to the sky, spying a plane, its lights flashing, soaring peacefully above the turmoil beneath.

Perhaps she could leave, get on an aeroplane and head out of London. Back to where she came from. And where was that? What would she find? What could she do when all she knew was these few square miles of an alien city she hated? Other parts of the world held populations who suffered far more than this one. War, famine and pestilence – those might be good ingredients. Perhaps she could live there, feeding off the pain and suffering, not caring because those people would die anyway. Better to make it quick, albeit more painful?

But Mia knew it wouldn't happen. She stayed for the same reason she didn't take her own life. Answers. The answers were here in London. The doctors were here. Her parents were here, those faces that looked like hers and had love in their eyes. Mia couldn't abandon even the smallest chance of seeing them again.

Shivering, Mia knew she was spiralling. Her months of routine were finished, her body was changing, her mind fragmenting. The insane often knew it, and Mia knew she was dancing on the edge; a wrong footstep could send her over. Insanity might be a welcome relief from her daily existence.

But there were no answers in madness. If she fell, there would be nobody to pick her up, and those responsible would get to live their lives knowing they'd ruined hers, confident in their ability to remain in the shadows.

Mia sucked in more cold air. She increased the pace. It didn't help. Her nausea increased and her heart tried to push up through her throat. Swallowing hard, she stopped, holding on to a lamp post, drawing several deep breaths.

A window of normality presented itself, her desire swirling back into the depths. She ducked into a store, grabbed chocolate and Coke, noted her cash supply was dwindling fast. Pausing on the street to shovel the calories into her body, she watched the bodies flowing by.

An old woman with a stick. A patient, perhaps heading to the hospital, which loomed ahead. She crawled along, her ankles creaking, sending waves of pain up her legs into her back and shoulders. Her eyes were downcast, focused on the pavement, careful to ensure how each footstep was placed. Once down, there might be no getting up again.

A young woman darted past. A doctor. Mia's eyes were drawn to her legs. She dragged them towards the woman's face, which was excited and stressed, the beginnings of sweat beading on her forehead. In a hurry somewhere, perhaps to a meeting with a boyfriend, a girlfriend. Mia wondered what that must be like, to have somebody rushing to meet you, so full of energy they ran and sweated just to see you.

A group of young men sauntered past, three abreast. The one in the centre was confident, sure of his own standing among his peers, his swagger letting them know he was the alpha. Mia caught a whiff – a complicated mixture of adolescent scents – as they reached her. The boy on the left was shorter than the other two. He was uneasy, his face twisted with concern. What troubled him, Mia would never know. She wanted to reach out and tell him life was painful.

The boys walked on and Mia sucked in a deep breath, necking the rest of her drink, throwing the can into a bin. She paused, looking left and right. What was her plan? She should use her time wisely. Would satiating her appetite now mean more time later? She doubted it. The regularity of her cravings was shot through. She couldn't predict if she'd need five fixes this week or a hundred. Perhaps the next month could pass without the need to satisfy herself at all.

Doubtful.

But now, in the moment, Mia increased her pace, heading for the hospital entrance. While she had clarity, she'd pursue her goal. Cravings aside, distractions aside, she had an opportunity to make progress.

CHAPTER THIRTY

London City Hospital. After leaving Grace's, Alex had driven for an hour or so before finding himself alongside the huge building. He parked in a visitors' space and sat for twenty minutes, his mind spinning.

Grace was right and he was wrong. As usual. But his addiction ran far deeper than she knew. It was not something that could be ended with a few trips to one of his colleagues. Treatments for anxiety were wide, varied and usually successful, but dragging somebody off a lifetime benzo habit at the same time was a mammoth task, and that was even without taking into account the risk to his professional reputation if he was discovered. As a psychologist with a benzo addiction, he'd be finished. No more private clients, no more forensics for the police. If he was lucky, he'd get an assistant psych job in a hospital after he'd been clean for a couple of years. Until then his life would be over.

Alex knew he wasn't up to it. He wasn't prepared. He couldn't do it. Not now.

He left the car and headed into the hospital with a vague idea of trying to clear his head. He'd screwed his personal life enough this week, but perhaps he could make progress in his professional life.

The hospital was quieter at this time of the evening. Official visiting time was over and families were starting to leave. Alex had no particular destination in mind, but he wanted to get closer to his subject. Mia had stalked these corridors. She was inextricably linked with this hospital, against her will, and Alex needed to feel it, to breathe the air and smell the chemicals and odours of thousands of people's lives. He wanted to hear the calls and the shouts, the hisses and the alarms.

He stood in the centre of the emergency department and closed his eyes, taking a moment, willing his anxiety to settle. *Give me a few hours*, he thought to himself. *Let me think. Let me focus.*

Alex started on the ground floor. After an hour he paused on floor five, finding a row of vending machines. He fished around for loose change, selecting a strong coffee, double sugar. It tasted as predicted but he sipped it anyway, wanting to stay alert. The alternative was to go home and drink, a not entirely undesirable prospect but one he wanted to avoid. He wanted to see how long he could resist.

Would Dr Tau be back? Would he turn up as if nothing had happened, back to his surgical lists full of patients? Alex thought not, but Laurie and the police seemed unwilling to pursue him. There was something not quite right, but he didn't want to push. He and Laurie had started off so well and it was her call. He needed to let her do her job.

The coffee finished, Alex coasted along to the lifts. The corridor was quiet, the lift empty. He watched the buttons light up, listening to the awkward robotic voice announcing floor three.

The doors opened and Alex shifted back. A young lady entered. She glanced at him but moved to one side. She was pretty, slim and athletic, but her face looked tired, stressed and pasty. Perhaps she'd spent too long on a visitor's chair. Her shoulders drooped. Perhaps she'd lost somebody. Alex found his gaze on her dirty trainers, then her jeans and floral top.

He stared at the floor, shifting his feet. They were aching and he stretched them, wincing as one of his tendons cramped in complaint. He sucked his breath in through his teeth, surprised when the woman next to him did the same.

She didn't turn, but Alex saw her shoulders tense.

He stared at her hair – mid-brown, but the roots were starting to show; only just, but enough to reveal a lighter shade underneath.

Alex stretched his leg again, feeling the pain from the cramp shoot from heel to calf, then disappear. He watched the woman's body jerk at the same time. As she moved, her left sleeve shifted up to reveal what looked like a makeshift splint, as though she'd hurt her arm and tended to it herself.

His heart skipped. Just one beat. It couldn't be. He scanned her again: five foot six, maybe; slight frame; thin enough and in baggy clothes to blend in. Her skin olive, but her complexion hard to place. Mediterranean. Greek, perhaps.

This woman had a purpose, a desperation about her, a furtive need for being here. Alex saw what he'd been trained to see over the past decades and the realisation hit him.

She turned. Their eyes met. Hers were dark, piercing, staring through him, but they widened. She read him, seeing his discomfort.

Before Alex could act, she lunged at him. A flash of her hand brought a knife to his neck. He thrashed out, his left hand hitting the panel. His fingers found a grip on the emergency alarm and he pulled it, causing the lift to shudder to a halt between floors.

He brought his right arm up and their bodies tensed, her strength incredible, his fear causing his muscles to lock; he was unable to force her away. Time slowed as she allowed him to tire. His arm shook, trembling with the strain before it relented. She pinned him to the wall. He was hers.

'Mia,' he gasped, conscious the knife was now at his jugular. Her face was inches away, her eyes darting over him. She sniffed, catching his breath. Alex was mesmerised, despite his terror. It was Mia. This was their killer.

'I'm not the police,' he said. Mia didn't answer. She continued to hold him, her weight pushing him against the cold metal of the lift. He smelled her musky body odour.

'I know what you're going through,' he went on, digging deep to find calm in his voice. Would she kill him? Not unless he was in pain. Or would the knife see to that?

She sniffed again, tilting her head, her eyes piercing then glazing over. An inner battle playing out. Which way would it go? Alex couldn't risk a wrong move.

'I know what they did to you,' he said.

Her eyes changed, growing wider. Surprise. Alex used it.

'It's not your fault.' It was the statement every victim needed to hear. Cliché, perhaps, but necessary and right. But would Mia acknowledge it? Would she know she was a victim? He saw her battle increase, her breathing become tense and irregular. Her eyes focused again and she stared at him for several seconds. Alex found himself locked in her gaze, a barrage of primal emotion emanating from her.

Her shoulders finally sagged. She'd made her decision, whatever that might be. Hopefully, to let him live. She relaxed her grip and the knife fell away by a few inches, enough for Alex to breathe.

She stared. Was she waiting for him to continue?

'Are you one of them?' she said. Her voice was thick and deep. Alex considered his reply. She was not here to make friends with those who'd abused her.

'No,' he said. 'I'm hunting the people who did this to you.'

She stepped back a fraction, but her eyes remained on him, narrow, untrusting. Why should she trust him? What could he say to make her believe him?

'Where are they?' she said. 'Where can I find them?' Her voice faltered. She was on the edge, Alex could see. The violence was masking grief, hurt and more. She shivered and her hand shook. The knife went to her side, but she kept her weight on Alex. He thought about trying to push her back but knew her size belied her strength. This woman was all muscle and was no doubt practised at using it. He wouldn't stand a chance.

'I don't know,' he said. 'I know you were in a crash. I know they treated you here. They experimented on you, Mia, with illegal drugs in an illegal procedure. They made you what you are. Created your urges.'

The hand came back up. The knife teetered, trembling by his throat.

'What do you know about my urges?' she said, her voice almost a whisper.

Alex's suspicions were confirmed. He was right. 'The pain, Mia. I know you need pain. To feel it and watch it. You can sense it in others. I'm trying to help you.'

But Mia shook her head. Stepping away from Alex, she leaned over and pressed the emergency button, silencing the alarm. The lift bounced back into action. The voice announced the ground floor.

'What is your name?' she asked, glancing at the doors as they opened. The corridor was empty. Shouldn't the security guards come running when somebody hit the alarm?

'Alex. Dr Alex Madison.' He stared into her eyes, trying not to focus on the knife in her hand which had so recently been at his throat. She could have killed him; or worse, she could have done what she'd done to the others. Alex shivered at the thought but tried to look confident. He needed her to trust him. 'I can help you,' he repeated. 'You won't get in trouble. You're sick. They did this to you.'

She wavered. He saw it. The hand with the knife swayed outwards. She turned her head towards the corridor. Indecision was written all over her face.

But it wasn't enough. She shook her head, backing out of the lift. The sorrow in her eyes hollowed and she took a few laboured breaths.

Then she turned and sprinted towards the exit. Alex remained in the lift. He considered shouting, calling 999 or the hospital reception.

In the end he just stood there as the doors closed, catching his breath, feeling his heart thudding in his chest.

CHAPTER THIRTY-ONE

Alex. He'd said his name was Alex.

Mia had gone to City Hospital without thinking it through. Her mind was murky and her actions clumsy. She had so little to go on. One last name and address in Dr King's black book. What if it was a dead end? The name was listed as *TK* in bold italics, the address somewhere in east London. Quite a trek. What if it didn't exist? That's why she'd headed to the hospital, risky though it was. One more search, one more pacing of the corridors and wards. Another chance for her mind to give up the truth.

The surgeons' offices were beyond her now – guarded, out of bounds – but she might see a face, inhale a smell, trigger some other memory. She didn't know what she'd find, but she had to look. And then she'd found him . . . Dr Madison.

Her desire began to surge. She held it at bay, picking up her feet, dragging them forwards at a greater pace. Putting distance between herself and the hospital was important. Her appearance would need to change again too. Did she have time? Could she afford not to?

Mia paused near a chemist's. She checked her pockets and found twenty-five pounds and some loose change. Another packet of hair dye reduced it to twenty. A pair of long-sleeved blue tops at a cheap clothing store reduced it to ten. The floral top disappeared into a wheelie bin but the jeans stayed. She'd change her hair as soon as she got back to the warehouse.

He'd said he understood. That he could help her. She trusted her instincts, but her mind was a mess.

A doctor. Mia had sensed several things about the man while she held him against the wall of the lift. His face was open, honest, but he hid many secrets. One of them caused him anguish – a physical craving not unlike hers. She'd smelled it on him, seen it in his eyes, his expression. His breathing was shallow and his jaw muscles clenched a little too tight, not just because of her but also something else, some inner battle. Some inner pain.

He'd said he could help her, but a doctor would say that. The doctors who'd turned her into this creature had probably thought the same thing.

But he could be telling the truth. What if? What if Mia had found somebody on her side?

Thirty minutes of fast walking and Mia reduced the pace. Sirens were ever present in central London. She never knew which were for her. Perhaps all of them. Perhaps none. She reached for a hood to tuck over her head, realised it wasn't there and hunched over instead, traipsing one of the many familiar paths back towards safety.

Dr Alex Madison. She repeated the name over and over. He wouldn't be hard to find. Nobody was. A quick search on a library computer or in an Internet café. She could have stayed and talked to him. She had the upper hand, the knife, the strength. He was of reasonable build, but his muscles were honed for sitting at a desk – she could tell by the arch of his back and pelvis. She could have kept him in check while she questioned him.

But then what? There was only one way a prolonged encounter would have ended. She'd done the right thing, the sensible thing. She'd think about it, mull it over.

She'd visit the last address in the book. If it came to nothing, perhaps she'd pay Alex Madison a call.

CHAPTER
THIRTY-TWO

The police sketch artist held up the picture and Alex nodded.

The artist looked as though he wanted more. He was a huge man with thick fingers, more like a boxer than an artist. He held the small stub of pencil delicately, adding a little more shading to the eyebrows.

'Yes,' said Alex, not convinced it was accurate. The nose was too big and the cheeks too prominent. The woman in the lift, Mia Anastos, was prettier – chiselled and petite. He found himself nodding, however, reluctant to correct the picture. A part of him suddenly didn't want the police to find Mia, not in their way. He thought he knew why but needed more time to mull it over.

'You're lucky,' said Laurie, putting two coffees on the table. She sat next to him in the small conference room, stirring three sugars into the dark liquid while the artist packed up his kit and left. 'We'll get it circulated,' she said. She smiled, waiting until the door had closed before speaking again. 'So now we know what our monster looks like,' she went on, sipping the coffee, waving her hand in front of her mouth to cool it.

Alex watched her. She was under stress. He could read all the signs, not least of which was her apparent exhaustion. Her face, normally a mask of youthful glow, was pale and oily. The bags under her eyes were growing by the day. He wondered how much sleep she was getting.

'She's not a monster,' he found himself saying. He picked up his own cup and studied the rim. Laurie remained silent and he glanced up, saw her watching him.

'Mia Anastos has tortured, mutilated and murdered at least six people,' said Laurie, her eyes wary, narrowing. 'She *is* a monster, Alex. How could you think otherwise?'

Alex put his cup on the table, twisting it around in his hands. How could he explain this? Laurie was right, in a rudimentary fashion. To an outside observer, Mia was doing exactly what monsters did.

Except there was a reason. And the reason was important. It separated her from the category the police and the justice system would no doubt put her into. Victor Lazar, the serial killer, had been described as a monster. In Alex's eyes, he was an experiment.

'She's sick,' he said.

'You're telling me,' said Laurie.

'She's a product,' continued Alex. 'Before her drug treatment, before what they did to her, Mia was an ordinary citizen—'

'She's here illegally.'

'That doesn't matter.'

'It doesn't? Oh well, that's good. I must have misheard the commissioner when she said an illegal immigrant murdering British citizens was a bad thing.'

Alex paused, counting his breaths. He knew why Laurie was angry and frustrated. She had her job to do, but he had his. Stopping Mia wasn't in question, but what they'd do with her when they'd done so suddenly was. 'She's an addict. We've never experienced anything like this before. She needs our help.'

'That's your theory,' said Laurie, blurting it out. She looked as though she regretted it, her eyes darting down, but she didn't take it back. 'Alex, your contribution is valued. It is. But this woman is already a violent monster in the minds of all the people here trying to catch her, except perhaps in yours. We must catch her, put her on trial, lock her up and make sure she never does this again. You'll be vital for the psych assessment as part of the case building. That's what we're paying you for. That's what the justice system is supposed to do.'

'What about the people who did this to her?' said Alex. He was defensive, his voice raised. 'Besides, locking up addicts, even normal ones, is the worst thing you can do, you all know that.'

'What do you suggest? Putting her in therapy? Weaning her off with a little torture twice a week? Letting her spend weekends on the cancer ward for good behaviour?'

The sarcasm was back. This time it was biting, but Alex understood. He didn't want to fight with Laurie. They needed to be on the same side, but as they closed in on Mia, he began to worry it wouldn't be possible.

He shook his head. 'We lock her up, obviously. But yes, she needs help. Treatment, therapy, whatever it takes to understand and reverse her condition. We need her to be sectioned and hospitalised.'

Laurie shook her head back at him. 'You know it won't work out that way,' she said. 'She's killed too many people. She'll hang, figuratively speaking.'

Alex worried she was right. He was one voice in a force of hundreds. The profile of this case was high and getting higher. If they didn't kill her taking her in, there was a good possibility she'd be sedated and thrown to the courts, which would do their utmost to demonstrate their power with maximum sentencing. Would she even get a proper psychological consult once captured? He'd heard of cases where the outcomes were already documented, the psych assessments pre-filled by a remote psychiatrist based on the police arrest report and no patient contact. Alex couldn't pretend the justice system wasn't sometimes as corrupt as the society it claimed to protect.

'You won't help her?' Alex sipped his coffee, lowering his voice, deciding confrontation was not the answer here. He tried not to plead.

Laurie's eyes said she wanted to, but he could see the battle in them. 'I need to go,' she said, standing. 'Get the image out there, get the CCTV checked and re-checked. Kick the butts of my team until they turn up with something.'

Alex paused. Laurie hovered at the table. She seemed to want him to say something.

'Sounds like a late night,' he said finally, knowing their disagreement was finished but not wanting to end on a low. He wanted to reassure Laurie she was doing well and that he was trying to help her. They were on the same side.

'I don't get many early nights,' she said.

'You should,' said Alex. 'Good for you. Sit back, have a glass of wine. Relax.'

'I don't like drinking alone,' she said, looking as though she was going to say something else, but then stopped. She shrugged.

'Then I'll take you for a drink.' Alex saw a brief spark in Laurie's eyes, but it was quickly hidden. His heart hammered. Was this a mistake? 'I mean, as a . . .' He stopped. 'I'm not sure, actually.'

Laurie smiled, genuine and warm. She seemed to relax, her shoulders dropping a fraction. 'That would be nice,' she said, tapping her finger. She shuffled her feet and chewed her bottom lip, glancing at him then back to the desk. Alex was familiar with this body language.

'But?' he said.

'But, I'm even more screwed up than you are, Alex,' she said.

Alex opened his mouth to protest but Laurie put her hand up.

'Yes, you are. And your timing is poor.'

Alex didn't know quite what to say. She certainly knew how to reject a man. He frowned, unsure whether to feel hurt or to laugh.

'I'm not saying you wouldn't make a wonderful drinking partner,' she continued, 'but perhaps not now.' She backed away and opened the door. 'Not never. Just not now. OK?'

'OK,' Alex replied, watching her leave, wondering what had just happened, hoping he hadn't turned a great new working relationship into an awkward one.

As Alex left the station he felt a brief thrill of excitement at the idea of taking Laurie out, but it was quickly dampened as his thoughts turned to Grace and Katie and the impact this would have on his future with them. What would Grace think? How would Katie react? His mind swirled in a mess and he began to feel guilty in advance of a date he hadn't even had with a woman who'd turned him down.

Get a grip, Alex, he said to himself, sinking into his car seat, pulling the door shut and closing his eyes. He realised he was exhausted, and would probably have dozed off had it not been for his phone, which started buzzing.

He reluctantly pulled it from his pocket and glanced at the screen. It was Mikey, his long-time friend and trusted drug dealer.

'I was getting worried,' said Alex.

Mikey laughed. 'That's what I'm here for – to worry you, then sell you the pharmaceutical answer to those worries.'

'Funny,' said Alex. 'No problems, I hope?'

'Never for you, Alex. Usual supply. I've been away, that's all.'

'Somewhere nice?' He heard a sigh.

'No,' said Mikey. 'My parents' place in Cornwall. I hadn't seen them in a few months, thought I'd put in some time. You know how it is. They aren't getting any younger.'

Alex knew what he meant. He checked his watch. 'You're back in London?' he said.

'Yep. Got back today.'

'Fancy a drink?' said Alex. 'It's been ages.'

'I feel privileged,' said Mikey. 'You're not taking some hot date out? You used to stand me up all the time.'

'No hot date,' said Alex, smiling at the thought of Laurie's rejection. 'Usual place?'

'Sure. Give me an hour.'

Alex hung up. It would be good to see Mikey, not to mention the reasonably priced six months' supply of Xanax he'd bring with him.

There was also another matter Alex wanted to pick Mikey's brains about. Mikey knew all about the pharmaceutical supply chains and players in the UK. He might know something about Nova, or at least give him a lead.

Alex pulled out into the traffic, heading for their usual restaurant, a small, independent Italian not far from Alex's house in Ealing. The food was good and the chef was authentic, from Naples. Alex often went there alone if he couldn't be bothered to cook; a takeaway for one was too depressing. It was quiet and the tables weren't packed together like at some chains. It was a good place for a date, a family meal, or in this case a drug deal.

◆ ◆ ◆

'Doctor!' Mikey's friendly voice boomed from the door. Alex turned and waved him over, pouring a second glass of Chianti and shoving it into Mikey's hand as he approached.

'Good to see you, Mikey.'

Alex waved to the waiter, a young Portuguese man called Fausto who was studying law at the London School of Economics. They often chatted and Fausto would insist on describing the latest medical malpractice case in the literature. He smiled at them both and delivered menus, bread and olives.

'You look tired, Alex,' said Mikey, taking off an expensive-looking blazer and draping it over the back of his chair.

'You're looking too chirpy,' said Alex, raising his glass.

They toasted each other's appearances and drank. Alex found the wine slipping down all too easily. His aim of reducing weekday drinking wasn't panning out so well, but Mikey's thirst seemed to match his. They ordered a second bottle and pasta to soak it up.

'So how's business?' said Mikey. 'You still treating hot footballers' wives?'

Alex smiled. 'I never did, and I certainly don't now.'

'No?' Mikey stuffed a chunk of bread in his mouth and rummaged through the olives with his fingers.

Alex slapped his hand away and grabbed a few for himself. 'I'm reducing that sort of work,' he said. 'Private clients. I'm taking on more with the Met and the CPS.'

Mikey swallowed and sucked his breath through pursed lips. 'Sounds serious.' He glanced around the restaurant, ducking his head. 'This isn't a sting, is it?'

Alex smiled. His addiction shouldn't be a joke, but the wine, mixed with Mikey's infectious joviality, was affecting his ability to keep a straight face. His friend was a pleasant distraction from the seriousness of life. Alex regretted their arguments and the distance there had been between them over the years.

'If it is, we're both in it,' he said. 'I'm finished.'

Their food arrived and they talked around the edges of their lives. Once close friends, Alex saw the strain in Mikey's face and knew Mikey would see the same in his. Neither of them had ready excuses for how they'd turned out the way they had. Both had had a privileged upbringing, a good education and were successful in their chosen professions. Both had failed in their own eyes to make the most of it but knew they still lived wealthy and fortunate lives.

'How's Katie?' asked Mikey.

'Great – growing up, getting too smart.'

'For you, no doubt,' said Mikey. 'But that's good. She'll need to be smart with you as a dad.'

'Funny,' said Alex, who spent altogether too long pondering Katie's future, the immediate and the distant. As much as he tried to hide his own issues, he knew that she picked up on it, and had done from an early age.

'Just be there for her.' Mikey pulled at a piece of bread. He paused. 'And sort yourself out.'

Alex nodded, staring into his wine. 'Like you have?' He wished he hadn't said it, and followed with a smile, but it was awkward. Mikey was right.

'I'm trying,' said Mikey, his own smile disappearing, his eyes flicking to Alex's. 'I've joined GA.'

'Gamblers Anonymous?' Alex looked at his friend. Was Mikey seeking approval or driving home a point? 'Does it help?' he said.

'It's a long road, but I think it will.' Mikey examined his wine, sipping more slowly. 'And you?'

He was making a point, then. Mikey had taken a major step in seeking therapy. A step further than Alex. This is where the arguments started – Alex's fault. He was too proud and stubborn, even with a close friend.

'Can I ask you something relating to my case?' said Alex.

Mikey's eyes narrowed. He wasn't finished but allowed Alex to change the subject. He nodded.

'We're trying to research a pharmaceutical company by the name of Nova AG. Do you know it?'

Mikey shook his head. 'Doesn't ring a bell. UK-based?'

'Don't know. It's not listed. But they're running clinical trials in the UK.'

'Then they'll be published on the MHRA website.' Mikey poured them both more wine. 'They all have to be.'

The Medicines and Healthcare Products Regulatory Agency was the UK government's executive branch, covering all medical regulation. Any company offering medicine or devices in the UK had to be registered, regardless of their country of origin. The rules were clear.

'I've checked and they're not on there.'

'Then they're illegal,' said Mikey, shrugging. 'The police can raid them and the MHRA will shut them down.'

'If we could find them,' said Alex. 'We have a few references to their activity, but not to the company.'

Mikey nodded, pulling out his phone. 'I'll make some inquiries,' he said, 'through my unofficial channels.'

'Appreciate it,' said Alex.

Mikey tapped out a long text message before putting his phone on the table. 'So I've done you a favour,' he said. 'Now answer my question.'

'What question?' Alex beckoned Fausto over again, asking for more water. Anything to distract.

Mikey huffed. He produced a small brown parcel from his jacket. 'Take it,' he said, 'but talk to me.'

Alex took the package, tucking it into his own jacket. 'Six months' worth?'

'You tell me,' said Mikey, wiping his mouth with the napkin, leaning over the table. 'We only met four months ago for the last lot.'

Alex stared at his empty bowl of pasta. It was hard to lie to Mikey – after all, Mikey must know that if he'd already run out, then things were getting worse.

'How many are you taking?' said Mikey.

Alex stared through the window. First Grace and now Mikey. They cared, he knew. But this was his problem and he'd fix it in his own time.

'You're getting help your way,' said Alex, 'and I'm pleased for you. Let me do my thing.'

'I get that, but you're taking more than the recommended limit,' said Mikey. 'I am a pharmacist, remember. Seriously, as a friend, let's talk about this. What's changed?'

Alex sank another half-glass of wine. What had changed? Nothing and everything. His pursuit of an acceptable work–life balance seemed to trip him up at every stage. Grace, Katie, his job, his attitude. Lots of things had changed and Alex never seemed to keep up. He had hoped to come out and forget about everything for a few hours, but now realised the futility of that. Two addicts sitting across a table. What were they expected to talk about?

'The world,' said Alex, 'and my ability to cope with it. The hours in the day. The race towards middle age. Time speeds up, Mikey. I look at the calendar and weeks pass, months. My daughter is a teenager. Grace is seeing someone. What's changed is that I can't react quickly enough. My thoughts plummet and I spiral. The drugs fix it. I know the dangers and I know the physiology and the psychology. I am a psychologist, remember?'

Mikey didn't smile, but he nodded, his eyes warmer, less confrontational. 'Did that help?'

'What?'

'Telling me all that. Have you told Grace?'

Alex sighed. Trapped by his friend. 'No.'

'You could tell a psychologist,' said Mikey. 'Not in the mirror, but another one. You never know what they might come up with.'

Alex knew exactly what they'd say. The first thing would be a plan to wean him off the Xanax. He wasn't ready. Still. Not yet.

A welcome reprieve came from Mikey's phone as it buzzed a couple of messages. Mikey picked it up, his brow creasing. He cleared his throat. 'Mmm.' He glanced at Alex. 'What have you got yourself into, mate?'

Alex could see the concern in Mikey's face, a touch of fear creeping in. Mikey tapped away at the phone, responding to the message.

'Looks like Nova AG isn't a pharmaceutical company after all,' he said. 'It's a front.'

'For what?'

Mikey shrugged. 'Could be anything. My contact isn't saying.'

'What's wrong?' Alex saw the phone buzz again.

Mikey shook his head and kept tapping away. His phone buzzed as the messages went to and fro.

'What is it?' said Alex.

'A warning,' said Mikey. 'From a guy I trust.' He put his phone down. 'To stay away.'

Alex sipped his wine, feeling the adrenaline surge. 'Who are Nova AG?'

Mikey grabbed his napkin and wiped his hands. 'No idea.'

'That's it?'

'What do you expect? My friend is keeping schtum. If he knows anything, he isn't saying. I'll ask around, but by the sound of it, I'd better not dig too deep.'

Alex sighed, draining the last of his wine.

'Thanks for trying.' He studied his friend, wishing he could talk more openly. Perhaps one day he'd learn how to do it. The conversation dried up and they finished their desserts and drinks in near-silence. Alex offered to pay the bill and Mikey didn't object. As they left the restaurant Alex held Mikey's hand and gripped his shoulder.

'It did help,' said Alex. 'Saying what I said. It was a step.'

Mikey smiled, embracing him.

'Don't leave it so long next time, OK? We addicts need to stick together.'

Alex smiled, looking for a taxi. How right Mikey was. It was exactly why he needed to find Mia.

An addict who needed his help.

CHAPTER
THIRTY-THREE

He was almost dead. Almost.

Mia stood over the man's body, soaring above, rapturous in the waves of pleasure coursing through her tired veins.

Unplanned but inevitable, Mia had succumbed to her urges and hunted her prey. Happenstance took her past a care home on the way to the address in east London. She'd paused at the sounds from the front garden, her ears pricking and her heart giving a thud, telling her she sensed what she needed.

The high hedge was broken by a small metal gate, which creaked open. A stone pathway beckoned. Mia closed the gate behind her and gazed across the grass. Three residents of the home sat together, two women on a bench and an elderly man in a wheelchair with a drip attached to a long metal pole. Mia saw pain in all three and forced her breathing to slow, conscious of the thumping in her chest.

'Can I help you?' A nurse blocked the path, appearing out of the front door of the large red-brick house. He was young, healthy and friendly. His tone was warm and his posture non-threatening. Mia needn't worry.

'I have a friend here,' said Mia. 'Over there, in the wheelchair. I popped in to say hello.'

'Oh, Cecil,' said the nurse, nodding thoughtfully. His eyes saddened and he touched Mia's arm. 'He's due to go back to his room. Do you want to take him?'

'Sure. Just remind me which one?'

'Room sixteen,' said the nurse, frowning.

Mia nodded, containing her smile. She touched the nurse on his arm, leaving it there long enough to remove the frown. 'I'll take him,' she said.

Mia suspected it shouldn't be this easy to enter a home for the sick and elderly. Pretty people, she thought. Pretty people got to go places others didn't. They brightened other folks' days.

Now she would brighten her own.

The wheelchair bumped up the path and over the threshold. With each jerk, Mia experienced the pain stabbing through the man's chest. She didn't know the cause, only that each breath this man took was agony and that movement made it worse. Mia wobbled the wheelchair left and right, jolting it to a stop at each door.

'Not this one,' she whispered, gasping at the sensations creeping up her legs. His pain was fragrant and lush, his sweat rich with the chemical by-products of a body in distress. Mia drew it in, writhing as she walked, dizzy in anticipation.

Each room the wrong number. Cecil tried to talk and turn his head, but Mia thrust the chair forward, almost dancing along the corridor in her glorious foreplay.

'Who?' The whisper emerged from the dear old man. His chest was pierced with agony and he coughed, rattles echoing down the narrow corridor. His voice cut through Mia's thoughts for an instant, creating a faint shadow of guilt, but she dismissed it. She'd feel it later. She'd have time later.

Cecil's room was small, containing a metal-framed bed, a white chest of drawers and a faux-leather chair. The brown carpet was thin, threadbare at the centre. An old TV was perched at an angle on the chest of drawers, switched on but with the volume muted. The channel was set to twenty-four-hour news. Mia watched the reporter for a moment before turning to the door. She closed it, realised it didn't lock from the inside, and pushed the heavy chair across the doorway instead.

Cecil remained quiet, even more so when Mia pulled the roll of tape from her bag and sealed his lips together. He tried to speak, a faint groan radiating from his throat.

Bracing herself, Mia wedged one foot under one of the wheels and lifted the arms of the chair as high as she could. Cecil was skin and bone and fell out of the chair easily, hitting the floor in a ball, rolling on to his side. His eyes darted up in shock but Mia was on him in a second, straddling the small body, shifting him on to his back.

'Cecil,' she whispered, bringing her face close to his. 'Look at me, Cecil.'

His eyes welled with tears. The fear was already overwhelming him and he sucked, drawing air through his nose, shaking as Mia rested her face on his. She breathed in the pain, stroking his skin, absorbing the moisture.

She leaned back and set to work with ruthless efficiency. His chest was the source of the pain, so she bunched a fist and pushed it into his solar plexus, jerking it against the bottom of his ribcage.

It hit the spot, causing a convulsion so strong Mia's body responded with an orgasmic shudder, the pleasure taking her whole body. She gyrated, her hips forcing her weight forward and back, her arm pushing harder into his chest, forcing his breath out, forcing the pain to reach unfathomable heights.

Mia rocked in pure bliss. The suffering of this body in front of her no longer mattered. It was a tool, a necessary cog in Mia's clockwork existence. She basked in every sensation seeping from what little life the man had left.

He held out for a surprisingly long time. A subtle shift in her pleasure signalled the end, then it stopped abruptly. Glancing down, she saw that Cecil had passed out.

Mia took a few moments to breathe. The after-effects would soon be with her, but she clung to the last remnants of pleasure as her body sweated and shivered.

She stood. Cecil was gone. Nearly dead. She doubted if he'd wake from this and wondered if it mattered if he did.

She always finished off her prey. Self-preservation, as a rule, but also to ensure closure. These bodies – their last moment of pain was hers and hers alone. It wasn't a trophy; she wasn't crazy. But it was hers. She needed to ensure these people's pain stopped for them when it did for her, that their lips were sealed for ever.

It was the only way she could do it. The only way she knew how.

Monsters didn't need to explain.

This time, as Mia stared at the old man, she knew he'd be dead by the evening. He couldn't suck enough air into his lungs to keep them functioning. Without knowing why, she left him on the floor and moved the heavy chair, stumbling with the dizziness that had arrived promptly and wouldn't now leave her for hours.

She left the care home, along the stone path and through the squeaky gate, without meeting the nurse or anyone else. Was she being careless? Was it intentional? Did she want them to find Cecil and give chase? Dead or alive, they'd do it anyway.

Mia walked away. She stopped after a mile or so, resting on a park bench, shivering as she plummeted into the near-darkness.

An hour, maybe more. Mia let her body recover slowly as the terror retreated. What now? She hadn't achieved what she'd set out to do

– she'd been full of the hunt, full of questions, but distracted by her primitive needs.

She needed to keep searching. Follow the scant information she had and find them. What other route could she take? She could leave. Run and hide herself in the maze of roads and buildings. But then what? She could find Dr Madison, hand herself in, allow herself to be shackled and tested, prodded and humiliated. He had said he wanted to help. Could he help? Could anybody help her, such as she was? Dr Madison was honest, he spoke the truth, yet Mia needed to find her own answers. That night in the surgeon's office had opened up the box she'd had closed since she first woke on the streets. It gave her hope that the answers would be out there. If she found them, if she knew what had happened to herself and her parents, perhaps then she would go to the friendly doctor. Perhaps then she would accept help and whatever came her way. It could be over. She could rest in peace.

Mia forced herself up. The road was quiet and cars drifted past her. She knew which direction to head in but struggled to move. Her high had been extreme and her subsequent low reflected it. She staggered and struggled not to vomit, the bile sloshing in her stomach, the nerves biting with every step. It was all she could do not to curl into a ball at the side of the road and howl.

Digging deep, Mia found the energy to keep walking. She knew she was being foolish. Even if she found the address, cornered somebody, what could she do to them?

Ask for the answers, Mia. That's all you want.

Mia trudged, eyes down, not paying attention to the road or the further thinning of traffic as she left the shopping streets. If she had, she might have heard the van earlier. As it was, the soft drone of the engine behind her continued for half a mile or more before she realised.

By the time she noticed, the vehicle had stopped at the kerb and two men had climbed out.

A black Transit van. New and shiny, with a sliding door on the side. Open. The driver moved fast, blocking the path ahead. He was tall and stocky, dressed in black trousers and jumper. Mia spun on her feet to find a second man blocking her retreat. He wore similar clothing, this time in grey and black, and large boots. The men's faces were stony and alert, far more so than Mia. Her vision jumped and danced. She staggered back and found herself against a wall. Blocked in on all sides, her only exit was the van and the open door.

The driver pulled out a mobile phone and held it up. Mia heard the sound of a picture being taken. They both waited. Mia tensed, readying her legs for a sprint she knew she couldn't do. Panic gripped her at the edges. The need to escape overwhelmed every other sensation.

Her eyes darted to the driver as his phone pinged. He glanced at the screen then nodded to his colleague, who reached behind his back and drew something from his belt.

Mia's heart jumped when she saw the long black barrel of a pistol.

'Wait!' she said, her voice sticking in her throat. It couldn't end here. Why here? She'd had no closure, no answers. These men had no right.

But he didn't wait. He raised his arm, pointed the gun at Mia's chest and fired. The gun made a dull pop and she felt as though she'd been hit in the chest with a golf ball. She raised her hand and found a feathered dart stuck deep into her skin. She tried to pull it out, but her hands felt powerless and weak. She couldn't grasp it and it slipped through her fingers.

She floated instantly, her head drifting above her body as the ground came up to meet her. She was vaguely aware of the men approaching as the light flickered out and her eyes closed. She never felt the rest.

CHAPTER THIRTY-FOUR

White. All white. Mia's eyes struggled to focus, the brightness dazzling. She closed her eyes and tried again. Blinking away the tears, she tried to move her head but found it stuck. Pressure on her forehead suggested she was restrained. When she tried to raise her hand she heard the squeak of leather. Her arm moved six inches, no more.

Her panic reflex was subdued, her reactions dumbed, but her mind chugged with the realisation of what had happened.

Drugged.

Captured.

The white ceiling tiles were broken by lights every other tile. Harsh but unavoidable. Mia swallowed, clearing her throat. She tensed her muscles, testing her movements. Her legs were also restrained and the bed rattled. A distant humming broke the silence: an industrial drone vibrating through the bed.

'She's awake.' A voice to her left. The sound of a laptop being closed and a drawer being opened. The voice was steady, not calm but in control.

'Are they ready?' Another voice, this time from behind her head. Mia tried to arch her neck backwards but her head wouldn't budge.

'I think so. I'm not sure.'

'Then find out.'

Mia held her tongue, but she watched and listened. The occupants of the room shuffled, their footsteps squeaking on the floor. She heard a door open and close, a lock clicking into place and a hiss of air.

She tried to move towards the sound but her whole body was strapped tight. Her eyes flooded with tears. The dizziness circled but seemed to hold off, perhaps because she was lying down. Her bladder needed emptying. She held it, feeling the discomfort in her belly.

Her head was pushed to the left, the strap was loosened and her neck felt light and free. She moved her head, feeling the ache. The room was smaller than she'd thought and resembled a private hospital room, clinical and bare, with artificial light and no windows she could see. To the left was a trolley holding several devices – an ECG and an EEG. A syringe pump and a stand for a drip. None of them seemed to be connected to her.

To her right, her gaze fell on a man. Standing, dressed in a white coat over a shirt and tie. His face was clear and instantly recognisable. It triggered a wave of emotion, flashbacks of sights and sounds. She smelled the bleach and the blood, felt the vibrations of the hospital bed and the bang of the doors against it.

The scar.

Below the man's right eye, pink and raised, it flashed like the bolt of lightning from her dream. This was him. This was the masked man who had gazed at her while she lay helpless and injured.

'I . . .' The words wouldn't come. She saw the man's eyes dart past her, to the left and right, then back to her face. He tried to smile but it was a mixture of complex emotions.

'You know me,' she said, seeing it as clearly as she'd seen in the last doctor she'd killed. But this time she was shackled and powerless. She couldn't attack this man; she was at his mercy. Terrified.

The scarred doctor folded his arms, leaning over the bed, studying Mia. His face was stern but not altogether hostile. Mia sensed confusion.

'You remember me?' The surgeon spoke perfect English – cultured, British. Mia watched the scar on his cheek. It wasn't a dream this time. She really was lying on a bed with him staring at her, minus the mask.

'Yes,' said Mia again, finding her wits. Her voice was hoarse and she cleared her throat.

'Can we get some water?' said the doctor. More footsteps, and another man came into view. Mia didn't recognise him. He helped support her head and held a tumbler with a straw to Mia's mouth. She drank the warm water until it was gone, licking her lips.

'I was captured,' said Mia. 'I—'

The scarred doctor ignored her, his eyes avoiding hers, instead looking at other parts of her face and body. He was examining her. Mia's heart sped up. She watched his eyes and his face. The doctor appeared tired, his clammy skin furrowed and pale. He huffed as he moved, fidgeting with his hands.

'Bloods?' he said to his colleague.

His colleague paused. Mia heard a drawing-in of breath. 'Results just in. They are . . . unexpected.'

'How so?'

Another pause. 'Should we discuss in front of the subject?'

The scarred doctor glanced at Mia's face. He frowned. 'Put her out then.'

A scratch. More darkness.

It was impossible to judge time. Mia came round, staring at the ceiling of the same room, which appeared to be empty apart from her. The head restraint had been left off, so she strained her neck, glancing around at the sterile white. She could see the door, solid with a small pane of glass woven with metal. Large rubber seals surrounded the frame.

Her bladder felt ready to burst. Whatever their plans for her, it didn't seem to involve basic comforts, and Mia's heart jumped again. Was this it? Would her search end with no answers, nothing but this white room? Prison would be no worse than this. Should she have trusted Dr Madison?

A click and a hiss at the door. Mia watched it open and two people enter. A man, large with a bald head. He wore a suit, not a white coat. Next to him was a woman, young and dark-haired with olive skin. Her eyes were full of intrigue. They both watched Mia, keeping their distance from the bed.

The man said something. Heavily accented, another language. Mia thought it might be Russian; the consonants were harsh. The woman responded in similar tongue. She shook her head, speaking in a language Mia didn't understand before approaching the bed.

She put her hand to Mia's head and gently smoothed her hair.

Mia watched the woman. Was she friend or foe? She found her voice. 'My name is Mia,' she said.

'I know who you are,' the woman said.

'Who are you?'

The woman smiled. Mia detected sorrow in it, a deep maturity suggesting that this young woman had lived and seen things Mia could never understand. She frowned.

'That, I'm afraid, you cannot know,' said the woman, 'but I'm interested. Please . . .' She leaned over, her fragrance wafting over Mia, a mixture of perfume and her natural odour. She gazed into Mia's eyes, her face no more than a foot away.

'Can you tell me?' she said. 'What do you feel? What do you sense?'

Mia was confused. She studied the woman's face. She had no pain, no discomfort. Her face was closed and her eyes held many secrets, an agenda she would never share with Mia. Mia shook her head. 'I don't know what you mean.'

The woman's eyes narrowed. 'I think you do,' she said. 'Look harder.'

Mia watched and read the woman's body language as best she could. The woman was furtive and her expressions controlled. She was as practised at hiding her emotions as Mia was at reading them. In the absence of pain, Mia could see very little. Why did it matter?

The woman straightened up, reaching into her pocket. She pulled out a small folding knife. Mia tensed, her fists balling. She couldn't move.

'What about now?' said the woman, extending the knife and sticking the point into her own fingertip. She grimaced as she held the knife there for a second. Blood dripped on to the floor. The man passed her a tissue.

Mia barely registered his movements. Her focus was on the pain.

The finger throbbed, sending a shock wave of pain up the woman's arm. It registered with a pulse and sent a myriad of reactions through her body. Mia responded automatically, tensing her shoulders and drawing in huge, deep breaths. The sluggish fog at the back of her mind departed as a rush of pleasure hit her. She smiled, enjoying the morsel thrown to her. Her mouth filled with saliva and she swallowed, desperate for more.

But the woman's expression changed. She turned to the man and they exchanged a few words in their language. He shook his head. They seemed to disagree. The woman shrugged before turning back to Mia. She looked sad. Her pain was dissipating and Mia felt it being torn away from her. This woman was teasing her, testing her.

'They want to start treatment,' the man said, this time in English.

The woman tilted her head. 'Yes,' she said, 'but not yet.'

They both turned and headed for the door.

'Wait,' said Mia. 'You can't . . .'

The door closed and hissed, a lock clicking into place. Mia was alone.

CHAPTER THIRTY-FIVE

Alex waved his patient out of the door of his office and paused next to the water cooler. He could have done with something stronger but resisted. It was eleven a.m. He'd already had one Xanax and two cups of coffee – a non-addict might have concluded that the caffeine cancelled out the Xanax, but Alex knew better. The Xanax quelled the rising anxiety always present first thing on waking. The coffee came later, when the anxiety had subsided and he needed a stimulant. Alex had had many years of practice at this, and his body chemistry management was down to a fine art.

Except, of course, lately he'd needed more and was mixing it with way too much alcohol. Mikey was right. Grace was right. Alex was slipping, on the edge of a precipice, the bottom of which he knew very well from his countless patients over the years.

He'd just closed the door on somebody who could easily be him. Generalised anxiety progressing to crippling panic attacks and agoraphobia to the point where it stopped him functioning. The patient who'd just left had lost his job and was fast en route to losing his family. It could so easily be Alex.

He drained a cup of ice-cold water. Forty-eight hours since he'd seen Mia Anastos in the lift at City Hospital. The flurry of activity following his description had faded. The CCTV was poor and the witnesses were unreliable. Mia had left the hospital and disappeared like she always did, blending in with a city of close to ten million people with ease. The police were frustrated and Laurie seemed distant, distracted by other cases and the demands of her superiors.

He'd thought about Laurie a lot. He already missed their daily encounters, her sarcasm and obvious buried troubles. He wondered when they might go out for that drink, but didn't want to push it. Keen was attractive, obsessive was not.

What he couldn't stop were the feelings that Laurie set off. Even if he could manage to date her without screwing it up, he couldn't fathom how he'd deal with Grace and Katie. He knew it was his problem, not theirs. Grace had already moved on, but he knew she still had feelings for him. If he moved on too, then it would be final, an admission that it was OK for both of them. It would make Grace think he was ready, that he'd given up on her.

The thoughts spiralled and he couldn't concentrate. Without thinking, he picked up the phone.

'Alex.' Grace's usually warm voice sounded strained. She hadn't forgotten his last visit. He had hoped it would blow over. Wishful thinking.

'Are you in?'

'Yes. Katie's at a friend's.'

Alex wasn't sure if that was a hint to stay away. 'Fancy a coffee?'

A pause. 'I have to go out in an hour or so.'

'I won't keep you.'

A sigh. 'OK. A quick coffee.'

The journey from his office to Grace's took twenty minutes. Alex raced through the traffic, cursing as he pulled up at a pedestrian crossing. A young mother and toddler started to cross. Halfway, the boy sat down in the road and started to cry. The mother, balancing two bags and a cuddly toy, struggled to pick him up. She glanced up, mouthing the word 'sorry' to Alex.

Alex sat impatiently, tapping the wheel. His phone rang and he hit the answer button, willing the mother to drag the boy by his feet if she had to.

'Yes?'

'It's me.' Mikey's normally cheerful voice was muted, serious.

'Mikey. I'm in a bit of a rush, actually.'

'I have something for you.'

Alex paused, shifting his gaze inside the car. 'What?'

'This Nova AG of yours. I tapped a few more contacts. Most had never heard of it, or at least pretended that way. One was a little more open. I think he'd had a run-in with them in the past. He says Nova is major organised-crime territory. Syndicates, global reach, political involvement. "Mafia shit" is what he said.'

Alex felt the adrenaline surge. 'And?'

'Don't get involved was the advice I was given. They're not a group you want to mess with if you value your life, your family and your friends.'

Alex valued all of those, but he wasn't planning to mess with Nova . He was planning on letting the police do that.

'Why did you call, Mikey?'

A pause on the other end. 'I have an old address for you,' said Mikey. 'If you insist, I'll text it over.'

Alex didn't need to think about it. 'I insist.'

'Give it to your detective,' said Mikey. 'Don't say where it came from. Don't go there yourself.'

Alex nodded. 'Sure thing.'

'I mean it, Alex,' said Mikey. 'I know some pretty shady characters – you make strange friends in the drug-running business – but this is another level. Give it to the police. Let them do what they will.'

Alex saw his phone buzz as the text message came through. 'Thanks, Mikey. I owe you.'

'Don't forget it,' said his friend, then hung up.

Alex felt his heart race. Finally, a lead that might give them some progress. A lead that might prove this wasn't all about Mia, that the guilt belonged to more than just one person. He smiled at the dashboard as a horn blasted at him from the car behind. He looked up to see the road empty, the mother and son some distance along the pavement, merrily on their way. He gunned the engine and sped off.

Alex rapped on the door and stood back, surveying the garden that used to be his. The lavender bushes were huge; he remembered planting them with Grace, trying to pay attention as she described the end result. She'd planned the garden landscaping front and rear, and her eye for detail had paid off.

'Come in.' Grace threw open the door and paused. She was dressed in a small blue summer dress, floral, mid-thigh, with detail around the neckline. Her hair was perfectly sculpted around her face, which was delicately made-up. Alex sucked through his lips.

'Wow,' he said, 'you didn't need to. We're only having coffee.' The joke masked his actual reaction, which was a burst of heart-thumping desire. He swallowed it away.

Grace pulled a face. 'You wish,' she said, laughing. 'I have a lunch date, actually. That's why I'm going out.'

Alex wanted to make a light comment about John, but the name stuck in his throat and nothing nice would come out. He choked it back. 'Anywhere nice?'

'Girly lunch,' said Grace. 'Seeing as the kids are all having fun, we reckoned we would too.'

Alex felt better but knew he shouldn't. Grace no doubt dressed up for her new man as well. The thought of it made him feel sick. 'Coffee, then?'

Grace led the way. Alex stared at her behind as she walked through the hall in her floaty dress. Inappropriate, no doubt, but he couldn't help it, and Grace probably figured as much. She perched at the breakfast bar and invited him to make the coffee.

'So, Mikey called me,' she said. Alex paused, his heart in his throat. They knew each other, of course, but Grace had never known about Mikey's role in his prescription drugs. Had he told her? Had he betrayed Alex? Why would he?

'He said you had dinner, caught up.' Grace tilted her head, her eyes bright and calm, not a hint of anger. 'He told me you opened up a little,' she said, 'about your health. He seems to think you're making progress.'

Alex nodded, waiting for more before he confirmed or denied anything.

'He said he was worried about you.'

Alex filled the cafetière, watching the black liquid swirl into foam. Mikey shouldn't have done that. He thought they had an understanding. 'Did he say anything else?'

Grace shrugged. 'No, only that he cares, and it had been too long since we'd all had a drink together. Oh, and he said if I don't marry anybody else, he'll marry me.'

Alex laughed before he could stop it. Mikey had always had a thing for Grace. It would be just like him to flirt a little. 'Well, I'll trust you to use your best judgement on that proposal,' he said.

Grace wiggled her eyebrows and smiled. 'But seriously,' she said, 'he was always a good friend of yours. You should listen to him.'

'I did.'

'And?'

'And what?'

Grace huffed. 'Christ, Alex, don't be such a child. About getting help. Have you found somebody yet?'

Alex didn't want to lie outright, but the only thing he'd progressed since seeing her last was to secure another six months of benzos. He could hardly tell her that.

'I'm making inquiries,' he said. 'It's not as easy as all that. I have my career to think of. It has to be discreet.'

Grace looked unconvinced, but she let it go. 'Do it for Katie?'

A direct stab to the heart, and she knew it. He poured the coffee, keeping his expression as non-committal as he could. He nodded. He'd do anything for them, he would. Why couldn't he do this? 'I'll try,' he said, taking a sip, realising he meant it. He wasn't sure how it would happen or when, but those small words were significant.

They drank and talked about Katie, a pleasant distraction from his mental health. Alex asked everything he could think of, and Grace answered. There were no secrets where Katie was concerned. Luckily for them both, she seemed to have her head screwed on and had fallen in with a decent group of friends. *One less thing to worry about*, he thought. At least one part of his life was stable.

Grace sipped her coffee, smiling as Alex teased her about the amount of pink in the house since he'd left. It seemed to be everywhere. He made a mental note to talk to Katie about it.

They laughed as the conversation tailed off. Silence followed, their eyes meeting. Grace chewed her lower lip, as she always did when she was apprehensive. She crossed her legs, causing her dress to ride up. Alex's head spun at the sight and he found his breath shallow. How long had it been since he'd touched her? How long since they'd kissed, tearing each other's clothes off? Once upon a time a dress like that wouldn't have stayed on Grace for long. She was fiery and seductive when she wanted to be. Always in control, she'd lure Alex in and drive him crazy before telling him what she wanted. He would succumb in an instant, begging her for the inevitable. They'd make love for hours, resting only when Grace decided she was satisfied. Those days had been bliss, and Alex found himself struggling to tear his eyes away.

When he did, he met hers again and found them sparkling but firm.

'I think it might be time for you to go, mister,' she said, sliding off the stool. She paused for a moment, standing in front of him. She bit her lip again but shook her head. 'Definitely time for you to go.' Her face flushed and she backed away, leading Alex out into the hallway.

Alex wanted to protest, to extend the moment, to scream that it wasn't over. These silences, these moments. These things happened to people in love. These weren't moments shared by exes who didn't want to be together.

But he didn't.

They hugged and pecked each other on the cheek.

'I'm glad things are improving,' said Grace, finding her voice. 'I'll support you. Anything you need, tell me.'

Alex smiled, knowing that what he needed was the one thing he couldn't ask of her. But it spurred him on. He drove off positive and in control. His love for Grace wouldn't fade fast but he must give her the space she wanted and in the meantime try to move on himself. She had hinted that he should, and however much it hurt, he was determined to do it, if only to prove he'd listened.

Putting his thoughts of Grace firmly back in their mental box, he reached for his phone.

'This isn't a date.' Laurie sat opposite Alex at the restaurant. Alex had called and persuaded her to come for a drink, insisting it was to discuss the case. She'd protested with the usual degree of sarcasm but agreed. She didn't have anything else planned that evening except cleaning the oven, so she said, but it was a close call between the oven and drinking wine with Alex.

'Obviously,' he said, pleased he'd taken the time to go home and change into an ironed white shirt and navy chinos. Laurie looked more casual than usual, in tight jeans and a top.

'I like your hair down,' said Alex. 'It looks great.'

Laurie blushed. She looked as though she was going to make a sarcastic comment but smiled instead. 'Thanks,' she said. 'It's a little long for work. Don't want to get it stuck in blood, bodily fluids, bad guys' fists, etcetera.'

'Nice image.'

'I try.'

Alex poured them both a glass of Malbec.

'But this isn't a date.'

'I get it,' said Alex, watching Laurie's infectious smile. 'So how about we talk shop instead?' He produced the address he'd been given by Mikey, careful to restrict any incriminating information. 'He has a lot of contacts.'

'With organised crime?' Laurie looked puzzled.

'Pharmacists know about the dodgy routes to market,' said Alex. 'They have to. This company is dodgy as hell.'

Laurie nodded, shrugging. 'So you want me to check it out?'

'Of course. Why wouldn't you?'

Laurie looked troubled. She sipped from her glass, glancing around the restaurant, staring at several other patrons until they stared back. 'I don't know if I can.'

'Why not?' Alex tried to rein in his irritation. This was a lead. He knew Laurie was focused on finding Mia above all else, but the police couldn't ignore the company or organisation behind this. 'This is criminal activity,' he said. 'If they experimented on Mia, they've done it on others.'

Laurie sighed. 'I know. What I mean is, *I* can't. I'm being pulled off the case. As from tomorrow.'

'What? Why?'

Laurie sighed, looking at him, her eyes full of puzzlement and fatigue. 'I don't know, Alex,' she said. 'Internal politics, management infighting. Perhaps I pissed off the wrong person.' She shrugged and took a gulp of wine. 'It happens all the time. I'm just a grunt in the hierarchy. They say, "Bullshit" and I say, "How much?"'

Alex was shocked, saddened at the thought of being split up so soon from Laurie. 'That's it?' he said. 'They can do that – reassign you? We're making progress. We know who she is. We know what motivates her. We have a lead on the organisation behind her condition . . .' He trailed off, watching Laurie's expression.

'Not enough and not fast enough,' she said. 'The hunt will continue, Alex, but you'll need to report to Hartley. I'll send her the address but let her decide how to proceed. I'm done, so I've been told.'

Alex didn't know what to say. Laurie was clearly angry and frustrated. His venting wouldn't help matters. He was sad for another reason too. It meant that whatever budding friendship they might have had was fading before it had properly started.

'We can keep in touch,' she said, as if reading his mind. They watched each other for a few moments, sipping their drinks, lost in their own thoughts.

'I'd like that,' he said, finishing his glass, checking the bottle. He glanced up. 'Seeing as we're here, do you fancy a bite to eat?'

Laurie narrowed her eyes. 'If you feed me and ply me with alcohol, you've only got yourself to blame for what happens.'

Alex stifled a laugh. 'I wasn't intending to ply you with anything.'

Laurie grabbed the bottle. 'Then I'll ply myself. Just keep your hands to yourself, Doctor. I'm far too much trouble, and you don't want it.'

Alex raised his hands in surrender.

'Got it,' he said. 'You're trouble.'

He watched Laurie for a few more seconds before burying his eyes in the menu, wondering if this type of trouble, this distraction, was exactly what he wanted.

CHAPTER THIRTY-SIX

Time passed in a blur. Mia had no frame of reference. She woke periodically, always drugged and groggy, always staring up into the small white room with the dazzling lights and the stench of bleach.

Her hands and feet remained strapped. Her makeshift splint had gone, replaced with a white cast. The doctors had fitted a catheter. She was fed and watered, like a zoo animal, she considered. Or like a prisoner.

How many days had she been here? Maybe just one. Maybe a week. Her mind struggled.

Mia craved answers but being here only raised more questions. Her memories were real and the people who created them were here, in this place. The doctor with the lightning scar – the man from her dreams – came and went, watching Mia but never speaking to her or touching her.

Mia mumbled; incoherent pleadings. Her voice barely escaped her dry throat. Starting as a hiss, it erupted into screams until the doctors left the room. The scarred doctor's expression remained fixed and unwavering. Did Mia observe sadness in his eyes, or was this simply a trick of the light?

The suited couple didn't return. The beautiful woman with the deep and complicated eyes preyed on Mia's mind, but she remained elusive. Mia wondered if she was there, lurking in the background. Her eyes had been full of knowledge, yet she had seemed sad at seeing Mia. Or had it been disappointment?

The room became smaller with each passing hour. Unrecognisable doctors and nurses checked on her at random intervals, keeping her off balance and agitated. The catheter was removed; her plaster cast remained. What were they keeping her for? What were they preparing her for? They left as soon as she asked.

Mia tried to quell her anxiety. Her desire would be back. It always came back. She closed her eyes, clenching her jaw, concentrating on her chest rising and falling. Her muscles tightened and her mind spiralled.

CHAPTER THIRTY-SEVEN

Alex's non-date with Laurie had ended without the trouble she'd promised. They'd parted at the taxi rank, rather inebriated but both sensible enough to call it a night. Alex promised he'd call. Laurie promised to pick up the phone if he did.

He resisted the urge to call the very next day. He'd had a somewhat vivid dream about Grace, during which Laurie had appeared, hands on hips, giving him a sarcastic reprimand on his priorities. The images of both were burned into his consciousness and the anxious guilt wouldn't depart, even with his morning Xanax. Two pills this morning.

He knew he should take the time to unpick it but instead called Hartley. Not sure what to say, he knew he couldn't rest. He felt loyal to Laurie, and progressing the case would help her.

His thoughts were also with Mia, snippets of their meeting flashing into his consciousness. Alex had been face to face with several killers in his time, but very few had generated the feelings of sympathy Mia had. She wasn't evil, far from it. She was desperate and out of control, crying for help. He needed to find her. She needed him. He still wasn't convinced Hartley and the police would handle it in the way he wanted. Alex wanted Mia to have treatment, and more than that, treatment under his management. This was another career-defining moment for him: to leave behind the legacy of the Victor Lazar case and finally break away from his private practice – to make a name for himself not just catching but helping the people they caught. The police were necessary, but as an instrument for deciphering the minds of killers they were blunt. They went for the prize but didn't stop to think about whether it was the right one. That was what Alex was there for, to temper their enthusiasm for the chase and focus on the real challenge – that these criminals were often created and could be cured. Those who created them should face justice. Society and science would learn something as a result.

'Alex!' Hartley's voice snapped him out of it. She sounded harassed. A busy lady, she was still running several major cases, so he'd heard. He was surprised she'd answered the phone at all.

Alex asked about the current status of the case. He tried not to sound too frustrated.

'Detective Laurie may be back,' said Hartley. 'She's good, but she's been reprioritised. It happens.' Hartley's tone sounded final.

'Back when?' said Alex. 'We identified the killer and we have a conspiracy of doctors who are responsible.'

'So you say,' said Hartley, her tone cautious.

'You disagree?' Alex wondered what Laurie's handover report had said. 'What about Dr Tau? He's the last contact we have at the hospital and his disappearance is not a coincidence.'

'I agree,' said Hartley, 'which is why my officers are pursuing inquiries as to his whereabouts.'

'A warrant?'

'We don't issue warrants for prominent NHS doctors who haven't committed a crime or been conclusively linked to one. Particularly a doctor who has friends outside my sphere of influence.'

'Meaning?'

Hartley cleared her throat. 'Please don't take that tone, Alex. Detective Laurie's report was thorough. She did mention your findings, as it happens.

We're putting all of our efforts into locating Mia Anastos. We have a virtual army of officers sifting through hours of CCTV footage all over London. Others are out interviewing NHS personnel and going door to door.'

'And ignoring the doctors.'

Hartley huffed. 'Alex, I'll tell you this because I think you're one of us. Things take time. Things can get political. If we don't follow your every recommendation, there is often a good reason for it, one we might not tell you straight away. OK?'

Alex paused. 'Political,' he said. 'Which bit?'

'The bit where we storm into a big multinational company's premises based on the word of a drug dealer.'

Alex's heart jumped into his mouth. He swallowed. Laurie's report had passed on the address Mikey had supplied, but she or Hartley already knew about Mikey. Dammit. He chose his words very carefully. 'He's a friend and I trust that his contacts are real,' he said. 'If you know about this company Nova, please follow it up.'

Alex heard Hartley tapping away at the other end. She sniffed.

'I've got to go, Alex. Time to end this conversation. My decision at this point in time is that we're not going to pursue the address you gave us. Nova is not to be pursued.'

'Why the hell not?'

'Because I said so!' Hartley shouted back.

Alex pulled the phone away from his ear.

She paused. 'I'll let you know, Alex. Keep working. We need a full profile for the CPS for when we catch this psycho. If you're at a loose end, start writing. In the meantime, stay away from Nova AG.'

'Not a psycho,' said Alex.

'What?'

'I said she's not psychopathic.'

Hartley coughed. 'Goodbye, Alex,' she said, hanging up.

◆ ◆ ◆

Alex was seething. He'd been put in his place and wasn't handling it like the seasoned professional they'd hired and continued to pay. But he had good reason and Hartley knew it. They'd both worked on the case of Victor Lazar and she knew the background, even if they'd never managed to find the perpetrators. Human experimentation was alive and well in the UK and Mia could lead the police straight to it, if they were willing to be led.

Political, that's what she said. Alex was not naive – he knew the machinations of big business, and there were few bigger than pharmaceutical companies. Hartley knew something about Nova. If the pressure was on her to stay away, then the police were having their hands tied. Alex found it hard to accept.

He calmed himself, pacing the soft carpet of his office, working the stress out of his body through deep breathing. He went over to the coffee maker, poured a large mug but set it to one side. Caffeine was the wrong drug. The right drug was in his pocket, but three Xanax would cause his head to muddy and he couldn't afford that.

Laurie was off the case. Hartley chose to chase the shadow of Mia Anastos but do nothing about the sinister group that had created her. The police had stalled themselves while the senior officers battled political games and favours.

But Alex didn't need to follow any of that, did he? He'd agreed to be an external consultant to the police precisely because it gave him freedom from their rules. It wasn't that he intended to break them all on a regular basis, but having no boss other than himself allowed him to be objective. It allowed him certain liberties.

He sat at the desk and pulled out his phone. He'd already put the address into his Notes, and now he cut and pasted it into the maps app. It pinned the location somewhere on an east London industrial estate. He thought back to Mikey's warning. Alex valued his health and his life, but this was London, not some Mexican slum. He could drive to an estate in this city and poke around without getting out of the car. He could at least see what this place might be, gather a little more intelligence ready for his next conversation with Hartley, or if all went well, Laurie.

The thought of Laurie gave his heart a brief murmur. He pictured her at the restaurant on their not-a-date, her shining eyes and her wicked sense of humour.

He decided to text her; tell her what he was doing. It was the sensible thing. He wrote: *Hartley battling politics. I'm heading to the Nova address to check it out.* He pressed send and put his phone on silent before she could reply and try to persuade him out of it.

The Merc spat gravel as he accelerated away, enjoying the sensation for fewer than five minutes before he hit the lunchtime traffic. He crawled around the northern edge of the city, wishing he'd brought a snack or a drink. He lowered the air-con, loosening his top button.

As he approached the location on the map his phone buzzed. A message icon appeared at the top of the screen. He ignored it, figuring it was Laurie telling him to stay away. He felt a little underhand for going against her advice but figured it would be good for her if he found a lead. Even a snippet of information about this Nova company could sway their investigation his way. It might even persuade Hartley to put her back on the case. Wishful thinking, perhaps, but his mind was made up.

He slowed as the entrance to the industrial estate loomed on his left. A billboard-sized map showed a bewildering array of company names and logos, all with numbers and roads. He pulled over, scanning for Nova, but couldn't see anything. An articulated truck stopped behind him and honked its horn. Alex pulled away, turning into the estate, arching his back to see the signs.

He was still half a mile from the address he'd been given by Mikey. Unfortunately, there was no number, just the name of the street: *Pickard.* Alex crawled along, seeing few companies he recognised. Technology and engineering firms seemed prominent. A biotech company called

Transcend with a DNA logo dominated three consecutive warehouses, all huge metal complexes set far back from the road behind razor wire. After ten minutes of crawling along then pulling over to let more trucks pass, Pickard Street appeared on his right and his left. Checking the map, the street appeared to stretch for miles in a grid structure. He drove past the turning for a hundred yards or so and parked, tucking in tight against the kerb, folding his mirrors in. He doubted any of the truck drivers would mind too much about hitting his car on their way past.

Alex stepped out of the car, locking it behind him. He swung his jacket over his shoulder and tapped his pockets, ensuring he had his keys and phone. He'd parked in front of a small unmarked brick storage unit. Nobody should mind too much, and it wasn't as if there were any traffic wardens around. There was nobody around, in fact, and Alex paused. This wasn't the sort of place he'd want to walk around alone at night, but surely it was safe in daylight hours?

Mildly reassured by his weak rationale, he walked back towards Pickard Street and turned left.

The pavement and road stretched on into the distance. Both sides held eight-foot-high wire fences topped with both barbed and razor wire. Beyond the wire was concrete, clean and empty, stretching for over thirty yards before the buildings rose up. Alex walked for five minutes, counting three warehouses. No names, no logos, just huge complexes holding their secrets. Whether they were sinister or otherwise, Alex was none the wiser. He paused, linking his fingers over the wire, staring through at one of the buildings.

Mikey can't have known what this place looked like. Did all of this belong to Nova AG? If so, it couldn't be illegal. Whoever owned or leased these buildings wasn't hidden. Discreet, maybe, and secure, but not secret. If the police wanted to, they could ask for a warrant and search any one of the buildings.

Except that Hartley didn't want to, or couldn't, which amounted to the same result.

Alex turned to face along the road. He squinted into the distance, where the road terminated at another high fence and beyond that a line of trees. The road between was empty.

The frustration welled up. There was nothing here to see, not without hammering at the fence or shouting through it. He'd expected something different, perhaps an open building, a reception area or a bustling loading bay he could slip into and sneak around. What he'd found was nothing like that; this estate was more like a military base, a deserted one.

Alex crouched, dusting the pavement before sitting at the kerb. It had been a wasted trip. He pulled his phone out and checked the screen. The message icon had doubled into two. Alex swiped and saw Laurie's messages. The first was as expected: *Leave it, Alex. Let Hartley do her job.* The second was surprisingly pleasant: *I'm finishing at six today. Fancy a drink?*

Alex responded to the second, feeling a rush of anticipation. She'd called him first. *Sure thing*, he replied. *I'll pick you up?*

The reply came through. *No, thanks. Mercs are for old men and pimps. I'll meet you at the restaurant. Same place as last time.*

Alex smiled, staring at the message. He was about to type a response when the sound of an engine caused him to look up. A black Transit van appeared at the far end of the road, where the fence and road disappeared. A gate had opened to let the van through and was sliding closed behind it. The engine gunned and the van headed towards him. Alex stood, stepping back from the kerb, watching the van approach. The cab held two figures, both in dark matching clothing.

Alex had no ready excuse for being here, but it wasn't a crime and, if challenged, he didn't have to say anything. The van might be security. Private contractors were often arrogant and intimidating, but they had to operate within the law.

He faced the van as it slowed, trying to make himself look unthreatening and lost. He hoped the van would drive straight past and was disappointed to see it stop right in front of him. He kept his phone in his hand, watching the two men step out.

The first – the driver – was tall and stocky. He wore black trousers and a turtleneck. Security, if Alex had to guess. The second man wore near-identical clothing, his grey trousers bunched over a pair of large black boots. Both had close-cropped hair and were clean-shaven.

'Sir,' said the driver, approaching Alex. The other man stepped on to the kerb to his side.

'This is a private estate, sir.' Alex noted an accent: South African, perhaps.

Alex nodded, already feeling intimidated. He tried to keep both men in view, but they separated and Alex found himself turning back and forth between them.

'I took a wrong turning,' he said, pulling his practised doctor's smile. He could do it on demand under any circumstances. The driver didn't return the smile, his expression alert and firm.

'May I see some ID, sir?'

Alex knew he didn't have to produce ID to a private security guard, but at the same time he realised he was on a deserted street in the middle of what looked like a highly secure industrial park. He should have thought of a reason for being here; the security firm was within its rights to challenge him. The police wouldn't be very supportive if he caused trouble. He could picture Hartley's face already.

He glanced past the men, feeling an urge to run back to his car, but the two guards looked rather athletic. If they were guards – which wasn't clear – he didn't want to give them an excuse to practise their restraining skills.

'My name is Dr Madison,' said Alex, keeping his wallet in his pocket. He had ID but didn't want to show it if he could help it.

The driver continued to stare. He tapped his ear and Alex noticed a small radio earpiece.

'What are you doing here, Dr Madison?'

'I took a wrong turning,' said Alex, broadening his smile. 'I . . .' To his right, Alex noticed the second guard approaching him. He stood two feet away, behind Alex and near the fence.

'My car's back there,' Alex said, pointing. 'I'll leave; see if I can find the right road.'

The driver tapped his earpiece again before nodding to his colleague. Alex backed away but found himself against the fence. The two guards approached, the driver in front and the other stepping to the side.

'Wait,' said Alex. 'Look—' He felt a scratch on his neck. The guard to his right had lunged so fast that Alex didn't have time to react. Alex saw the needle come away and the guard reaching out to catch him as he fell. His knees buckled as his vision tunnelled. The grey gave way to black. The last thing Alex heard was his phone falling out of his hand and hitting the concrete.

CHAPTER THIRTY-EIGHT

Alex woke with a thumping headache which crept from the back of his neck through to his eyes. He found himself in a dimly lit room, small and featureless with a faint chemical odour. The left-hand wall was mirrored, reflecting Alex and a dirty white Formica table in front of him. Alex stared at his reflection. He looked washed out and grubby, his shirt creased, with the top three buttons undone. He leaned forward to stand but jolted back again; his hands were restrained, attached by thick leather straps to a metal chair which didn't budge. It was fixed to the floor and as he looked down he saw his feet were also restrained, long straps snaking out of the legs of the chair.

Panic rose up, lurching into his throat, a mixture of claustrophobia and confusion. He writhed and yanked at his arms. His legs moved but he couldn't get more than a few inches off the chair before collapsing back again. He paused, hyperventilating. His face flushed with heat and the throbbing in his head became more intense. His heart thumped and his mouth dried up. Closing his eyes, he took a deep breath and blew it out, feeling the hot air on his lips. He repeated it four times, trying to calm the rising anxiety, trying to think straight. *Calm yourself, Alex,* he thought. *Don't fight it.*

He opened his eyes.

The two men in the van, they'd knocked him out with something. A fast-acting sedative. By the headache, it must have been Etorphine or similar, which meant he could have been unconscious anywhere between a few minutes and a few hours. What type of security guard carries that sort of drug? One who worked for Nova, or whatever Nova really was. Alex had told them his name and they'd relayed it over the radio. They were told to take him. Ordered to sedate and capture him.

By whom?

Kidnapping was an extreme crime, risky as hell and with mixed outcomes. Alex shivered at the possible ways this could end. A memory of Victor Lazar sprang to the surface, the man who had kidnapped Katie and threatened her life in front of him.

But this was no individual out for revenge. If Nova was a front for illegal activity, Alex was considered too risky to be left poking around on the street outside but too valuable to kill outright. He took some solace in that fact. If these people had wanted him out of the way, he'd be six feet under somewhere, never to be found again. The fact he was in this room was significant and he needed to use it.

But did they know who he was? Had Dr Tau relayed his fears about the police investigation and Alex's part in it? *Be reasonable*, he thought. *Help them out. Get out of this unharmed.* He drew breath, trying to figure out his tactics.

He didn't have long. They must have been waiting for him to wake up. He glanced at the mirrored wall, wondering who was watching.

A loud click came from the door. A large man with a bald head in a grey suit entered first, followed by a young woman with dark hair and olive skin. She wore all black – tight trousers, top and ankle boots. The two were talking to each other in Russian, thick and deep. The woman shook her head, glanced at the mirrored wall before flicking a switch by the door. The dim room lit up in dazzling white. Alex squinted, holding his eyes shut until they became accustomed to the light.

'Dr Alex Madison.'

The soft female voice penetrated his consciousness like a blast of warm air, although his skin prickled with the effect. He opened his eyes and saw the woman who spoke. Her face was beautiful, her eyes deep and complex, but there was something more – her voice and appearance stirred something in Alex he couldn't understand. Recognition. A distant memory, but almost childlike in its vagueness. Alex could have sworn he'd never met this woman, yet he felt a closeness to her, more than an acquaintance, less than a friend.

'I . . .' His eyes darted over her body. She was slim but her posture was all strength; she was very like Laurie in her stance. Powerful and athletic, she crossed her arms and narrowed her eyes as she examined Alex.

Visions of a prison cell entered his mind. He could see Victor Lazar, the serial killer, his squat body on the bed, whispering to Alex through the cell door, teasing him. Flashes of an orphanage – the final stand-off with Victor, where Alex had rescued his daughter and the police had lost Victor. He was never to be seen again and the police blamed Alex.

Memories, so vivid and violent, jostled in his mind, confusing and distracting him. Why now?

'Who are you?' he said, realising the feebleness of his voice. He cleared his throat, trying to calm the rapid thump of his heartbeat. 'Why do I know you?'

The woman's cool expression flickered for a second. Her eyes widened in surprise before she got it under control. Alex saw it. She hadn't expected him to recognise her. Why not?

'You don't know me, Dr Madison.' Alex saw her eyes dart to the mirror and back. She bit her lip. She'd lost her composure for an instant.

The man in the suit, his expression stony, said, 'We found Dr Madison outside complex E.'

The woman tilted her head, examining Alex. 'I see.' She cleared her throat. Her composure was back. 'But you didn't find what you were looking for?'

Alex thought carefully about his reply. There was much more to this situation than he could fathom. However, they seemed to think he was worth talking to.

'I think I did,' said Alex, knowing his lies needed to be few and far between. He was looking for them and they knew it. But who was this woman? A doctor, a surgeon? Had she been at one of the hospitals – London City?

But the woman shook her head. 'I'm afraid you didn't,' she said.

The man murmured a few words in Russian and she shook her head again.

'The police know I'm here,' said Alex. He watched her expression. Again, her eyes darted to the mirror. Alex's eyes followed. The mirror was huge. From Alex's seated position he could see it was dirty, smudged around the bottom below the table line. It had a hairline crack in the bottom-left corner. He looked away, back to his captors.

'Dr Madison's phone?' she said.

The man slipped a hand into his jacket pocket and produced Alex's phone. He offered it to the woman.

'Leave it,' she said. 'Dr Madison can't do us any harm.'

The man shrugged and dropped the phone on to the table. Alex wasn't sure whether or not that was a good thing. Probably not. His mouth dried and his breathing became more shallow.

'Car?'

'Moved. Two blocks away.' The suited man turned to the woman. 'If the police are coming, we need to prepare.'

The woman nodded. A fresh wave of anxiety took Alex. Prepare for what? Alex had seen a whole road of huge warehouses. Did they all belong to these people? Which one had they taken him to? It was possible he wasn't even in London. If he'd been sedated for several hours, he could be anywhere in the country by now.

He recoiled as the woman approached. She sat on the desk, leaning in. She examined his face, peering into his eyes. Alex found himself unable to look away. Her gaze was both scary and mesmerising.

Again, Alex's mind wandered. Memories of Katie being held by Victor Lazar, his hands at her throat, the knife poised to take away Alex's daughter. Alex blinked, suppressing the traumatic visions. What was this woman doing to him?

'Will you deal with him?' The man's gruff voice broke Alex's trance. 'Take care of his . . . interfering?'

The woman continued to stare. She rested her hand on Alex's shoulder. He flinched but then relaxed. Her touch was light and she slid her fingers over the muscle, gently caressing him before pulling her hand away.

'No,' she said. 'There's no need for that.'

The man huffed, seeming to disagree. He spat something in Russian and the woman snapped her head around, responding in kind. The man put his hands up in submission.

No to what? Alex wondered. What was involved in *dealing with him*, and why had she saved him that ordeal?

'He will stay here,' she said. 'And take off his restraints. Dr Madison isn't dangerous. He could be useful.'

Alex tried to hide his surprise. The dynamic between the two was puzzling. He was a problem, but they didn't agree on what to do with him. The man approached Alex and tore the straps off his wrists and ankles, leaving them hanging. He didn't seem at all worried that Alex might try to fight. Being twice Alex's size, Alex couldn't blame him.

'Why are you keeping me here?' Alex risked the question. He directed it at the woman but watched the man for his reaction. 'Is Dr Tau here?'

Neither answered. They whispered a few words to each other. The man stiffened and nodded.

'Do you know Mia Anastos?'

Both of them stopped talking, turning to stare at Alex. The man raised his eyebrows, but the woman shook her head again, uttering more Russian. They argued for several seconds, but while the man got more agitated, the woman became calmer and more composed. She finished their argument with a string of soft Russian words.

'*Da*,' said the man, looking defeated. Without glancing at Alex, he headed for the door. He exited and left the door open. The woman paused. She nodded to herself, watching Alex.

'You've stirred up trouble, Alex,' she said. 'You should never have come here.'

Alex was about to speak but she shook her head and put her fingers to her lips. His mind went blank. Whatever he was going to say evaporated from his mind as the woman turned and exited the room.

CHAPTER
THIRTY-NINE

Mia was woken, jolted out of sleep by a nurse who refused to look her in the eye. She was told to use the bathroom and wash herself.

'Why?'

The nurse shook her head. Two muscular men in grey boiler suits entered the room. They unstrapped Mia in silence and frogmarched her out into a long white corridor with doors every few yards. They stopped at the third door along, ushering her into a bathroom. It was clinical, reminding Mia of a hospital ward and shared facilities. How many other people were here? she wondered. Were there others like her? Scores? Hundreds?

Mia asked the guards and was met with silence. They both stood in the bathroom with her, pretending not to watch as she pulled her clothes off and scrubbed her skin under the open shower.

She sat on the toilet, dabbing her plaster cast with a towel, staring at the military-style boots of the closest guard, wondering if she could take both men. She doubted it. Her head seemed clearer – had the drugs stopped? But she was no match for both. One by surprise, perhaps, but not both. She had no weapon and, despite the strength and fitness she'd developed from months surviving on the streets, superior numbers always won in brawls. Two six-foot men versus one woman. Mia didn't like the odds and so continued to sit, emptying her bowel and bladder, her modesty gone.

She stood waiting in front of the guards. The one on the left held out clean underwear and a gown. He made her wait, casting his eyes over her naked body, the smallest smile cracking at the edges of his lips. Mia stared through him, waiting. She had no advantage here and fighting would make it worse. She must bide her time and wait. They might kill her; they might let her go. She had no idea.

There was suspense in the air. Confusion and indecision on the part of both doctors and guards, and the scarred doctor refused to answer her questions and she remained captive and in the dark.

What to do with the monster? Mia hoped they didn't rush their decision.

The guard holding the clothes turned to his colleague. 'Give us a few minutes, yeah? Wait outside.'

The guards rarely spoke. This one sounded English, cockney. Mia recognised many accents, and this place held more than most.

His partner frowned, breaking his frosty professional gaze. He appeared to consider the request.

'I don't think I can do that.' Not English. German, perhaps; a mild accent but distinctive.

Cockney sniffed. He approached Mia. Before she could move he grabbed her, his hand sliding around to her bottom. He gripped it hard and pulled her towards him. His fingers slipped inwards, searching, rough between her legs. Her heart hammered. This wasn't about to happen, was it? Of all the things she could suffer, she hadn't expected this.

She turned to the other guard, her face trying not to plead, her mind whirring. If the other guard left, it would be just the two of them. Could this man overpower her? Was it that easy for him? Mia would fight, she'd have to, but he was huge, his muscles rippling under his T-shirt. She saw desire on him, a surge of excitement. He had one single thing on his mind today, and Mia started to prepare herself. Her body lurched into fight-or-flight mode, the latter impossible, the former her only option.

The German guard stepped forward. 'I can't let you do it. Leave her be.'

Cockney snapped his head around. His hand remained on Mia, but his fingers relaxed their grip. She stepped back and his hand fell away.

The two guards squared up, face to face, but the German one fingered the radio on his hip.

'Don't make me do this, my friend. Let's put it down to a lapse in judgement, keep it between the two of us.'

Cockney paused. His face screwed up but Mia knew he was done. He huffed, throwing the gown and pants on the wet floor.

'Get dressed,' he said, turning away, taking his position at the door once again, and this time his gaze fell on the wall, away from Mia.

Mia crouched to pick up the clothes. She glanced at the German guard, but he wouldn't look at her either. He was chewing on gum, staring straight ahead, recovering from the near-conflict.

Mia dressed and stood and let herself be escorted to her room. The German guard strapped her to the bed while Cockney waited by the door, his face like thunder.

Once Mia was secure on her back, both of them left. Mia saw Cockney glance her way, just for a second. His eyes were wild and violent, but he left before German, who gave the room the once-over before closing the door. It hissed and clicked behind him.

Mia stared at the closed door, wondering what would happen if she found herself alone with Cockney. She wondered if she'd have a chance to defend herself, a chance to escape.

Wishful thinking, and Mia knew it. She had no power here. Her power lay in the shadows, sneaking around, staying hidden, taking her prey when she needed it and disappearing when done. Here, she was a captive, an exhibition, an experiment.

But what would happen when the experiment ended?

CHAPTER FORTY

Mia's heart rate had dropped. The guards were gone. It felt late in the day. She hadn't slept for several hours. Her mind was clearer still. No more sedatives, she assumed.

The white of the ceiling was tiring on her eyes. She closed them, slowing her breathing, feeling her craving tickling at the edges. *Count your breaths, Mia. Slowly in, slowly out.*

The door clicked. *Please not the guards*, she thought. Keeping her eyes closed, she pretended to be asleep, hoping they'd leave. She heard footsteps and the squeak of one of the stools being dragged across the floor.

'Is she asleep?'

Not the guards. A doctor. Familiar.

Mia kept her eyes closed and her breathing slow. The voice belonged to one of the scarred doctor's colleagues. It wasn't the woman; if it had been, Mia would have spoken. Instead she let them think she was asleep. Perhaps they'd leave her in peace.

'Shall we wake her?' The same voice.

'No.'

The second voice caused the flash in Mia's mind. A lightning scar and then darkness. The scarred doctor who had treated her. It made Mia hold her breath for a second. She tensed, then forced herself to relax. If she was a monster, he wasn't far off one himself, but she didn't want to speak to him. Not now.

A few moments of near-silence passed. Mia heard feet shuffling around, heavy breathing and the huffing of the doctor.

'It's OK, Aubyn, they're not listening.'

'You sure?' The doctor called Aubyn sounded weak, scared. It worried Mia.

'They're shipping out.'

Mia risked a peek. Opening her eyes a fraction, she watched the backs of the two doctors. Both wore white coats and were hunched over the work surface by the wall, scribbling on to forms. She snapped them closed when Aubyn turned to look at her.

'And this one, Dr Tau? What do we do?'

Mia let out a hiss. Dr Tau. The scarred doctor's name. He wasn't in the black book, but here he was, the monster responsible for Mia's condition. He had a name. It almost made him human.

Dr Tau coughed. 'We do as we're told,' he said. His voice was weary. It was obvious he didn't agree with his orders, but it generated little sympathy in Mia. Given the opportunity, she'd take his life in an instant.

More scribbling. Mia's heart thumped in her ears.

'What are her latest oxy readings?'

'The chart says elevated nine hundred per cent. Stable.'

'That's incredible.'

'I agree.'

'But they're willing to risk losing her?'

'Yes.'

Mia swallowed. Their voices were loud in her ears and she struggled to comprehend. Her throat tickled, a result of the drying effect of trying to keep her breathing slow and sleep-like. She feared opening her eyes again, puzzled by what she heard yet desperate to hear more. They were talking about her. They knew about her addiction. They had caused it.

'When is she getting the new compound?'

'Today. Later.'

'But it doesn't work.'

Mia heard a sharp intake of breath. Dr Tau huffed, clearing his throat before responding.

'It'll work on the endorphin production.'

'But we haven't tested it. We don't know what it'll do to her.'

'She'll feel pain. Hers, other people's. She'll be in a world of pain.'

Feel pain. Hers? Mia's confusion deepened.

'But it won't stop the addiction. The latent withdrawal will continue. We haven't even begun to get that stabilised. She'll do what the others did to themselves. She'll be dead within twenty-four hours.'

'Stop telling me things I already know,' snapped Tau.

A snort from Aubyn. 'This doesn't bother you?'

Mia's breathing trembled, along with the rest of her body. She followed what they were saying but didn't understand it.

Tau's stool squeaked. Mia risked another look. He was off his stool and pulling together several papers from the worktop.

Tau sniffed. 'Let's not talk about it. Let's do our jobs. We give her the compound,' he said, 'get the results. Regardless of what happens, we've been ordered to hand her over. They'll deal with her.'

Aubyn also stood up. The two doctors were animated. Mia's eyes were wide open, watching these two discuss her fragile life. Should she speak? Scream? Would it make any difference?

'You can't let them have her,' said Aubyn. 'I know this is the frontier, Tau, I'm not an idiot. I know there are sacrifices. I've made enough of my own. But this young lady . . . We could save her, treat her. We haven't finished.'

Mia lifted her head from the pillow. She couldn't help it. This was it.

'Christ, you're naive, Aubyn,' hissed Tau. He turned away, silently gathering his papers. He made for the door. Aubyn gathered his own and followed.

'This was your plan?' said Aubyn.

'Don't be obscene,' said Tau. 'This was their plan. I follow orders, and so must you.'

Neither of the doctors even glanced at Mia as they exited the room. If they had, they'd have seen her trembling, hyperventilating as the panic shook her body. Only when the door closed and locked did she utter a sound – a long, slow sob as she contemplated the end of her life, and what that meant.

CHAPTER FORTY-ONE

Mia slept fitfully, drifting in and out of exhaustion, but now her head rushed with heat and speed. She tried to lunge upwards, only to jolt when the straps yanked her arms. Her shoulders cracked, the joints protesting at the stress.

'Nearly,' said a voice.

Mia's ears rang. High-pitched like tinnitus, it changed tone and faded.

'No,' said another voice. 'One more.'

Again, a shot of heat went through Mia. It jerked every muscle in her body and she strained against the straps. Her vision sparkled with stars and her hearing disappeared, to be replaced with a fresh high-pitched whine.

'That'll do it,' said the first voice.

Mia's heart thumped through her chest. She blinked rapidly, trying to focus on the shapes in front of her. They came into focus: two white blurs, two white-coated doctors. Dr Tau and his colleague, Aubyn.

Tau stood back. He held a metal-pronged device in each hand, each one attached to thick black cables snaking away to a black box on the worktop. The box hummed. Electric. What had he done to her?

Mia shook her head. The room spun. She felt sick and tilted her head to the right. Her stomach heaved and bile filled her mouth. She spat it on to the bed, but more followed. She heard the doctors swear and one of them threw a towel next to her face, another on the floor.

'Get the orderly in here,' said Tau. 'I can't work around that stench.'

Mia heard the click and hiss of the door. When it opened she heard more sounds – a mixture of an alarm and machinery. She heard shouts, people moving. The noises were new. Normally, it was all quiet when the door opened. Something was happening.

The door closed but opened again almost immediately.

'Well?'

Aubyn shook his head. 'It's just us,' he said. 'I think they're leaving.'

Tau huffed. He shuffled over and kicked the towel around the floor, mopping up the contents of Mia's stomach. She waited until he'd finished then spat, turning her head to face the ceiling. The bastards had electrocuted her, along with whatever else they were talking about. What had they pumped into her? Whatever it was, it seared through her mind like wildfire. Her muscles twitched, stabilising after the shock. Her broken arm ached. Her neck ached. She moved it but winced as a nerve caught. It hurt and she tried to stretch.

Wait.

Mia paused. Her heart fluttered. She moved her neck to the left, feeling the muscle pull with tension. Then to the right and . . .

The pain shot through her body, a jolt so pure Mia groaned.

She did it again, wrenching her neck, feeling the nerve catch. The wave of trauma flooded her brain, causing another gasp.

Pain, glorious pain.

Mia was confused. She paused. Her heart hammered so fast her chest hurt. It hurt. She willed it faster.

'Tachycardia,' said Aubyn. 'Jesus. It's over two hundred.'

'It'll calm down,' said Tau. Both doctors stood back from Mia, staring at the screens, checking their notes.

'If it doesn't, I'll need to—'

'No,' said Tau. 'She gets the N13 compound and the trigger. Nothing more.'

'But . . .'

Mia jerked. The familiar call of desire leached up, like a creature awakened from its slumber. It crept out of her stomach into her chest, hearing her heartbeat, feeling the morsel of pain in her neck. It wanted more, it wanted satisfying. It wanted feeding.

She monitored her symptoms. She usually had no choice but to wait – to battle the creature until she found her prey, someone in pain who could transfer the glorious sensation to her. But now . . . Mia had almost forgotten what it felt like. Almost.

She clicked her neck. Another fragment. Her addiction snapped it up, the pleasure centre of her brain lit up and the waves juddered through her body.

'More,' she whispered, snapping her neck as hard as she could. The pain and pleasure came together, like a couple in an intricate dance, like lovers wrapped around each other. No sooner had the pain registered than the pleasure smoothed the edges, shooting to her extremities and erogenous zones.

The outside of her neck tingled, as if an ice cube were being run up and down it. In contrast, her lips swelled, her tongue scorched and ready. The tingling danced over her stomach, all the way down, where it met a rush of heat flowing up the inside of her thighs. Mia writhed on the bed, straining at the straps, searching for more pain. For more pleasure.

'Jesus,' she heard Aubyn say, distant behind the white noise in her ears, the blood rushing as her heart pumped faster and faster, her blood pressure climbing to lethal highs.

Tau coughed. Mia opened her eyes, but the two figures were blurred. Her eyes burned and everything was tinged with red.

'Strap her head,' said Tau, and two pairs of hands grabbed her, pulling her neck straight as a cold strap was placed on her forehead. She heard a buckle being fastened and the two doctors stepped back.

Mia faded. The pain seeped away and the pleasure danced, teasing around before fading also. Mia tried to crack her neck, to start it again, but her head was fixed and she couldn't move even an inch.

The doctors shuffled forwards, tightening the straps on her arms and legs until she was rigid and immobile. No matter how hard she strained, her limbs and head were solid, fixed.

An instant chasm. Like a darkness behind her eyes, it grew larger, taking in her chest and gut. The pain was gone, and so was the pleasure. She knew this feeling well. Her comedown, her darkness. The calm after the storm, except that Mia wanted the storm.

'No,' she said, panting, to the ceiling. 'No. Let me. Please let me.'

Her heart rate remained high, but she could already feel it slowing. With her sensations curtailed, her body frantically tried to return to normal, her body churning out toxins, flushing itself clean.

'Please,' she whispered. To be given a taste of ecstasy and have it snatched away was a cruel experiment. But she realised, even through the haze, that this was what this was.

It was what she was.

'Why?' she asked.

Neither doctor answered. The smell of her vomit wafted over. A distant hum and clatter filtered in through the thick door.

'Are we complete?' Aubyn's voice. It was clearer as Mia crawled from the depths into the land of the living.

'We did what they asked,' said Tau.

Mia could feel the doctors' discomfort, even over the deep thud of her own body's protests. These men were unwilling and on the edge. Whatever they thought they were doing had turned sour, and the result in front of them was not what they wanted. Not what they'd dreamt of for their perverted scheme.

Mia opened her eyes. She stared at Tau and they locked eyes. Mia knew hers were full of anger and hate; what else could she feel for this man? His were full of frustration and latent arrogance. He'd failed, and Mia knew that part of him blamed her. Even now.

But Mia couldn't let this be the end. She needed closure and being taken from this place now wouldn't give it.

'Where are they?' she whispered, trying to make her eyes warmer, less hate-filled.

Tau frowned. Genuine surprise. 'Who?' he said.

The first time he'd spoken directly to her. His conscience finally starting to kick in? Mia swallowed. Did she want to hear it? Could she?

'My parents. The others in the car.' She never knew for sure if it had been her parents. She only had her dreams and visions. But as Tau's eyes widened she knew she was right. His face gave it away so clearly, and Mia read his expression of horror.

Tau shook his head. His colleague, Aubyn, frowned, darting his head towards him.

'What does she mean?' asked Aubyn.

'Nothing,' said Tau. 'She's delusional.'

'Please,' said Mia. She could threaten and scream, but it would do no good. All she wanted was honesty. What they'd done to her was clear, and her life was finished. She would leave here and die – they'd made that explicit. But she had to know. Through the darkness and the haze of her body trying to right itself, the longing for her family had never left her. 'Tell me what happened to them.'

Tau gathered up his things from the workbench, pushing papers into a brown folder then into a messenger bag. He switched off the ECG machine, nodding to his colleague. Aubyn slowly gathered his own things together, glancing at Tau and Mia but keeping silent.

Mia heard the rustling of papers and listened to the silence from the doctors. Her eyes welled up and the tears dripped down her cheeks. Pain of a different kind. The pain of torment and secrets.

'We're done.' Tau's voice. Aubyn nodded.

They paused at the door. Tau looked back. 'We were trying to help you,' he said. He frowned, some inner battle playing out. 'It wasn't supposed to be like this.'

The two doctors left. The door shut.

Mia was alone again.

CHAPTER FORTY-TWO

Mikey had warned him. *If you value your life*, he'd said. Hartley had warned him too, for other reasons, but they amounted to the same thing: stay away.

Alex didn't doubt for one moment that both had been serious, but if they knew him, they'd know he'd follow his gut and not let this go. This case wasn't about Mia's killing spree, grotesque and horrific as it was. This case was about far more. The doctors and the organisation behind Nova were the real prize, and that should have been their focus. If only he could have convinced them.

This was about the woman in black.

Alex racked his brains, trying to figure out how he knew her. A case? A patient? An ex-colleague? Alex had worked across a diverse field, meeting many hundreds of professionals during his clinical tenure. But he'd remember someone like her, with those eyes so deep they'd swallow you whole and leave you gasping for air. Alex had made a habit of remembering beautiful women during his early days. His marriage breakdown could attest to it and his ever-present guilt about Grace and Katie was a constant reminder. If that woman and Alex had ever worked together, Alex would know her name at the very least.

But the woman was a criminal and her business was serious organised crime. Alex's patients had never come close.

She'd used his first name. It had rolled softly off her tongue, familiar and warm. She knew him and he knew her, but his memory wouldn't cooperate. Each time he pictured her face his thoughts became muddled. He heard her voice, but the sounds twisted and changed in tone and tempo until he couldn't recall what she sounded like, or even the pitch of her voice.

His left hand was shaking. He looked at it, making a fist. How long had it been since his last Xanax? Too long. His body knew it and his mind would soon catch up. He clenched both hands into fists a few times then released them. Get the blood pumping until the shaking stopped. His jacket was gone and so was his wallet. His trouser pockets were empty. No Xanax, no quick fix. He prayed he wouldn't be here long enough to suffer the consequences. Benzo withdrawal was unpleasant and debilitating. It was something he'd promised he'd put himself through, but not today. Not under these conditions.

He picked up his phone from where the Russian man had left it on the desk. The screen flashed on but couldn't find a signal. He tried 999, but nothing. Were they intentionally jamming radio signals? He tucked the phone into his pocket.

Alex realised he'd remained seated for a long time after his two captors disappeared. Unrestrained, he risked standing, stretching his arms and legs, examining the small room again. Apart from the single chair and desk, the walls were blank white except for the one composed of mirrored glass. He glanced at it, hunting for a recording device or a camera. There was neither on this side, so he stepped up to the glass and tried to peer through.

If it was one-way glass, the type seen in police interrogation rooms and, from Alex's experience, mental health assessment centres, he might catch a glimpse of something on the other side. All it took was a glimmer of light to spoil the privacy. He let his eyes relax, cupping them with his hands for several seconds, looking left and right.

Nothing. The room beyond was in total darkness. Whether or not it contained anybody was impossible to tell. Alex turned his head and placed his ear against the glass, realising how absurd he'd look but not caring much. He'd compartmentalised the kidnapping and his curiosity was returning. The woman, whoever she was, didn't want him dead and didn't even consider him dangerous enough to restrain.

He heard nothing, which told him nothing.

He checked the door. Locked and solid. The handle didn't move and there was no keyhole on the inside. Putting his ear to the door, he heard a faint thud of footsteps and distant machinery. Diesel engines, perhaps. Lorries?

Alex had to assume he was still on the industrial estate where they'd captured him. They'd seen him snooping around and brought him inside. He could only guess at which building, but it didn't matter either way. He only had one choice to make: whether to sit and wait or try and find his own way out.

He paused, judging the risk. How long would he have to be missing before somebody raised the alarm? A day? Two days? He'd already stood Laurie up, but she might just shrug it off. She didn't seem the type to chase men.

Grace would expect to hear from him at least once a week, but she'd left him a message saying she was going away for four days with Katie – a pampering retreat in Surrey. He texted Katie most days, but there were plenty of occasions when work had kept him distracted and he hadn't been able to.

Hartley would expect him to check in, but she'd only just told him to back off. It might be a week before she called.

Living alone sucked. Alex realised that several days could pass without a major alert. That ruled out rescue, leaving him with his original options: wait or force the issue.

Waiting would be safer, but Alex realised his choice had already been made by the growing frustration in his gut, present even before he had entered the industrial estate. The strange woman had distracted him, intrigued and confused him, but now his frustration was turning to anger. He'd been here before, with his father and the arrogant criminals who thought nothing of human experimentation and the suffering they inflicted. These pharmaceutical companies and the people working on university research programmes considered themselves gods, playing games with their subjects, manipulating and subjecting innocent people to the bizarre and the grotesque. They concocted their hypotheses and devised their experiments knowing full well that the ethics of modern medicine would never allow it. So they ignored ethics and they ignored the law. They ran their experiments with reckless abandon, leaving death and suffering in their wake, leaving people like Hartley and Laurie and Alex to pick up the pieces. These people called themselves doctors but in reality they were an abomination. They must be stopped.

Alex couldn't wait.

Putting his fists against the door, he thumped repeatedly.

'Hello?' he shouted at the top of his voice, the sound echoing in the confines of the room.

'Hello?' He paused, then called and hammered for a minute or more, until his fists started to hurt and his throat was sore. He was about to stop when the door shuddered. He heard the lock click and it hissed open. Alex stepped back, not wanting to appear threatening.

The door opened a fraction. A man's face appeared. He was dressed in white – a lab tech.

'Who are you?' said the tech.

The question was significant. It had been a gamble on Alex's part, and if a guard had appeared, he might have been shackled again to the chair. But Alex suspected that his presence here was not well known. Given the size of the complex, there would be hundreds of staff, and as with most fronts for serious crime, the majority wouldn't even know the true purpose of the business. Alex had wagered that the first person to open the door wouldn't know who he was. He was right.

'I need to make a call,' said Alex. 'My phone is—'

Another person barged into the room. Another white-coated clinician. He pulled the first man away, grabbing him by the arm, eyeing Alex with suspicion. He looked older, with grey hair and long stubble. He wore a stethoscope around his neck.

'Why did you open this door?' He spoke to the bewildered-looking lab technician, his face flustered.

'I heard thumping,' said the tech, trembling. 'I thought somebody was stuck in here. I'm helping with the asset move. We've been told that all N-class assets are to be loaded within the hour. I was assigned over here with temporary clearance.'

The technician fumbled with his ID badge and produced it. The doctor examined it with a scowl.

'Then go and do your job,' he snapped. 'This is a secure area, for Christ's sake. Behave like a fucking professional.'

The technician nodded frantically and hurried out of the door. The doctor remained for a few moments. He cast his eyes around the room, shaking his head. His eyes narrowed at Alex as he backed away out of the room. The door closed and the lock fell into place.

Alex found his heart thumping after the brief encounter. He tempered his anger. He'd failed, but the contact had been useful. They were moving everything out of this place in a hurry. People or materials? And why? Did they know he was working with the police? Had Alex's appearance here spooked them enough to leave? It sounded chaotic out there.

Alex paused, slowing his breathing. He could try again, thump and shout. But he had a feeling that the next time the door opened the person wouldn't be quite so friendly. Alex wondered if the doctor would report the incident and have Security come back again.

He turned to examine the mirrored wall – something he'd noticed earlier on the bottom part of the mirror. He crouched, checking the glass. The right-hand corner was clear, smudged but intact. The left-hand corner, however, had the beginnings of a hairline crack, perhaps from careless manufacture or from when it had been fitted, which had widened to create a weak spot. It was unlikely ever to be a problem, judging by the steel chair bolted to the floor and the leather straps. Most occupants of this room would never get near the mirror.

Alex tapped the crack with his finger. It felt as solid as the rest of the glass. He bunched his fist, giving it a firm thump. He thought he heard the slightest of scratching noises above the thump, like two edges crunching.

He stood up. He had a lot to lose. His life, for one thing, but he still didn't think it would come to that. He had been put here to keep him out of the way. The woman said he'd caused trouble, but she also said he was harmless. His punishment might depend on whether that trouble could be cured, but Alex was convinced he didn't want to wait and find out.

He braced himself against the table, lifted his foot and stamped at an angle into the glass. The hairline crack shot up a foot or so, widening, and the corner of the glass crumbled. Alex paused, listening. If there was anyone in the room behind, they'd have taken action by now. They'd be restraining him, sedating him, whatever other methods they might have.

But nothing.

He stomped again. The crack widened further and a piece of glass the size of a side plate shattered. He kicked it through with the toe of his shoe, wincing as the fine leather of his brogue scratched and ripped. If he lived through this, he'd need a new pair of Barker's.

It took him five minutes to kick out a hole big enough to crawl through. The glass was safety rated and didn't break all in one. It shattered and splintered into manageable chunks. He tried to kick as many as possible out of the way before crouching on to the floor.

The hole let through enough light to see into the observation room. Hardly larger than the room he'd left, it held a few chairs and a table, a video camera on a tripod and a directional microphone. Alex stood, checking the camera. It was on, but on standby, not recording. He left the light off and went to the door, placing his hand gently on the handle. Leaning in, he placed his ear against the cold surface. He thought he could still hear footsteps, but this door, like the other, was thick and solid. He'd have to risk it.

The handle turned and Alex breathed a small sigh of relief mixed with a fresh wave of anxiety as he stepped out into the corridor.

The corridor was white, empty and smelled of disinfectant. It stretched for fifty yards or so before disappearing through opaque glass doors. Familiar, like a clinical ward, a hospital or testing facility. He assumed the latter. Distant hums of machinery and a klaxon came from his left. He heard a speaker, a voice barking orders.

Overhead, red lights flashed at three-second intervals. Alarms? The red lights bathed everything in a pinkish glow for a fraction of a second before disappearing. The effect was one of urgency and danger.

How long until somebody came through those doors and saw him? He had no way of fighting and no easy story to tell. He could run and he could hide, but he needed to get moving.

He checked his phone. Still no signal, so Alex turned right and headed towards the glass doors. He found himself keeping in tight against the wall, running his fingers across each door. He'd counted five so far. The doors were metal-framed but had traditional turn locks on the outside. He'd been kept in one of them. Who or what were in the others?

He stopped at one, leaning in to listen. He heard nothing and rested his hand on the lock. If he could escape this place, he could call Hartley and the police would descend. At least, that's what he hoped. Hartley couldn't ignore a kidnap attempt, even if she had told him to stay away. But how long would they take, and would the people here manage to cover up what they were doing before they arrived?

The doctor had said they were moving assets within the hour. Moving them where? A fleet of trucks flowing out of the industrial estate could easily get lost in among the traffic. The police would scream past them without a second look. Alex doubted the lorries had *Nova* stamped across the side of them. More likely, they'd be using nondescript transport designed to blend in.

As Laurie kept saying, evidence was what they needed. Perhaps the kidnap of Alex would stick as a charge; perhaps it wouldn't. With the organisation's word against his, they could argue a security incident and that they had been keeping Alex restrained until they gathered more information. They could argue a chemical leak and say he was kept in a locked room for his own safety. As it stood, he had precious little on this place other than his presence here.

He needed evidence of their activities.

He unlocked the door and slipped through into the dark room. Flicking the light switch by the door, he was presented with an empty hospital bed and a range of standard equipment you might find in any NHS ward. The room, like his own, was windowless, but without the mirrored wall. The workbench to the side was clean and uncluttered. Alex opened the drawers and checked the cupboards, but they were empty.

Evidence of a sick bay? Evidence of a post-treatment room? Perhaps. It wasn't enough.

Alex exited and kept walking. The sound of machinery grew louder and he paused, picking the next room at random, turning the lock and entering.

The same, except this time the bed had sheets on it. They were ruffled, stained in places with dark red and brown. Apart from that, the room was empty. Alex once again checked the cupboards and drawers. Not a single piece of paper. No documentation, nothing to indicate who had been in this room and why.

He peered at the sheets without touching them, aware he was putting himself at risk. A criminal pharma company might be experimenting or shipping toxic or biohazardous materials. If that was blood, it could be infected with Christ knows what.

He backed away and exited the room.

Reaching the end of the corridor, Alex approached the glass doors, which hissed open in front of him. He peered left and right. To the left, two white-coated women hunched over a hospital bed. They were some distance away, so Alex couldn't see what they were doing, but the bed was occupied, the prone body covered with sheets. A drip hung above the bed, an ECG machine off the side.

Alex stepped back, out of sight, his heart hammering. A patient. An experiment? Was this one of the assets they were moving? He risked another peek. That was evidence right there, but he was dismayed to see a third person enter the corridor from a side room. A largish man in grey coveralls. He grabbed the end of the bed, pulling it along, away from Alex. The bed, the patient and the three persons disappeared through another set of glass doors.

Alex gave them thirty seconds before following. He crept along, conscious of his hard soles tapping on the lino floor, echoing off the walls. His eyes darted to the strip lighting and back to the endless doors – all identical: white, metal-framed with locks on the outside. The atmosphere unsettled him – his neck hairs stood on end as he realised why. During his clinical training he had spent several months in a secure psychiatric facility. Distinctly different from a normal hospital, the wards were quieter and more compartmentalised, with scores of secure rooms with metal doors, all locked from the outside. This place resembled one of those, down to the hardened security personnel and white-coated clinicians.

A psychiatric testing ward, in the middle of an east London industrial estate.

Alex tried another door. The room was identical to the others. Empty. No sheets. He tried another, then another. The next five looked as if they had been recently occupied, with dirty sheets ruffled, some on the floor. It disturbed him to see that three of the five beds had heavy restraints hanging at the sides. Worn-looking brown leather straps, including some for the head and torso. He shivered again. Evidence that this place was being used for live patient research. Without the proper licence and regulations, that was illegal enough to get it shut down.

He kept walking. He stumbled across two more doctors, both looking stressed, hurrying towards what Alex guessed was the exit, where the humming was loudest and the klaxon alarm could be heard.

The clock was ticking on this place; Alex could feel it. As soon as they realised he'd escaped, he had no doubt that the security protocol would kick in and he would be trapped inside.

One more door, he thought, then he'd have to try and find the exit, evidence or not.

He picked the last one on the corridor. The lock clicked open and the door hissed as he pushed it open. A new smell hit his nostrils in this one. Musty, sweaty. A very human smell. An occupied room.

Alex stared at the bed and held his breath as his heart jumped through his chest. A young woman lay there, her head, legs, arms and torso strapped down so she couldn't move. Her eyes were open, blinking up at the ceiling.

Mia Anastos.

CHAPTER
FORTY-THREE

Mia heard the door open. This was it. She didn't try to strain to see who it was. They were coming for her, and her life was over. They'd said so. Would they put her to sleep or let her experience it all? It would be karma, she guessed, given how many lives she'd taken. Strap the monster up and let it suffer. That wouldn't be unfair. Nothing was fair in Mia's world, and she knew what she was.

How much pain would there be?

How many ways were there of killing a human? Mia knew many and knew some were far quicker than others. It depended on your goal. She saw regret in Dr Tau, but his innate arrogance never left him. He still believed he was right, that what they were aiming for was worth it. It was a shame Mia had turned out this way, but it wouldn't stop them. Would Tau watch to the end?

She heard a gasp. The door closed and footsteps approached the bed. Hard soles, not like the others. Was the woman back? Her Russian companion? Had they changed their minds?

The face leaning over hers was red, flustered and instantly recognisable. The eyes darted in horror and surprise. He whispered to her.

'Mia,' he said.

Dr Madison, she thought.

So he was involved. She'd read him wrong. At the hospital she could have sworn he was innocent, that he wanted to help her. Mia was never wrong about such things and the doubt hit her hard. Was he the executioner?

But his eyes confused her yet again. They spoke of empathy and innocence. He looked stressed and anxious, but not like Dr Tau. Dr Madison's body language was more immediate, hurried. Mia closed her eyes, her thoughts in disarray.

'Mia,' he said again, 'my name is Alex.'

Why tell me his name? she thought. Why should she care, if she had minutes or hours to live? Better to think of other things – her parents, her mum's smile. What pleasant memories could Mia make surface that would distract her until the end?

'Can you walk?'

The strap loosened around her head. The torso strap followed. Relief washed over her as her ankles were unshackled, the blood flowing beneath her skin. Her feet itched with heat.

Why did it matter if she could walk?

'If I let you go, will you try to hurt me?'

Mia's eyes snapped open. She turned her head, shifting on the bed to get a better look at Alex Madison.

What she saw wasn't right. His clothes were messy and creased, his shirt untucked and his trousers grubby, a rip near the bottom near his shoe, which was scuffed and damaged. His face and hair were dirty and sweaty.

Mia peered closer. She sniffed. His right foot ached. Minor but noticeable. But Alex's real trauma was hidden, mental and suppressed. He suffered inside; she could smell it on his breath. Not the raw pain

Mia desired but a deeper, more complicated set of emotions and hurt. This man was troubled, and he was speaking the truth.

'I won't hurt you.' Mia realised she meant it. Her first conclusion held – this man was on her side. Every part of his physical presence screamed it, and his eyes were the final confirmation.

Alex paused before reaching over and undoing the wrist straps. Mia waited for a moment before sitting, swinging her legs across the bed. Alex flinched but held his ground.

'I'm also a captive,' he said. 'I escaped my room.' He glanced at the walls and the door.

'I doubt we have long,' he said, peering at the huge picture of the storm on the wall. Mia jumped off the bed. Her feet were unsteady, shuffling on the floor.

'Why?' she said.

'Why what?'

'You're a captive here. Why? Do you suffer from . . .?'

She watched his expression. 'No,' he said, 'I'm not like you. I work with the police.'

Mia froze. Would she be trading one captor for another? If that was the choice, which was it to be? The people in this place had made their intentions clear. Death was the likely outcome. What would the police offer? Not death, certainly, but would incarceration be better or worse?

'You're arresting me?'

Mia knew she could overpower this man if she needed to. He was physically able and well proportioned. If Mia was so inclined, he'd be quite attractive. But he wasn't strong or athletic. Not a fighting man.

He shook his head. 'No,' he said. He appeared to think about this, frowning, his eyes darting around the room. 'I don't think that's the right thing,' he said, almost to himself. It puzzled Mia. If he was working for the police, why didn't he want her arrested?

'Then what?'

Alex Madison stared at her. 'I need to get you away from here,' he said, 'then I need to think.'

'Away where?'

'I don't know,' he said. 'Do you know this place? How to get out?'

Mia shook her head. 'I think we're at 121 Pickard Street,' she offered. 'Marshall's industrial estate in east London.' She'd memorised the address from the black book.

'One twenty-one?' said Alex. 'I only had the street name. I didn't see the numbers.'

'You think we're still there?'

Alex shrugged. 'I hope so,' he said.

Mia watched Alex. He withdrew into himself, pacing the small room, checking the door, even though there was no way of locking or unlocking it from the inside. Should she leave and take her chances? If she could get out of the building, she could go back to her warehouse, hide away until the heat died down, go back to normal . . .

The pain.

There was no normal, was there? The pain. The thought of it caused Mia's eyelids to flutter. She remembered her experience on the bed. Her sore neck. The nerve pain and the pleasure that followed.

Her heart rate increased. Her body liked what her mind was doing. The thoughts triggering neurons triggering hormones triggering action. A chain reaction, unstoppable once it had started, like lighting some touchpaper. Stand back or get burned – the flash would be the last thing her victim ever saw.

Resist. Every fibre in her body screamed at her to resist. There would be time for pain – glorious, sensual pain – but not now. These precious minutes should be used for action of another kind. Escaping this place must be her priority. Giving in to her desires could wait. It must wait.

She walked to the door and opened it. Alex flinched again, darting behind her as she peered into the corridor.

'Nobody here,' she said. The faint alarms she'd heard while lying in the bed were more urgent, clearer and nearer. The corridor smelled fresh compared to the small room. She realised her odour was strong. It wasn't long since she'd showered, but since then rivers of sweat and tears had flowed.

'To the right,' said Alex. 'Let's go.'

Exit, and trust this man. Mia's mind was set, with one important caveat. If she lived to escape, she didn't intend to hand herself over to the police. Alex Madison might offer to help, but Mia knew she could take better care of herself than any prison.

For now, Alex was an ally. Once they were out, perhaps not.

Mia led the way. Alex seemed to jump at every sound. She sympathised, to a limited extent. He didn't have her experience of creeping along corridors like this, keeping to the shadows, listening for the telltale sounds of footsteps and breathing in the dark. Mia took several large strides before stopping, pausing, listening to the building. She waited for the sounds to become familiar and rhythmic. The klaxon could be ignored. The machinery too. Diesel engines roared, several individual ones revving at different rates. It was the human sounds she needed to listen for. They were varied, muffled by speakers and distorted by distance.

This part of the building was maze-like, the corridors in a grid. But it was quiet, and Mia saw the signs – it had been deserted. Hospital trolleys were parked against the wall, but scattered, out of line. She saw laptops, powered on, lids half closed. Alex kept pausing, checking the laptop screens, huffing when he didn't find what he wanted.

Mia raced through another set of doors and stopped. This corridor was different from the others. On the left, the wall was white and unbroken, stretching towards a marked fire exit. On the right, however, was a glass observation window running the full length. A single door was positioned halfway along.

Mia put her hands against the glass and stared into what looked like a hospital ward. There were four beds in the ward, two of them empty. The third and fourth in the row were occupied. Between the beds stood a woman in a white coat. She was staring at a tablet, swiping at the screen.

The red lights in the ceiling continued to flash. Mia determined that they switched on at the same time as the klaxon sounded and ignored them. The alarm was sounding, but not for them. The building was frantic for some other reason.

She walked closer to the occupied beds, running her hands along the glass, tracing it with her fingers. The doctor was facing the other way.

'The fire exit,' said Alex, behind her. 'Let's go.'

Mia was about to turn when she saw the face of one of the patients. A young man with bushy blond hair and an ashen face turned his head towards the glass. He was in pain.

Mia sagged against the glass, leaning her forehead into it with a dull thump. She felt the sensation – her own pain, a quick shock through her head.

The man in the bed gulped and opened his mouth to speak. Mia saw his eyes and watched his body convulse with a full body wave of agony. His face contorted and his head snapped back on to the bed.

Mia's knees wobbled as the tingling crept up her legs. She needed to see him, to get closer. She needed to touch him and caress him, push him and find the source of the pain. It was pure and wonderful.

'Mia.' Alex's voice broke her reverie, but it was short-lived.

'They're in pain,' she said, unable to keep her smile in check. 'Him, over there. He needs . . . I need him. Let me see him.'

'Mia.' Alex placed his hand on her shoulder and she snapped around, grabbing his fingers. They crunched under her grip and he yelped. His pain shot up his wrists before he wriggled free. He backed away, putting his hands out in front of him. She hadn't hurt him badly. She didn't want to.

Mia knew she was sinking. She stared at Alex and shook her head. This was wrong, all wrong, but she couldn't help it. The waves hit her and the surge of desire engulfed every limb. She turned to the door and kicked it open.

The doctor spun around on her feet. Her eyes widened in fear and darted to the wall. Mia saw a red alarm button above every bed. The doctor lunged for one but Mia was faster. She leapt at the woman, planting her fist into her chin with all her weight. The female doctor collapsed against an ECG machine, sending it clattering on to the floor. A hospital trolley overturned to her left, scattering scalpels and other steel implements. Out cold, the doctor remained prone on the tiled floor. Mia watched her for a second then crouched to pick up one of the scalpels. She held it tight, blade outwards. If the doctor woke, it would be her life. Better to stay down and stay asleep.

The patient angled his head towards her. Their eyes met and she saw understanding and acceptance. This man was dying. His pain was symptomatic of a deeper trauma. Mia pulled away the sheets and saw that the man's chest had recently been opened and stitched back up again. A cruel fold of skin ran from his neck to his solar plexus. His entire ribcage had been cracked open and his torso damaged beyond repair.

'What did they do to you?' she whispered, watching his breathing. His lungs struggled; the left one seemed to have collapsed. His gut was distended and his skin clammy. Sepsis was setting in. Easily remedied in a facility like this, but they'd chosen not to. Why?

Mia's hand hovered above his abdomen. His pain attacked her senses, like the finest meal placed in front of a starving mouth. She inhaled, twirling the flavour around her tongue, filling her lungs with his agony.

'Mia, please.'

Alex Madison had entered the glass room behind her. Distracted, Mia hadn't seen him approach. She spun around, her arm hitting the bed as she did so. The scalpel in her hand jabbed inwards to her thigh and the sharp blade passed through her gown, digging deep into her skin.

She looked down. Pulling the scalpel out of her leg, she watched the blood darken the fabric. A small cut and clean, yet it created an alien sensation. A sensation rippling up her leg, causing her to shiver.

Pain. Small – a flutter, no more. But pain.

Mia looked at the scalpel. Its fine blade was clean, a few drops of blood blemishing the steel. She lifted it up, her mind whirring, spinning out of control. The man next to her groaned. His chest heaved as mucus became dislodged and caused his lungs to attempt to clear themselves.

Mia felt his pain, then she felt her own.

She pushed the blade back into her leg, below the other cut. A sharp scratch followed by a thundering ache. Her eyes watered at the pain and her jaw clenched.

Her pleasure centre went into overdrive.

Mia twisted the scalpel. The pain was intense, excruciating. She cried out, staggering back towards the wall. The blood gushed on to her hand over the handle of the knife as the rush of pleasure screamed through her nerve endings. Her body tingled and her vision sharpened, the colours deepening in contrast. Her ears popped and a rush of sounds hit them; she could hear her own heartbeat and that of the patient in the bed. His laboured breathing was like a howling wind, her own like the hurricane that followed.

Mia stabbed again. She pulled the knife out and moved it to her torso. The lower gut hurt – it always hurt in others. Mia needed to see how much it hurt on her own body.

The scalpel stabbed and twisted. She pulled it out and repeated. Her high grew steadily, but she had a long way to go. Her arms were next. Her fingers. She jammed the tip of the scalpel under the nail of the index finger on her left hand and twisted it away, laughing and screaming at the same time.

She was vaguely aware of the blood. Her hand was slippery and so was her body. Looking down, her clothes were stained deep red. The white tiled floor was growing red as the blood seeped out of her many cuts.

Still she continued.

Her vision blurred as she reached the apex of her high. In a frenzy, stabbing repeatedly, she saw Alex dancing around, trying to get near her. Whenever he got close she swiped at him, stabbing the blade towards his face. Specks of blood flew off her arm and hand, spraying the doctor's white coat. He was shouting, screaming at her, but she couldn't make out the words. Mia was lost in her high.

This was beyond the pleasure of others. This was her own pain, and it was exquisite. Twenty wounds. Twenty-one. With each, the pain increased and so did the pleasure. A twisted dance of complementary opposites. Yin and yang so perfectly entwined they created a perfect balance of euphoria. Mia panted, closing her eyes, groaning at the effect.

Dizziness. To be expected, of course, but this was faster and more disturbing than her normal highs. She shivered. Why would she feel cold? The building was hot; hospital wards were always warm.

Vertigo and chills swamped her body. As if being bathed in ice on a spinning top, Mia sank to her knees, slipping on the floor as she fell. The blood coated everything. Her eyes were red.

The blood. Of course.

The blood is what kept her warm.

She stared down at her body. The blood pumped out of it. Her blood. How could she have stopped it?

The red faded to black. Mia's high was complete. She closed her eyes. A dull, pleasurable thud welcomed her head to the floor.

CHAPTER FORTY-FOUR

The red from the overhead lights flashed against Mia's skin. It oozed with blood, creating a horrifying vision before Alex. She was alive, but unconscious. On initial inspection, he didn't think it was loss of blood, but as he put his hands on her, he realised how deep some of the wounds went. One in particular, on her thigh, seemed to pulse with blood. A nicked artery. He looked around, finding a roll of tape on the floor where the hospital trolley had overturned. He grabbed it and tore off a few strips, trying in vain to stick them over the bleeding wound. It was no use, so he grabbed the roll and wound it round her leg three or four times. The tape held against the wound, but he'd bought time, nothing more.

He had managed to push his anxiety deep down while he focused on Mia's frenzy, but now it lurched up and he found himself trembling. 'What have you done?' he whispered, holding her limp body. His hands were slippery with her blood, his shirt covered and his trousers soaked.

Alex was on the verge of panic. He could leave her. She was a killer and this is what karma would demand. This is what the public would demand, and the police wouldn't protest too hard.

But as he stared at her young face his heart tugged with fury. This wasn't her fault. This poor girl had been transformed into a monster and couldn't be left to die. Alex owed her more. He'd failed to catch her, then failed to rescue her. He couldn't let his third and last failure be her death.

'Mia,' he whispered. 'Please wake up, Mia.'

She remained unconscious, breathing slowly. Her eyelids fluttered. Alex rested her against the side of the bed. It wobbled and the occupant groaned, but his voice was weaker than before and Alex didn't have time to check him. He would be a casualty of this battle. Alex had other priorities.

He crouched, searching the room. What did he need? He crawled to the unconscious doctor and checked her pulse. It was strong, but the crack on the jaw had rattled her enough to keep her under. Alex rummaged through her pockets but found nothing except a mobile phone. It was half charged, locked but had full network signal. He dropped it and pulled his own phone out. Full signal too. He must be out of range of whatever jamming technology they'd been using.

He paused for a second, thinking through his next move. He'd considered it from the moment he saw Mia strapped to the bed. He'd thought about it from the day Laurie had made it clear what would happen when they caught their killer. It might not be the right move, but Alex knew he would do it anyway.

He looked up the correct number and went to hit the dial button.

'Put the phone down, Alex.'

Alex froze, his thumb hovering over the screen. He turned in his crouched position to see the dark-haired woman at the doorway. She held a small pistol pointed at his chest. Behind her stood the same bald man who'd been with her before, plus two guards, all blocking his exit.

The woman tilted her head, peering at Mia propped against the bed, bleeding on to the floor.

Alex kept his hand on the phone but didn't touch the screen. He held it up in surrender. Would she shoot? She didn't have the eyes of a killer, Alex thought he could tell that much. She held the gun but there was hesitation in her stance. She was tense, indecisive. Alex saw her frown as she took in Mia's condition.

'Where are you taking her?' asked the woman.

'Hospital,' said Alex. 'She needs help.'

The woman raised her eyebrows. 'Apart from stating the obvious. Why would you take her away? She can only be treated by us.'

Alex dropped his hands to his side. The gun remained trained on him.

'But you're not keeping her . . . here. And you're not taking her.' Alex nodded past her, to the corridor still flashing with red lights. 'You're leaving.'

The heavyset man leaned in, whispering a few words. 'The police,' he said, 'they are at Compound E. We need to get you out of here.'

The woman nodded but didn't move. She tore her eyes off Mia and stared at Alex. 'You think putting her in police custody will help her?'

Alex shook his head. He didn't know how to answer. 'She's killed so many,' he said. 'What would you expect me to do?'

To his surprise, the woman laughed. 'Expect from you? I have no idea. You always were a little unpredictable.'

Alex felt hot. Her laugh triggered a vivid memory. He saw himself on the floor of an abandoned building, cradling his daughter, Katie, promising it was over; promising her that Dad had found her and it would all be OK. He smelled the brick dust and the plaster, the stale air and the cold breeze whistling up the stairwell.

It was the memory of Victor Lazar's final stand, when he took Alex's daughter and held a knife to her throat. Victor had held Alex within his control, total and unwavering, and was on the verge of killing them both, father and daughter, in revenge for his own suffering.

And then Victor had disappeared and Katie was in Alex's arms.

'I'll help her,' said Alex. 'That's what I intend to do. If you let me go.'

The woman stared through him. Her eyes were deep and Alex was losing himself in them. She sighed, tilting her head one way then the other.

'You don't remember me, Alex,' she said, 'but I remember you. It was intentional, the way it had to be. Perhaps one day I'll explain, but that day has not yet come.'

The man hissed into her ear.

The gun lowered. The woman spat a few words at her companion, who backed away, disappearing out of sight towards the rooms and the corridors Alex had just escaped from.

'I must leave,' she said, lowering the gun. 'This place is in chaos – because of you.'

Alex swallowed. What was her game?

'You brought me here,' he countered. 'I didn't ask for it.'

'Oh, but you did,' she said, her tone losing its warmth for an instant. 'Because you were warned away and you didn't listen. Your leash is too long, Alex.'

Alex paused. His mind raced. He stared and she met his gaze. They locked eyes for an age, unable to break away. Alex's breathing become shallow and his heart rate increased. He was on the edge, his anxiety peaking. She seemed to draw it up, pulling his panic to the surface.

He felt suspended in time, held by her in the moment. She barely moved, only her chest expanding and contracting with each breath. Alex felt his own breathing falling in rhythm, mirroring her, controlled by her.

And then, in an instant, she let him go. Alex's shoulders fell like a marionette dropped by its puppeteer.

Her expression changed. She looked deep in thought, casting her eyes on Mia then cocking her head, listening to the background hum of increasing mayhem. She made her decision quickly.

'Take her,' she said. 'The fire escape.' She gestured behind her. 'Turn right and follow the path along the side of the building. At the very end, go left and you'll find a gate in the chain-link fence.' She threw Alex a swipe card on a lanyard. 'Use that to open the fire escape and the gate.'

Alex bent to retrieve it. He wanted to speak, to say something. Not thank her, but ask her why. A thousand questions presented themselves and he stumbled over his words, trying to find the first.

'Goodbye, Alex,' she said, 'or, perhaps, *au revoir.*'

The woman turned and headed back into the building.

'Wait!' shouted Alex. She paused.

'What's your name?' he said, hoping it would trigger his memory.

Again the woman laughed. 'That depends,' she said. 'But I like Talia.'

Her laugh faded and she turned away, striding after her colleague. She didn't glance back, leaving Alex alone in the room with Mia bleeding on the floor and two dying patients in their beds.

Alex didn't pause this time. He shoved his phone and the swipe card into his pocket and knelt, heaving Mia over his shoulder, ignoring the blood and the stench of her body. With some difficulty, he stood, heading to the fire exit doors, blindly trusting the word of the woman who'd kidnapped him and held a gun to his chest.

Talia. A woman he knew yet had no memory of. Another part of the puzzle, but one he'd have to leave for another day. Today, he had to save Mia Anastos and figure out his next move. He had a plan to put into action, and by the increasing wail of the alarms, very little time to do it.

CHAPTER
FORTY-FIVE

The woman who called herself Talia was true to her word. Alex didn't know why she'd let him go or helped him, but he didn't question it. Not today.

The path led Alex to a razor-topped fence sheltered behind a short, squat brick building. The swipe card opened the gate and he stepped through, still carrying Mia. The complex behind him rang with the sound of alarms. Diesel engines gunned and he could hear gearboxes crunching as lorries started up.

Beyond the alarms came the welcoming sound of sirens. Police? It had to be. They were near, although the pitch was changing – the cars were still moving and distant.

Compound E, the Russian man had said. A different part of the estate? How would the police know where to go?

Alex struggled with Mia across a rough patch of scrubland. The grass was thick and within it lay hidden rubble and other detritus. Alex stumbled several times. Mia fell and he caught her. Checking her pulse, he forced her back on to his shoulder and pushed on.

Glancing around, Alex realised they must be on waste ground on the other side of the complex, a long way from the road where he'd been captured. Behind him lay a row of dark buildings, but the appearance to the rear was disordered, not the clean lines that the facades presented to the road. The buildings looked even larger from here, intimidating in their height and cold exterior.

He couldn't see far in any direction. Trees to the left and high corrugated-metal fences surrounding low brick structures to the right. The police sirens still screamed in the wind but they were fading. How big was this estate? Were the sirens even for him?

Alex found a path between two high fences. He wasn't sure how much longer he could carry Mia, but if he didn't hurry she'd be dead and all of this would be wasted effort. Nova was packing up and anything of value might be gone soon.

The alley continued for some distance until Alex found himself at the kerb to a different road in the estate, this one flanked by more familiar industrial units, their logos standing proud at each entrance, customers and workers milling around the parking lots. The razor wire gave way to low fences with wires strung between wooden posts. The Nova buildings seemed distant and foreign. How easily they hid among the rest.

Alex paused, stepping back into the alley, out of sight. He lay Mia against the fence and pulled out his phone.

Mikey answered on the third ring.

'Alex?'

'Listen, Mikey. I need a huge favour.'

Mikey found them without too much trouble. Alex relayed the names of all the businesses he could see and Mikey plugged them into his satnav. He arrived in less than thirty minutes. Alex stayed hidden until he saw Mikey's BMW approaching. He jumped out of the alley to meet him.

'Shit, man,' said Mikey as Alex emerged with Mia in his arms. 'What the hell?'

'Open the back door,' said Alex.

Mikey hesitated, but only for a second. Their friendship covered all the unanswered questions. Alex would explain everything later. Right now, there was no time.

'You're paying for the cleaning,' said Mikey, watching the blood smear over the ivory-coloured leather of the car's interior. 'Is she alive?'

'Just,' said Alex. 'Give me a pen and paper.'

Mikey rummaged in the glove compartment. 'Here.'

Alex scribbled his instructions on one sheet, taking his time to get them right, glancing nervously at Mia. Putting his plan on paper was more difficult than he'd thought. He scribbled out and rewrote several sections, aware of the seconds ticking away. Distilling everything he knew, all of the conclusions he'd reached. A tentative diagnosis, more guesswork than science. It would have to do.

'Check her pulse,' he said to Mikey.

'Still strong,' said Mikey, reaching over and holding Mia's wrist. He wiped his hand on his trousers afterwards, watching the blood stain his chinos. 'How many times was she stabbed?'

Alex shook his head and kept writing. He folded the paper three times, writing a name in capital letters on the outside of the fold.

He grabbed another piece of paper and wrote an address on it.

'I need you to take Mia here,' said Alex, giving Mikey the second sheet. 'Hand her over to this doctor, and only him. He's a friend – you can trust him. Give him this note.'

'Wait,' said Mikey, peering towards the back seat. 'You're not coming with me?'

'No,' said Alex. 'I need to do something else. Promise me you'll do this. I'll explain everything later.'

Mikey looked bewildered at the thought of driving across town with a blood-covered fugitive on his back seat, but he nodded, pulling a blanket out of the trunk and covering Mia as best he could.

'You know what you're doing?' he said. 'I've got . . . product in the car. That's all.'

Alex understood. A car containing stolen drugs and a stab victim would be the end of Mikey if he happened to be pulled over. The fact that Hartley knew about Mikey's antics was not something Alex decided to share at this point in time.

'I think so,' said Alex, not at all convinced, but he was committed. Once Mikey drove off, he would set himself on a path that couldn't be changed. If he tried, he'd be joining Mikey in the police cell. He nodded.

'Go,' he said.

Alex watched Mikey drive off before withdrawing to the alley. He sat against the fence, checking the time on the phone, deciding to give it another twenty minutes. Long enough for Mikey to get a good head start.

His heart thudded. His anxiety had been tempered by the exertion and focus of carrying Mia. Still out of breath, he now used it to burn the adrenaline, thankful he was still coping. He should have asked Mikey for some Xanax, but in the heat of the moment he'd forgotten. He cursed, clenching his jaw, grinding his teeth while the minutes ticked on.

His plan had been rapid and was full of holes. It was simple, though, and in Alex's experience, simple often won out. He'd find out soon enough.

The sirens had almost disappeared. It was hard to tell at a distance, the Doppler effect changing the pitch and tempo and the wind carrying the sound and reflecting it off the buildings.

No one came along the alley, which was one thing to be thankful for. Trying to explain his blood-soaked clothes would be difficult.

The twenty minutes passed. Alex gave it two more for luck, figuring he'd need as much as he could get, before dialling again.

The call was answered immediately.

'Alex?' Laurie's voice was high-pitched. Alex could hear the sounds of a car engine and a siren.

'Where are you?' he said.

A pause.

'Where am *I*? Where the hell are *you*, Alex?'

Alex heard the siren cut out and the screech of tyres as Laurie stopped her car. He took a deep breath and started from the beginning, from his decision to approach the address at the industrial estate and his detainment under sedation by the security guards to his escape. His carefully crafted story accentuated every little detail about the facility and his suspicions of what was happening there. He described the observation room in which he'd been held and the patient rooms he'd spied on his way out, some of them recently occupied. He described the final ward through which he'd escaped, holding two near-death patients, one of whom had been subjected to very recent and barbaric surgery.

He laid out his theory that these buildings were being used for illegal drug trials on human subjects, and that his presence here had started a frantic clean-up operation to ship out subjects and pharmaceuticals.

Most importantly, he told Laurie he'd found Mia Anastos strapped to a bed in a secure room. Nova had got to her first and had been holding her captive.

His story was detailed, crafted and delivered with the right amount of urgency. Alex left out only one detail.

He left out the fact he'd taken Mia with him.

CHAPTER
FORTY-SIX

Alex replayed the story in his head. He'd been accurate and hadn't faltered. *It needed to be this way*, he told himself. *You did the right thing. A doctor's first priority is the patient.*

Always.

His body shook with exhaustion and stress, but a roar of engines made him peer out into the road. Four large articulated trucks were speeding towards him. They were white, unmarked, bumper to bumper. Alex stayed hidden as they passed him by but watched with interest. The trucks were travelling rather too fast for their size. In a great hurry, it seemed. Alex thought of the revving engines he'd heard during their escape. How many exits would there be on a complex the size of Nova's? Several, he guessed, cursing at the sight of the last truck's rear end.

He hoped he wasn't too late, but his heart skipped a beat when two black Transit vans appeared from the same direction. He ducked into the shadows and they passed without stopping, following the trucks. He stared after them, counting the seconds, thinking he'd left it too late. Part one of his plan was complete, but the second part – finding evidence at the Nova complex – was looking more doubtful with every second. If they'd cleared out, he'd be left with nothing.

A few minutes later Laurie's unmarked car screamed to the kerb. The temporary blue light flashed on the roof but the siren was muted. She jumped out and Alex met her at the entrance to the alleyway.

'Christ, Alex.'

She ran her hands over his chest. 'Where are you bleeding?'

'I'm not,' he said, gripping her wrists, pulling them away. She was clearly worried, in near-panic. When Alex glanced at his shirt he could understand why – there was barely a patch not covered in blood.

'It's not mine,' he said, waiting for her to understand, to calm down. She took her hands away and stepped back.

'You scared the shit out of me,' she said. Her eyes hardened, as if this was now his fault. Alex supposed it was but didn't offer his apologies.

'A patient in the facility.' He indicated the alley and the way he'd come. 'I tried to help him – he was bleeding out.'

Laurie nodded, backing away. She pulled out her phone and made a call. Alex guessed who was on the other end.

'Yes, ma'am,' she said, 'I've got him here. No, he's fine.' Laurie nodded a few times, staring at Alex. 'Yes, possible casualties.' She listened for a few moments. 'Our suspect. Yes. Anastos. Alex says she's in one of the warehouses.'

Alex's heart jumped, but his poker face was well rehearsed and he stayed calm.

'Where?' asked Laurie, glancing up.

'Pickard Street is where they took me,' said Alex, 'but that whole place is high security – the buildings are all behind razor wire.'

Laurie nodded, frowning. 'I know, and it's not just one street. These industrial estates were designed by idiots. Pickard winds around and back on itself for two miles. Several roads are called Pickard and no fewer than eleven different multinational companies own property along them. We've been parked at the various gates for hours. We haven't managed to get a warrant for even one of them yet.'

'A warrant?'

'Yes. All we had was your word. Hartley let me take three cars to check it out after I lost my temper, but we can't force entry without probable cause.'

'Like a murder suspect inside?' Alex remembered the number Mia had given him. 'It's warehouse 121 you want. The main compound. That's where Nova is and where they held me. It's where you'll find Mia Anastos.'

'One twenty-one?'

Laurie relayed it over the phone. Alex could see her swearing under her breath. She hung up and breathed out slowly through her lips.

'You lost your temper over me?' he said.

'Shut up,' said Laurie.

'Is Hartley angry?'

'You could say that. She's happy you're OK, but yes, she's fuming. I believe she told you not to come here.'

Alex swallowed. Laurie didn't seem to share Hartley's anger, but she would struggle to take sides against her boss and Alex couldn't ask her to.

'When did you raise the alarm?' he said.

Laurie flushed. She looked embarrassed. 'Not until this morning. I was angry after you stood me up.'

Alex smiled. 'You think I'd stand you up?'

'You did!'

'I was sedated and strapped to a chair.'

Laurie shrugged, tucking her phone into her pocket with a wry smile. 'I wouldn't have stood you up,' she said, indicating the car. 'Get in.'

'We need to go back,' said Alex.

'We are. Hartley is spinning the plates. Now we have a location and a murder suspect inside we don't need a warrant.'

'So you're back on the case?'

Laurie huffed. 'No, I'm not. But Hartley is letting me tag along because she's under-resourced. It's just for today. Once we get Mia, I don't know what will happen.'

Alex jumped in beside her, his heart in his throat. He felt guilty for lying to Laurie and Hartley but remained convinced he'd done the right thing. The fact that he was deliberately misleading a murder investigation was disturbing, but he tried to push it to one side. The more important focus was Nova and their facility – to catch the people working there – any of them – and expose what they were doing. That was Alex's priority.

As Laurie's car screamed away on the concrete, his thoughts turned to the woman who had given her name as Talia – who she might be and what she might want. He realised he hadn't told Laurie anything about her and her Russian friend, except that they'd questioned him. Should Alex describe this strange woman who claimed to know him? Could the police help him find her?

As they swerved through the dusty roads back towards Nova and Pickard Street, Alex decided to keep Talia's words to himself. It was a vulnerability, something personal and hidden he needed to discover first before sharing. Talia was intriguing, and Alex didn't feel threatened, but he had a strange feeling he hadn't seen the last of her.

Pickard Street. Laurie shot past the two parked patrol cars and headed towards the far end, where the road stopped and a large gate barred the entrance to a winding private road shielded by a row of trees. She pulled to within an inch of the gate and jumped out.

'Satnav says this is 121.'

Alex stepped out. He stared back towards the two patrol cars, which were turning in the street and heading towards them. If the white lorries had exited via this route, they would have been seen, in which case they must have gone out on a different road.

A third car, unmarked, appeared in the distance. Alex squinted. It was Hartley's BMW.

'I was picked up by Security at the other end of this section of road,' said Alex, remembering the black van. It had been yesterday but felt like an age. The sedative had messed with his head; his sense of time was off.

Laurie stood over a small metal box set into the frame of the gatepost and pressed the single black button. A distant buzzer sounded through the tinny speaker.

She waited a few seconds and pressed it again. The same buzzer sounded. Nobody answered.

'OK,' she said. 'We'll do it the hard way.' She waved at one of the approaching patrol cars. It pulled over and she had a word with the two officers. One of them retrieved a pair of heavy bolt-cutters from the trunk and went to work on the gate.

'There's something you should know,' said Laurie, watching Hartley's car. 'A member of parliament close to the commissioner has been linked to the Nova group. An investment fund of some sort.'

Alex thought about it. 'So that's why Hartley told me to stay away?' Laurie nodded.

'Is that why you were taken off the case?'

Laurie shrugged. 'The MP will be investigated, but this is sensitive, OK? Hartley was in an impossible position. Don't mention it.'

'Noted,' said Alex, feeling for Hartley's position while at the same time furious at the situation. He wondered if there were any medical corporations out there that weren't rotten to the core. He didn't hold out the same hope for politicians.

At least it meant his decision about Mia was reinforced. There was no telling what would have happened to her in the system. If politicians were pulling the money strings, the current task force could be replaced with a puppet team whose only purpose would be to lock Mia up tight and make a good story for the press. He couldn't trust them to do the right thing.

Hartley pulled up as the gate swung open. She stepped out of the car and approached Alex and Laurie.

'Christ, Alex,' she said, looking at his clothes. 'I hope none of that blood's yours?'

'Thankfully not.'

Laurie turned to Hartley. 'Alex says the guards may be armed. Should we wait for SCO19?'

Hartley shook her head. 'I've made enough enemies today. Let's take this access road, carefully as we go. Any hint of firearms, and we withdraw and I'll put in the call. Until then, it's just us.'

Alex shadowed Laurie and Hartley. They left the cars at the entrance and proceeded on foot, flanked by the four officers from the patrol cars. They were exposed as they reached the line of trees, pausing as a flock of birds took off in fright, singing their displeasure at the group of officers.

Alex was astonished at the size of the compound in front of him beyond the trees. Straight ahead was a metal building the size of an aircraft hangar. To the left and right, joined by covered walkways, were more lightweight buildings with corrugated white plastic roofs. They looked futuristic and alien. The road they were on split into three, one ending in front of the hangar and the other two circling around to the left and right of the complex.

Trying to get his bearings, Alex figured that he must have been kept towards the north-eastern corner. Exiting there would have taken him to the opposite fence and through to the road where he'd met Mikey. That must also be where the trucks and black Transit vans had exited.

He tried to explain this to Hartley as they walked. She glanced at him, her face stony but troubled.

'I hear you, Alex,' she said. 'We'll enter the building based on your statement. If Mia Anastos is in there, we'll all go home happy, job done. But I'm not sending half of London's patrol cars out looking for unidentified white lorries. This is an industrial estate. This is London. Did you even get their registration numbers?'

Alex conceded that he hadn't. A stupid oversight, but in the moment he'd been more concerned about staying hidden. He seethed but kept his mouth shut. Nova couldn't have cleared out everything. There would be something – a file, a sample. Some record of what they were doing.

They all stopped in their tracks as a small door rattled open in the hangar. They watched two suited men walk out to greet them, accompanied by a single security guard in a blue outfit, nothing like the clothing worn by the men who had captured Alex.

'Hello!' shouted one of the suits. He had a posh voice and a broad smile. He wore an ID badge on his chest, as did his colleague and the guard. He walked up to Hartley and extended his hand. He looked nervous and apologetic. 'I'm afraid our gate intercom is broken, but we saw you on the camera as soon as you turned the corner.' He glanced at the assembled officers, who had their hands on their batons and were spacing out. 'I do hope everything is alright?'

It took three hours in total. At first, the suits introduced themselves as Mr Gray and Mr Shaw and led them into the reception area of the building. Both were shocked as Hartley laid out the situation and looked genuinely confused, asking her to clarify Alex's claims.

'We're a conglomerate transport company,' said Mr Gray. 'Nova is not a name I recognise, but our investors and company divisions are international – wide and varied. I'd be happy for one of our legal team to discuss our portfolio with you, but I'm not sure we can help. Your story,' the man went on, glancing at Alex, 'is wildly . . . scary? I've never heard anything like it.'

Alex shouted out in disbelief, but Hartley stopped him. 'They're lying,' he said, his eyes darting from the suits to the reception area they'd been invited into. Pictures of ships and cargo planes dotted the walls. An uncomfortable-looking sofa stood under the window. A water cooler sat empty next to the reception desk, behind which the security guard had taken up position, his face blank, all emotion hidden.

'This estate is a maze, to be honest,' said Mr Gray. 'There are millions of square feet of warehouses, offices and industrial plants. Perhaps you have the wrong place.' He tailed off. His bright smile was fading and Alex noticed his eyes darting towards the corner of the reception area. Alex saw a small camera there.

'Who's watching?' said Laurie, who must have been following Alex's eyes.

Gray reddened. 'Nobody,' he said, and smiled. It was forced and weak.

'We're going to examine this facility,' said Hartley, 'because we have reason to believe a murder suspect may be here, whether with your knowledge or without. I would advise you to assist us. If you don't, I'll bring a hundred officers here with a warrant and shut you down for a week. Your choice.'

Gray's already thin smile became thinner.

'If you say so, DCI Hartley.' He turned towards the guard. 'Take them where they want to go.'

The guard nodded. Alex noticed an almost imperceptible look pass between the two. Alex was screaming inside. These men knew. Were they stalling for time?

The guard's right hand went to his pocket. 'Very well,' said the guard.

'I want to see the medical block,' said Alex. 'The patient rooms. Treatment rooms. Observation rooms.'

The guard looked puzzled. He glanced over to Gray then back to Alex. 'I'm afraid we don't have anything like that here,' he said. 'Just warehouses full of crates. Thousands of them. We do ship a lot of medical supplies into the UK, for the National Health Service. I'm happy to show them to you.' The guard's stony face broke into a sneer.

These people were playing with them, brazen in their defiance. Alex glanced at Laurie. Her eyes were narrow; she was studying the suits and the guard. The four patrol officers stood back, watching this play out, ready to step in if Hartley needed it.

Alex had a thought. He rummaged in his pocket to make sure.

'I have a security pass,' said Alex, remembering he'd kept it after exiting through the gate. He produced it, waving it in the air. 'I was given it by the armed woman who let me go after my detainment in one of your holding rooms. Perhaps we could see where this gets us? Unless she's still here? She could tell you where we were.'

Time slowed. Alex saw Mr Gray's eyes widen at the sight of the card in Alex's hand. His head snapped left to the guard, who was pulling something small and black from his pocket. Behind the guard, Mr Shaw spun on his feet, turning to run.

Laurie moved first, throwing herself at the guard and pushing her arm into his neck, taking him down. Two of the other four officers jumped on top, while the remaining two secured Mr Gray. Mr Shaw crashed through the double doors at the back of the reception area, his footsteps thundering away. One of the patrol officers gave chase. The scuffle lasted under ten seconds, during which time Alex stood frozen, holding the security card.

Laurie wrestled with the guard's hand until he released his grip. Fearing a gun, Alex let out his breath when he saw it was a small mobile phone. Laurie sat on the guard's stomach and checked the screen.

'Who were you messaging, if you don't mind me asking?'

The guard clamped his lips shut and smiled. He looked unhurt by the scuffle and resolute in his silence.

Alex glanced at Hartley, who already had her own mobile to her ear.

'Where do you want to start?' he asked.

At that moment the fire alarm went off.

◆　◆　◆

It didn't take them long to find it. The smoke was already billowing above the complex and they followed it around, jogging alongside the warehouses to the rear. They left the patrol officers with Gray and Shaw. The guard was shackled against a chair until backup arrived.

Alex suspected he knew what had happened, but it was still a shock when they rounded a corner to see a smaller, squat brick building on fire. He recognised the double exit and the path towards the fence at the northern end of the complex. This was the building he'd left not an hour ago. This was the medical block where he'd been held, where Mia had been held, and where human subjects had been experimented on.

He approached the building, feeling the heat pouring from it. Whatever accelerant had been used to start the fire was doing a good job. The roof was already burning and what few windows broke the charred walls had shattered, the flames licking out on to the scorched brickwork.

Laurie gripped his shoulder.

'That's far enough, Alex,' she said.

He shrugged it off and took another step, feeling his skin burning under the raging heat.

The final clean-up. What did they have left? Mia. A handful of doctors and suits who would no doubt tie them up with expensive lawyers for months. A building burned to the ground. A multinational company with a thousand secrets they'd never give up.

Alex crouched, staring at the concrete, listening to the roar of the flames mixed with the increasing wail of sirens in the distance. Too late, he thought. Nothing would survive a fire like that. Nova knew what they were doing. Extreme, perhaps, and a setback, but they'd move on and set up somewhere else.

Alex had failed again. His timing had been off. In his rush to save Mia he'd misjudged how quickly these people would cover their tracks. He'd expected the people to flee, but the complex itself . . . His visions of computer files and medical records faded into the flames. His plans of following the money trail back to the sponsors – the puppet masters – vanished into the smoke. He couldn't meet Hartley's eyes. She knew all of this. They would discuss it over the coming days. Right now, it was best left unsaid.

He sat. Laurie gave him some space, rushing back to liaise with the new officers on the scene. The fire trucks honked their way around the edges of the complex. He heard them driving up nearby but he didn't turn to look.

He was about to stand when his phone started ringing.

He pulled it out and answered. 'Hello?'

The line was crackly. 'Alex? Is this you? Your friend gave me your number.'

Alex swallowed. He was desperate for good news but didn't want any record of this on the airwaves. There could be no trail, however small. 'Yes, it's me. Don't say anything. Hang up.'

There was a pause on the other end. '*Qui vivra verra*. Goodbye.'

The line went dead. Alex looked at the phone. He sighed, but a smile crept in at the edges.

Qui vivra verra. A French phrase he and Dr Larry Van Rooyen had used back in their clinical training days when they'd witnessed a particularly harrowing but rewarding case. The patient's outcome was unknown, but there was hope.

That was the message from Larry today. Mikey had found him and handed over Mia.

Qui vivra verra. Who will live, will see. Or rather, the future will tell. Mia was safe.

CHAPTER
FORTY-SEVEN

The next few days were a blur. The lawyers descended and the knots started being tied around Hartley's investigation. The shipping company fought back and the police withdrew, inch by inch, until there was nothing left.

The primary purpose of the raid – to apprehend the serial killer Mia Anastos – had failed. The secondary purpose, to gather evidence of illegal medical experimentation, was there only because of Alex's reckless pursuit – Hartley's words, not his – and had not just failed but had brought scrutiny on Hartley and her team, damaged her relationship with the police commissioner and used tens of thousands of pounds of resources and time while they searched and catalogued a major shipping hub in east London which was found to contain nothing illegal in the first sweep. Subsequent searches were on hold, postponed due to issues with warrants and international treaties. They all knew what it meant. The lawyers would tie things up long enough for anything incriminating to be moved out of the UK. They didn't have the resources to monitor every truck and van in and out.

No trace of Mia Anastos was found in the charred remains of the building. No traces of any bodies whatsoever. The building appeared to be an office block with old-fashioned rooms, all empty apart from the odd plastic chair. No beds, no sheets and no medical equipment or drugs.

There were no cameras or CCTV in that part of the complex. The recordings from the rest of the compound were unavailable, lost in a server backup error, blamed on the fire and an electrical surge which also took out several weeks of logs and shipping manifests.

Alex's claim that there was an observation room was explored but couldn't be confirmed. The police believed him, of course they did. He was one of them. But there was nothing physical to support his claims. Traces of acetone were in every room and corridor. The building had been doused, according to the firefighters, a claim the lawyers instantly denied, citing shipping containers full of acetone being stored at the facility. Accidental fire was their claim. The battle raged. Alex had more than an inkling of who would win.

All Alex had was his story, and as the hours went by he began to conclude that wasn't a bad thing.

The links between Mia and her victims, Dr Tau, City Hospital and Nova were tentative and weak. They all rested on an admission of guilt or hard evidence, neither of which was forthcoming.

The suits at the entrance and the few guards they'd picked up were saying nothing. Their lawyers probably cost more than their salaries, but they were all released on bail within twenty-four hours and had disappeared within forty-eight.

All the effort was on Mia. Find the killer, save face. That's all everybody wanted.

Alex made no mention of Talia, and as the hours passed she began to drift into the background, a puzzle needing to be solved, but a solitary one, once he was back in his comfort zone. Away from the anxiety of the interview room.

On the third day, Alex sat in one of the many conference rooms at the Met HQ nursing a cup of bad coffee. He watched the drips beading on the rim and took another sip.

'Nothing?' he said.

'Dr Tau hasn't turned up,' said Laurie. She sat next to Alex in front of her laptop, scanning through the endless reports. 'Another doctor from St Mary's – connected to Tau – has disappeared too. We're tracing his whereabouts. Tau's remaining colleagues at City Hospital appear to know nothing. Tau has been offered representation by the shipping company legal team in his absence. They said he was employed as a consultant on the correct shipping procedures for surgical equipment and pharmaceutical supplies.'

'Bullshit,' said Alex.

'Of course,' said Laurie, 'but it pre-emptively ties up any connection we might find between them. Clever.'

Alex raised his eyebrows.

Hartley, sitting across the desk, also absorbed in her laptop screen, let out a snort. She peered over at him, closed her laptop and crossed her arms. 'When we spoke a couple of days ago, I hinted at the complications I was facing.'

'When I mentioned Nova Pharmaceuticals?'

Hartley nodded. 'Those complications haven't gone away. If anything, they have increased.' She paused, glancing at Laurie. She was about to say something when Laurie cut in.

'The forensics team say they're missing your clothes,' said Laurie. She frowned and glanced up. 'Sorry,' she said to Hartley.

'My clothes?'

'Yes. The blood-soaked ones. We need them for DNA matching. I thought that would be obvious.'

Alex swallowed. He knew that. Which is why he did what he did. 'I, er, I washed them,' he said, 'when I got home. Sorry, I wasn't thinking.'

Laurie's jaw dropped.

Hartley's phone rang. She excused herself and left the room.

'You washed them? Evidence of a person you told us was bleeding out on a hospital bed?'

Alex met her eyes. He held them, his mind screaming at him. Of course he couldn't let Mia's blood go to the forensics team. His story didn't support it and he wanted as few traces of Mia left behind as possible. He'd thought about it carefully. He could have said she was bleeding and he helped her. But the amount of blood would invite too much scrutiny. She would have to have been dying.

What did you do with her? You say she was strapped to a chair and bleeding? How did you get covered in it? Let's start again, Alex.

No. The simplest story was one in which he saw Mia during his escape but didn't go near her, didn't speak to her and didn't touch her. He had to keep to the story, and the blood was an inconvenient element that needed to be washed away. Literally, in this case, going through a boil wash three times.

Laurie rested on her elbows. Her eyes were piercing but Alex's conviction carried him through.

'I wasn't thinking,' he said. 'I was stressed. I'm sorry.'

Laurie shook her head, her eyes narrowing. She chewed her bottom lip. Alex could almost hear her mind churning away, calculating, sifting through everything she knew about the events of the last few weeks.

Eventually, she sighed. 'Well,' she said.

'Well, what?' Alex forced his voice to remain light, friendly. The stress of the last few days had intensified his feelings for Laurie, but the situation he'd created, the secret he now held, meant he couldn't see how a relationship could work.

'That's it for me,' she said. 'I'm off the case. Hartley allowed me in to help with all of this,' she said, indicating the forms and reports on her laptop screen, 'but I'm back in Holborn tomorrow. Hartley is leading from here. Mia Anastos is hers.'

She huffed and closed the screen. The suspicion in her eyes hadn't departed, but she tilted her head. 'So, about you standing me up . . .' she said.

Alex smiled.

Somebody knocked at the door and an officer poked his head in. 'Dr Madison? Your wife and daughter are here.'

Grace stood at the reception desk with her hands clasped together. Katie stood next to her, face buried in her phone.

'Alex,' said Grace, as he stepped out of the lift. He grinned and she punched him in the chest before throwing her arms around his neck. Her touch was warm and electrifying. Alex embraced her, burying his face in her neck.

'Hi, Katie,' he murmured.

'Hi, Dad,' said Katie.

Grace pulled herself away. 'Why didn't you call?'

'You were being pampered,' said Alex. 'Spa weekend, wasn't it?'

'You should have called,' she said. 'I don't like getting text messages saying you were involved in a police raid and a fire, then signing off with an emoji!'

Alex smiled. The mixed emotions after they'd left the compound had resulted in a hastily typed message to Grace. A cry for attention, perhaps, or a cry for love. It was worded in a way that conveyed altogether the wrong mixture of light-hearted anecdote and near-death experience. He regretted sending it but didn't regret the result – Grace and Katie turning up to see him.

But he didn't want to burden Grace with his work. He'd involved them far too much over the years. Katie, in particular, he wanted kept away from his murky world. He could shield her from it, but he found it hard to keep Grace away.

'Are you free for lunch?' asked Grace.

Alex checked his watch. Hartley was busy for the moment and Laurie wouldn't be too bothered if he stayed away for a couple of hours. The sight of Grace made his head spin anyway. Thoughts of Laurie were jostled out of place and he found himself sinking back into his old feelings.

'John not around?' he said.

Grace's eyes flickered. She swallowed, her delicate neck tensing.

'Not at the moment,' she said. Alex could see hurt in her eyes. Had John hurt her?

'Do you want to talk about it?'

Grace shook her head and smiled. 'I'm OK. John's OK. He's away for a couple of weeks, that's all. Now,' she said, turning to Katie, 'where for lunch?'

They linked arms as they walked out of the Met headquarters.

'You're not baggage, Dad, are you?' said Katie, as they stepped on to the pavement. They headed east in search of an Italian.

Alex raised his eyebrows at Grace. 'John said that?'

Grace shrugged and clasped Alex's arm even more tightly. 'He said I talk about you too much.' She sniffed and linked her other arm with Katie's.

Alex glanced at them both and his smile widened. She talked about him. Too much. His heart skipped a beat, despite the heavy weight on his chest from the previous days and the difficult path ahead. Just for now, however, in this moment, he felt happier than he'd felt in years.

The three of them, a family, going for lunch. What could be more normal?

CHAPTER FORTY-EIGHT

The second glass of wine sank more easily than the first. The Xanax had blanketed Alex and he relaxed into his leather chair with a sigh.

He needed the alcohol to temper his swirling emotions. He knew it was temporary, and with each sip the problems seemed more distant but became more urgent. But he couldn't stop it.

Off the case. First Laurie, then Alex. Hartley had broken the news that afternoon. She hadn't even invited him into the office but had preferred a phone call full of huffs and awkward throat-clearing.

Alex said all the right things. He valued her valuing him and agreed that his professional conduct had started solid but ended up verging on careless. He'd helped them to an extent, and it was noted. His relationship with the Met would continue, but on this particular occasion his name was being mentioned in the wrong places by the wrong people. A change of guard was necessary.

Alex staged a reasonable protest but conceded gracefully. He considered the key reasons to fight but came up empty. Laurie was back in Holborn. She hadn't called and Alex's brain performed one U-turn after another as he struggled to figure out what he wanted. His suggestion of a determined attack on Nova and the paper trail through the shipping company had been put on the backburner. Despite everything, Hartley had been nudged away, and her new team would follow. The case was a traditional manhunt. Find the killer. Lock her up. Standard.

Except they'd never find her.

Alex wrestled with his decision. Mia was a killer. Always would be, perhaps. Her victims deserved justice. But would justice ever have been served by apprehending her? Mia was a machine, an automaton. She couldn't control her actions any more than a spider could control the instinct to pounce and kill the bugs struggling for their lives in its web. When Alex witnessed her frenzied attack on her own body he knew death would find her quickly if he handed her over. He thought she deserved more than that – the chance to find out the truth and have it put right. There might not be a quick cure for her mangled nervous system, but there might be a slow one, and Alex had decided she deserved to try it out.

If the police wanted to stop her, it had been achieved. Mia wouldn't kill anyone, not any more. Would the victim's families be satisfied if they knew? Certainly not, but neither would they be able to grasp the enormity of what had happened before. The cause, not the effect.

The group behind all of this, whether called Nova or by another name, was bigger than Alex and bigger than the police. It was bigger than one experiment. Alex had witnessed it first with Victor Lazar, and now with Mia Anastos. Both had been subjected to brutal medical experimentation and found their way into Alex's path. Whether or not the cases were related was impossible to say, but Alex knew that medical research at the highest levels was a small and secretive world, ruled by a few and financed by an unknowing public. As long as the cures kept coming, the public were happy in their ignorance. If they could truly understand the price of such progress – how many innocent subjects like Mia had suffered in the making of their drugs – would they still be happy?

Perhaps. Perhaps not. It wasn't a referendum anybody would be willing to hold.

But deeper still was Alex's certainty that this wasn't about medical progress. The results of these trials were specific outcomes that, if one were to posit them in more sinister terms, could be used for more menacing objectives. The ability to read or control people, the absence of pain, an empathy so deep you could smell a person's emotions from across the room. Such outcomes were not purely benign treatments for an eager public.

Alex refilled his glass, settling back into the chair. His mind wasn't done.

State actors were involved. Hartley had hinted at it, and the hint would be as much as he ever heard from her on the matter. Laurie had been more direct. Government meddling in the industrial world was hardly news, or a secret. Most governments had their own research programmes, ostensibly open to audit and scrutiny by the political party of the day. The reality was far away from smiling lab recruits holding test tubes for a front-page shot in the *Daily Telegraph. Join the civil service. Make the world a better place.*

And that was where Alex's interests lay. His focus and his drive, from this point on.

He'd continue as usual, of course he would. He had a medical practice to run and criminal cases to work on. Hartley had already forwarded him a piece of profiling work for an incarcerated sex offender going through an appeal. It was important work, interesting work, and it paid the bills.

He had a mortgage and expensive tastes to nurture, not to mention a loving family who might just let him closer if he put in the work. And he fully intended to do that. Grace had offered to help with his addiction and, this time, he'd accept it. His heart would be Grace's if she wanted it. Until then, he would live the best he could. He was only human.

But in the background he would search. They were out there. Talia was out there. The Russian connection was impossible to ignore. His father's work was ripe for reanalysis – his contacts and research programmes were in the past, but fragments would remain, out in the ether and in parts of the world where the scrutiny was lower and the results quicker.

Alex would hunt, and he would piece together what he could. His target was movable and his aim wouldn't be true. But he'd try, and hopefully, he'd find supporters along the way.

Once in a while, he would make a visit to someone who might be interested. His first ally.

Mia Anastos, when she was ready, might accept him as a visitor. And perhaps they could talk. Perhaps she might be willing to help.

EPILOGUE

Dr Boucher savoured the fresh air coming through the open window. He resisted the urge to stare out at the mountains. The village of Beaufort-sur-Doron enjoyed the most incredible views of the Alps and Dr Boucher never tired of it. Only when the skiing season was at its peak did he sometimes close the window against the bustle and noise of the tourists. Even then he considered it hardly unpleasant.

You didn't get many unpleasant people in Beaufort-sur-Doron. Unless you counted the town planning officials, he thought, which was a little unfair, although their scrutiny of his planning applications was always tiresome.

The quiet private medical facility which he owned and ran was in a converted chateau of nineteen rooms with ten private patients. The other rooms were given over to state-of-the-art treatment resources along with a medical staff of five, three of whom lived on site, the rest in the village below.

His facility was unique and well respected. The service he offered was straightforward and discreet. A fully capable psychiatric and therapeutic treatment centre for the most exclusive and special of cases. What determined *special* status was a combination of the patient's condition and who was asking. He'd accepted a range of patients from celebrities to government officials and military personnel. Spies and oil company executives all got a place if he thought he could help them and he had room.

On occasion, he took referrals from all over the world as a favour to people he knew and trusted.

Last week he'd taken one of the latter, and this morning was examining the patient referral and financial accounts. He was a doctor first and foremost, but he was also running a business. The cost of his residential treatment was high and beyond the means of most people, although the rates were flexible, determined in large part by what the patient could pay and how interested he was in their condition.

A knock at the door disturbed his scanning of the single page of notes. He turned over the thin sheet to find the back of it blank. He huffed.

'Enter,' he said.

Dr Henri Durand, his close colleague, a medical doctor and also the company accountant, stepped into the room, closing the ancient door with a creak.

'I've been to see our new patient,' said Henri. He swallowed, thinking hard. Dr Boucher didn't interrupt. If Henri was thinking, the topic was important.

Henri squinted at Dr Boucher, his old eyes dancing over the top of his glasses. 'She's intriguing,' he said.

'I'll say,' said Dr Boucher. 'How are her wounds?'

'Staying shut,' said Henri. 'Most of them. The blade must have been clean. No sign of infection.'

Dr Boucher nodded. 'You've read the notes?'

Henri snorted. 'What notes? There's one page of hasty conjecture.'

Dr Boucher nodded. Henri wasn't convinced, but they hadn't run any tests. If what was written in the notes by the English doctor could be confirmed, this would be the most exciting patient he'd had in years.

'Have we received payment?' he said, knowing Henri was a devil for the practicalities of running their business.

'Yes,' said Henri. 'Six months upfront plus a monthly commitment if needed.'

'What's the account name?' said Dr Boucher, surprised at the upfront payment. He grabbed a pen. He liked to know who was paying for his patients, particularly this one. He'd rarely get in contact with them, only in emergencies. Only if he and his colleagues failed with their treatment.

'Dr Madison,' said Henri, watching Dr Boucher as he scribbled it down. 'Dr Alex Madison, clinical psychologist, resident in the UK. He is paying for this young lady as her guardian, not as her clinician. Looking at the state of her, I do hope he has deep pockets.'

Dr Boucher smirked. Henri had a way with him. 'Shall we fix a drink, *mon ami*? I'd like to discuss the initial treatment plan.'

Henri agreed, sitting across from Dr Boucher on the leather sofa. Both men enjoyed these moments: fine surroundings, fine wine and a fine professional challenge ahead. As they sipped from their glasses they discussed the main points, what they could extract from the hand-written note that had been delivered with the patient in a creased and bloodstained envelope.

'If the prognosis is correct, we have our work cut out,' Dr Boucher said to Henri. 'I have never seen anything like it.'

He saw Henri raise his eyebrows. His friend cleared his throat and poured another glass, tapping his pen on paper.

'I take it you have?'

Henri shrugged. 'Rumours, nothing more. I'll make some inquiries. In the meantime, I have some ideas. This young lady is not lost. I think we can do a lot for her and I think she may come out of this with some semblance of normality, if not a complete remission.'

Dr Boucher leaned back, enjoying the warmth of the alcohol in his body against the cool breeze. It reinvigorated him, giving him the energy he always welcomed at the start of a new patient's journey. He had a feeling this particular one would be long and difficult.

'Very well,' he said, taking a deep breath. 'Let us begin.'

The new patient enjoyed the fresh air. Everything had been dull. The journey had troubled her, but the pain and the fog had kept her senses blunted. She'd been medicated – she didn't know what with, but her body and mind both felt numb, distant, as though she was watching herself from afar.

Forty-eight hours passed with little change. The drone of an aeroplane, the vibration of a car, then the silent brisk air as she was carried in the dead of night into a building that smelled a thousand years old and looked older.

'*Bienvenue, mademoiselle,*' were the first words she heard. Everything smelled different, from the air to the furniture to the people. Everything was soft and calm. The voices were friendly and they cared.

She drifted at first. Her head spun and the nausea bounced around her body until she begged for help. They provided it, and her body relaxed. Her mind followed until she was in a dream. The pain disappeared and her cravings subsided.

For now, at least, she was at peace.

Her room had a window, a wardrobe and a bed. The bed was wooden and the sheets soft. The straps were loose and they allowed her to sit, if she wanted. A simple bell on the wall allowed her to summon a nurse, who would smile and tend to her demands, few though they were.

She knew what had happened, what she'd done to herself and what had transpired that day. She remembered the words of the doctors and the game they were playing. But here, a world away, her pain was tempered and her addiction, while ever present, was held at bay, caged beneath her consciousness. The soothing voices of the nurse explained what she had to do, and she smiled at them. She couldn't remember the last time she'd smiled.

But she remembered her saviour. He had come for her once and she had shunned him. He had come for her again and she had shown him what she was, the monster and the woman inside, desperate to escape.

He'd watched her sink into the depths of her frenzied feeding and still he'd lifted her out again. If she ever saw him again, she'd offer him her life, because he'd saved it. It was his.

She'd got her answer. He'd whispered it to her as he carried her bloody body across the grass and concrete. She'd heard. She was still conscious, unable to move or speak, but she could hear what was going on. He was almost as frantic as she was, telling her she'd been abused, that her condition was not her fault. Mia knew this, but the next answer hurt more than the stab wounds. He said that her father was dead but her mother had survived. The car accident wasn't a dream. They'd been separated and her mother might still be out there somewhere. That's all he knew. He said he was sorry.

Dr Madison, thought Mia, as she gazed out at the snow-covered mountains under the starlit sky of a foreign land that had taken her in and offered her protection. Alex Madison, the timid man who had pursued her to the end.

Thank you, she thought.

You saved a monster, but you saved me as well.

ACKNOWLEDGMENTS

Some claim that writing the second book is more difficult than writing the first. I disagree, for the simple reason that all of the wonderful people who worked with me through the publication of my first book, *Trance*, were with me once again, as professional and supportive as ever.

Thank you to my agent, Julie Fergusson, who continues to be my trusted friend and advisor on every aspect of my writing – the first port of call for every one of my questions and ideas. Julie sifts through the noise and gets the absolute best out of me.

Thank you to the Amazon Publishing team, who continue to be the most fantastic and energising bunch of professionals I've ever had the pleasure of working with. A huge thanks to Jack Butler, meticulous in his analysis of what makes a great story and steering me in the right direction. Also special mentions to Laura Deacon, Martin Toseland, Monica Byles, Harriet Stiles, Nicole Wagner, Alexandra Levenberg and Jodi Marchowsky – all of whom worked their magic on both *Trance* and *Pain*.

Thank you to my parents, Brian and Mary, and my sister, Lucy (and Tim, Charlotte, Millie and Alice), who have been so encouraging and enthusiastic throughout the process.

Thank you to my wonderful wife and daughters, Kerry, Isla and Daisy, who continue to provide the perfect home in which to write, offering patience, time and the motivation to keep going.
Lastly, to the real psychologists out there dealing with real patients – your job is fascinating and hugely challenging. I sincerely hope you never come across anyone as damaged and damaging as my antagonists, but if you do, please help them. Thank you!

ABOUT THE AUTHOR

Adam Southward is a philosophy graduate with a professional background in IT, working in both publishing and the public sector. He lives on the south coast of England with his young family.

Printed in Great Britain
by Amazon